throughout the world and ... shopaholics and people in credit card debt everywhere. *What's Your Number?* is her first novel and was originally published in 2006 as *Twenty Times a Lady*. Born and raised in Chicago, Karyn now splits her time between New York and Los Angeles. She's now at work on a third book.

www.**transworldbooks**.co.uk

Also by Karyn Bosnak

SAVE KARYN

and published by Corgi Books

WHAT'S YOUR NUMBER?

Karyn Bosnak

CORGI BOOKS

TRANSWORLD PUBLISHERS
61–63 Uxbridge Road, London W5 5SA
A Random House Group Company
www.transworldbooks.co.uk

WHAT'S YOUR NUMBER?
A CORGI BOOK: 9780552165006

First published in Great Britain
in 2006 by Corgi Books
an imprint of Transworld Publishers
as TWENTY TIMES A LADY
This edition published as WHAT'S YOUR NUMBER by Corgi Books 2011

Copyright © Karyn Bosnak 2006

'Three Times a Lady' Words and Music by Lionel Richie © 1978, Jobete Music
Co Inc/Libren Music, USA.
Reproduced by permission of Jobete Music Co Inc/EMI Music Publishing Ltd,
London WC2H 0QY.

This book is a work of fiction and, except in the case of historical fact, any
resemblance to actual persons, living or dead, is purely coincidental.

A CIP catalogue record for this book
is available from the British Library.

Addresses for Random House Group Ltd companies outside the UK
can be found at: www.randomhouse.co.uk
The Random House Group Ltd Reg. No. 954009

The Random House Group Limited supports the Forest Stewardship
Council (FSC®), the leading international forest-certification organisation.
Our books carrying the FSC label are printed on FSC®-certified paper.
FSC is the only forest-certification scheme endorsed by the leading
environmental organisations, including Greenpeace. Our paper-procurement
policy can be found at www.randomhouse.co.uk/environment.

Typeset in 11/14pt Garamond by Falcon Oast Graphic Art Ltd.
Printed and bound by CPI Group (UK) Ltd, Croydon, CR0 4YY

2 4 6 8 10 9 7 5 3 1

To everyone who's ever second-guessed
a decision they've made.
Our past makes us who we are.
Have no regrets.

Prologue

Stop the Insanity

So I feel like I'm at a twelve-step meeting, like I stood up just as you opened this book. You're staring at me, waiting for me to introduce myself, waiting for me to tell you why I'm here. And I'm sweating, sweating because I'm nervous, sweating because I don't belong here, sweating because never in a million years did I imagine I'd end up this way. But seeing as I did and seeing as you're here, I might as well come clean and explain myself, so here goes: My name is Delilah Darling. I'm twenty-nine years old, I'm single, and well . . . I'm easy.

There, I said it. I'm easy, I am. Now you know.

I've always suspected I was easy but never knew for sure, not until about six months ago, when I broke up with a guy named Greg, a guy I like to refer to as Greg the East Village Idiot. Although it was my decision to end things, I was angry about the break-up for two reasons.

For one, I wasted four months of my life on him, a guy who didn't even have a real job. I met him while walking through SoHo one day. He walked up to me, all cute and charming, and was like, 'Excuse me, can I ask you a question about your hair?' Yes, he was one of *those* guys – a young, good-looking stud hired by a local beauty salon to butter me up so I'll buy a bunch of coupons. I fell for his spiel and for him. But forget all that now, forget that he had the face of a Baldwin (Alec or Billy in their

7

younger days, not those other two jokers) – where was he going in life? Nowhere, that's where. I might've overlooked this minor flaw if he had a personality, but he didn't. Talking to him about anything other than hair was like talking to a *box* of hair. He was dull, wrapped in a pretty package. He was a foxymoron.

The second reason I was angry is that even though I knew our relationship wasn't going anywhere, I slept with him. Normally this wouldn't be a big deal, which, ironically, is how it ended up becoming a big deal. To be honest, I was getting a little self-conscious about my 'number'. It was getting kind of high, and sleeping with Greg didn't do anything except make it higher. When I say my 'number', I'm of course referring to the number of men I've slept with.

Exactly what number is considered high for a woman my age? you ask. Well, it's hard to say, because people rarely tell the truth about their number. They don't; it's no secret. Men usually up it, believing if people think they've slept with forty women even though they've only slept with four, they'll appear to be a bigger stud than they are. Women, on the other hand, usually lower it, leaving out the guys they'd like to forget. (You know . . . the one they met on spring break, the two who were brothers and the three who are now gay.)

I'll admit, I'm just as guilty as the next person when it comes to fibbing about this. In fact, my number even changes depending on who I'm talking to. For example, every boyfriend thinks my number is somewhere around four. (They also think they're the only one of those four to give me an orgasm, but that's beside the point.) My gynecologist thinks it's closer to seven, all done with protection, of course. (Oh, come on . . . everyone's had at least one slip-up, and you know it.) My mom – even though I prefer not to talk about sex with her – thinks it's somewhere around two. (I needed someone to pay for the pill when I was in college.) Even my best friend thinks my number is a little lower than it really is, because no one – I repeat, no one – tells even their best friend everything.

All these numbers are primarily the reason I was so worried about my own. It seemed high, yes, but with all the lying that goes on, who's to say?

The *New York Post*, that's who.

On the very day Greg and I broke up, my favorite newspaper printed the results of the world's largest ever sex survey. I had just finished reading a thought-provoking piece of journalism (two blind items on Page Six) and was about to learn how to get the most from my MetroCard (how to find love on the F train), when I ran across the incriminating piece of information. It was right there, nestled in between the average age people first have sex (17.7) and the average time spent on foreplay (19 minutes).

The average person has 10.5 sexual partners
in their lifetime.

Yes, 10.5. I almost had a heart attack when I read this because the truth is . . . well . . . Greg the East Village Idiot was the nineteenth guy I slept with. Yes, nineteen, as in there were eighteen others before him. My number was almost twice as high as the national average.

Needless to say, after reading this I quickly realized that I needed to take control of my number before it got any further away from 10.5 than it already was. Like Susan Powter, my favorite infomercial star, once declared, I had to stop the insanity. If I kept doing what I was doing, if I kept having sex at the current rate, then my number would be seventy-eight by the time I turned sixty. Yeah . . . *ewww.*

Afraid of what my future held, I made what I thought was a wise decision: I would stop having sex. Not *forever*, don't get me wrong, I just decided to put a limit on my number, a cap, if you will. After thinking about this for a bit, considering the current situation was so dire, I decided to make that limit twenty. Yes, twenty. I was giving myself one more chance to get things right. If I blew this last chance (excuse the pun) and wasted it on some random Tom, Dick or Harry (excuse that pun, too), then I'd force myself to live a lifetime of celibacy.

Maybe setting a limit is crazy, but there comes a point when one drop of water will send a full glass overflowing. I was at that point, enough was enough. Twenty was it; it was as simple as that.

Twenty.

No more.

Not ever.

Chapter One

Beep

Del, it's Mom. Listen, hope you're not upset Daisy got engaged before you. Green's never been your color . . . it makes you look more washed out than you already are. Can't wait to see you tonight at the party. Bye!

Beep

Hi, Mom again. I meant to ask . . . Patsy was in Manhattan recently and thought she saw you buying a dozen cupcakes at Magnolia Bakery. She waved but said you didn't wave back. You must not have seen her. In any case, she said it's normal for people to overeat when they're depressed, and thought you were looking a bit hippy. Like I said, hope Daisy's engagement isn't upsetting you. Okay, see you tonight.

A List by Delilah Darling   Friday, 1 April

A list. Tony Robbins is telling me I need to make a list. A list of things that are wrong with me. Issues. Problems that need fixing. You see, I don't have a therapist, so I rely heavily on self-help books (usually the audio version, downloaded into my iPod) to work out my problems. I wouldn't make a list for just any self-help guru, but Tony's my favorite, not only because he uses sexy phrases like 'pathway to power' and 'avenue of excellence' but also because he's freakishly huge and has really white teeth. According to him, if a man with artificial hands can play a piano (which, apparently, he can), then a perfectly healthy woman such as myself can overcome a few issues. But first I need to come up with a list.

Since I'm at the office I probably shouldn't be doing this, but it's late Friday afternoon and a mandatory staff meeting is beginning in twenty minutes so it's useless to start a new work project. What's not useless, however, is to start a personal project, so I grab a piece of paper and begin writing. Time is tight, but I think I can finish my list before the meeting begins; I just need to focus.

Things Wrong with Me
A list by Delilah Darling

1. I can't focus.
2. ~~My boss Roger is a lying, fat pig who is holding me back.~~ I'm too judgmental.
3. I'm jealous of my younger sister, Daisy. (I'm not really, but my mom thinks I am, so I should look into it just in case.)
4. I'm starting to look more and more like Sally Struthers every day.

There, finished. To be honest, this is usually where I stop. Although I say I 'rely heavily' on self-help books, I usually just read/listen to whatever the guru has to say and nod in agreement, like, 'Yep, that's me. I sure *am* a mess!' I don't actually take the necessary steps to fix the problem I'm addressing; I usually lose interest by that point. It's part of the first thing on my list, not being able to focus. But today is the day I'm going to change all that. Today is the day I'm going to explore these issues a bit further.

Okay, one, the focusing problem. I think the reason I can't focus is because I have a mild case of undiagnosed ADD. I'm not sure if ADD just didn't exist when I was younger or if my doctor was a complete moron, but whatever the reason, I'm pretty sure I have it. For example, I can simultaneously play computer solitaire, read *Glamour*, instant message multiple people, paint my nails, talk on the phone, and work better than anyone else I know. I call this multi-tasking. I also have a hard time finishing things I start, like projects, for example. Considering my job title is 'Project Manager', this can be a bit of a problem.

I work at a company called Elisabeth Sterling Design (ESD for short), a company that designs and manufactures a popular line of household products. Elisabeth Sterling, a woman from humble beginnings, started her now-public company just fifteen years ago in a small Harlem studio apartment. She's an artist who painted modern geometric designs on dishes that she sold through neighborhood boutiques. The dishes became all the rage in New York City, so much, in fact, that she couldn't keep up with the demand. Being the savvy businesswoman she was, rather than just hire an apprentice to help keep up, she hired a publicist to create some more hype and then a manufacturer and distributor to produce the dishes in mass quantities. Soon thereafter, Elisabeth Sterling Design was born.

To cut a long story short, the line that began as dishes today includes just about every household product you can imagine – from cleaning to decorating to gardening – and is available exclusively at Target stores across the country. Four years ago, in what has become one of the biggest IPOs in history, Elisabeth took the company public and became a billionaire. Elisabeth Sterling is a household name. Elisabeth Sterling is an icon.

But let's get back to me not focusing.

In addition to multi-tasking and not finishing projects, I tend to go off on tangents and speak in circles. (I sometimes speak in parentheses, too.) And also, footnotes.*

Okay, now that I've explored one, let's move on to two. Yes, I feel like I'm being held back at work, but after re-reading what I wrote about my boss being a fat pig, I feel like I should address the fact that I'm a tad judgmental first. I know it's wrong to judge others, but when it comes to people like Roger, I feel that doing so is justified because he's a slime ball who once tried to steal an idea from me. About six months ago, I had to come up with a unique color name for a pair of light-green oven mitts my team had just designed (to Elisabeth nothing is ever just

---

* I wonder if people with ADD are eligible for workers' comp. If so, then I need to get a proper diagnosis right away so I can take advantage of the perks.

14

orange, it's *pumpkin* or *persimmon* or *harvest moon*) and was looking out of the window, staring at the Statue of Liberty, when suddenly, it came to me. 'Oxidized copper,' I said aloud. Although 'oxidized copper' might initially evoke thoughts of something rust-colored, copper turns green when it oxidizes, which the Statue of Liberty so beautifully demonstrates. 'Oxidized copper.' It's a smart and clever color name, and I knew Elisabeth would love it because she's smart and clever herself.

Since Roger is my immediate boss, I report to him, and then he reports to Elisabeth. When he told her about the color name for the mitts, she loved it so much that he somehow ended up taking credit for it. When I found out and confronted him, he started whining pathetically, saying 'She didn't give me a chance to explain, and now it's too late . . .' and *blah blah blah*. Lucky for me, my best friend and co-worker Michelle is a tough cookie from Queens who refused to let Roger get away with what he did. To help me get the credit I deserved, she and her frizzy red hair marched into Roger's office and demanded that he confess to Elisabeth, saying she had proof that I came up with the color name and not him.

'What kind of proof?' Roger asked nervously.

'If you must know,' Michelle warned, 'I was testing out the memo recorder on a new interactive date book my team is designing and happened to be in Delilah's office recording when she came up with the name.'

Yes, it was a far-fetched lie, but being the gullible sap he is, Roger believed it and fessed up to Elisabeth the next day. Although she was angry when he did, she didn't fire him because she said she believed in giving people second chances.

Anyway, this is why it should be okay to call Roger a lying, fat pig. This is why it should be okay to make fun of his toupee and bad fashion sense.* This is why it should be okay to send him evil subliminal messages.† Roger is trying to hold me back. I want to be a designer, not a project manager; that's what I went to school for. A project manager is a middleman. All I do all day is shuffle papers; it's hardly an outlet for all my creative energy.

You know, the more I think about this, the more I think being too judgmental isn't such an issue after all. Yes, in addition to Roger, I sometimes judge other people, but I don't do it very often, and when I do, I do it only in my head and who's that hurting? No one. In fact, it might be helping people because every time I say or think something really evil, I give money to charity to balance out any bad karma it might bring. If I stopped, the food supply in Third World countries might be negatively impacted. Looking at it this way, I think it's clear what the real issue is:

* Roger is a holiday dresser of the worst kind. Some of the offending accessories I've seen him sport include a Santa tie, reindeer horns, a blinking shamrock button, Easter Bunny ears, Dracula fangs, American flag suspenders and, yes, a pilgrim hat.
† I frequently stare at the permanent eyeglass indentions above his ears while silently chanting the word 'loser'.

I mean, come on – that's really what the problem is. Every time I do or think something that's not considered 'nice', I think God is going to strike me down. Twelve years of Catholic school didn't teach me much, but it sure did ingrain in me the fear of eternal damnation. I haven't been to church in years, either. I've forgotten the Ten Commandments, I've forgotten the Seven Deadly Sins – I've obviously forgotten about the evils of premarital sex – why can't I forget about burning in hell? I mean, there's really no reason I should be hanging on to this.

Anyway, on to three. I'm not jealous of my sister, Daisy, and I know it. Yes, she's younger than me, and, yes, she's getting married before me, but I'm not bothered by it. What I am bothered by is that, like my mom demonstrated in her voicemails, everyone assumes I'm jealous and/or upset by this and therefore feels sorry for me. Tonight, my mom is throwing an engagement party for Daisy and her fiancé and I'm dreading going for this very reason. It's going to be one big celebration for Daisy and one big pity party for me. Back pats and words of encouragement will lurk around every corner.

To be honest, ever since I've been a little girl, things have always come more easily to Daisy than to me, and I've gotten used to it. For example, she doesn't have the greatest job in the world (she sells wallets at Saks Fifth Avenue), but she never has money problems; she lives in a huge loft apartment in the West Village but barely pays any rent (it's rent-stabilized); and she never diets or exercises but has the body of a supermodel (she could be Cindy Crawford's twin). Daisy's blessed, yes, but she's so friendly and down-to-earth that it's impossible to hate her for being lucky. So there, that's settled, I'm not jealous. Once again, looking at this issue more deeply, I think it's clear what the true problem is:

<u>Things Wrong with Me</u>
A list by Delilah Darling

1. I can't focus.
2. ~~My boss Roger is a lying, fat pig who is holding me back. I'm too judgmental.~~ My Catholic guilt is out of control.
3. ~~I'm jealous of my younger sister, Daisy.~~ My mom is crazy.
4. I'm starting to look more and more like Sally Struthers every day.

She is, believe me.

Finally, on to four. I'm getting fat. Not *fat* fat, just *chunky* fat. I look a little like Sally Struthers looked in all those feed-the-children commercials she did, a little bloated. You can still see the thin person floating around inside me, so I'm thankfully not a lost cause, but if I don't do something about my weight soon, I will be. (Just to make it clear, this is the *only* similarity I have to Sally Struthers; I look nothing like her otherwise. I stand about 5 feet 5 inches tall, and have long brown hair and big brown eyes.)

Anyway, I know why I'm getting chunky. Ever since I decided to stop the insanity, I began consuming large amounts of chocolate because I heard that doing so releases the same feel-good endorphins into the brain as having sex does. My thinking is this: if eating chocolate keeps a steady supply of these endorphins pumping through my brain while I hold out for Mr Right, then I'll be less likely to seek out other ways to activate those endorphins, i.e., having sex with another Mr Right Now.

Women use all sorts of methods to keep themselves from having sex. Some wear grandma panties when they go on dates; others put off bikini waxes and refuse to shave their legs.* I eat chocolate. It's my version of the patch.

So that's it. Those are my issues, things I'd like to change about myself. Although I haven't come up with ways to fix these problems, I still feel a sense of

---

* I once met a girl who would write the word 'slut' in permanent marker on her belly before every first date to prevent herself from hooking up. Harsh? Yes. Effective? Absolutely.

accomplishment because I was able to focus long enough to finish exploring them before my meeting begins. I'm already making progress. Tony would be proud, I bet. And you know, in some strange way, I think the man with artificial hands who can play the piano would be proud, too.

Evildoers

The meeting is being held in the large conference room, so Michelle and I walk there together. We both started working at the company around the same time three years ago and have been inseparable ever since. We eat lunch together, we take breaks together, and since we live in the same apartment building (she lived there first and gave me a heads-up when the old lady above her died), we frequently travel to and from work together as well. Michelle's good people, which is why she's my friend. She's a very practical person with a strong voice of reason and she always expresses her opinion about what I do, whether I like it or not. This can be irritating, but at the same time, it's nice to have a friend who cares.

Although we aren't exactly sure what the meeting's going to be about, we have a pretty good idea. About a year ago the company's CFO, Barry Feinstein, was indicted on several counts of fraud for allegedly reporting inflated company profits to shareholders. According to the newspapers, the SEC has evidence that will likely convict Barry, but offered to lessen the charges against him if he cooperated with their investigation. He agreed and ratted out Elisabeth, saying she pressured him into fixing the books. Because of this, Elisabeth was indicted as well and has since stepped down as the company's CEO.

Although not everyone believes it, rumor is that Elisabeth is innocent, that Barry ratted her out only to save his own ass. I believe the rumor and feel bad for Elisabeth. Not only is she on the verge of losing control of the company she built, but she's also on the verge of losing her good name. The trial is set to begin in a couple of months.

After giving our names to a human resources lady taking attendance at the door, Michelle and I grab two empty seats near a large picture window. As I look around the room, I can't help but think that a few things about this meeting are strange. First, not everyone on the staff was invited. Second, the people who were invited are an oddly selected group – a few from this department, a few from that department. And third, I can't remember the last time attendance was taken at a meeting, or if it ever has been. Although I would normally worry about this, I decide not to. Things have been so weird here lately, there's really no point in trying to make sense of it.

At quarter after four the meeting finally begins. As Roger wobbles up to the front of the room, the human resources lady passes out envelopes to everyone, asking us to wait to open them until she's finished. Since I've never been good at waiting, I quickly open mine anyway. My guess (and hope) is that there's a bonus or gift certificate inside, rewarding us dedicated employees for sticking with the company through this trying time. Elisabeth's always doing nice things like this for the staff. I pull out the piece of paper and begin reading, and—

Whoa, wait.

This isn't a bonus; nor is it a gift certificate.

Oh no. Oh no, oh no, oh no.

In big bold letters across the top of the page are the words TERMINATION OF EMPLOYMENT. Suddenly, it's like I have Tourette's.

'*What the motherfuck is this?*' I yell.

Oops! I quickly cover my mouth but do so too late. Everyone in the room has already turned to stare at me, including the human resources lady, including Roger. Looking back down, I quickly scan the rest of the memo. (The ADD makes it difficult to read anything completely from beginning to end.) From what I gather, owing to a decline in profits, the company is downsizing and laying off 25 per cent of the staff.

Oh. My. God.

I look back up. 'We're getting fired? Are you kidding me?'

Roger looks at me with pity. 'We prefer to call it being *laid off.*'

'Oh yeah? Well, I prefer to call it *bullshit.*'

Roger shakes his head. 'Delilah, I understand your frustration, but please watch your language.' He turns to the group. 'Listen, I know this might come as a shocker to most of you, but there's nothing anyone could've done to prevent it from happening. These layoffs were inevitable. This isn't your fault.'

No, it's not my fault; nor does it have anything to do with my multi-tasking, as I briefly suspected when I read 'Termination of Employment'. For a split second I wondered if it was possible that someone was monitoring my computer use, reading my instant messages. I wondered if maybe there was a hidden camera in my office, behind my desk, watching me read *Glamour*, watching me paint my nails. But no, none of that has been happening because this *isn't my fault*.

I look around the room. Since no one else is speaking up, I appoint myself the spokesperson. 'So what are we supposed to do now?' A few co-workers nod when I speak. I feel proud to be their leader.

'Well, I'm sure you all wanna run right out of here, call your family and friends, and fill them in on what's going on,' Roger says. 'But I shouldn't have to remind anyone about the confidentiality agreement you signed when this whole mess began. Please avoid talking to anyone about this, particularly the media. The last thing I want is for the details of this meeting to end up on Page Six and—'

'Excuse me,' I interrupt, 'but I wasn't asking how we should break the bad news to our loved ones and the press. I meant what are we supposed to do now? Like when's our last day?'

'Today's your last day,' Roger says quietly.

Today? I'm so shocked I can't respond.

'Listen, I know this is hard for everyone to understand,' Roger continues, 'but it wasn't an easy decision for us to make. This is something we've been mulling over for the past few weeks. The company's tight on money; these lay-offs were inevitable.'

Inevitable? My head begins to spin, I get dizzy with anger. A few weeks ago, when rumors of possible layoffs circulated, Roger denied them, and now all of a sudden he's saying they were inevitable? I stand up.

'Then you shouldn't have lied to us a few weeks ago,' I say angrily. 'We're loyal employees who stuck with this company during uncertain times when we could have been out looking for more secure jobs. How can you let this happen? How can Elisabeth let this happen?'

'Elisabeth fought this tooth and nail, but she's unfortunately no longer in control of this company. The board overruled her.'

'Then *the board* needs to do something more to take care of us.'

As a few co-workers yell out from the back of the room, I suddenly begin to feel like Sally Field in that movie where she works in a factory and starts a union. What's it called? *Norma Rae*. Yes, that's it.

I am Norma Rae.

The attendance-taking human resources lady must sense that the 'union' is about to take over because she cuts Roger off and explains to everyone that employees who've been at the company for over three years will receive a severance check equal to two weeks' pay for each year of employment. I quickly do the math in my head but can't remember when I started. It was at least two years ago, but was it three? It's hard to say.

'What if we haven't been here for three years?' I ask on behalf of my union members and myself.

'Those who don't receive a severance check can file for unemployment.' She then gleefully points out, 'It's up to four hundred dollars a week now.'

Four hundred dollars a week? *Ooh, party*! Four hundred dollars a week in New York is pennies. This is not good, not good at all. Not only do I not have a savings account,

I also don't have any investments. The only thing I've ever invested in is a good pair of black pants.

I glare at Roger. He's such a liar. He's an evildoer, I tell you! Who does he think he is, standing up there in his high-waisted khaki Dockers that balloon at the knee from being worn too many times? He looks like a carnival act, for God's sake, a clown. I wouldn't be surprised if at any minute he started making balloon animals. And that belt he's wearing . . . that ugly braided belt. Who wears braided belts any more? Who has since 1995? No one, that's who. It's so horrible, the way it's pulled too tightly around his fat belly, pinching him in the middle – it makes him look like the number eight.

When other people begin asking questions, I stop channeling Norma Rae and stare out the window at a large white cloud that's hovering in the distance. If I could hop on it and fly away from this mess, I'd fly past all the office buildings in Manhattan, watch other people being fired, other people aside from me, and offer them words of encouragement.

'We'll all be okay,' I'd say. And then they'd smile. And then we'd all go back to my place, work on our résumés, and write one another letters of recommendation. We'd help one another fill out job applications, and in the empty space after DESIRED SALARY, we'd write '$1,000,000' and have a good laugh at our witty reply.

I'm not sure how much time passes, but eventually the meeting ends. When it does, two ladies from human resources start calling everyone in the room over to a table alphabetically to answer questions and let us know if we've made the severance cut. As Michelle and I wait for our turn, we debate when we started working for the company. I started a few days before she did, but neither of us is sure if it was over three years ago.

Michelle and I get called over to the table at the same time. Her last name is Davis, so she always comes right after me in anything alphabetical. After waiting anxiously for the human resources lady to review what I assume is my file, I find out that I made the cut by four days.

Kick. Ass.

Not only should I get a check equivalent to six weeks' salary in the mail sometime next week, but my health insurance will also last six more weeks. After thanking the lady, I turn to Michelle, who's standing next to me.

'I made it by four days,' I sigh, relieved. She looks up.

'I missed it by two.' By the look on her face, I can tell she's disappointed and feel horrible about it. We do the same thing here – we're both project managers – it doesn't seem fair that I should get severance pay and not her.

'I'll split my check with you,' I say quickly. 'And you can split your unemployment check with me. We'll pool all our money together and cut it right down the middle. That way we'll make the same amount for the next six weeks.'

Michelle shakes her head. 'I'm not taking your money, Delilah, that's not right.'

'Yes, it is,' I say, grabbing her by the shoulders. I try to reason with her. 'You've helped me out so many times that I probably wouldn't still have this job if it wasn't for you.' It's true, she's always keeping me on track, always reminding me of things. 'I owe you for that. Please let me do this.'

Michelle stares at me. I know she wants to take the money but feels badly. She needs to be pushed. 'Michelle, have you ever read *Chicken Soup for the Soul at Work?*' I ask.

'No,' she says, rolling her eyes. She hates when I quote self-help books.

'Well, I did, and in that book was a quote by a very wise woman named Sally Koch. Do you wanna know what she said?'

Michelle nods, indulging my need to share the wisdom.

'Great opportunities to help others seldom come along, but small ones surround us daily.'

Michelle smiles. 'You're crazy, you know that?'

'Yes, yes I do,' I respond.

'Okay, fine,' she says, eventually giving in. 'You can give me your money if that's what you wanna do.' She then leans in to give me a hug. 'Seriously, thanks,' she whispers. 'It means a lot. I'll figure out a way to make it up.'

'Don't worry about it.'

After wiping away a few tears, Michelle and I clean out our desks in twenty minutes flat – there's no reason to hang around the office any longer than necessary. I have to admit, part of me wants to do something bad before I go, like leave a piece of meat in a desk drawer or put a ham steak in the drop ceiling, but I decide against it. I'm a nice Connecticut girl who only thinks bad things – I don't actually do them.

Rumor around the office is that everyone, fired or not, is going to a bar in Midtown known for its relaxed atmosphere and stiff margaritas. Although I don't have much time before having to hop on the train to Connecticut to go to Daisy's engagement party, I figure I can squeeze in one drink. I want a drink, I need a drink, I deserve a drink . . .

Pity Party

. . . or four.

When I get to my mom's house around nine o'clock, I find that I can't focus and realize it has nothing to do with my ADD and everything to do with my LOM – my love of margaritas, that is. Yes, I'm drunk. And not only that, but as a bonus, because I'm clumsy and didn't go home to change, I'm wrinkled and covered in tequila. I know it's wrong to show up at my sister's engagement party in this condition, but if I didn't show up, Daisy would be disappointed and people would begin to speculate.

'She just couldn't bear it.'

'Yeah, I hear she's eating herself silly.'

'And to lose her job on top of it . . . what a life, that poor girl.'

Details of the big layoff topped the evening newscasts, so I'm no longer just going to be the single, older sister tonight, I'm now going to be the *jobless*, single, older sister.

My mom and step-dad, Victor, live in the same large, white Colonial house I grew up in, forty miles north of New York City in the woodsy town of New Canaan, Connecticut. The party looks hopping, so without hesitation I head inside to join the fun.

When I open the front door, an overwhelming smell of

garlic and perfume fills my nose. I almost sneeze but don't, which irritates me. Almost sneezing is like almost having an orgasm. Sure it tickles getting there, but if you don't get the release you were hoping for at the end, then what's the point?

I see Daisy standing in the corner and head her way. She looks fabulous – a thin layer of tulle is peeking out from underneath the cream-colored circle skirt she's wearing; the rhinestone buttons on her pink cardigan are sparkling. Engrossed in conversation with someone I don't know, she doesn't see me sneak up. I whisper softly in her ear: 'There's more St John in here than a Park Avenue plastic surgeon's office.' When she hears my voice, Daisy jumps and turns around.

'Delilah!' she screeches. Her teeth are as white as the china, her beautiful brown hair as bouncy as her boobs. She flings her arms around me. 'I'm so glad you're here.'

'Me too,' I say, giving my sister a big squeeze. And I mean it. Despite my apprehension about coming to this party, I wouldn't have missed it for the world.

'Let me ask you something,' Daisy says, turning us both around to face the party. 'If this party is for me, then why aren't any of my friends here?'

As I look out at a sea of middle-agers who look like they walked right out of *Town & Country* magazine, I smile. It's so like my mom to throw a party for Daisy or me yet invite only her friends, many of whom we don't even know. It's not that my mom doesn't keep old friends, she's just always making new ones.

'Who are these people?' I ask, only half joking.

Daisy shakes her head. 'I have no idea.'

'Oh, Daisy, Mom's just proud and wants to show you off.' I mean this – she and her friends are always trying to one-up one another with their kids.

Daisy rolls her eyes. 'Yeah, yeah, yeah, whatever.'

'Hey, is Grandpa here?' I ask, looking around.

'No,' Daisy replies, looking slightly disappointed. 'Apparently there was some schedule mishap at work.'

Our dad died when we were younger, right after Daisy was born, in fact. When he did, our grandpa – his dad – became like our father. He signed report cards, went to parent/teacher conferences, you name it. He was around more than some of our friends' dads, always making sure we didn't miss out by not having a father. Daisy and I were in grade school when my mom started dating Victor. When they decided to get married, my grandpa didn't take it very well. Thinking Victor would try to take his place, he pulled both Daisy and me out of class one day and tried to convince us to move to California with him. He wasn't trying to kidnap us or anything, it wasn't anything creepy like that, it was more funny and sweet than anything else. Funny because my grandpa rarely leaves the East Coast. Sweet because, when Daisy and I told him that no one could take his place, he smiled and then cried.

'He said he'd try to get off early,' Daisy explains, 'but wasn't sure he'd be able to.' Grandpa's a bagger at the A & P grocery store in Danbury. It's his retirement job, the thing he does to keep himself from going crazy with boredom. I'm disappointed he's not here, but I have a feeling the reason has more to do with the fact that he doesn't care for the hoity-toity New Canaan crowd my mom and

Victor hang out with, than a schedule mishap at work. My grandpa's very blue collar, very practical.

'Gee, hungry?' Daisy asks, hearing my stomach grumble loudly.

'Starved,' I say, snatching a beef-kabob off a tray on a table behind us. My mom owns a catering company – Kitty Cannon's Catering – so I've had the kabobs before. They're pretty darn tasty. As I pop the large piece of steak into my mouth, Daisy holds her left hand out in front of my face. Hanging off her finger is quite possibly the largest, most brilliant diamond I've ever seen. I practically choke.

'Four carats,' Daisy says matter-of-factly, as the diamond twinkles in her eyes.

'Fourmf? Ohmf . . . wowmf,' I say, with a mouth full of meat.

'I know. I almost passed out when Edward gave it to me. It's almost too big, you know?'

Ignoring Daisy's comment, I listen to the Rock Report (four carats, Asscher cut, platinum band) and then anxiously look around for Edward. I haven't yet met him; no one in the family has. Daisy and he have had a bit of a whirlwind romance – they met just six weeks ago. I feel stupid not knowing anything about him, but every time the two of us talk, Daisy gushes so much about how fabulous he is that by the time she regains her composure, her other line rings or something else happens and one of us has to go. The only thing anyone in the family really knows about him is that his name is Edward Barnett, he works on Wall Street somewhere and he's ten years older than Daisy.

'So where is he?' I ask. 'Is he here?'

'Of course he's here,' Daisy says, looking around. Smiling when she spots him, she nods in his direction. 'He's over there talking to Victor.'

I turn around and spot Victor in the corner talking to a man wearing a light-blue shirt. Although his back is facing me, from what I can tell, he appears to be tall, dark, and handsome, and – oh yippee! He's turning around. As I get a better look at him, I realize that sure enough, he's tall, dark, and hands—

Whoa, wait.

Back to dark.

Edward's black.

My eyes light up. Well, hallelujah, Daisy! Turning back to my sister, I see a cheeky grin come across her face. 'Okay, this is so not a big deal,' I say, 'but I can't believe you didn't tell me!'

Daisy laughs. 'I know, I know,' she says quickly, trying to explain. 'And I knew you wouldn't care, it's just that I didn't want Mom knowing until she met him.'

'Oh my God . . . what did she say? Tell me everything!' My mom isn't racist by any means, it's just that not many black people live in New Canaan.

'Well, when I first introduced them, she stared at him for a few seconds with her mouth slightly ajar, but then I kicked her and she snapped right out of it!'

'Daisy, be serious!'

'Okay, fine, I didn't kick her, but she did stare for a bit.'

'And?'

'And honestly . . . she's fine with it. You know, I'm an adult, he's an adult, she could care less. But Patsy on the other hand . . .'

As Daisy says this, I look over at Patsy – our bitchy, humorless, no doubt sexless neighbor – and see her scowling at Edward. Patsy has never liked Daisy and me, so her obvious distaste for Edward probably has more to do with the fact that he's made one of us happy than anything else.

After turning back to Daisy, I listen to her go on and on yet again about how much she's in love, when it suddenly dawns on me that she can probably shed light on whether there's any truth to a very popular myth. 'So is it true what they say?' I ask coyly, when she finally exhales.

Daisy looks at me confused. 'True about what?'

I didn't think I needed to explain what I was referring to, but apparently I did. 'About his . . . you know. Is it big?'

Daisy's cheeks turn red. 'Delilah! I can't believe you'd ask me something like that!' She quickly looks around to make sure no one heard my question.

'Well, sorry,' I say, defending my curiosity, 'but since he's only known you a month and already knows he wants to spend the rest of his life with you, I assume you did something right.'

'For your information, we're waiting to sleep together until we get married,' Daisy sniffs. Holding her shoulders high in the air, she stands as tall as she can.

'Waiting? Why on earth would you do a thing like that?' Obviously, this concept is foreign to me.

'Because we have a lifetime to have sex, that's why. Why rush it?'

I have to admit, Daisy's behavior goes against the image I had of her. She dates way more than I do – way more – and I'm not saying that I think she's easy, but only a prude would hold out on her fiancé. I'm going to get to the bottom of this . . . in a roundabout way.

'Hey, did you read the results of that sex survey in the *Post* a few months ago?' I ask. Daisy shakes her head.

'No, what survey?'

'It was really interesting. It said the average person first has sex at the age of seventeen.'

Daisy thinks about this and then nods. 'That sounds about right.'

'It also said the average person has about 10.5 sexual partners in their lifetime.'

'10.5?' Daisy wrinkles her nose.

'Yeah . . . that doesn't seem right, does it?'

'No, not at all!'

I feel relieved. Maybe the survey is way off. Maybe having a number like nineteen isn't that bad and I've been worrying for nothing. However, maybe Daisy is saying this because she thinks 10.5 is too high. If so, then I'm worse off than I thought.

'Wait – what do you mean by that?' I ask.

'I mean only a total tramp would sleep with that many guys.'

'A total tramp?'

Oh no. Oh no, oh no, oh no! My relief turns to nausea.

'Yeah,' Daisy continues. 'I mean, I don't know anyone who's slept with that many men.' After looking around and seeing that no one's within an earshot, Daisy leans in closer to me. 'I mean, between you and me,' she whispers, 'I've only slept with four.'

Four?

FOUR?

Holy Sweet Mother of God!!!

Before I have a chance to ask Daisy if she's kidding (oh, who am I kidding? I'm sure she's not), a breathy voice interrupts us. 'Delilah . . . you don't return my phone calls . . . you've got me worried sick!'

Oh no, it's my mom. Reluctantly I turn around and find her staring at me pathetically. Her hair is perfectly coiffed and colored, her head slightly lowered.

'Mom!' I exclaim, raising my voice an octave, trying to sound excited to see her. 'How are you?'

'Never mind me,' she says, patting down the wrinkles in my shirt. '*You*. How are *you*?'

'I'm—'

'Come,' she says, not letting me finish. 'Come to Mama.'

As my mom embraces me, she hugs me hard, squeezing me so intensely that I can barely breathe. Although I try to pull away, I can't, so for the next minute, I find myself gasping for air as she silently rocks me back and forth. Even though she's not saying anything, I know her well enough to know that her inner dialogue is jabbering away. You see, in her world, if a woman is single and thirty, it's because she's either a lesbian or a loser. Since my thirtieth birthday is three months away, she's trying to figure out which it is and, more importantly, what she should tell her friends.

What's wrong with Delilah? Why can't she meet a man? Is she a lesbian? No, no, she's not a lesbian, she can't be. Although she did like Joan Jett an awful lot when she was younger. And I swear I caught her listening to Melissa Etheridge last time she was home. I sure hope she wasn't fired today, because if she was, then my excuse as to why

she's still single – she works too much – is no longer valid,
which means that all my friends will assume she's single
because she's a lesbian. It's not that I don't like lesbians, I
do. Lesbians are funny. Look at Ellen DeGeneres. They can
be successful, too. Look at Hillary Clinton. Oops, she's not
a lesbian . . .

Yes, the pity party has officially begun.

'Honey,' she says, finally breaking her silence, 'did you lose your job today?' She's talking to me like I'm a dog.

'Lose her job?' Daisy pipes in, confused. 'Why would she lose her job?'

'Daisy, honey, watch the news once in a while, will you?' my mom says as she finally (thankfully) releases her hold on me. 'There were big layoffs today at ESD.'

'Layoffs?' Daisy gasps loudly. Glaring at me, she slugs my arm. Hard.

'Ouch!' I scream.

'Oh, ouch nothing!' Daisy says. 'Why didn't you tell me?'

'I don't know,' I say quietly. 'I didn't—'

Suddenly sensing we're not alone, I stop talking and turn around. Just as I suspected, all of my mom's friends have gathered around, waiting to hear what I have to say. Like I said, Elisabeth is an icon, so to hear the scoop on the day's events from an actual staff member is exciting. All of their big owlish eyes (the result of overzealous plastic surgeons) are on me. All of their big black pupils (the result of one too many Vicodin tabs) make me nervous. I feel like I'm in *Rosemary's Baby* or an episode of the *Twilight Zone*. I don't know what to do, I don't know what to say, so . . . I lie. (And with such grace, I might add.)

'I didn't tell you because I didn't lose my job.'

My mom lets out a huge sigh of relief. 'Thank the Lord!' she exclaims. 'When the news said almost twenty-five per cent of the staff was let go, I thought for sure you were a goner!'

'Thanks for the confidence, Mom,' I mutter. Ignoring me, she turns around to address her friends.

'Did you all hear that?' she asks gleefully. 'She said she didn't lose her job!'

I turn back to Daisy and roll my eyes.

'C'mon,' she says, putting her arm around me, 'let's go meet Edward.'

After chatting with Edward for the next hour (who couldn't be more perfect, by the way), I spot waiters making rounds with my mom's famous chocolate bonbons and excuse myself to go to the kitchen, to the source. Since I've started using chocolate as my patch, I've built up quite a tolerance and know one won't be enough. After grabbing a handful, I head upstairs to eat them alone in my old bedroom, and pass by Patsy on my way there. Glancing down at the pile of bonbons I'm holding, she shakes her head in disgust. Slightly embarrassed, I ignore her and continue on my way.

When I get to my room, I close the door behind me and take a deep breath. Gosh, what a day, what a night. Leaning against the door, I look around and become melancholy. My room hasn't changed since the day I left home for college. The Laura Ashley wallpaper still matches the Laura Ashley bedspread, which still matches the Laura Ashley curtains. Posters of REM and Pearl Jam still hang on the wall. It's a room frozen in time, a room frozen at a time in my life when the world was one big opportunity waiting to happen.

Thinking about my life, I can't help but feel like a loser. I mean, I always imagined things would be perfect by now. I wouldn't just have a job – I'd own my own company. I wouldn't just rent an apartment on the fourth floor of an East Village walk-up – I'd own my own loft in TriBeCa. I wouldn't still be single – I'd be happily married with a big family.

Looking at my dresser, I see a pile of stationery sitting on top, so I walk over and pick it up. Covered in stars, it says FROM THE DESK OF LITTLE DARLING along the top. My grandpa used to call Daisy and me that when we were little girls: Little Darling. It was his nickname for us. I look into the mirror, and wonder if the girl who used to live in this room – Little Darling – could write a letter on this star-studded stationery, I wonder what she'd say to me today. After thinking about this for a minute, I plop down on the edge of my bed and reach for a bonbon. Instead of eating it right away, I stare at it for a while and feel sorry for myself. Then, a few moments later, something hits me – a thought.

I'm pathetic! I'm completely, utterly and totally pathetic!

What kind of loser sulks in a childhood bedroom while eating bonbons on a Friday night? Moping about what I don't have and what I didn't do isn't going to make my life any better. Neither is eating a dozen bonbons. I just lost my job, for God's sake. I should be out with my friends and co-workers, letting loose and acting like an idiot, not sitting alone contemplating my self-worth. I can deal with the real world tomorrow and the day after that, and the day after that.

Although I was planning on staying the night, I decide not to and call Michelle to see if she's still out. Sure enough, she is, as are all my co-workers. Deciding I should be with them, I stand up and throw all the bon-bons out the window. I don't need food – I need a drink!

I tell my mom and Daisy that I received an emergency phone call from work and have to leave immediately to prepare for an early-morning crisis-control meeting. They're both very understanding. After that, I call a taxi to take me to the train station and hop on the 11.40 train back to Manhattan. I arrive at Grand Central just before one o'clock and head straight out to meet Michelle at a bar in Hell's Kitchen.

For the rest of the night (morning?), Michelle, my former co-workers and I reminisce about the past, toast to the future, laugh, cry and eventually . . . sing karaoke. After that, we go to a bar in the Meatpacking District, then to another in Chelsea, and then . . . then I'm not so sure what happens.

Chapter Two

FROM THE DESK OF LITTLE DARLING

Dear Delilah,
You're a huge
fuck-up.
Sincerely,
Little Darling

Oops! . . . I Did it Again Saturday, 2 April

Thump, thump, thump.

I hear a loud thumping at the door and wonder who's visiting me at such an ungodly hour. I'm not really a morning person, and all my friends know this.

Thump, thump, thump.

Oh, there it goes again. When I open my eyes to look at the clock next to me, I quickly realize three things: one, no one's knocking on my door – the thumping is a pounding headache; two, it's not some ungodly hour – it's one o'clock in the afternoon, and three, the clock that tells me so is not mine – nor is the table it's sitting on. I have no idea where I am.

The sun is pouring in from a window behind me and beating down on my neck. The smell of alcohol, which I assume is coming from me, fills the room. As I look around, I notice some familiar things . . . my brown purse, my shoes, my crumpled-up skirt, and my—

Whoa, wait. That's not mine.

Could it be . . .? No, it couldn't possibly be . . . *a braided belt?*

Oh God, no. Say it isn't so.

Please tell me it's not.

I mean, I wouldn't. I couldn't!

Please tell me I didn't . . . shack up . . . *with Roger!*

'Hey there, sexy,' says a familiar and somewhat scratchy voice from behind me.

Holy shit, I did.

No! No! No! No! No! No! Noooooooooo!

I try to remain calm but can't. My mind is too hazy from last night's margaritas and I'm completely naked, lying one

42

foot away from the man I despise most in the world. How could I have let this happen? I mean, no amount of liquor could make Roger even remotely desirable. He's not cute, he's not funny – he's Roger, for God's sake! He must have slipped me a Mickey last night because there's no way I would've voluntarily chosen to come back here with him.

As a wave of nausea comes over me, I bolt out of bed, scramble to gather my belongings, and run to the bathroom. Once I arrive, I lock the door behind me and turn around to find myself face-to-face with –

Oh, Lord . . .

– the hairiest toilet I've ever seen. I'm barely able to kneel before getting sick. While throwing up, with tears streaming down my face, I pray . . .

Dear God, why me? Why have you chosen to punish me this way? Is it because I despise Christian rock bands? I know they spread your good word, but let's be honest – most of them suck. Is it because I eat meat on Fridays during Lent? Is that it? If so, I'll never do it again, I swear. Please, God, whatever I did, whatever it was, I'm sorry! Please, God, just make last night go away and I promise . . . I'll never drink again!

After saying three Hail Marys and five Our Fathers, I close my eyes and click my heels, hoping that, like Dorothy, I'll be magically transported home. No such luck. When I open my eyes, not only do I find myself still kneeling in front of the world's hairiest toilet, but, to make matters worse, I'm now connected to it by a long string of spit.

I've become one with the hairy toilet.

I get sick again.

Afterwards, I try to remember the previous night, I try to remember how this happened. The last thing I remember is singing along to 'Survivor' by Destiny's Child. I was good, too. People were cheering me on, hands were in the air – it was like *American Bandstand*. I even stood on a table while belting out the end of the song to make sure I went out with rock-star status. And then I think I saw Roger . . .

Yessssss. Oh shit, yesssss! Yes, I did!!!!

I remember it a little more clearly now. After singing, I was feeling positive and optimistic about my future, when Roger showed up with another co-worker. People weren't being very nice to him and I thought it was funny, thought he deserved every snide remark he was getting. But as people became more rude, I started to feel bad. Someone threw a piece of ice at his head, and then, while a group of people were singing the 'Copacabana', someone else changed the words and sang, 'His name was Roger, he was a jackass. He pulled his pants way up his butt, just to get them over his gut.' Roger tried to laugh it all off, of course, but I could tell he was embarrassed – anyone would be. I walked over and said hello.

As we started talking, I got the feeling that Roger was a little more shocked about the layoffs than he let on at the meeting and I began to look at him in a different light. I saw his vulnerable side, and it made me like him a little bit. He's just a person, after all, who does what he needs to do in order to get by.

Roger asked me to dance and I said yes. To be honest, I didn't expect much more than two left feet, but Roger surprised me. He might have clodhopped his way through the hallways at work, but he was as light as a feather on the dance floor. He was smooth – he spun me around like a ballerina. He kept doing this thing where he would send me whirling out into the crowd and then quickly snap me back in to him at the last second. He was like Tony Manero in *Saturday Night Fever* and I was like . . . I was like . . . I was like the girl in the movie . . . whatever her name was. Gosh, it was so much fun!

After a while of dancing, I remember coming in off a whirl and landing in Roger's arms. With my back to him, he held me close while we danced as one. I don't even remember what song was playing. I just remember the beat of the music: *Ba dada ba da da. Ba ba! Ba dada ba da da! Ba ba!* When the song ended, I turned around and looked into Roger's eyes. He looked sweet . . . and lonely.

The next thing you know the two of us were outside the bar, hopping into a cab. Our plan was to go to another bar, but when the driver took a sharp turn and I ended up in Roger's lap, those plans changed. What happened after that is somewhat of a blur. I remember being carried up a few flights of stairs on piggyback, I think . . . and then . . . and then . . . and then it happened. Yes, *it*. A little mattress mojo. Twice, I think.

Oh, God. I can't believe I did this. I can't believe I did *it*.

I'm so stupid – I'm so, so stupid! I didn't just sleep with Roger last night, a man who wears a braided belt, a man who doesn't wash his pants as frequently as he should – it's worse than that. I didn't just sleep with Roger last night

– a man who owns a musical Rudolph tie, a man who owns a pilgrim hat – it's worse than that. In sleeping with Roger last night, I screwed him *and* myself!

Roger was #20.

He was it.

IT. IT. IT.

How could I have blown my last spot – the spot I was supposed to be saving for my future husband – on him? On Roger? What in hell was I thinking?

While trying to block the photographic memories of last night from my mind, I stand to wash my face. I'm so ashamed at my lack of self-control that I can't even look at myself in the mirror. I feel like a failure.

But then, while getting dressed, something suddenly occurs to me. What if I'm supposed to marry Roger? What if last night was a sign from God, telling me Roger wasn't the fat pig I always thought he was but a nice guy who just needs to start counting points or controlling his carbs? Maybe last night happened for a reason. We were listening to Destiny's Child after all. Maybe last night was destiny.

I quietly open the bathroom door and look at Roger lying on the bed, heavily breathing in and out. As his whole body rises to the occasion and then sinks back down, I wonder if I could learn to love him. Thinking about this, I watch him for a while. I watch him lie there. I watch him roll over. I watch him scratch his back. I watch him scratch his ass.* And then I watch him bring his scratching hand to his nose and . . . smell his fingers?

---

* This bad 'man habit' can be unlearned or at least controlled, so I let it slide.

Ewww!

I mean, really . . . *ewww!*

That was so disgusting! When Roger smelled whatever he . . . *smelled,* the corners of his mouth turned up in a half-smile – I think he enjoyed it!

I quickly slam the door shut.

Who am I kidding? Roger's not the one! Last night was no sign! I can't believe that I blew my last spot on him! For the love of chocolate, what have I done?

Suddenly I realize – that's it. This happened because of chocolate, or, I should say, the lack of chocolate. This happened because I threw all those bonbons out of the window and didn't have enough endorphins in my brain when Roger came-a-knockin'! Those endorphins were my patch. I was patchless!

Why, oh why, oh why me?

As I plop back down on the ground and curl up into a ball, I think about what I've done. I don't mean to sound dramatic, but I don't think I can go on. I've had sex with twenty men – twenty – and I'm never going to have sex again. Never, ever.

For a moment I try to imagine what my life as a celibate woman will be like. I try to imagine myself as one of those born-again ladies who goes on talk shows and travels around the country lecturing teenagers about the evils of casual sex. Maybe I can do this; maybe I can.

Who am I kidding? No, I can't.

I can't handle this – not alone, not in my condition. My head is pounding. My ears are ringing. I need to talk to someone. I need to talk to someone now.

Papa Don't Preach

I can't believe I'm here. I didn't plan on coming, it just happened. On my way home from Roger's, my taxi driver started eating something curried, and the smell made me nauseous.* We were somewhere in Little Italy at the time, which is pretty close to where I live, so I paid him and hopped out. I intended to go straight home, but when I turned around, I found myself standing in front of a Catholic church. I mean, what are the odds, right? It had to be a sign from God, no doubt, so I walked inside.

I don't know what I'm looking for, maybe a solution to my problem or a divine intervention of some kind to make my twenty become nineteen again. I don't know. All I know is that things can't get much worse than they already are, and I need to talk to someone. Going to confession isn't exactly what I had in mind, but it's my only way in to see the big man.

'Bless me, Father, for I have sinned,' I say. 'It's been . . .' *Twenty-nine minus eighteen equals . . .* 'nine years since my last confession.' No wait, that's not right. 'I mean eleven.' I never have been good at math.

'What are your sins?' the priest asks. Although his voice is soft and he sounds nice, I'm still nervous. Thank heavens there's a screen between us because I don't think I'd be able to tell him if this was one of those face-to-face confessionals.

'Well, Father . . .' There's really no easy way for me to tell him other than to just spit it out, so I close my eyes,

---

* Note to cab drivers: when someone with puke on their shirt gets into the back of your cab and asks you to crack a window, it's not a good idea to pull out greasy food.

take a deep breath and go for it. 'I've slept with twenty men.'

There, I did it. I'm already beginning to feel relieved. I wait for a response.

And wait.

And wait.

The priest, however, does not give me one. The longer we sit in silence, the more I begin to worry, but then something dawns on me . . . maybe he misunderstood my confession.

'Not all at once,' I clarify. 'Twenty separate men at twenty separate times.'

There, that's better. That should get him talking.

But it doesn't.

As more time passes, as the priest still says nothing, as the silence weighs heavier, something else dawns on me . . . maybe he knows I'm not telling the whole truth.

'And one girl,' I add. 'But I'm not counting her. It was college, strictly above the belt, and well . . . you know how that goes.'

You know how that goes? Why did I say that? Of course he doesn't know how that goes – he's a priest! Jesus, I'm so stupid! Oops! Sorry for taking your name in vain!

While I wait and wait for the priest to say something – anything – a vicious cycle begins: I become nervous, which makes me sweat, which makes me smell like liquor, which makes me more nervous, which makes me sweatier, which makes me smell like liquor more. I feel like I'm in one of those 'and so on and so on' commercials. Madonna songs then begin running through my head and I go with it because it takes my mind off the silence.

'Papa don't preach . . . Like a virgin . . .' Oh, who am I kidding?

I wonder if he's still there. 'Hello?' I ask quietly.

The priest clears his throat. 'I'm here,' he says. 'I'm just thinking. Let me ask, are you sorry for sleeping with these men?'

I think about it for a minute. 'Well, some of them were tragic, for sure. But no, I'm not sorry for all of them.'

'Then why are you confessing?'

'Because I'm sorry for them as a whole. I'm sorry for sleeping with twenty men, you know, collectively, but I'm not sorry for each of them individually.'

'Well then, why did you come here today?'

I think about it for another minute. 'Because I don't have a therapist?'

Obviously unhappy with my answer, the priest exhales loudly. That's it. I'm done here. This was a bad idea. I don't need to be judged, not right now, today. I'm going home. I stand up.

'Wait, wait, don't go,' the priest says, hearing. 'I'm just a little confused because, well . . . I'm not sure why you're here.'

'You already told me that,' I say loudly. As the 'and-so-on-and-so-on' cycle starts once again, my face gets hot. Honestly, I've had a hard day – why couldn't this have been easy?

'You're right, I did,' the priest says. 'And I'm sorry. Why don't you tell me the reason you're upset instead.'

'The reason?' I hesitate before continuing. 'Well . . . there are a lot of them.'

'I have time,' the priest says. 'Come on, I'm here to

help.' He sounds sincere; he sounds nice; his voice is comforting. 'Tell me everything.'

'Everything?'

'Everything.'

'Are you sure?'

'Positive.'

'Okay.' With that, I plop down on the floor of the confessional and begin to tell him everything – everything. I don't think about what I'm saying or who I'm saying it to; the words just pour out of me. Pour. I tell him about 10.5, multi-tasking, chocolate and endorphins. I tell him about Tony Robbins, Elisabeth Sterling, bonbons and Roger. I tell him about Norma Rae, Destiny's Child, my mother and her friends. And I tell him about Edward, Daisy and her magical number four. I tell him everything – everything. In one big run-on sentence, I tell him. When I finish, I once again wait for the priest to say something – anything – but he doesn't. At least he's consistent.

I think I know why he's silent this time. However, I'm pretty sure I'm going to hell and he doesn't want to tell me. Yep, I'm pretty sure that's it. After taking a deep breath, I accept my fate: a lifetime of celibacy followed by hell.

Just as I'm about to walk out of the confessional, the priest finally speaks. However, he doesn't say what I'm expecting him to say, he doesn't say that at all. He says my name.

'Delilah?'

Frozen with fear, I stop. Not only have I never been to this church before, but I didn't even know it was here until today.

'Um, how do you know my name?' I ask slowly, nervously.

'Oh, uh, I uh . . . I'm sorry, I just . . .' The priest can't answer.

Suddenly, I realize something. His voice isn't comforting because it's kind; it's comforting because it's familiar. 'Do we know each other?' I ask.

'You could say that,' the priest responds.

'How?'

'Well . . . we went to school together.'

'School?' I'm confused. 'What school?'

'High school.'

'High school?' I don't believe him. 'In Connecticut? We went to high school together in Connecticut?'

'Yes. It's Daniel. Daniel Wilkerson.'

Daniel Wilkerson? *The* Daniel Wilkerson? A priest?

Oh no. Oh no, oh no, oh no.

'You're a . . . a . . . a priest?' I ask.

'Yeah . . .' he says quietly. My stomach drops. 'It's been so long, Delilah. The last time I saw you we were—'

'Having sex!' I screech, cutting him off. We were. We were having sex in the back of his mom's wood-paneled Wagoneer. You know how Greg the East Village Idiot was #19 and Roger was #20? Well, Daniel was #2. Suddenly, I feel faint – how can this be happening? How is this possible? Of all the people to hear me confess that I've slept with twenty men, it's one of the twenty? I'm mortified! And oh yes, I'm so going to hell! I exit the confessional and head toward the front door as quickly as I can. As I do, I hear footsteps behind me.

'Delilah, wait,' Daniel says. 'I'm sorry. I shouldn't have said anything, but I wanted to stop you before you said too much.'

'Before I said too much?' I laugh. 'If that's the case, then you should have stopped me at "Bless me, Father, for I have sinned"!'

'Yes, you're right, but I didn't realize it was you until you started talking about your mom and Daisy.'

Arriving at the door, I stop walking and turn around. I can't believe this. I can't believe Daniel is a priest. Standing in front of me with his dirty blond hair and green eyes, he looks the same as I remember. Well, except for the outfit.

'I'm so sorry, Delilah,' he says softly. 'Really, I am.' I can see the remorse in his eyes, but I'm still disappointed.

'Yeah, so am I,' I say, turning back around. As I reach for the door handle, I feel his hand on my shoulder and freeze. As I do, thoughts of our one night together rush through my mind like flashbacks in a movie. The images play one after another like a slideshow.

It's fall 1993. I'm home from college for a weekend. My friends and I are laughing. We're at a Santana concert at Jones Beach. We're laughing because we have no idea who Santana is. (This was long before he had the big comeback.) We've only gone to the concert to chase boys. *I've* only gone there to chase boys. *A* boy. *One particular boy.* Not Daniel. I sleep with Daniel only to make that boy jealous.

It's so awkward.

Daniel and I have left the concert early and are pressed up against each other in the back of that Wagoneer, that wood-paneled Wagoneer. He can't look at me – his eyes are closed, his face is all scrunched up. For some reason he can't look. But I don't ask why, I prefer not to know, pretend not to see.

Remembering this now and learning how he ended up makes me wonder. Did Daniel not enjoy having sex with me because he knew he wanted to become a priest? Or did Daniel become a priest because he didn't enjoy having sex with me? Turning back, I reach up and touch his little black-and-white collar.

'Did I do this to you?' I ask. I need to know.

Daniel shakes his head. 'No, no, you didn't do this to me, Delilah. I swear.'

'Are you sure?'

'I'm positive.' Taking both my hands in his, Daniel pleads with me not to go. 'Please, please, come back and talk to me,' he begs. 'I wanna help you work this out. I do.'

Looking at Daniel, I feel sorry for him. I feel sorry for me. I feel sorry for both of us because this is so incredibly awkward.

'I already know everything,' he says. 'You might as well.'

I let out a sigh. He's right. 'Fine,' I say softly, after a bit. Daniel smiles. As he leads me toward a quiet area in the back of the church to talk, I can't help but point out, 'You know, I'm usually much cuter than this.'

Daniel smirks. 'I'm sure you are.'

For the next hour Daniel and I talk about my problem in a little more depth. Although I didn't initially come for forgiveness, I find myself getting angry because Daniel won't give it to me. Even though I keep telling him that I'm sorry, he keeps insisting I'm not.

'Delilah, if you didn't have sex with Roger last night, then you wouldn't be here today confessing. Am I right?'

'Well, yeah, probably.'

'Exactly – you weren't sorry for any of them until you slept with the last one. And the only reason you're as upset as you are about all this is because you've hit some self-imposed limit.'

'So what? I'm still sorry now. Isn't that the point?'

'No, because if you set your limit at twenty-five, then you wouldn't be here and you wouldn't be sorry. You'd be at home, nursing your hangover, trying to forget about the gross man you woke up next to. You're not truly sorry.'

I look down, Daniel's right.

'Listen, there's a deeper issue here that you need to explore, and until you do that, until you figure out why it is you keep going through men, I'm not going to forgive you for any of these guys.'

'How am I supposed to do that?' I ask, beginning to sulk. I mean, this hardly seems fair.

'Well, you could start by going home and making a list of the twenty men.'

'A list?' I ask skeptically.

'Yes, a list. I think you should figure out why you slept with each guy on it and then analyze why things didn't work out.'

'Analyze?'

'Yes.'

I shake my head. 'That's not gonna work. I mean, I can

make the list, but that's about it. The whole analyzing part isn't going to happen. I have undiagnosed ADD.'

'Okay, then.' Daniel shrugs. 'Just know that one day you'll become that sixty-year-old woman who's had sex with seventy-eight men.'

I glare at him. He's not being funny.

'Del, there's no quick-fix to make this go away. You're gonna have to work at this, or you'll keep making the same mistakes over and over again. Make the list, will you? Then come back and see me.'

'Okay, fine,' I say, giving in. 'Confessing was so much easier when I was a teenager, you know? When the worst thing I did was swear every once in a while.'

'You're forgetting we grew up together,' Daniel jokes.

I laugh and then change the subject. 'Hey, do you still talk to Nate by the way?'

Daniel shakes his head. 'No, we lost touch years ago. How about you?'

'No.'

Nate was Daniel's best friend in high school. He was the boy I went to the Santana concert to chase. He was the one I was trying to make jealous by sleeping with Daniel. Nate was my first, my #1.

As Daniel walks me to the door, he asks if he'll see me at mass tomorrow.

'Yeah, maybe . . .' I say, clearly lying.

'You should come, really. You need Jesus in your life, Del.'

'I need a lot more than Jesus.'

Bubble Gum and Puppy Dogs

My apartment is on the fourth floor of a brownstone in NoHo, a neighborhood in the East Village. As I climb (crawl?) the three flights of stairs, I try to be as quiet as I can. I don't want Michelle to know I'm home. I haven't decided if I'm going to tell her about Roger yet.

By the time I get to my floor, I feel like I've climbed Mount Everest and collapse on the floor. I lay there for a moment and catch my breath when suddenly my neighbor's door flies open, scaring the bejesus out of me. Before I have a chance to stand, four men who appear to be in their fifties walk out, three of them uniformed New York City policemen. When they see me, they smile.

'I guess Colin wasn't the only one gettin' into trouble last night,' one of them says.

As I struggle to my feet, my neighbor Colin appears in the doorway wearing nothing but a pair of black boxer briefs and a thin, white T-shirt. Running his hands through his short, dark, messy hair, he smirks when he sees me.

'Ah, don't listen to him,' Colin says in a thick lyrical Irish brogue. 'He's just kidding.'

I smile and nod. I don't know Colin very well. All I know is that he moved here a few months ago from Dublin and is gorgeous. He's got big, brown, puppy dog eyes with the kind of devilish twinkle in them that makes women melt and husbands worry. He has kind of an edgy look to him, a little bit Johnny Depp in his younger days. My guess is we're around the same age.

'Delilah, this is my dad,' he says, gesturing to the man

standing next to him, the one not wearing the police uniform. I'm surprised he remembers my name – we've met only once.

Rather than say hello, Colin's dad turns to him and hits him on shoulder. 'Jaysus Christ, don't be such a fecking disgrace, son! Go put your trousers on before talking to the lady, will ya?' He also has an Irish brogue.

'Ah, quit having a conniption,' Colin says, looking down at what he's wearing. 'I'm covered up, for Christ's sake.' He then looks over at me. 'Delilah, does my outfit bother ya?' he asks, pronouncing *my* like *me*, which I think is cool. (Little things always amaze me when I'm hungover.)

'No, it's fine,' I say, trying not to stare. His boxer briefs are actually the highlight of my last two days.

Colin turns to his dad and smiles. 'See?'

Colin's dad shakes his head, then walks over and takes my hand. 'Jimmy Brody,' he says, introducing himself. 'Nice to meet ya. Delilah, was it?'

'Yes,' I say, nodding.

Jimmy smiles and turns to his friends. 'Delilah, these are my friends. They're all Jimmys too.' Starting with the one on the left, he goes down the line. 'This is Jimmy Callahan, this is Jimmy Murphy, and this is Jimmy O'Shaughnessy.' He then addresses them as a group. 'Jimmys, say hello to Delilah.'

All the Jimmys say hello. They're obviously Irish, but unlike Colin and his dad, they have New York accents, so I'm guessing they're not from Dublin. After shaking everyone's hand, I turn to Colin. 'I guess I know who to call next time I'm in trouble.' Everyone laughs.

'Please,' bellows Jimmy Murphy, pointing to Colin. 'As if our hands aren't full enough with this one.'

'Hey, I've never done nothin' wrong,' Colin says, defending himself, but the guilty smirk on his face suggests otherwise.

'Oh right,' Jimmy O'Shaughnessy says loudly. 'Do I have to remind you about public intoxication and disturbing the peace?' He turns to me. 'He's had two run-ins already since he's been here, Delilah.'

'Yeah, you've got a criminal living next door to you,' Jimmy Callahan adds, winking.

'Oh, don't go scaring the girl,' Colin says. 'I'm no criminal. The first disturbance it was my birthday.'

'And 'twas it the second time, son?' Colin's dad asks, although it's obvious he knows.

Covering Colin's mouth, Jimmy Callahan answers for him. 'I remember, it was the first snowfall of the season, and after making a snow angel in the middle of Park Avenue, your son started going on about how important it is to love the Mother Earth, and woke the whole block in the process.'

As all the Jimmys erupt in laughter, Colin's face turns slightly red. 'Yeah, yeah – laugh all you want,' he says, smiling. 'I'm thankful to be here and don't take this earth for granted, what can I say?'

'Jimmys, we need to get going,' Jimmy Brody says after a bit. 'It was nice to meet you though, Delilah. I look forward to the next time.'

'Yeah, me too,' I say.

As the Jimmys head down the stairs, I say goodbye to Colin and unlock the door to my apartment. Just as I'm inside, Colin calls out to me, so I turn around. He's still standing in his doorway. In his underwear. 'Yeah?' I ask.

'I mean this in the nicest way,' he says, peering at me closely, 'but you look a bit green.'

'Green?' I let out a laugh. 'Since you're Irish, I'm going to assume that's some sort of compliment and let you off easy.'

'I'm sorry,' he says, letting out a laugh. 'What were you drinking last night?'

I hesitate for a second, afraid to say it. 'Tequila,' I finally whisper. Colin shudders and looks at me with pity. 'I lost my job yesterday,' I explain.

'Ah . . . sorry 'bout that. 'Tis a good reason to get drunk out of your head though. Good luck gettin' through the day.'

'Thanks,' I say, and then we both close our doors. Before proceeding any further, I lean against the wall for a second to catch my breath. Gosh, he's cute. Even though we have the only two apartments on this floor (mine's in the front of the building and his is in the back), I rarely see him and forgot what a looker he was. I hear him – he's always coming and going late at night, always having people over at three o'clock in the morning – but never see him. I think he's a bartender or something. We share a very thin wall, so I can pretty much hear everything. The other day I caught a glimpse of him carrying a hula hoop up the stairs, and then later that night, around three in the morning or so, I heard people laughing in his apartment along with an occasional 'Boing!' of the hoop hitting the wall. I think he was having some kind of late-night hula hoop party.

After gathering the strength to walk to the kitchen, I pour myself a glass of water and then plop down on the couch. Grabbing a pen and a piece of paper off a side table, I decide to do what Daniel suggested and make a list of the twenty guys. On the left side of the sheet I write numbers one through twenty and then begin to fill in some names. The first guy I ever slept with was my high school boyfriend, Nate. The second was his best friend, Daniel, Daniel the priest.

I can't believe I had sex with a priest.

Roger was the most recent, #20. Greg the East Village Idiot was #19 and—

Suddenly there's a knock at the door. I bet it's Michelle wanting to hear the scoop on last night. I bet she saw me leave with Roger. Even though I still have no idea what I'm going to tell her, I stand up, walk over to the door and look through the peephole. Hmm. It's Colin. And he's still in his underwear. I wonder what he wants. When I open the door, he holds out a shot glass filled with some kind of amber-colored liquid. Whiskey, maybe?

''Twill take the bite away,' he says.

The bite? Although I'm touched by his thoughtfulness (if bringing alcohol to someone who's hungover could be considered thoughtful), my mouth waters just looking at it. I think I might get sick.

'Thanks, but I can't drink that,' I say, shaking my head. 'In fact, I'm not sure I'm ever gonna drink again.'

'First, you can drink it,' he says. 'And second, sobriety's a deplorable affliction, so no going on the wagon.' He winks.

'Honestly, I don't think I'll be able to keep it down,' I

say, letting out a slight giggle. 'Besides, doing shots when you're hungover is a guy-thing, not a girl-thing.'

Colin waves his free hand in the air. 'Ah – guy-thing, girl-thing – I'll hear none of it. C'mon, just close your eyes, hold your nose, and you'll be fine.' When I don't respond or move, Colin reaches over and wraps my hand around the shot glass himself. 'It'll make you feel better, I promise. And if you think it's a guy-thing, I'll close my eyes while you drink it.'

I think about it for a second. Maybe it will make me feel better. People I know are always doing this – having a beer or doing a shot the morning after a crazy night – and swear it works. I reluctantly give in. 'Okay, fine,' I say slowly. 'But don't watch.'

Colin smiles and closes his eyes. 'I promise, I won't.'

Since Colin's not looking, I take the opportunity to check out his legs. I didn't want to stare earlier, but I caught a glimpse and they looked really nice. Looking down, I'm impressed at what I see. They're tan but not too tan, muscular but not bulky, and hairy but not too hairy. They're more than nice; they're perfect, actually. His toes are nice too. They're not all gangly like some guys'—

'What are you doin'?' Colin suddenly asks, startling me. When I quickly look up, I'm relieved to find his eyes still closed. Thank God.

'Oh, uh . . . I'm just thinking, that's all.' Okay, enough with the legs – it's time to get down to business. I hold up the shot glass. Although I'm tempted to toss its contents over my shoulder, I decide not to, so I close my eyes and think of happy things. *Bubble gum and puppy dogs, bubble gum and puppy dogs, bubble gum and puppy dogs, bubble gum and—*

Down the hatch it goes!

My mouth begins to water, just as I suspected it would, so I shake my head for a few seconds until it stops. When I open my eyes, I see Colin standing back a few feet from where he originally was, with a pained look on his face.

'You said you wouldn't look!' I exclaim.

'I'm sorry, but when I heard ya shakin', I got worried,' he explains. 'Are ya gonna get sick?'

I shake my head. 'No, I don't think so.'

'Attagirl,' he says, smiling big. He looks proud and, you know, *he should.*

For the next few seconds, the two of us stand in awkward silence, not sure what to say. 'So, is your dad a policeman?' I eventually ask, after racking my brain.

'My dad? Oh, no,' Colin says. He once again runs his hand through his messy hair. 'He works with them a lot though. He's a private investigator, owns a big company here in New York, has for years. They find cheating spouses, bust people for ripping off insurance companies, stuff like that.'

'Oh, he's not from Dublin? His accent is as heavy as yours.'

'Well, yeah, he *is* from Dublin, but he's lived here in New York for the last twenty years or so. Divorced parents. He should've lost the accent long ago, but hasn't. I joke with him about it all the time, accuse him of faking it to charm the ladies.'

'Ah, I get it.' I smile. 'So is he why you moved here?'

'No, actually, I'm an actor.'

'An actor? Really?' I ask, intrigued. 'What kind of stuff do you . . . act in?'

'Well I had a really small part on *Law & Order* last month, but other than that, I can usually be seen playing a bartender at the new vodka bar on Rivington.' I laugh.

'*Law & Order* – that's exciting.'

'Yeah, I s'pose.' Just then my phone rings, startling us both. 'I'll let you get that,' Colin says.

'Yeah.' I look at the shot glass and hand it back to him. 'Oh, and here. Thanks.'

'Any time. The color's already coming back in your face.' Colin turns to walk away, but then quickly stops and turns back around. 'Oh, Delilah?'

'Yes?'

'So, what'd you think?'

I'm confused. 'Think of what?'

Colin smirks. 'Think of my legs?'

His legs? Oh my . . . he was peeking. I feel my face flush. 'I don't know what you're talking about,' I say, trying to cover.

'Oh, sorry. My mistake,' Colin says, still smirking. He totally doesn't believe me. 'Have a nice day.'

'Yes, you too,' I say, trying to keep my cool.

After closing the door, I shake my head. The nerve of him! To peek is one thing, but to call me out on it is another. It's kind of . . . well, arrogant, to be honest.

Hurrying over to the phone, I look at the caller ID and see that it's my grandpa. I take a deep breath, raise my voice an octave – hoping to sound chipper, not hungover – and answer. 'Hi, Grandpa!'

'Hey, Darlin'! Sorry I missed you at Daisy's party last night, but by the time I got there, they said you left.'

'Oh!' I exclaim, disappointed. 'I didn't think you were coming.'

'Yeah, well, I got off work a little early.'

'Sorry I missed you.' I plop down on the couch. 'Hey, what did you think of Edward?'

'Oh, I liked him. He's good man,' he says. 'And you know what they say, you choose your friends by their character and your socks by their color.'

I smile. I love that my seventy-five-year-old grandpa is so open-minded. Suddenly I realize there's a spark in his voice. He's usually pretty chipper, but this spark is different. Something's up. 'Why do you sound so happy?'

'Well . . . I'm moving to Las Vegas!' he gleefully exclaims.

'Las Vegas?' I sit up, slightly stunned. Like I said, my grandpa rarely leaves the East Coast. 'Why?'

'I met someone. Or I should say I re-met someone. Do you remember Gloria from when you and Daisy were kids? We took you to the Bronx Zoo once, the time you cried because a llama peed on you in the petting zoo.' I remember Gloria, I remember the zoo, but I tried to bury the memory of that evil llama long ago. The thing practically attacked me.

'Yeah, I remember.'

'She lives in Las Vegas now, in a retirement community, but has been in town for the last few weeks visiting her family. I ran into her at the Holiday Inn Lounge – I go there dancing sometimes – and we got to talking. I don't know, we went to dinner, one thing led to another and now I'm gonna move in with her!'

Move in with her? Move away with her is more like it. This is not good, not good at all. From what I remember, this Gloria woman hung hippie beads all over her house, always burned incense and had carpet on the walls. When I point out to my grandpa that she might be a *stoner*, all he says is, 'Oh, Delilah, settle down. They give marijuana to people with glaucoma. It's not that bad for you.'

I'm truly dumbfounded. For a moment I feel like Carol Brady in that *Brady Bunch* episode where Greg becomes a hippie and moves into Mike's den. Except in this case it's not my son, it's my grandpa, and he's not moving into the den, he's moving to Vegas. Suddenly I hear background music through the phone – 'We built this city!' – and realize that my grandpa is listening to Jefferson Starship.

'I love this song,' he says. 'They play it at the lounge sometimes. It's good, huh?'

'No!' I shout. I mean, is he kidding? 'It's horrible and so is this idea of you moving! You belong in Connecticut with your family, not in Las Vegas with some stoner hippie lady you re-met while dancing to Jefferson Starship!'

My grandpa is silent. My negative reaction is obviously not what he was expecting. After a few seconds he takes a deep breath and speaks.

'Delilah,' he says softly, 'Connecticut gets cold in the winter; it makes my joints hurt. It's warm year-round where she lives – people drive around in golf carts, for crying out loud. I don't even need a car. I wanna hang out with people my own age. I need a change in my life.'

'Yeah, but—'

'Yeah but nothing,' my grandpa says, refusing to listen

to what I have to say. 'I'm doing this whether you like it or not, and I'm not calling for your permission but your blessing.'

I'm silent for a minute. My grandpa's moving away? What a shitty ending to an already crappy day. 'Are you sure you wanna do this?' I ask.

'Positive.'

Ever since Daisy and I were little, my grandpa has always told us that you know you're in love when your heart goes 'boom'. The way he explained this 'boom' is that it's not the giddy feeling you get when you first meet someone; it's deeper than that. It's more of a low, bellowing boom that resonates in your body the moment you realize you need someone, you love someone. It's more a boooooooom than a boom! I have yet to feel it; Daisy says she felt it with Edward, and my mom thinks my grandpa's crazy. But he's not crazy – he's just romantic.

'So did you feel—'

'Not yet,' he says, cutting me off. 'But I'm hoping I will. The two of us really clicked.'

My grandpa sounds happy when he says this, more happy than I've ever heard him sound. I don't want him to leave, but it's silly to expect that he'd stay just for me. If I re-met some old flame and fell in love, I'd probably move to wherever he lived to be with him. I want Grandpa to be happy, I do.

'Okay, fine,' I say reluctantly. 'You have my blessing, but don't let this Gloria woman boss you around because you're gonna be living in her house.'

'I won't,' he says. 'People change, Delilah.'

After getting the details of when he's leaving and

67

making farewell dinner plans, I hang up the phone and stare at the ceiling for a while. Thinking back to that day at the zoo, I never thought Gloria would be the one able to convince my grandpa to leave the East Coast. He's left before, yes, but only when my grandma was alive, which was way before my time. I never would've guessed she'd be the one he'd click with, but people change, I guess.

People change, I guess? Hmm. Suddenly getting an idea, I sit up.

I wonder what would happen if I re-met the twenty guys I slept with, if I bumped into any of them while I was out, listening to Jefferson Starship. I wonder if we'd click. Thinking back, I don't think any of them was the one, but people change, I guess.

I pick up the list Daniel wanted me to make, the list that I started but didn't finish, and look at it. If I were to end up with one of the twenty guys I already slept with, then my number wouldn't go up and I wouldn't have to live a lifetime of celibacy.

Call me crazy, but I really think I'm on to something here.

All I'd have to do is find out where they all live, if they're single, and then arrange to bump into them somewhere. I could do that – I totally could. I've got more than enough time on my hands now. I'm at the beginning of what's basically a six-week paid vacation. I could just get in a car, go find them all and pick the best of the bunch to settle down with. It's not such a wild idea. I was attracted to all of them at one time or another.

Yes, I really think this could work . . . I do!

I grab my pen and begin filling in the rest of the blanks on my list, which, to be honest, isn't as easy as it sounds. Sure, the first few and the last few were easy, but the middle's a bit foggy, specifically the college years, a time when, owing to a lack of sleep and vitamin-enriched foods and an overabundance of mind-altering substances like alcohol and recreational party drugs, I wasn't at my sharpest. It's easy to forget details, like someone's name for instance, when you're trying to break your roommate's record for the most upside-down margaritas done in one sitting. However, I don't let that stop me. I scribble and scribble and scribble . . . for the next hour I scribble.

When I'm done, after I've written down names, nick-names, and whatever else comes to mind, when I look at the list of twenty men who make up my number, an array of emotions run through my body. Despite the odd things that I remember about some of them, on my list is a man for all seasons. There's the one who looked good on paper and the one who just looked good . . . the one who couldn't get it up and the one who couldn't keep it down . . . the one who became my best friend and the one who became my worst enemy . . . the one who made me sweat with anticipation and the one who left me out in the cold. There's the one-night stand, the one-week fling, the pity lay, and the good one who got away. There's the one I lived for, the one I lusted after, and the one I thought I loved more than anyone else in the world. They're all there.

Tony Robbins says what separates the good from the great is the ability to take action, so that's what I'm going to do – take action! I'm going to get in a car and find these guys one by one. Yes, I'm going to do this and it's going to work! Celibacy is not an option, damn it – it's not!

Daniel said there wasn't a solution to my problem, but by God there is. And telling me I need Jesus – who does he think he is? I don't need Jesus.

I need Google.

Chapter Three

Mergers and Acquisitions*
A (very long) list by Delilah Darling

1. <u>Nate Syracuse</u> — High school boyfriend.
2. <u>Daniel Wilkerson</u> — Now known as Father Dan.
3. <u>Cowboy Shaner</u> — Frat boy who loved cowboy hats & Coors Light.
4. <u>Zubin Khan</u> — Quiet Indian Resident Advisor of my freshman-year dorm.
5. <u>Tim the Townie</u> — One half of the 'Thompson Twins' (not the 80s band); rumored to have a big one, didn't.
6. <u>Ian Kesselman</u> — Weirdly obsessed with his mom.
7. ~~<u>Kate Scott</u>~~ — It was college, I was curious, she doesn't count.
7. <u>Henry Parker</u> — One-night stand, used to prove to Kate I was straight. Aka 'Henry the Do-Gooder'.
8. <u>Oliver Leet</u> — Dapper Brit; cheated on me with a girl because he 'fancied her sparkly hose'.
9. <u>Tom the Townie</u> — Other half of the 'Thompson Twins'; rumored to have a big one, did.
10. <u>Nukes</u> — Don't know his last name. Or his first. Spring-break fling involving a trampoline. Came from an 'A' state. Arizona?

This is how long the average person's list would be. But I'm not the average person, I'm a tramp, so mine continues on the next page.

* Code name in case anyone finds this list.

11. <u>Foxy Blond</u> — Real name: Matt King. Aka 'The Stoner Who Couldn't Keep a Boner'.
12. <u>Delaware Pepper</u> — Yes, it's his real name. Smelled like macaroni.
13. <u>Alex Wolfe</u> — Triple threat: funny, smart, good-looking. Aka 'The Good One Who Got Away'.
14. <u>Wade Wojosomething</u> — Aspiring stuntman.
15. <u>The R.O.D.</u> — Real name: Rod Verdicchio. Booty-call Boyfriend. Obsessed with his D.O.G.
16. <u>Abogado</u> — Real name: Diego Soto. Barcelona fling; serious language barrier.
17. <u>Grody Gordy Peterson</u> — Lying S.C.U.M. (Self-Centered Urban Male) with 1 wife, 2 kids, 3 girlfriends and a 4-inch penis.
18. <u>Kyle Luxe</u> — Aka luxeynluv; result of innocent work e-mails spiraling out of control.
19. <u>Greg the East Village Idiot</u> — Not the sharpest tool in the shed.
20. <u>Roger Lipschitz</u> — Already got his second chance; blew it. Or scratched it and smelled it.

So there you have it. The twenty men who make up my number, all summed up on one page. I mean two. Yikes.

Things to Do for Road Trip
A list by Delilah Darling

1. ~~Buy road map for car.~~ Get car.
2. Buy road map for car.
3. Buy big black sunglasses, hat and binoculars for stakeouts.
4. In anticipation of lots of downtime during stakeouts:
   a. Buy lots of tabloids.
   b. Buy comfy clothes, like cotton underwear and flip-flops. No one likes stinky feet and the other thing.
   c. Load up on snacks and tasty beverages.
5. Bring camera and laptop to document journey. (If things work out with someone, photos taken will be great to show the future kids how Mommy and Daddy ~~met~~ re-met.)
6. Download music into iPod. In addition to getting music that brings back memories of each guy, get:
   a. Good sing-along music: John Denver, Kenny Rogers, Neil Diamond, Peter, Paul & Mary, and of course . . . Lionel Richie.
   b. Good kick-ass girl music: Pink, Gwen Stefani.
7. Based on a TV report on dirty hotel rooms:
   a. Buy pillows, sheets and blankets. (Hotel bedspreads are covered with grody things.)
   b. Buy rubber gloves to handle things like doorknobs, alarms clocks, telephones and remote controls. (Ditto for these things.) Note: Gloves can also be used to go through garbage if necessary.
8. Buy pink quartz Chinese love bracelet from old man on Canal Street, guaranteed to bring success.

'This is the craziest idea I've ever heard!'

Michelle is screaming in my ear, but I ignore her because I've read *The Success Principles: How to Get from Where You Are to Where You Want to Be* by Jack Canfield. According to Jack, many people will try to talk me out of my vision and say I'm crazy, but I'm not supposed to listen. I would tell Michelle this, but she'd probably just yell at me and tell me to quit quoting self-help books, so I'm going to keep it to myself and fumble with the windshield wipers on a blue Ford Focus I'm considering renting.

'Driving cross-country to find all the guys you've had sex with just so you won't have to up some crazy self-imposed limit is nuts.'

Obviously I ended up telling her what happened with Roger. And Daniel. And 10.5. And my twenty. And Daisy's four. And about being a tramp. I had to. I couldn't take off on a road trip by myself without telling anyone; that would be irresponsible.

'I can't believe you're actually considering doing this,' she snaps.

'I'm not considering – I'm doing. I'm taking action.'

'Then *take action* like any normal person would – pick up the phone and call these guys.'

'I'm not gonna call them!' I shriek. 'That'll look desperate.'

Michelle shudders with confusion. 'And showing up on their doorsteps won't?'

I roll my eyes. 'Michelle, Michelle, Michelle – I'm not just gonna go knock on their doors and ask them how they've been,' I explain. 'I'm gonna stake these guys out, figure out where they work, what they do, and then work my way back into their lives.'

'So you're gonna stalk them.' She stares at me incredulously.

'If that's what you want to call it,' I shrug.

'Delilah, stalking is a criminal activity – you could go to jail!'

'I'm not gonna go to jail; there's nothing illegal about what I'm doing. Curiosity is human nature. I have an enquiring mind.'

'Then buy a tabloid.'

'I did. I have a whole stack back at the apartment to read during my stakeouts. It was number 4a on my to-do list.'

'What to-do list?' Michelle asks nervously. Reaching in my purse, I pull it out and hand it to her. Gosh, for a person who rarely makes list, I can't believe I've made so many in the last few days.

When Michelle finishes reading, she glares at the pink bracelet on my wrist. 'Is that it?' she asks. 'Is that your Chinese love bracelet?'

'Hey, do you think this thing has anti-lock brakes?' I ask, trying to change the subject. I don't want to hear it.

'Delilah, pay attention! You're not thinking this through – you're rushing into it.'

I roll my eyes. I have thought it through – for three whole days I thought it through.

'Have you even thought about how much this is gonna cost? It'll be a fortune. I hope you know that.'

'No, it won't,' I insist. 'I'm giving myself six weeks to

make it work, which is technically how long our paid vacation is.'

'Del, we're not on a paid vacation. We've been laid off. You should be looking for a job, not for a . . .' Michelle stops talking to search for the right word.

'A life partner,' I offer. Michelle rolls her eyes. 'Jobs will always be there, Michelle; the opportunity to do this won't. Besides, even if it takes the entire six weeks to work, the most I'll end up spending is a little over five thousand dollars, which I have *and which you have*, thanks to my severance check, plus whatever the private investigator costs.'

Michelle rolls her eyes. 'Oh right, the private investigator. I can't believe you dragged your crazy Irish neighbor into this.'

You see, although Google helped me find out where many of the guys have been – running races, participating in charity events, winning cars in radio station contests (one of them did, I swear) – it wasn't much help in finding out where they are right now. Even if it was able to locate where they are *physically* (home addresses, work addresses), I need to know where they are *romantically* before I drive cross-country to re-meet them. I need to know if they're married, I need to know if they're gay. (One of them was a little bit questionable.) The only way for me to find out this stuff was to hire a private investigator.

After spending hours yesterday calling around to different ones to get quotes and finding out that they're too expensive, I decided to knock on Colin's door to see if his dad could give me a deal. He didn't answer, so I taped a note to it that said:

Colin,

I need to locate about fifteen old friends for a party I'm having. If I give you old addresses, nicknames, etc., do you think your dad could find them for me? I was quoted $150 per person and was hoping to spend less.

I just need the basics . . . current address, marriage history, sexual orientation. Let me know.

Thanks, Delilah
(your neighbor)

I said fifteen old friends because Roger and Daniel are out of the running for obvious reasons, I already know that #18, Kyle Luxe, is single and living in Los Angeles, and two locals – #17 and #19, Grody Gordy Peterson and Greg the East Village Idiot – don't need locating. In fact, like Roger and Daniel, I already eliminated them both from the running.

I 'coincidentally' bumped into Greg the East Village Idiot at the grocery store yesterday morning and, after a minute-long discussion, realized not much had changed. I had just finished reading an article in a magazine about euthanasia, living wills, and the like, and asked Greg to share his thoughts on the issue. After looking at me blankly, he mumbled something to the effect of not understanding what little kids in Asia had to with living well.

'No, no – living *wills* and *euthanasia*,' I clarified. 'It's been a hot topic in the news lately.'

Greg shrugged. 'Sorry, you lost me.'

Later that afternoon I went jogging and coincidentally ended up in front of the building where Grody Gordy

Peterson works, right around the time he used to leave for lunch every day. Grody Gordy and I dated for three months a few years back. At the time, he told me he was single, which he very much wasn't. Not only did he have a wife and two kids, but he had two other girlfriends besides me. I found all this out one day when one of those girlfriends called to yell at me for dating her married boyfriend. Yes, it was all a little bit screwed up. Anyway, because of this, even if Gordy was suddenly single, I doubt I'd consider dating him again, but I had to explore all my options.

Long story short, Gordy is definitely not suddenly single. All in the matter of a lunch hour, I watched him canoodle with an unknown woman in the back of a cab, snuggle up to a second in a Starbucks, and then kiss his wife hello as she greeted him at the door of their Gramercy Park brownstone with a sandwich. Poor woman. I hope she spends all his money and then leaves him.

Anyway, this is why I need Colin's dad to find only fifteen guys – I've eliminated four already and found one on my own. So back to my note. Like I said, I hung it on Colin's door around seven o'clock and then went to meet my grandpa and Gloria for a farewell dinner at Chili's. (My grandpa goes bananas for the 'I want my baby back, baby back, baby back . . . Chili's baby back ribs!') After a pleasant reunion with Gloria and a tearful goodbye with my grandpa, I got home around eleven and found a return note taped to my door. It said:

To my dear neighbor Delilah—
Talked to my father. Yes, can give you a deal. I'm

working tonight, so put all the info you have under my door. I'll have a price for you tomorrow, stop by around 6.00.

Cheers, Colin

PS Sexual orientation? What kind of a party is this?

So, anyway, I'm planning to go see him after I rent this car. With that, I slap the dashboard. As far as famous road trips go, a blue Ford Focus isn't exactly on a par with Thelma and Louise's cool blue Thunderbird, but it's more reliable and more economical. After honking the horn wildly to celebrate, I lean out the window and yell to the car rental guy. 'I'll take it!'

Mr Lucky Charming

Around 6.30, when I hear the *vroom* of Colin's old beat-up Vespa, I look out the window. His scooter really is a clunker; I always hear him coming and going on it. After giving him a few minutes to settle in, I freshen up – smear a little gloss across my lips, give my hair a fluff – and then head over to his apartment. I'm not trying to impress him or anything. It's just that the last time he saw me I had been crying and barfing all morning, and I don't want anyone to think I really look like that.

After I knock, it takes Colin only a second to answer the door. He smiles when he sees me. Unlike Saturday, he's dressed in a gray vintage-looking T-shirt and an old pair of Levi's. His feet are bare again though, and his toes are still clean. 'Welcome, Delilah,' he says, waving me inside.

Colin's place looks like a typical guy's apartment. Everything in it is pretty much brown and blue, crumbs and empty beer bottles decorate the floors and counters, and nothing decorates the walls. Oh, and yes, there's a hula hoop in the corner. It's bad but not as bad as some apartments I've seen. For one, it's IKEA-free, and two, a full set of All-Clad pots and pans hang from a rack in the kitchen. 'Do you like to cook?' I ask, motioning to the cookware.

'Ah . . . yeah,' Colin says, nodding at the pots. 'I'm a master chef. I like to mix leftovers together. I make good goulashes and fries with them.'

'Goulashes?' I ask. I don't even know what goulash is.

'Yep.' Colin nods. 'And fries.' He then motions to the couch. 'Please, sit yourself down.'

'Thanks,' I say, doing just that.

'So, how are ya? Ya good?' he asks, sitting down himself.

'Yes, great. Thanks. And you?'

'Couldn't be better,' he says, picking up a pile of papers.

While waiting for Colin to flip through the stack and find what he's looking for, I look around his apartment some more. Sitting on the table in front of me is a script of some sort. I want to look, but don't want to be nosy. Looking back at him, I study his face. He definitely has the looks of a leading man, but I wonder if he has any talent. You know, maybe it's the Irish accent, maybe it's the first name, maybe it's because he's an actor as well, or maybe it's because he's so darn sexy – whatever the reason, Colin looks a little less like Johnny Depp to me now, and a little more like—

'So, you're having a party, are ya?' he asks, interrupting my thoughts.

'Huh? Oh, yes – a party. It's a . . . reunion party of sorts. Old friends getting together.'

'A reunion party? With all guys?'

'Pardon me?'

Colin looks up. 'The list you gave me was all guys.'

'Oh, uh . . . it's kind of a singles thing, too. I have a bunch of girls already lined up.'

'I see,' he says, drumming his fingers on his knee. 'I s'pose it's none of my business anyway. Okay, here's the deal. Based on the info you gave me, it'll be fifty dollars a person.'

'Fifty dollars a person?' I ask excitedly. That's *way* less than I expected. 'Really?'

Colin nods. 'Yeah. Most of it's pretty basic – some computer work and a couple of phone calls. In fact, I can probably do a lot of it from here.'

From here? 'Wait, *you're* gonna do it?' I ask uneasily. 'I thought you were an actor.'

'I am, but when things are slow, like they are now, I help out my dad.'

I don't want to offend him, but . . . 'Colin, don't take this the wrong way, but I was hoping to hire a real private investigator, someone like Magnum, P.I.'

'If you want me to grow a mustache, I will,' he teases.

I laugh. 'That's not what I meant.'

'Yes, I know. I'm just kidding. But listen, seriously, if you want someone at my dad's office to do this for you, then fine, but it'll cost you more. Me doing it instead helps us both out. For one, I get to keep whatever I make, and because of that, I can charge you whatever I want. I was doing you a favor with the fifty bucks because I know you just lost your job. Anybody else is gonna charge you more.'

Hmm, what to do, what to do? If I don't let Colin do this, not only will I have to fork over at least a thousand more dollars than what he's charging me, but he'll also be out seven hundred fifty dollars. I begin to feel guilty.

'Have you done this before?' I ask. 'Do you know how to find people? And find out if they're married? And find out if they're gay?'

'Of course I do,' he assures me. 'Don't worry.'

I stare at Colin long and hard. I'm still not sure. I'm putting a lot of energy into this, and if he gives me the wrong information for anyone, it's going to be a big waste of time.

'So what do you think?' he pushes. 'Do we have a deal?'

Oh, what do I have to lose? I'm sure it's not brain surgery. 'Sure,' I say, exhaling loudly. 'I mean *yes*, we have a deal.'

Colin smiles. 'Excellent.'

'So how long will it take?'

'Well, when's your party?'

I draw a blank. 'What party?'

Colin cocks his head. 'The singles party? The reason you need to find all these guys?'

Suddenly I remember my excuse. 'Oh, right! *That* party. It's soon, really soon.'

Colin shakes his head and looks back down at the papers – he so knows I'm not having a party. After pilfering through the pile once more, he pulls out a few sheets and hands them to me. 'I found these three guys already, and they're all single and straight.'

My eyes light up. 'Three? In a day? Already?'

'Yeah, well, I didn't have anything else to do today, so I thought I'd get started.'

When I look at them, I can barely contain my excitement. He's already found #14, #15, and #16, Wade Wojosomething, The R.O.D. and Abogado. Wade's in Chattanooga, Rod's in Philadelphia, and Abogado's in New Orleans. I look up at Colin and smile. I feel bad for doubting him. 'Wow, you're good!'

He winks. 'That's what they tell me.' He looks back down at the list. 'I'll probably have a couple of questions along the way, but I have one now. Do you mind?'

'No, not at all,' I say. 'Shoot.'

'One of the names on the list you gave me is a guy named Nukes. Is that his real name?'

Ah yes, Nukes, #10 on my list. Nukes wasn't exactly one of my longer relationships. He was a spring-break fling. I was a senior in college at the time and went to Cabo San Lucas with my friends for a week. After a long day of drinking Coco Locos in the sun, I hooked up with Nukes on a trampoline on a beach. I know it sounds like fun, but the trampoline was so bouncy and the Coco Locos were so strong that the sex wasn't even memorable.

Neither was his name.

'Not exactly,' I tell Colin. 'I believe Nukes was a nick-name based on his last name, but I can't be certain because I don't remember his last name.'

'How about his first?'

I shake my head. 'Nope, sorry. But hey, I wrote down some other information that might help you find him.'

Colin looks down at the piece of paper. 'Right, you

did . . . ' Looking bewildered, he reads the information I gave him. 'In 1997 he was anywhere from eighteen to twenty-one years old. You think he played football for Arizona State, but you might be wrong, it might've been Arkansas or Alabama.'

I nod. 'Right. I just remember that the state began with an *A*.'

'What about Alaska?' Colin asks. 'Alaska begins with an *A*.'

Alaska? Oh crap. I never thought about Alaska. No, no – if it was Alaska, I would've remembered asking about Eskimos and polar bears and things. I shake my head.

'No, I'm positive it was Arizona.'

'Or Alabama. Or Arkansas.'

'Right.'

Colin smirks. 'Sounds like this is gonna be some party.'

After exchanging phone numbers and e-mail addresses, Colin walks me to the door. As he says goodbye, he puts both arms over his head and stretches big, causing his shirt to lift up a few inches, exposing the sexiest abs and treasure trail I've ever seen. Without thinking, I stop and stare – I'm entranced by it – then quickly snap out of it. When I look back up, Colin is frozen, arms still in the air, with a smirk on his face.

Oops. I think I've been busted. Again.

'You were checkin' out my abs, weren't ya?' he asks, laughing.

Yep, I've been busted. Again. Deny, deny, deny.

'Abs? No, I wasn't doing anything of the sort.'

'Yes, you were. You were totally checkin' 'em out and I caught ya. First it was my legs, now it's my abs – you're beginning to make me feel like a piece of meat, Delilah.'

Oh jeeze, I'm so embarrassed, but I stick to my guns. 'I'm sorry but I don't know what you're talking about.'

He nods. 'Right . . .' He then extends his hand to me. 'Well, goodbye.'

'Goodbye.' After giving my hand a quick, firm shake, Colin hangs on to it for an extra second and gives it a little squeeze. I blush. After he lets it go, I turn around and walk to my apartment. As I open the door, I hear him call out my name again, like he did Saturday. I don't turn around because I know what's coming – he's going to ask me what I thought of his abs. 'I'm not falling for it again,' I say confidently. Colin laughs.

'Thought I'd try.'

Once I'm safely in my apartment, I close the door behind me and lean against the wall. Damn . . . what a flirt. But damn . . . what a good private investigator! When I pull out the pieces of paper and read them again, adrenaline rushes through my body – I can't believe I'm really going to do this. I sit down and clearly lay out how much time and money I have.

	$ 7,264	Amount of my severance check.
+	$ 2,000	Estimated amount of Michelle's unemployment.
	$ 9,264	
÷	2	We're splitting . . .
	$ 4,632	
+	$ 538	My checking account balance.
	$ 5,170	
–	$ 1,032	Monthly car rental.

$$\overline{\$\ 4,138}$$

$-\quad \underline{\$\ 150}$ Money paid to Colin (3 guys @ $50 each)

$ 3,988

I have $3,988 and forty-two days to find sixteen guys. I can do it . . . I can do it! Standing up, I run to my room and begin packing. I'm going on a road trip! Philadelphia, here I come.

Chapter Four

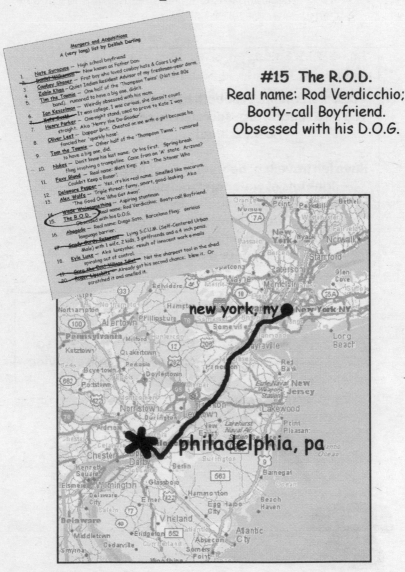

Mergers and Acquisitions
A (very long) list by Delilah Darling

1. Nate Syracuse — High school boyfriend
2. ~~Daniel Wilkinson~~ — Now known as Father Dan.
3. Cowboy Shaner — Frat boy who loved cowboy hats & Coors Light.
4. Zubin Khan — Quiet Indian Resident Advisor of my freshman-year dorm.
5. Tim the Townie — One half of the 'Thompson Twins' (Not the 80s band), rumored to have a big one, didn't.
6. Ian Kesselman — Weirdly obsessed with his mom.
7. ~~Kate Scott~~ — It was college. I was curious, she doesn't count.
   Henry Parker — One-night stand, used to prove to Kate I was straight.
8. Oliver Lest — Dapper Brit. Aka 'Henry the Do-Gooder'.
   fancied her 'sparkly hose'
9. Tom the Townie — Other half of the 'Thompson Twins'; rumored
   to have a big one, did.   Spring break
10. Nukes — Don't know his last name. Or his first. Come from an 'A' state. Arizona?
    thing involving a trampoline. Aka 'The Stoner Who
11. Foxy Blond — Real name: Matt King. Aka 'The Stoner Who
    Couldn't Keep a Boner'.
12. Delaware Pepper — Yes, it's his real name. Smelled like macaroni.
13. Alex Wolfe — Triple threat: funny, smart, good-looking. Aka
    'The Good One Who Got Away'.
14. ~~Wade Watersomething~~ — Aspiring stuntman.
15. The R.O.D. — Real name: Rod Verdicchio; Booty-call Boyfriend.
    Obsessed with his D.O.G.
16. Abogado — Read name: Diego Soto. Barcelona fling; serious
    language barrier.
17. ~~Scotty Gordo Patterson~~ — Lying S.C.U.M. (Self-Centered Urban
    Male) with 1 wife, 2 kids, 3 girlfriends and a 4 inch penis.
18. Kyle Luxe — Aka luxeyluv; result of innocent work e-mails
    spiraling out of control.
19. ~~Greg the East Village Idiot~~ — Not the sharpest tool in the shed.
20. ~~Roger Upadhye~~ — Already got his second chance. blew it. Or
    scratched it and smelled it.

#15 The R.O.D.
Real name: Rod Verdicchio;
Booty-call Boyfriend.
Obsessed with his D.O.G.

new york, ny

philadelphia, pa

Beep

Del, this is Mom. Elisabeth herself sent you on a special, top-secret assignment? How exciting!

Have fun traveling, dear, and don't forget - drink lots of water and moisturize liberally. Airplanes really dehydrate your skin, which is something you can't afford. I noticed you've been getting some fine lines around your eyes. Have fun!

Beep

Hey, it's Daisy. Got your message. I'm so jealous you're going away - Mom's driving me crazy. Call me.

After slipping a check for one hundred fifty dollars under Colin's door, I leave early the next morning. Philadelphia is a good city to start my search in for one main reason: it's close to New York and I'm a really bad driver. I'm okay when it comes to driving around town (I find comfort in all the stopping and going that comes along with it), what I don't like is the highway. Not only am I afraid to drive fast, but when things get too still, like when I'm cruising along with all the other drivers, I become paranoid. I hear funny noises – clicks, hums and rattles – that aren't really there, and I assume that a tire's about to fall off or the engine's about to blow. Because of this fear, I'm cautious when driving, perhaps too cautious. I'm the driver everyone hates on the highway, the one who drives forty miles per hour in a fifty-five-mile zone, with my hands at 'ten and two'. I'm a total mess.

Since I didn't want the simple fact that I can't drive to prevent me from going on this road trip, I convinced myself that all I need is a little practice. I am hoping I'll get better. Until that happens, to deter my mind from obsessing, as well as to drown out the clicks, hums, and rattles, I tune my iPod to the playlist that contains songs from the year 2000, for that's when I met the reason I'm going to Philly. As sounds of *NSYNC fill my ears, I say 'Baby, bye, bye, bye' to New York, and begin to remember #15 on my list, Rod Verdicchio.

I don't know if *dated* is the right word to use when describing my relationship with Rod. He wasn't a one-night stand, but he wasn't a boyfriend either. In fact, he never even took me to dinner. What can I say, guys like this happen.

I was twenty-five years old at the time and had a very active social life. Every weekend my friends and I would go out to whatever the hottest Manhattan club of the moment was and dance our sweaty booties off till dawn. Everywhere we went, no matter where it was, we always ran into Rod and his friends. The reason we initially noticed them was because they were big guys, guys who didn't fit in with the rest of the scene. You see, when a place in Manhattan is considered *hot*, the average Joe can't walk in off the street and have a drink. In order to get inside, either you have to know someone and get your name on a list, or you have to look amazing and impress the doorman, which is easier said than done – he's usually an asshole, especially to guys. Rod and his friends weren't pretty boys, nor did they dress particularly well, so I'm not sure how they got into half the places we ran into them, but somehow they did. They were at every club, every opening, every party. And they stuck out like sore thumbs.

Rod was over six feet tall and about two hundred pounds. He was Italian, really Italian, born and bred in South Philly. He was a little bit of a meathead, however, not in the 'I like to work out' kind of way but more in the 'I like to pig out' kind of way. He liked pizza and power tools, football and fixing things, which is actually the reason I was attracted to him. In New York, a city of metrosexuals, Rod was one of the few 'guys' left.

Rod and I always said hello to each other and quickly became friends. He was a born salesman and very charming. One night he invited me back to his place for a nightcap after the bar closed, and I eagerly accepted. We kissed and hooked up that evening, but didn't sleep together. Before I left, we exchanged phone numbers, but neither of us called the other. I'm not sure of Rod's reason for not doing so, but as for me, although I liked him, I didn't get butterflies in my stomach when I saw him. He was just a funny, nice guy, someone to hook up with.

The next time we ran into each other, the same thing happened. We went back to his place after the bar closed, hooked up, and then neither of us called the other. This proceeded to happen again and then again – both times with no post-hookup phone call. Once we finally slept together is when the phone calls started. As much as I'd like to say they were daytime 'What are you doing this weekend?' phone calls, I can't because they were night-time 'Do you wanna have sex?' phone calls. Yes, Rod was my booty-call boyfriend.

For as much fun as I had with Rod, I knew I'd never develop feelings for him because I found him slightly irritating, which is why he was perfect for this. For some reason, he'd always refer to himself in the third person, and would spell out his name while doing so. For example, if we were out and he wanted to go home, he'd say, 'The R.O.D. wants to leave.' Or if he was telling me about a particularly grueling day, he'd say, 'The R.O.D. is wiped.' This kind of talk bothered the D.E.L.I.L.A.H. (It doesn't work as well with longer names.)

Another thing that bugged me about The R.O.D. was that he was completely obsessed with his D.O.G., a black Lab named M.A.X. Apparently, Max had a medical problem and almost died when he was a puppy, and ever since, Rod had become infatuated with him. 'I almost lost him,' he'd say, when recalling the gruesome details of Max's lifesaving surgery. Rod worshiped Max. He talked about him all the time and took him everywhere he went. They were inseparable, the two of them. Inseparable. Case in point: Rod allowed Max on his bed while we were having sex. It was so awkward. He'd sit down by our feet and watch us, I swear.

Because Max totally ruined the mood for me, I asked Rod if it was possible to make him wait outside the bedroom until we were finished. When I did, he, of course, said no and pointed out, 'You're in his bed, you know.' Yeah, it was covered in dog hair, I knew.

After weeks of begging, I finally convinced Rod to at least make Max get off the bed during sex; however, doing so backfired on me. Realizing he was being slighted, Max would sit at the edge of the bed and stare at me. Holding his head one foot away from mine, he'd breathe his smelly dog breath on me and occasionally drool on the sheets. It was horrible.

'Just ignore him,' Rod would say. *Pump, pump, pump.*

Ignore him? I couldn't ignore him. Every so often I felt his cold wet nose rub against my elbow, and one time he even leaned over and gave me a kiss.* Eventually I started to hate Max, and I like dogs too, so that's saying a lot. My hatred ran deep, so deep in fact that it freaked me out because I didn't know where it came from. As time went on, however, as Rod and I continued to have sex, I slowly

---

* I have a friend who was having sex once and, in the middle of it, felt something wet on his rear. When he turned around to see what it was, he realized his dog had just licked his butt cheek. Different cheek but a similar story. Pets and sex don't mix; they just don't.

figured it out. I didn't hate Max because he was always hanging around; I hated him because he got more of Rod's attention than I did. I was jealous.

When I got involved with Rod, I knew what I was getting into. It was just sex – he didn't want anything from me, and I didn't want anything from him. But when I saw the way he acted with his dog, when I saw how much he cared for him, I couldn't help but feel something more. It was attractive the way he took care of Max. In the morning he'd take him for a walk and make him a steak breakfast, and then afterward, he'd rub his belly and brush his coat until it was shiny. Rod never did any of those things for me. He never rubbed my belly, never fed me steak, never brushed my hair. I wanted the attention Rod gave Max.

It's a funny thing. When it comes to having sex, I try to convince myself that every once in a while I can have it like a man, with no strings attached. Sex is fun; it can be purely physical. I'm a single working woman in New York City, for God's sake; I need to work off stress. But more often than not, doing this backfires on me, much like making Max get off the bed during sex did. I'm not a man, I'm a woman, and we aren't wired the same way, it's a fact. We have some kind of hormone that makes it difficult to have unemotional sex. I read it in a book. I'm not saying all women are helpless romantics who fall in love with every guy they sleep with, but it's not as easy as it seems to shut off every last bit of emotional attachment. This is what happened with Rod. I went in thinking it was just sex but ended up developing feelings; I ended up wanting more.

I didn't want to put Rod on the spot and tell him how I was feeling because I didn't think it was fair. I signed up for a booty-call relationship, after all, and felt it was wrong for me to expect anything more. I hinted to him a couple of times about the possibility of us doing something when it was light outside, but he didn't really respond to the idea, so I let it go.

Since I kept thinking and hoping that Rod would fall in love with me, I didn't put an end to the booty calls. I still went to his apartment at all hours of the night and still had sex with him while his dog watched and waited for us to finish. Afterward, sometimes, I'd lie in his bed and feel sorry for myself.

Then a funny thing happened. One morning, while I was doing just this, Rod got up to take a shower. When he did, I looked down at Max, who was lying at my feet, and gave him a sad little smile. Max wagged his tail, and then came over and licked my arm. It was like he was giving me a kiss, telling me it was going to be okay. It was so sweet. I never realized how cute he was until that moment.

When Rod got out of the shower, for some reason, Max stopped what he was doing and hurried back down to the foot of the bed. Once I smoothed out the covers, we both closed our eyes like we had been sleeping the whole time Rod was gone. When he came back to his room and got dressed, we peeked at each other a couple of times, like we knew we had shared a moment, but neither of us wanted Rod to know. I'm not sure what Max's reasons were, but I didn't want Rod to think I was using his dog to get closer to him, like 'Your dog likes me, so you should, too'.

The next time I was at Rod's, it happened again. When Rod went to the kitchen to get something to eat, Max laid down next to me and the two of us hugged. It was great – not only was Max warm and cuddly, but he had a lovely scent to him, too. He smelled a little bit like butterscotch. Once again, when we heard Rod walking toward the bedroom, Max hauled-ass back down to the foot of the bed, just like he did the previous time.

From this point, things spiraled out of control. I started booty-calling Rod more and more, just so I could see his dog. And every night after sex, rather than feel sorry for myself, I'd look forward to the morning, look forward to Rod's shower, look forward to having another quickie with Max, my little Maxi-pad. During the time we spent together, I told Max all about my life, all about my problems. I talked and talked and talked, and he blinked. Max knew about my friends, about my family – Rod didn't know about any of those things. For once it was so nice to have someone who listened.

As I started delving into deeper issues with Max, I realized that Rod's showers weren't long enough. (Ten minutes is hardly enough time to contemplate the meaning of your life, you know?) To allow myself more time with him, I started doing things to get Rod out of the apartment. Not only would I send him out for coffee and doughnuts in the morning, but a couple of times I even hid his box of condoms and then forced him to go out in the middle of the night to get more. Poor Rod had no idea what was going on; it was like Max and I were having an affair behind his back.

One day I realized I didn't care about Rod any more. All

the feelings I thought I had for him were gone. But I didn't want to stop the booty calls, no way – I was totally attached to his dog. I wasn't sure what I should do. I was stuck between a dog and hard place.

Then once again a funny thing happened. One night Rod got a little carried away during sex. Right before he was about to . . . get there, he yelled, *'Give it to the R.O.D! Right-O!!!!!'* at the top of his lungs. Max must have thought Rod was hurting me because he started barking ferociously at him – he even bared his teeth. It was awkward. Rod's dog had turned on him to protect me.

That was the last time I saw either of them. Not only did Rod ask me to not stay the night that evening, but the next time I booty-called him he said he didn't think it was a good idea if we saw each other any more. Just like that, our relationship was over. I'd be lying if I said I wasn't a little saddened by this, but I'm pretty sure I missed the company of Rod more than I missed Rod himself. I mean, sometimes it's just nice to be with someone, even if you know he isn't the one.

Right around the same time, my friends and I stopped going out every weekend. I got sick of the scene, sick of getting decked out, sick of the same old, same old every single weekend. I was getting older and didn't find it as exciting as I once did.

According to Brody, P.I. (insert bad 80s TV theme song here), Rod and Max have been living in Philadelphia since 2002. Despite the awkward way things ended, I still have fond memories of the time we spent together. I miss his warm body next to mine and I'm excited to see him again. Rod too.

My drive to Philadelphia goes off without a hitch, but as I pull up to my hotel, I quickly realize booking it before I left New York might not have been such a good idea. Although it's not far from where Rod lives, the locale leaves something to be desired. Situated in South Philly by the stadium, the neighborhood looks like the one Rocky used to live in before he beat Apollo Creed's ass and moved into the mansion. However, I'm not going to be high maintenance. I can stay in a room that smells like smoke in a gross hotel in a rough neighborhood, I can. I'm not on a vacay; I'm on a mission.

After settling in, I decide to drive by Rod's, so I put on my sunglasses/baseball hat disguise and head out. The house he lives in is located off Passayunk, a main street that runs through South Philly, and the closer I get to it, the nicer the neighborhoods become. In fact, when I pull onto Rod's street, I have to stop and take a breath because it's so pretty. Beautiful brownstones fill the tree-lined street, flower baskets bursting with color hang from windows. It's blooming with life. As for Rod's house, it's large and gray. He's obviously doing well. After finding a parking spot across the street, I pull in, turn off the engine and wait.

And wait.

And wait.

By ten o'clock that evening, Rod still hasn't made an appearance, so I head back to the hotel. From what I remember, he used to take Max for his morning walk around seven o'clock, so I decide to go back then.

The next morning, sure enough, Rod emerges from his

house with Max at seven o'clock on the dot. When I see them, I instantly smile. I can't help it – this is all so exciting! As I watch them walk down the street, I notice that both of them seem to have put on a little weight. However, they don't look bad – they look good.

When they disappear around the corner at the end of the block, I turn on my car and nervously follow. Michelle was right. Saying I was going to do this was one thing, actually doing it is quite another. My hands are shaking so much that I can barely hold the wheel. Two blocks away, Rod and Max enter what seems to be a dog park, so I pull my car over to the side of the road and watch them play for the next twenty minutes or so.

Rod seems confident, which to me is the biggest turn-on. Confidence has a way of making me want to tear the clothes off even the most average-looking man.* After deciding he's worth a second chance, I ponder my next step. I believe our relationship ended because Rod thought Max liked me better, because Rod felt Max's loyalty might have resided with me and not him. I came between them, and I need something to show Rod that it won't happen again. It's clear to me what I need, it is . . .

I need my own dog.

Bitches and Studs

Later that morning, around ten o'clock, I walk into a pet store on Passayunk and begin to look for my new best

* Note to men: there's a very fine line between confidence and arrogance. Don't mistake the latter for the former.

friend. I know I can be impulsive, but getting a dog is something I've thought about for a while, ever since Max actually. The only reason I never took the plunge is because I was working so much. But I don't have that problem anymore. Yes, I realize a road trip probably isn't the best time to get a dog, but that's beside the point.

Since I live in a small apartment, I think a little dog is the best way to go. However, to avoid comparisons to irritating people like Paris Hilton and Tinkerbell (Sorry, Tinks . . . your mom bugs me way more than you do), I will not dress my dog up like a doll, carry it around in a bag like an accessory, or raise my voice a gazillion octaves and talk to it like a baby ('puppy-talk') – because it's not any of those things. In my opinion, 'puppy-talking' is the worst of these crimes – it's demeaning to both you and the dog. I never spoke to Max that way, and I think he respected me for it.

Toward the back of the store, behind a big glass wall, are dozens of puppies sitting on display, waiting for someone to take them home. There are puppies of every color – puppies playing, puppies sleeping, puppies pooping – puppies, puppies, puppies everywhere. As they look out at me with their big dark eyes, I can't help but feel sorry for them because they're all cute, every one of them, it's just how cute they are compared to the others that determines whether or not someone takes them home. It's all about the competition in a pet store, just like it was in all those Manhattan clubs I'd go to when I met Rod. You feel confident and sexy when the doorman gives you the green light to enter, but once you get inside and realize you're one sexy person amongst a thousand and experience just how fierce the competition really is, it's a bit disappointing.

Working my way down the cages, I pass three Malteses sleeping on top of one another, two Jack Russell terriers chewing each other's ears, one Bulldog taking a dump, and oh wow . . . the cutest chocolate-colored Lab ever. Yes, I want a small dog, but this one sure is a cutie. When I kneel down to take a good look, the dog wags its tail and presses its nose to the glass, then lies down and rolls over on his back to expose his belly and—

Oh, Jesus!

The dog – obviously a boy – is very excited. I quickly look away, feeling like I've just seen the centerfold in *Puppy Playgirl*.

Standing back up, I leave the chocolate Lab hanging in the breeze (both figuratively and literally) when a young kid who works in the store walks over to me. Maybe eighteen years old, he has pimples on his chin, a pair of Harry Potter glasses on his nose, and a silver smile (braces) that stretches from ear to ear. He's wearing a name tag, but I don't look at it because I don't want to know his name. For some reason, I've decided that his name is going to be The Kid.

'Can I show you a puppy?' The Kid asks.

'Yeah . . . but I'm not sure which one I want to see yet. The only thing I'm sure about is that I don't want a boy dog. I want a girl dog.' No way am I getting a boy, not after what I just saw.

Before The Kid has a chance to respond, I hear a scary, shrill voice come from behind me. 'You mean you want a *bitch*!' When I turn around, I see an ugly old hag of a lady standing behind a counter.

'Excuse me?' I ask.

'They're not called *girl* dogs,' she huffs. 'They're called *bitches*! And the *boy* dogs are called *males*!'

Bitches and males? That doesn't seem fair. 'Why aren't the boy dogs called *bastards*?' I ask.

'I don't know,' the old lady says defensively, throwing her hands in the air. 'Sometimes they're called studs – it's just the way things are.' Bitches and *studs*? It still doesn't seem fair.

'Well, it's not right,' I tell her, 'and I'm not gonna perpetuate it.' I turn back to The Kid and speak loudly. 'I'd like to see a *girl* dog, please.' The Kid smiles.

'I have a really great girl dog downstairs, let me go get her.'

As I wait for The Kid to return, I think of two more reasons why this place is just like those Manhattan clubs. Not only are they both filled with bitches and studs, both also come equipped with an asshole. The Manhattan hot spot usually has one at the door; this place has one behind the counter.

The Kid returns and motions for me to come to the back of the store. When I arrive to a one-on-one puppy playroom, he's holds up a tiny black and brown Yorkie for me to see. 'She weighs four pounds,' he says.

Although she's a little scruffy and scraggly, she's cute, so I take her from him. When I do, she looks up at me. Long eyelashes set off her big brown eyes, her button nose is as black as they come. She looks like Chewbacca with one heck of a handlebar mustache.

'She's cute,' I tell The Kid, 'but I was hoping for something a little bigger than four pounds.' Hearing me say this, the Yorkie begins blinking incessantly. It's like she can understand and is batting her eyelashes, flirting, trying her hardest to show me how adorable she is. Seeing her work it makes me smile at her. When I do, I swear to God . . . she smiles back. My mouth drops open.

'Oh my God!' I exclaim, looking up at The Kid. 'Did you see that?'

'See what?'

'She smiled at me – I swear, she did!'

'Oh, you don't have to convince me. She does it all the time. That's why I wanted you to see her. If you look back down at her, she'll do it again.'

I look back down at the puppy, and sure enough, she smiles a second time. Suddenly a voice comes out of my mouth that I do not recognize: '*Hewwwo you wittle poopy poopy poo!* I screech. '*Who's so pwetty today? Whooo? You are, dat's whooo!*' Looking up, I cover my mouth in horror. 'I always said I'd never do that!' I say to The Kid, in my normal voice.

'It happens.'

'*Whooo's my butter wutter babycakes?* I squeal again, looking back down. By God, he's right. It does. '*You are, dat's whooo!*'

Hearing my high-pitched voice makes the puppy cock her head. Call me crazy, but I think she can understand what I'm saying. 'She's so adorable,' I say, laying her in the crook of my arm. I then rock her like a baby. When I bring my finger up to her nose, she bats it with her paws and tries to bite it. 'How much is she?'

'I'm not sure, but I know she's on sale,' The Kid says. 'The old lady marked her down.'

Bending over, I put her on the ground. Holding her head high in the air, she scampers around. 'Marked her down?' That's odd. 'Why?'

'She's old.'

'Old?' Reaching down, I turn her collar until I can read her birthday. She was born six months ago. 'You're not old,' I tell her. She stops and stares at me intensely. A few seconds later, she backs up ever so slowly and then charges toward me like a bull.

Ruff, ruff, ruff!

Oh my, she's got the most ferocious bark I've ever heard.

'Compared to the other dogs here she is,' The Kid says. 'Most of them are around three months.'

Scooping the puppy back up, I stand. 'So she's been banished to the basement and marked down? How horrible!' I look at her. Poor thing, pushed out by all the younger bitches, kept downstairs in the basement because she's older than all the other available pups. Telepathically, I tell her that I know how she feels. I felt the same way after Rod and I stopped seeing each other, when I stopped going out. I was older than all the available bitches out there too, and the competition just got too fierce.

'I don't know why she's still here,' The Kid continues. 'A lot of people play with her, but for some reason, no one commits.' *A lot of people play with her, but no one commits?* Once again, I telepathically tell her that I know how she feels. As she bats her eyelashes at me again, I can't help but feel like I'm looking into a mirror. If dogs lived in a parallel universe, then this puppy would be me.

'So what do you think?' The Kid asks.

What do I think? I think the connection I have to this dog is too deep for me to leave her here, no way, not after learning her story. They say people get dogs that resemble themselves, but I always thought they meant in the looks department. I look up at The Kid. 'I'll take her.'

'Oh goodie!' he exclaims, smiling a smile that's so big the bad overhead lighting reflects in his braces and practically blinds me. 'I'm so happy she's finally getting a home!' He reaches out to take her.

'No!' I snap, pulling her in closer. 'I'm just gonna hold her. She needs that. Trust me, I know.'

The Kid smiles; he understands.

Since a new dog isn't in my budget, I hand over my credit card. (She's one of life's little emergencies.) After filling out the paperwork and signing on the dotted line, I parade my pup past all the other bitches on display. I know it's not their fault for being so young and cute, but I want them to know just who's going home today.

On my way out, I glare at the ornery old lady behind the counter. 'No one puts baby in the corner!' I yell to her. 'Or the basement!'

Bringing Up Baby   Friday, 8 April

'Baby' is from Budapest, that's what The Kid told me. I don't know why and I don't want to know why, so I didn't ask. All I know is that I'm going to be getting some Hungarian papers in the mail instead of AKC papers. To be honest, I think it's kind of cool and I feel proud that

I'm creating a family that's culturally diverse. I feel like Angelina Jolie.

When I first learned about Baby's past, I pictured her wearing a babushka and talking with an accent, but then decided that she's much too fabulous for a babushka. Baby's more like a Gabor – both Zsa Zsa and Eva are from Budapest.* In fact, I'm going to name her after one of them – Baby can be her nickname. Hmm. Eva or Zsa Zsa, Eva or Zsa Zsa . . .

Okay, I've decided.

Drumroll, please! (Drumroll begins.)

Everyone, I'd now like to introduce, direct from Budapest via South Philly . . . Eva Gabor, the four-pound Yorkie!

(Deafening applause.)

The next morning, after praising Eva for sleeping through the night, I shower and change into a casual outfit to wear to the dog park – low-waisted jeans, a vintage T-shirt and super-cute open-toed sandals. After that, Eva and I head out the door. On the drive there, she sits on my lap, which kind of freaks me out. I mean, if someone were to hit me because I was . . . let's say . . . driving too slowly or something, she'd fly right through the windshield. Eva needs a baby seat – it's as simple as that.

After parking my car around the block, I attach a leash to Eva's harness and attempt to walk her to the dog park, but quickly realize that walking on a leash isn't something that's instinctual with dogs. After running around in a circle and darting from left to right, she's plopped down

* As is their forgotten older sister, Magda.

in the middle of the sidewalk and started chewing on her leash. Thinking she'll catch on, I give her a little tug and try to walk forward, but I end up dragging her. Realizing this is going to take some practice, I pick Eva up and carry her.

Rod and Max are already at the dog park when we arrive, as are five other dogs and owners. Since I'm not exactly sure what I should do, I decide to wait for Rod to recognize me and put Eva down on the ground to play. When I do so, all the dogs in the park, including Max, run over and head-butt one another as they try to get close to her butt. When I say hello to Max, he kisses my hand over and over again – I'm sure he remembers me. Although I get tears in my eyes, I fight them back. I can't get too attached to him. I have my own dog now. I need to leave that space in my heart open for her.

In the end, an Italian greyhound wins out and ends up getting the most intense sniff of Eva's butt. As he does, the people in the park walk over to claim their dogs, including Rod. The closer he gets to where I'm standing, the more nervous I become. As he grabs Max by the collar and pulls him away from Eva, he looks up. This is it, the moment I've been waiting for. He's going to see me and be pleasantly surprised. I hope. He's going to tell me how good it is to see me. I hope. He's going to tell me he misses me. I hope.

'Sorry,' Rod says. He then turns and walks away.

Okay, that didn't go exactly as I imagined. I know he saw me, he looked me straight in the eye. Why didn't he say hello? Before he gets too far away, I realize I have to make a move.

'Cute dog,' I say, trying to initiate conversation.

Glancing over his shoulder, Rod looks me right in the eye again, and smiles. 'Thanks.' He then turns around and continues to walk away.

Why is he doing this? Is he doing that thing people do when they see someone they don't want to see ... gosh, what's it called? Oh yes – *ignore them*. Is that what he's doing? If so, I'm not going to let him get away with it. I stayed two nights in a shitty hotel and bought a dog for him, damn it – he's going to talk to me! I boldly call out to him. 'Rod?'

Hearing his name, Rod turns around again. 'Do we know each other?' he asks. He looks confused.

'Yeah, you could say we do,' I say, after letting out a pathetic laugh.

Suddenly having a moment of realization, Rod hits himself in the head with the palm of his hand. 'I'm so sorry!' he exclaims. A sense of relief comes over me. I mean, if he didn't recognize me, it would be the most embarrassing thing ever. 'It's Darcy, right?' Not remembering my name, however, runs a pretty close second.

'Delilah,' I respond smugly. I mean, is he kidding?

Rod hits himself in the head again. 'Delilah, right. Gosh ... sorry. I'm not good at remembering names and faces.'

'How about hooters?' I ask, as I lift up my blouse to flash him. Kidding, I don't really say or do this.

Rod bends down to look at Eva. 'Is this your dog?'

I nod. 'Yeah, isn't she cute?'

'She sure is,' he says, picking her up. 'She's so little. How old is she?'

107

'Six months. I just got her yesterday.'

'Yesterday? Wow . . .' Eva looks like a football in Rod's big hands. 'What's her name?'

'Eva Gabor.'

'*Hewwwo*, Miss Eva Gabor!' Rod says in an extremely high-pitched puppy-talk voice. I laugh. It's funny to hear him talk like this, he's such a big guy.

'Sorry,' Rod says, blushing slightly. He puts Eva down. 'It happens.'

'That's what they tell me.'

Rod looks me up and down for a second, and then shakes his head. 'Delilah . . . wow. What a surprise. You look great.'

Now I blush. 'Thanks,' I say, 'so do you.'

Rod points to a nearby bench. 'Hey, do you want to go sit down and catch up? I'd love to hear what's going on in your life.'

'Sure.'

For the next two hours, Rod and I chat happily. He tells me all about how he moved back to Philly a few years ago for a job and how he's happy to be here, as is Max. If he remembers what happened the last night we were together, he doesn't let on or seem threatened in the least by me being near Max. When he asks why I'm in Philadelphia, I tell him pretty much the same story I told my mom and Daisy – that I'm here staking out locations for a possible store Elisabeth is thinking about opening. As for why I'm in this particular dog park, I wing it and tell him that my hotel accommodation got screwed up and I got stuck staying in a yucky cheap one by the stadium. Although Rod totally buys my stories, he expresses concern for the security of my job, since the future of the company is so up in the air.

'With everything I keep seeing about Elisabeth on the news, you should have a back-up plan, you know, in case you lose your job. Do you have one?'

You mean other than to chase down all the men I've ever had sex with? 'No,' I say.

'Well, you should. I've been through enough jobs to know that losing one isn't fun. It's important that you be in control of your future.'

'Yeah, maybe you're right.'

'I am right. Don't let someone else predict your future. Take it into your own hands. I'm serious.'

Rod seems genuinely concerned about me, and I can't help but be touched. I think he's interested in me, too. When I complain that my back is sore from the crappy mattress at the crappy hotel, he offers to rub it for me. And when we play with Max and Eva, he tackles me. (Yes, I land very close to a large pile of dog poop when he does, but still.) Looking at Rod, I think I could be happy with him. He could totally be the one.

Around nine o'clock or so, Rod says he has a big day of running errands ahead of him and gets ready to leave. As he does, he turns to me. 'Hey listen, if you're not busy tonight, I'd love it if you joined me for dinner.'

Dinner? Really? I smile. 'That'd be great!'

'Awesome.' Rod punches both my cell and hotel phone numbers into his phone and says he'll call with details.

After saying goodbye, I watch Rod and Max walk out of the dog park and disappear around the corner. When they do, I turn to Eva. 'Can you believe it?' I ask her. 'He's finally taking me to dinner.'

Puttin' on the Ritz

After driving to Center City (a nicer part of Philly), I find a cute boutique and buy a pink and green argyle dog bag for Eva. Yes, I realize that doing so brings me *thismuch-closer* to being compared to Paris Hilton, but since I'm buying the bag for safety reasons, I decide it's okay. My thinking is that I can put Eva in the bag, and then secure it to the passenger seat with the seatbelt. That way she's not bouncing all over creation every time we go somewhere.

The bag might also make sneaking her in and out of the hotel easier to do, which I'm about to find out because I've just walked inside and am heading toward the elevator. After successfully making my way there (A victory! Hoorah!), I push the button and wait for a car when suddenly, the front-desk attendant calls out to me. Worried I've been busted, I slowly turn only my head around. 'Yes?'

'A note arrived for you,' he says, walking over. He hands me an envelope.

'Oh, thanks,' I say politely, taking it. As the man nods and walks away, the elevator door opens, so I quickly jump inside. As the doors close, I sigh with relief and then open the envelope. I read the note inside.

Delilah,
   I've arranged for you to stay in a nicer hotel in Philly, guaranteed to have a mattress that won't make your back ache tomorrow morning. Check out of that

dive you're in immediately, and go to the large white marble building @ 10 Avenue of the Arts. Everything else will be taken care of.

Rod

PS Meet me in the lobby @ 8.00 for dinner.

Oh my ... dinner and a nicer hotel? What's gotten into Rod? Is he trying to make sure I'll sleep with him tonight? If so, here's a newsflash, Rod – I'm kinda easy. I don't know if you picked up on that during the relationship that we *didn't* have, but I am.

To be honest, although I'm unsure of Rod's intentions – or if he even has any – I'm tickled pink that he cares so much about me and my back to do something like this! He must really regret brushing off my suggestion to do something when it was light outside. He must really like me! My plan is working! Yippie!

After quickly packing and checking out, I drive to the address on the note and pull up to the big white marble building that looks like the Pantheon in Greece. Huge columns support the front and a big ol' dome tops it off. As I give my car to the valet out front, he tells me that the building was built over a hundred years ago and is a historic landmark. Apparently, it used to be a bank, but today ... it's a Ritz–Carlton! Sweet bejesus! I've never stayed at a Ritz before in my life – this is so cool!

The Ritz is dog friendly, so I don't have to hide Eva. As I parade her through the lobby, several people stop me to say how cute she is, making me feel like a proud mother. When I check in, the woman behind the counter says they've been expecting me and hands me a key. That's it – no credit card on file, nothing. They just hand over a key and that's it. Nice.

When Eva and I get to our room, we can hardly contain our excitement. Decorated in peachy tones, it's warm and inviting. I immediately plop down on the big fluffy bed, and am thrilled to find it comfortable. What a difference, what a dream. While lying down, I notice a large gift basket filled with all sorts of beauty products sitting on the dresser, so I stand up and walk over to it. I see a small gift card attached, so I open it up and read.

Delilah,
Enjoy! Also, as part of the Ritz's pet program, I've arranged for Eva to get the works. Her appointment begins at 3.00, someone will come up to get her.

Rod

Dinner *and* a nicer hotel *and* a gift basket? My life rocks.

I call Rod to thank him, but he doesn't answer, so I leave him a message. When I'm done, someone from the hotel comes to take Eva for her bath (I feel so bad giving her away – she didn't want to leave), so I draw one of my own in the large tub and begin to unwind, begin to work out the kinks in my back. I feel like a princess.

A little before eight o'clock, as I'm just about ready to go, I hear a knock on the door and open it to see a Yorkie that I do not recognize. Not only did the Ritz give Eva a bath and haircut, but they tied a little scarf around her neck and painted her nails red. It's like she's

112

Cinderella – she's the most beautiful puppy I've ever seen in my life!

I'm so touched by all this – the hotel room, the basket, the puppy bath – that I suddenly begin to worry. What if I do something tonight to blow it? I've never been one of those women who expects things from men. Boyfriends don't give me credit cards, they don't send me shopping. But all this is so nice – The R.O.D.'s come a long way.

After giving myself a once-over in the mirror (black skirt, fuzzy blue sweater and heels that are sex-kitten purrrrfect. *Meow!*), I give my Chinese love bracelet a little rub for good luck and head downstairs.

Rod takes me to a small, romantic Italian restaurant in South Philly that's very crowded and dimly lit. They're expecting us when we arrive and show us to a table in the corner. He smells good tonight, like cologne, and it's a huge turn-on. Guys don't seem to wear as much cologne today as I remember them doing when I was little. I mean, yes, my grandpa still wears Old Spice, but I'm talking about guys my age and I'm talking about good cologne.

'So, how'd you like the basket?' Rod asks, once we get settled.

'Oh, I loved it, thank you!'

Rod smiles. 'Nice stuff inside, right?'

'Oh yes! It was all so wonderful!'

Since Rod's been to the restaurant before, he orders for us. Generously, I might add. In addition to splitting a bottle of wine, we have steamed mussels, a fennel salad, goat cheese tortellini, grilled prawns, and, for dessert, chocolate hazelnut cake with a warm orange sauce. The food is delicious and I'm stuffed by the time we're through.

As for the conversation during dinner, it couldn't go better. It's like Rod and I are on the same wavelength. We talk about our hopes and dreams and what we want out of life – the same stuff I used to talk about with Max, actually. I never knew Rod could be so deep. I don't know if it's the wine, or the candlelight, but he looks so cute tonight, so handsome, and I'm incredibly attracted to him. We have such a connection.

After dessert, Rod orders two shots of sambuca and says he wants to talk to me about something important. I get both nervous and excited. 'Delilah, you might have noticed that I wasn't rushing off to work when I left the dog park this morning. Do you wanna know why?' he asks. I nod. 'Because I make my own hours, that's why. Life's too important to me to live by someone else's schedule. If I wanna go golfing, then I go golfing. If I wanna take a long weekend, then I take a long weekend. Do you get what I'm saying?'

I nod again. 'Absolutely, Rod.'

'Great. Let me ask you something. Do you wanna work less?'

'Well sure, yes.'

'Do you wanna live life to the fullest?'

'Most definitely.'

'Do you want kids?'

Kids?

Whoa, wait.

'Rod, where are you going with this?' I ask. I have to admit, I'm a little taken aback.

'Delilah, I'm asking you all these things because I want you to know that my lifestyle can be yours.'

His lifestyle can be mine? As Rod reaches across the table and takes my hands in his, my heart goes pitter-patter. Is he going to ask me to move in with him? To have kids with him? To share his life? To become his wife? 'Rod, what are you talking about?'

'I'm talking about a partnership, Delilah.'

A partnership?

Rod *is* asking me to move in with him, to have his kids, to share his life, to become his wife! He must be going through the same phase I am. He must be sick of the game and ready to settle down, too. I can barely contain my excitement and Rod can tell – he smiles.

'Does that sounds like something you'd be interested in?' he asks.

'Oh yes, absolutely, Rod!' I exclaim. 'Absolutely!' I'm booming. I can't believe this thing worked on the first try! Michelle is going to eat her words.

'Great,' Rod says. 'Del, when I see something I want, I go after it, and I see that same thing in you.'

I mean, I know it's all very sudden, but I'm so ready to try to make this work with Rod. I can already imagine our life together – Rod and Max, me and Eva – the four of us will make such a happy family.

'In fact,' Rod continues, 'that's why I brought you here tonight, Delilah. I wanna tell you about a great opportunity.'

Rod will make us all breakfast in the morning and then—

Whoa, wait.

Great opportunity? I'm confused. 'What do you mean by great opportunity?'

'Delilah, have you ever heard of Amway?' Rod asks.

Amway? Oh no. 'You mean like Amway, the pyramid scheme?' I ask.

'We prefer to call it a business opportunity. Pyramid schemes are illegal, and there's nothing illegal about Amway. It's a multilevel marketing system.'

Oh no. Oh no, oh no, oh no. Please tell me what I think is happening isn't happening.

For all the multilevel-marketing-system-challenged people out there, Amway is a company that makes and sells all sorts of products – beauty products, vitamins, home-care products, and such – and then sells those products to distributors. The distributors make money by not only reselling these products to consumers (they get a percentage of their sales), but by also recruiting their friends to become distributors as well (they get a per-centage of their friends' sales too) – that's the 'multilevel' part. It's like Mary-Kay or Avon.

'Yeah, I've heard of it,' I tell Rod. 'What's your point?'

'Delilah, I think you've got a lot of potential. You're charismatic, personable—'

'Rod, did you invite me here to get me to sell Amway?' I ask, interrupting.

'Well, yes. Yes, I did, Delilah.'

Oh. My. God. What I think is happening is really happening.

I almost laugh. And then I almost cry.

'The products are wonderful,' Rod says, going for the hard sell. 'In fact, that whole basket I gave you was filled with them. Did you try them out? What was your favorite?'

'My fah-fah-favorite?' I stutter. Rod nods. 'Well, the bubble bath was nice.'

I mean, I don't get it. Rod rubbed my back, he got me a hotel room – I just don't understand.

'How about the foot lotion?' Rod asks. 'Did you try that?'

'Yes.'

I can't believe myself – I'm so stupid. I should've realized this. To think Rod would've changed, to think he would all of a sudden want a relationship with me.

'Good, you'll find it does wonders for those scratchy feet of yours.'

Rod never wanted anything with me when we were together. Why would I think he would want something now? Wait . . . what did he just say?

'My scratchy feet?' I ask. Did I hear him correctly?

'Yeah,' Rod says, nodding. 'From what I remember, those things were like sandpaper! *Scraaaa-cheee!*'

'No, they weren't!' I yell, defending myself. 'No, they're not! My feet are not scratchy!'

'Well, to each his own,' Rod says, raising his eyebrows. 'Our definitions of *scratchy* must be different. But anyway, like I said, I put stuff in the basket that I knew you could use.' As Rod says this, the contents suddenly rush through my mind. The basket was filled with bottles of face lotion for oily skin, wrinkle cream, vitamins to increase metabolism, teeth-whitening gum, products for dry, brittle hair with split ends, and . . . Oh my God . . . cellulite cream. Suddenly my ears ring, my face gets hot, and I can't help myself – I hurl a left-over roll at Rod's head. 'You asshole!' I scream.

'Hey! What's your problem?' Rod yells, holding up his hands to protect himself. People sitting at nearby tables stare as I stand up.

'My problem? My problem is you, Rod!' I begin to gather my belongings. I'm so outta here.

'I don't understand,' Rod says, looking confused. 'What did I do? Why am I the problem?'

'Rod, you didn't bring me here because you liked me or because you wanted to spend time with me. You brought me here because you want to sell me stuff and get me to sell stuff for, for . . .' I begin hyperventilating. 'For fat people! That's why you're my problem, Rod!' Rod's eyes widen – he finally gets it.

'Delilah, I'm so sorry. Did you think I brought you here on a date?'

'Yes!' I scream. 'And why shouldn't I have thought that? I mean, you rubbed my back; you got me a room at the Ritz. Wait – why did you get me a room at the Ritz if you just want me to sell Amway?'

'Well, if you signed up to be a distributor . . . I could've comped it.'

Comped it? Okay, I'm not only embarrassed any more, I'm angry now, too. I'm so fucking angry! Looking at Rod, I don't know what to say, so I say the first thing that comes to mind. 'Max liked me better than you when we were sleeping together!'

'What?'

'You heard me!' I scream. 'Your dog liked me better! He did! When you showered, we would cuddle and he would listen to my problems, and I know, I just know, he liked me more than you!'

Rod looks at me like I'm crazy, which basically, I am. As I turn around and leave, I hear him behind me. 'Delilah, wait.' But I don't stop. I don't wait. I walk right out the front door and hop into the first available taxi I see.

When I get back to my room, I collapse on the fabulous mattress and cry into the fluffy pillows. I don't cry because I care about Rod but because I feel like an idiot. I mean, what am I doing? Seriously? Seeing my face scrunch up makes Eva nervous. Sitting next to me on the bed, she doesn't know what to do with herself. She keeps looking at me skittishly, not sure if she should approach. When she finally musters up the courage to do so, she sniffs my face for a couple of seconds and then backs away and begins to pant.

For the next hour, Rod calls my cell phone and the room phone, but I don't answer. I don't want to talk to him – I don't have anything to say. Around midnight, when the calls finally stop, I begin to feel better. As my sadness turns back into anger and adrenaline pumps through my body, I become motivated. I want to get out of here. I want to get out of the Ritz. I want to get out of Philly. With that, I pack my belongings, making sure to leave the gift basket, but clear out the minibar.

Comp that, you asshole.

$3,766, 39 days, 15 guys left.

Chapter Five

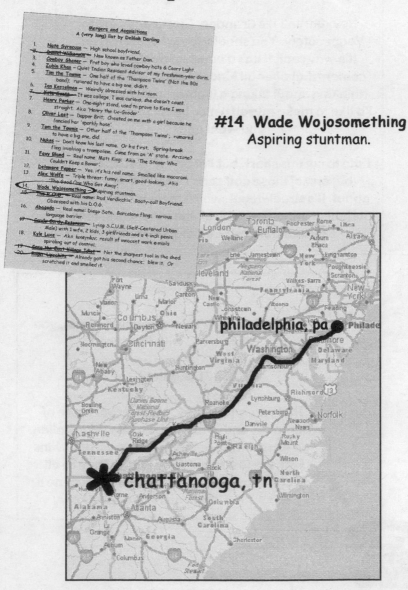

Mergers and Acquisitions
A (very long) list by Delilah Darling

1. Nate Syracuse — High school boyfriend.
2. Daniel Wilkerson — Now known as Father Dan.
3. Cowboy Shaner — Frat boy who loved cowboy hats & Coors Light.
4. Zubin Khan — Quiet Indian Resident Advisor of my freshman-year dorm.
5. Tim the Townie — One half of the 'Thompson Twins' (Not the 80s band); rumoured to have a big one; didn't.
6. Ian Kesselman — Weirdly obsessed with his mom.
7. Katy Gold — It was college, I was curious, she doesn't count.
8. Henry Parker — One-night stand, used to prove to Kate I was straight. Aka 'Henry the Do-Gooder'.
9. Oliver Leet — Dapper Brit; Cheated on me with a girl because he fancied her 'sparkly nose'.
10. Tom the Townie — Other half of the 'Thompson Twins'; rumoured to have a big one, did.
11. Nukes — Don't know his last name. Or his first. Spring-break fling involving a trampoline. Came from an 'A' state. Arizona? Couldn't keep a Boner.
12. Foxy Blond — Real name: Matt King; Aka 'The Stoner Who Couldn't Keep a Boner'.
13. Delaware Pepper — Yes, it's his real name. Smelled like macaroni.
14. Alex Wolfe — Triple threat: funny, smart, good-looking. Aka 'The Good One Who Got Away'.
15. **Wade Wojosomething** — Aspiring stuntman.
16. The B.C.B. — Real name: Rod Verdicchio; Booty-call Boyfriend. Obsessed with his D.O.G.
17. Abogado — Real name: Diego Soto. Barcelona fling; serious language barrier.
18. Gordy Gordy Peterson — Lying S.C.U.M. (Self-Centered Urban Male) with 1 wife, 2 kids, 3 girlfriends and a 4-inch penis.
19. Kyle Luxe — Aka luxeynlux: result of innocent work e-mails spiraling out of control.
20. Gary the East Village Idiot — Not the sharpest tool in the shed.
21. Nigel Upchitts — Already got his second chance; blew it. Or scratched it and smelled it.

#14 Wade Wojosomething
Aspiring stuntman.

philadelphia, pa

chattanooga, tn

Beep

Hey, Darlin'! It's Grandpa. Gloria and I got to Vegas safely. You should see where she lives. It's *way* cool! It has a bunch of pools and rec centers that offer all kinds of classes. I've been thinking about taking a leather-carving class. I'd like to make myself a nice belt. Let me know if you want one.

Hate to cut this short, but I'm on my way to check out one of those golf carts I was telling you about. It's street-legal, which means I can drive it right on the street with all the other cars. Ain't that something? Call me! Love ya!

Beep

Hey, Delilah . . . it's your neighbor Colin, you know . . . with the abs.

Laughter

That was a joke. Hey, I found four more of your fellas and e-mailed you the information. Ian Kesselman, Delaware Pepper, and twins with the last name Thompson. They're all single, in case you're wondering. Give me a knock next time you're around. Later.

'I'm in heaven, West Virginia, blue-tinged Mountains, Shannen Doherty river . . .' Oops, that's not right. I'm in Virginia, not West Virginia, but the highway runs right along the border of the two states, so I'm close enough to sing this song and mean it. 'Country roads, where I roam, to the place, I call home!' Oh dear, that's not right either. Anyway, rest in peace, John Denver, you musical genius you.

Even though Chattanooga's a twelve-hour drive away from Philly, the adrenaline from being angry at Rod, lots of coffee and sugar, and of course the motivational tunes keep me driving through the night and into the morning. Yes, I'm a little upset that my first try at this thing was a bust, but I can't let one bad experience stop me from moving forward, so I try to let it go.

After a brief excursion to Dollywood, I arrive in Chattanooga around two o'clock in the afternoon.* Even though there are a lot of inexpensive hotels to choose from, I opt to stay at a slightly more expensive Holiday Inn inside the old train station because there's a real Chattanooga Choo Choo inside. It's kind of embarrassing to admit, but who knew Chattanooga Choo Choos were actual trains? I thought it was just a song.

While checking in with an older woman at the front desk, I'm asked if I want a 'thtandard room' or a 'rethtored train car'.

---

* After talking two people into buying a set of Dollywood salt and pepper shakers, I realized that, owing to a lack of sleep, I was unfit to mingle with the public and quickly left.

'Pardon me?' I say.

'Well, in addition to the thtandard room, you can thtay in an actual rethtored Victorian railroad car inthide a train.'

I realize she has a lisp. 'Really?' I ask.

'Oh, yeth,' she says, 'they're beautiful. They look jutht like they did at the turn of the thentury.'

Although the rethtored train car costs almost twice as much as a thtandard room that's just a little more expensive than the inexpensive hotels, I decide to take it. I don't see myself coming back to Chattanooga anytime thoon – I mean soon – so I doubt I'll get another chance to do it.

The hotel/train isn't dog friendly, so I sneak Eva inside in her new bag. My room/car is long and narrow, not much wider than the queen-sized bed inside. Its dark decor is busy with patterns. I'm surrounded by swirls, paisley and plaid. To be quite honest, it's all so nauseating that if the car was moving, I'd probably barf. The only cool thing about it is the metal luggage rack that hangs above the window, so even though my bag is heavy, I lift it and store it up there just for kicks.

I plan to begin my search for Wade tomorrow, so after stripping the bed, I lie down and close my eyes. I have to admit, of all the people to come after Rod, I wish it was someone with a little more potential. Wade was always a bit odd, to say the least, and we didn't exactly leave on the best terms. But people change – they do – and everyone deserves a second chance. With that, I drift off to sleep and recall the last night we saw each other.

In my list of twenty men, Wade Wojosomething is #14. He came right before Rod, both literally and numerically,

I guess. Unlike Rod, he was an actual boyfriend, not just a booty call. And yes, I know what his last name is, I just could never spell it or pronounce it correctly when I first met him, so as a joke I started calling him Wade Wojosomething and it stuck.

Even though Wade and I were the same age, he seemed much younger than me. I know I'm not exactly a vision of maturity, but Wade's immaturity was different from mine. He liked to do little boy things, like go on scavenger hunts and play with Power Rangers. I mean, if there was Cub Scouts for men in their twenties, Wade would have been a member, no doubt.

Initially, I found Wade's boyish charm attractive, but eventually it annoyed me. One of the things that irritated me the most about him was that he loved playing a wide variety of mime games, especially charades. Now, I've played charades before, we all have, and the occasional game is fine. It can even be fun. But Wade didn't want to play the occasional game, Wade wanted to play *all the fucking time*. Even something as simple as going to a movie turned into a game. One night I remember asking him which movie he wanted to see. Rather than answer me, Wade held up one finger (first word), pulled his ear (sounds like), crouched down and waddled forward, bobbing his head and flapping his arms.

'A duck? A swan? A turkey?' I guessed. Honestly, I had no idea. 'A chicken? A hen?' (An idiot?)

I'm not going to make you go through what I had to – it was a goose, the first word that sounded like it was deuce, which meant that he wanted to see *Deuce Bigalow*. Since I was not about to see *Deuce Bigalow*, ten minutes later we were back at square one. Wade started pulling his ear, trying to get me to guess his next movie choice. Honestly, what kind of person has time for this?

I think the reason Wade liked charades so much centered on the fact that he wanted to be a stuntman. So 'pretending' to do something – whether it was falling down a flight of stairs or acting out a TV show title like *Walker, Texas Ranger* – was in his blood. It was his calling, his dream.

Yes, Wade was weird, so why did I date him? It's simple: he was nice. He was non-threatening. He was cute, in an Alex P. Keaton kind of way. He looked like he walked right out of a Sears catalog. Guys like Wade don't care if you wear Keds or heels. Guys like Wade don't care if you spill spaghetti sauce down the front of your blouse. Guys like Wade are easy to date.

The last time I saw Wade was Christmas Eve of 1999 when he invited me over to his family's house for dinner. Things between us had been a little tense in the weeks leading up to it – we were growing apart, becoming less tolerant of each other – but neither of us had yet said anything about it. We were still going along like everything was fine, which is why I agreed to go.

From the moment I arrived at Wade's parents' house that night, I knew it was a mistake. Wade was rude to me, as was his entire family. He must have told them that we were having problems because none of them talked to me. No one offered me a drink. No one took my coat – they acted like I wasn't there. I felt like an invisible ghost floating around a strange family's house.

And strange they were.

For some reason Wade's family was obsessed with him. Obsessed. All night, his two younger sisters gazed at him with stars in their eyes, like he was a celebrity or something. So did his older brother. He kept shouting out requests to Wade like he was Wayne Newton. 'Show Mom your Jim Carrey impression, Wade!' he'd yell, and, 'Show Dad how you can beatbox!'

As for his parents, you would have thought Wade was a war hero the way they treated him. Every time they looked at him they got teary-eyed and would say things like, 'We're so proud of you, son!' and, 'We're just so happy to see our boy!' Not to be mean, but I wasn't sure what it was about Wade they were so proud of. Although Wade wanted to be a stuntman, he wasn't – he was the assistant manager of a T.G.I. Friday's. And also, Wade didn't live in Russia. He lived in Manhattan and saw his parents every single weekend. Seriously. It interfered with our social life.

When dinner was served that evening, Wade's feeble old grandma came down from upstairs to join the family at the table. No one spoke to her or even acknowledged her presence. I felt sorry for her – if only the family loved her as much as they loved Wade. She sat next to me and since no one was talking to either of us, we bonded. Well, kind of. I kept trying to make conversation, but the concept of that seemed lost on her. She appeared to be listening to what I was saying all right, but when it came to responding, she'd open her mouth like she was going to say something, but then wave her wrinkly hand in front of it and look away, as if to say, 'Ah . . . forget it.'

After dinner Wade's family had a tradition of 'giving thanks'. Basically, this is how it worked: everyone grabs a partner, and the family goes around the table one by one and tells their partner why they're thankful for them. Wade's mom chose his dad, his little sister chose his other little sister, and Wade, rather than choosing his girlfriend, the stranger he had invited over for dinner, chose his brother. That left me with grandma.

Now, I appreciate a close family, but these people made me want to barf. For the next twenty minutes, I watched as everyone, with tears in their eyes, told their partner how special they were while Wade's dad exclaimed, 'The spirit of Christmas is in the air!' When it was my turn, I turned to Grandma and said, 'You must be a really special lady to have raised such a loving family.' As I spoke, Grandma smiled and nodded, which made me feel good. From the look on her face, it was apparent to me that she didn't get this enough. When I finished, I waited for her to return the kind words and was shocked when, instead, she got up and left the table without saying anything. Everyone laughed, they thought it was so funny. 'That's Grandma!' Wade's dad yelled. For a minute I was some-what relieved, thinking Grandma's odd behavior might have served as an ice-breaker between us all, but when no one stepped up to take her place, I realized I was wrong. After clearing the table, everyone rushed into the living room for the after-dinner festivities and left me sitting there all alone. No one volunteered to tell me how special I was – I got gypped.

Needless to say, I was angry. What they did was just plain bad manners. Just as I was about to tell Wade that I was going home, his mom cracked open a bottle of wine and announced it was time to play charades. When I saw how the family reacted – they nearly peed their pants with joy; apparently Wade's love of the game was genetic – I changed my mind. What better way to spend an evening than to get drunk and watch a bunch of people make asses of themselves, right? I grabbed an empty glass and told Wade's mom to fill 'er up!

Since it was a holiday, Wade's dad announced he was going to 'spice up the game', so he had everyone tear out random pages from old copies of *Reader's Digest* and put them in a hat. 'Instead of guessing the usual movie and song titles, we'll act out the article titles!' he exclaimed. This threw the family into a frenzy. Everyone started wildly stomping their feet and clapping their hands.

As the hat was passed around the group, everyone took turns acting out their titles, titles like 'Vacations on the Fly' and 'Stop Cop Killers'. They were all having such a good time, miming and guessing, and likewise, I was having a good time drinking and heckling. Yes, heckling. I had been taking cold medicine, and it must have interacted with the wine because one minute I was fine and the next minute I was heckling Wade's family. *Inappropriately* heckling Wade's family. Yelling things like, 'How could you not get that, you dumb bastard?' and, 'You call that a rhinoceros, you stupid asshole?' I'm not proud of my behavior, but screw them – I was special too, damn it!

When the hat landed on my lap, I announced I was going to sit this one out and tried to pass it to the next person, but the family wouldn't have it. Grandma was sitting on a La-Z-Boy in the corner, staring at the wall – she wasn't playing. Why did I have to? I made eyes at her, hoping to get her attention, hoping she'd stick up for me and tell them to back off since I told her how special she was, but no. She did the same thing she kept doing all through dinner. She opened her mouth like she was going to say something, then waved her wrinkly hand in front of her face and looked away, like, 'Ah . . . forget it.' Needless to say, I had to play, so I reached into the hat and pulled out my title. Of all the titles in *Reader's Digest*, of all the two-word and three-word titles, I got . . . 'Landing Pads for Extraterrestrials, Druid Temples, Sacrificial Altars: What are these Monuments from a Prehistoric Culture?'

Seriously. The pros got titles like 'Vacations on the Fly' and 'Stop Cop Killers' and I got 'Landing Pads for Extraterrestrials, Druid Temples, Sacrificial Altars: What are these Monuments from a Prehistoric Culture?' Since there was no way I was going to act it out, I laughed and threw it back in, and then went into the kitchen to get some more wine. After pouring myself a glass, I turned around and found Wade's mom standing behind me, holding my coat. Apparently it was time for me to go.

'I'm surprised you and Wade are a couple,' she said, as she ushered me toward the front door.

'Why's that?' I asked.

'Well, you don't seem like a girl who wants to get her hair wet, and my Wade is such an adventurer!'

After she said this, I turned around to say goodbye to Wade, who was in the middle of doing the Macarena with his brother. I watched him for a bit, and oh . . . what an adventurer he was. The way he put his hands on his shoulders, then his head, and then his hips – he was a regular Indiana Jones. I opened my mouth to say good-bye, but then thought twice.

'*Ah . . . forget it,*' I said, then turned around and walked out the door.

New Beginnings   Sunday, 10 April

The ring from my cell phone wakes me up. For a moment I forget where I am, but then I remember – Chattanooga, Wade Wojosomething. I reach for the phone and answer.

'Are you alive?' It's Michelle. She's screaming.

'Yes,' I grumble. 'I forgot to call you when I got in, sorry.'

'Oh, don't worry about it,' she says sarcastically. 'I just thought you were dead, no biggie.'

I quickly realize it was a bad idea to tell Michelle I was driving through the night. After apologizing, I assure her that I will check in more frequently and then change the subject. 'So, have you started looking for jobs yet?'

'Kind of,' she mumbles. 'I've updated my résumé. I just haven't sent any out yet. But you know what I heard? You know Vintage Vogue?'

'Vintage Vogue the furniture store?' I ask.

'Yeah. I heard through the grapevine that they're expanding their line to include all sorts of housewares to compete more with Martha Stewart and Elisabeth and I think they're gonna start interviewing soon.'

'Really? That's cool,' I say, sounding less than enthused. 'I like Vintage Vogue. They have nice furniture; it's washable.'

'Yep. Aren't you worried at all about a job?'

'To be honest, I haven't even thought about it.' I can't. I need to focus on this and only this.

'That's just crazy to me.'

'Well, it's not to me.' I sigh. 'Anyway, good luck with the job search.'

'Thanks. And good luck to you with Wade Wojowhatever.'

'Wojosomething.'

'Whatever.'

I flip my phone shut and decide to get an early start on my day, so as Dolly would say, 'I tumble outta bed and stumble to . . . err . . . *my train-car bathroom*, pour myself a cup of . . . *bad java brewed in a mini-sized Mr Coffee* and yawn, and stretch, and try to come to life.' Stalking nine to five, what a way to not sleep with any more men!

It's a bright sunny morning in Chattanooga and the air smells like spring. I feel refreshed. Any memories of The R.O.D. are long gone. Wade lives about a ten-minute drive away from my hotel in a medium-sized subdivision filled with two-story white town houses that look identical to one another.* After figuring out which town house is his, I put on my hat and sunglasses and then, just like I did in Philadelphia, park out front and wait.

Wade's car, a brown two-door Honda, sits in the driveway, so I'm pretty sure he's home. The reason I know it's Wade's car is because when I Googled him, I found out that he won the car in a radio contest about two years ago. For being new, it's a total disaster, the sides are all

* I always wonder if people who live in subdivisions like this have a hard time finding the right house after a late night out. I mean, it can't be easy.

scratched up, the front end is crumpled and the fenders are dented. It looks like someone's a worse driver than me.

For the next hour, while I wait, I tell Eva all about Wade. She's my partner in crime now, so it's important she knows what's going on. Although I can't be certain, I think she's listening because she keeps blinking incessantly and cocking her head. Even though going to see Rod was a big waste of time, if I hadn't gone, I wouldn't have gotten her. Everything happens for a reason, I guess.

Around ten o'clock I see movement at Wade's – the blinds open – and get nervous so I pull my car a little out of the way into the cul-de-sac at the end of the street. About thirty minutes later he emerges from the house and gets in his car. He looks more mature than he did the last time I saw him and I'm pleasantly surprised. When he backs out of his driveway and pulls away, I put my car in drive and slowly follow him. Lucky for me, the backseat of his car is jam-packed with stuff, so he can't see me (or anyone) in his rear-view mirror.

At the entrance of the subdivision, Wade makes a right onto the main road and, after a quick two-minute drive, pulls into the parking lot of a Winn-Dixie grocery store and goes inside. I decide to follow.

I quickly locate Wade in the produce section picking through onions. Grabbing a basket, I head in his direction, stopping when I get to a wheelbarrow filled with vibrantly colored apples. After picking through a few, I begin to read the nutritional label on the back of a bag and slowly inch my way toward where Wade's standing until I end up literally bumping into him. 'Oops, sorry,' I say, as I do.

Wade glances up. 'Oh, don't worry.' He looks back down, but then quickly back up. 'Wait . . . Delilah?' Hearing him say my name, I stop reading the bag and look up. When Wade and I make eye contact, I let out a fake gasp and press my hand to my chest for dramatic effect.

'Oh my gosh . . . Wade?' (I'd like to thank the Academy . . .)

'Yeah,' he says, smiling. 'It's so nice to see you!' He looks dumbfounded.

'You too!' I exclaim. I'm not sure why, but I throw my arms around him and give him an enormous bear hug. When I let go, I stand back a little and shake my head in disbelief. 'What a coincidence – I can't believe this.'

'I know . . .' he says. 'Do you live here in Chattanooga?'

'Me? Oh, no. I'm still in New York. How about you?'

'Yeah, I live about five minutes down the street.' Actually, it's more like two, but I don't correct him. 'Why are you here?'

'For work.'

'What kind of work brings you to Chattanooga?'

I tell Wade the story about Elisabeth's store and he believes me, like my mom and Daisy did, like Rod did. He asks where in Chattanooga the store might go, and since I'm not sure what to say, I tell him it's top secret.

'How about you?' I ask. 'How long have you lived here?'

'A couple years,' Wade says. 'I love it here. I can't imagine living anywhere else, especially back in New York. The people here are so nice and so much more approachable.' I never have agreed with this, that New Yorkers are rude. I've always found them to be the nicest people anywhere, but to each his own, I guess. Wade and I stare at each other for a few seconds in awkward silence.

'Well, it was nice seeing you,' he eventually says. He then turns away, but doesn't exactly leave. I remember him as being shy when we first started dating, and I have a feeling he doesn't know what to do right now, so I decide to make a move.

'Hey, Wade, before you go, I'm in town only until tomorrow and don't have anything to do today. Are you busy?'

Wade turns back around and smiles. 'That's so funny – I was just gonna ask if you wanted to come for a bike ride with me. I mean, it's so nice outside today, and I have an extra bike.'

I perk up. 'A bike ride? That sounds like fun.' Suddenly I remember Eva. 'Ooh, wait – I have a dog, though,' I say, pointing to Eva in her bag. Looking down, Wade jumps when he sees her little black nose pressed up against the mesh panel.

'Oh my gosh, I didn't know there was a dog in there!' He laughs. 'I thought it was a purse.'

'That's the point. I don't think dogs are allowed in grocery stores, so I snuck her in.'

'She's so cute,' he says, peering at her. 'You know, the second bike has a basket in the front. Maybe you could put the bag inside the basket and I could strap it in.'

I make a face. That doesn't sound safe. Wade senses my uncertainty.

'Come on . . .' he says. 'I'll make sure she's totally safe and we'll make it an easy ride. I'll even pack a lunch and we can have a picnic.'

The more I think about it, the more I'm sure Eva will be fine. I smile. I'm convinced. 'Yeah, okay. Sounds like fun.' I look at Eva. 'Right?' She looks at me and blinks, which I think means yes.

After driving back to my hotel to change, I meet Wade out front around noon. Once Eva is securely zipped inside her bag, I place it inside the bike basket, making sure to face the mesh opening forward so that she can see where we're going. Then Wade secures it with an elastic bungee cord and the two of us head toward a nearby park.

For the first mile or so of our ride, Wade cycles slightly ahead of me so he can turn around and check on Eva. Every time he looks at her, he bursts into laughter. Apparently she's having the time of her life – her tongue is hanging out of her mouth and her hair is blowing in the wind. Since I can't see, I give him my digital camera to take a picture. When I see the photo, I also burst into laughter. Not only is *she* the cutest thing on earth, but *I* look like the biggest moron. I'm riding a bike with a Yorkie in a pink and green argyle doggie bag strapped into a basket on the front of it.

Wade and I ride around Chattanooga for about an hour. Although I have a nice time, it's hard for me to tell if he's changed. I can't exactly talk to him. Thankfully, around two o'clock or so, we stop at a park near the Tennessee River to have our picnic. When I let Eva out of her bag, she runs around like a little hooligan. She's so funny, she keeps kicking dirt back like a bull, like she did the day I got her. The bike ride revved her up. She's so sassy!

While Wade spreads out a blanket, I ask him where he's working nowadays, silently praying it's not Amway. 'I'm managing a restaurant in town,' he says, much to my relief. 'I'm not crazy about it, but you gotta stick with what pays the bills, you know?' He sounds a bit glum as he says this. I hesitate for a minute, not sure if I should ask the one big thing I want to ask, but it's burning inside me so I decide to go for it. 'So what happened to your dreams of becoming a stuntman?'

Wade gives me a thin-lipped smile. 'It didn't really work out.' He then gets red in the face. 'It was kind of a pipe dream.' I feel bad for him; he looks so embarrassed.

'No, it wasn't,' I say, trying to make him feel better. Wade stops what he's doing and gives me a look that says, *Yes it was and you know it.* 'Okay, maybe it was a little,' I say, smiling.

By God, I can't believe it. Based on the little conversation that Wade and I have had, he seems to have changed; he seems more mature. However, I'm not sure I buy his new persona. Something tells me that the little boy is still lurking inside him somewhere. I need to test him. I need to see if this is all an act or the real deal, so I devise a plan. First up, Shania Twain. While Wade unpacks our lunch, I plug tiny portable speakers into my iPod and tune it to 'Man! I Feel like a Woman'. As soon as it comes blaring out of the speakers, I bite my lip to stop from giggling and watch Wade closely. He used to lip-sync this song to me when we dated. If anything is going to bring out that little boy, it'll be this. When Wade hears Shania's voice, he stops what he's doing and stares into space. Come on, Wade, you can do it. But Wade doesn't do anything; he just stares. Come on, damn it! But again, nothing. I move on to twenty questions.

While eating lunch, I begin to ask Wade all sorts of questions – stupid questions, questions with one-word answers – purposefully trying to get him to break into a game of charades. If I asked the old Wade what his favorite color was, he'd pull his ear and hold up his shoe. (Sounds like *shoe* . . . means *blue*.) Here goes.

'What's your favorite color?' *Blue*.

'Who's your favorite president?' *Kennedy*.

'Where's your ideal vacation spot?' *Africa*.

'What's the first thing you'd buy with a million dollars?' *A house*.

'Which superhero do you secretly want to be?' *Superman*.

Much to my amazement, Wade answers all my questions vocally. Honestly, I'm astounded; I can't believe it. He doesn't even look like he's fighting the urge to mime. Wade seems to have grown up. Wade seems to have (gulp) . . . become a man.

When we finish eating, Wade pulls out two cookies that he picked up at a bakery near his apartment. They're sugar cookies, shaped and decorated like tulips. The petals are iced with pink and yellow frosting, and the stems and leaves are covered in green sprinkles that glisten in the sunlight. 'To celebrate spring,' Wade says. 'A time of new beginnings.' He then holds my gaze for a minute. I think he's trying to tell me he's changed.

After smiling at Wade, I scarf down the cookie even though it's almost too pretty to eat. Seeing that the sprinkles have turned my tongue and lips green, Wade teases me. 'You look like Kermit the Frog!'

'No, I don't!' I say, hitting him.

'Don't be offended,' Wade says. 'It's a compliment.'

A compliment? *Wait, huh?*

Whatever

Around four o'clock, Wade asks if I'd like to see where he lives and I immediately say yes. If he's still hanging on to any old quirks, they'll surely come out there. While following him home in my car (ladies: always make sure you have a getaway car just in case), I try to remember what it was like having sex with him, if it was any good, but my mind keeps drawing a blank. The only thing that I can recall is that he was overly animated – he'd always make 'sex faces' while we were doing it, like one second he'd close his eyes and grit his teeth and the next he'd open his mouth wide, like he was a roaring tiger. He always looked intense.

I park on the street outside Wade's town house then walk up to meet him at the front door. I still have Eva with me, asleep in her bag. She's had a big day and is wiped out. While I wait for Wade to unlock the door, I think about our day together. If Wade is normal, I think I could seriously make this thing work with him. If I could only figure out a way to get rid of his family . . .

Kidding.

Maybe not.

Anyway, I'm so excited about the possibility of him being normal, that I can't help but grin as I enter Wade's apartment. As I do, he turns around. 'What's with the smile?' he asks.

'I don't know,' I say, blushing. 'I guess I'm just happy.'

'Happy why?'

'I don't know,' I say coyly. 'Happy I ran into you. You're so nice and norm—'

Whoa, wait.

Perhaps I spoke too soon.

As I walk into Wade's living room, I see something incredibly disturbing: about a dozen stuffed animals, in all different shapes and sizes, are hanging from sticks fastened to the wall above his couch. They're big, like the size of a forearm, and freaky, so freaky that I have a feeling they'll be an integral part of my nightmares for years to come. And did I mention that they're staring at me? They are. Every one of them is staring at me. I'm frozen in fear.

'Um . . . what are those?' I ask uneasily, pointing.

Wade looks at me, then back at the wall. 'Those?' he asks. I nod. 'Oh, those are my Muppets.' He says this very matter-of-factly, like he's talking about a wall shelf.

'Your Muppets?' I ask. Wade nods. 'You mean like puppets?'

'No,' Wade says. 'Muppets and puppets aren't the same thing – you use your left hand to operate Muppets, and your right hand to operate puppets.' He points back up to the wall. '*Those* are Muppets.'

There has to be some sort of logical explanation to this. 'Are they some new kind of art or something?' I ask.

'No, no, they're not some new form of art,' Wade says, chuckling. 'I'm a Muppeteer.'

I shake my head, not sure if I heard him correctly. Did

he say he was a Mousketeer? 'I'm sorry, what did you just say?'

'I said I'm a Muppeteer. I put on Muppet shows on the weekends.'

Oh. My. God. I knew it, I knew it, I knew it. And I jinxed it – by almost telling Wade he was normal, I jinxed it. Wade isn't normal. He never has been. He never will be.

'I know it might sound funny,' he explains, 'but adult puppet shows are becoming really popular. At least they are in Knoxville, which is where my buddy Jed lives – he taught me how to work them. I met him in clown school.'

'Clown school?'

Wade nods. 'Yeah, when I realized the whole stuntman thing wasn't gonna pan out, I had to quit living in a dream world and get a real job, so I went to clown school. I've always loved to perform, you know?' I nod – yeah, I know. 'I did the whole clown thing for a while – you know, birthday parties, bar mitzvahs, and such, but the make-up made me break out really badly, so I had to cut back.'

'Break out?'

Wade nods and points to a pimple on his cheek. 'Yeah, see? It happens to all clowns. It's a real drawback to the profession.' I'm guessing not the only one.

Okay, this isn't just not normal – this is plain weird. Weird beyond any weird I've ever encountered in my life. And I've been to a Michael Jackson concert before. And I watched Diane Sawyer interview Whitney Houston. And I'm aware of the trials and tribulations of Courtney Love. Wade was a clown? And now he's a Muppeteer? It takes everything I have inside me not to run out the door.

'Yeah, someone needs to make better clown make-up,' Wade continues, as he sashays over to the couch and plops down. 'Because what's out there right now is way too thick.'

'Did you ever think about being that someone? Did you ever see this problem as an opportunity to make a little money?'

Wade looks at me like I'm crazy. 'Develop clown make-up? No way – who has time for that?'

Who has time for that? *People who have time to play with puppets have time for that.* Wow. I mean, *wow.*

'Muppeteering comes naturally to me,' Wade says, as he brings his wrists together. 'I always loved making shadow puppets as a kid.' Gracefully waving his hands up and down, he pretends they're a bird soaring through the air to demonstrate.

Oh Jesus.

After breathing in and out heavily, like I'm in yoga, to prevent myself from hyperventilating, I begin to look around for cameras because, even though I'm not famous, I'm positive I'm being punk'd. I have to be – there's no other explanation. Ashton Kutcher's behind this – he's gotta be. There's no way my ex-boyfriend is a Muppeteer.

'What are you looking for?' Wade asks, as I peer under his couch.

'Huh?' I ask, turning back to him. 'Oh, uh . . . I'm just checking out the rest of the place.' I suddenly feel Eva rustle around in her bag. When I look down, she peeks out at me with sleepy eyes and then lazily glances over at Wade. When she sees the Muppets hanging on the wall behind him, she cocks her head, raises her ears and lets out a low grumbling growl.

'Eva, no,' I say, trying to quiet her down, but she doesn't listen. Within seconds she breaks into a barking fit and won't let up. The only way I can get her to stop is to turn the bag away from the wall so she can't see the Muppets, so that's what I do. As Eva silently retreats back into her bag, I apologize to Wade. 'Sorry.'

'No problem,' he says. 'She must be freaked out by the Muppets.'

'Yeah,' I nod. And she's not the only one.

Wade motions to the empty spot next to him on the couch, directly underneath *them*, and asks if I want to have a seat. 'Um, sure,' I say, as I cautiously sit down. Positioning myself at the edge of the sofa just in case one of them flies off the wall and decides to eat me, I put Eva's bag on my lap.

'So, Wade, where do you' – I search for the right word – '*Muppet* at?'

'Most of the shows I do are held at the local play-houses,' Wade explains as he reaches up to take an old man Muppet off the wall. He begins to play with it. 'But the last one I did – my personal favorite – was held at a church not far from here. Called Equestrians for Christ, it was a modern-day re-enactment of the Crucifixion. Basically, it was my version of *The Passion of the Christ*. It was a big undertaking – there were so many Muppets that I had to get some of the local high school kids to help.' Wade stops talking for a moment and becomes melancholy. 'You should've seen the end,' he says. 'All the Muppets rode atop horses while chanting, "We ride because Christ died." It was really powerful.' Turning around, Wade points to one of the Muppets. 'There he is. See?'

I turn around and look up and, low and behold, see Jesus in Muppet form, hanging from a wooden stick. Once again. Poor Jesus.

'But truth be told,' Wade continues, looking back at me, 'non-religious people didn't respond to the theme, so I canceled the show, and well . . .' Wade hesitates, like he's afraid to continue.

I prod. 'Well . . .?' *Come on, Wade, spill the beans.*

'Well, I figured I had to make a show that was a little racier, so I put together a more adult show, about a cranky, undersexed old man who has a crush on his neighbor. It's really fun and kinda sexy. I tested it out last month at the National Day of Puppetry Convention and got a lot of positive feedback. So I'm gonna try and book myself a couple gigs at the playhouse in town and see if people respond to it.'

A sexy puppet show? An undersexed puppet? Is he kidding?

Ewww! Ewww, ewww, ewww!

I watch in horror as Wade continues to play with the puppet he's holding. With his hand inside, he's turning it every which way, moving its mouth, moving its arm, making it blink. I wish I had a camera on my lapel to capture all this because no one's going to believe me when I tell them, no one. It's so bizarre. *He's* so bizarre. Wade needs his own reality series.

Realizing I'm staring, Wade scoots closer to where I'm sitting, if I'm not mistaken, to try to kiss me. Since I don't want any part of that – there's no way I'm going to let a man who just described a puppet show as being sexy kiss me – I shift my body away from him, hoping to send the signal that I'm not in the mood. Wade, however, doesn't get the hint. Moving the puppet off his lap, he puts his arm around me, sending chills through my body. 'You know, Delilah,' he says, looking at me intensely, 'I think we have a real connection here.'

As Wade begins to move his lips toward mine, I realize that this is it – he's going in for the kiss. I need a panic button. I need to stop him. 'You mean like a rainbow connection?' I joke, hoping to make him laugh. Wade immediately freezes. As he slowly leans back, the look on his face changes from one of seduction to one of what-the-fuck's-your-problem? *Oops.* I think I offended him.

'Are you making fun of me?' he asks.

Yep, I've offended him.

'Making fun? No,' I say, 'I was just making a joke.'

'A joke? It's kind of an odd time to make a joke, don't you think?'

'An odd time?' He's lecturing *me* about being odd?

'Yeah,' he says, nodding, 'I was just about to kiss you.'

I look at Wade for a bit, then decide to come clean. He has to understand. 'Wade, to be honest . . . I'm a little put off by the puppets.'

'They're Muppets,' he snaps.

'Whatever,' I say dismissively.

'No, not whatever,' Wade shoots back. 'The two are totally different.'

'No, they're not. Regardless of whether you stick your right or left hand in them, they're stuffed animals on

145

sticks.' Hearing me say this, Wade begins blinking rapidly. By the look on his face, you would've thought I just told him there is no Santa Claus. 'Wade, put yourself in my position,' I say, trying to explain. 'You're an old boyfriend, an adult, and you have puppets hanging from your wall.'

'Muppets!' he screams.

'Whatever!'

Wade rolls his eyes. 'I should have expected this,' he says pissily, slapping his knees. 'I should have expected this from *you*, the girl who got drunk and heckled my family.'

'Pardon me?'

'Oh, you heard me, missy,' he says, narrowing his eyes. 'Did you think I forgot about that? Well, I didn't.' As Wade shakes his head and looks away, I realize it's time for me to get on my launching pad and fly away.

'Wade, thanks for the picnic today,' I say politely. 'But I think I'm gonna go.'

'Yeah, good idea.' He stands up.

As I turn Eva's bag around on my lap and get ready to put it on my shoulder, she spots the old man Muppet sitting on the couch and, without so much as a warning growl, lunges toward it. Suddenly, it's like she's possessed. After landing on top of the Muppet, Eva takes it in her mouth and begins thrashing it from side to side, yanking out its yarn hair in the process. When Wade turns around and sees what she's doing, a look of panic comes over his face.

'Noooooooo!' he screams.

Reaching for the Muppet, Wade tries to pull it away from Eva but is unable to do so – her teeth are clamped firmly around its head. 'Stop her!' he screams, as complete chaos erupts. 'Stop her now!'

I try to pry Eva's mouth open but can't. I think Wade's panic is fueling her – she's out to kill. 'Wade, let go of the puppet!' I tell him. 'If you let go, she might too!'

'No!' he screams. 'Make her stop!'

'I can't! You're freaking her out! You're making it worse!'

'No, I'm not! Make her stop!'

As Wade picks up the Muppet, causing Eva – who still refuses to let go – to dangle in the air, I begin to panic. Seeing my puppy staring danger in the eye, I do what any good mother would do – I begin to kick the shit out of Wade's shins.

'Put her down, you animal!' I scream. 'Put her down now!'

'No!'

Wade begins to shake the Muppet up and down, and Eva bounces in every direction but doesn't seem to mind. She doesn't let go. She doesn't care – she's fearless. The Muppet must die, that's all she knows.

'Stop kicking me, you bitch!' Wade yells, suddenly feeling the sting in his shins.

'I'll stop when you put the puppy down! She's a living creature, for God's sake! What's wrong with you? You're gonna yank her teeth out! Let go of that stupid puppet!'

'Muppppetttt!'

'Whateverrrrrrrrrrrrrrr!'

That's it. I've had it. With everything I have, I give Wade one final kick – a karate kick. My foot meets his hip, and I hold on to Eva for dear life as Wade loses his grip on the Muppet and flies across the room. When he hits the wall,

Eva looks over at him, dropping the Muppet in the process. Staring at Wade, she chews on a few pieces of yarn hair she pulled out. When she swallows them, a look of satisfaction comes over her face. I swear to God, if she could burp, she would. Turning away from Eva, I glare at Wade.

'You're such a psycho! She's just a puppy, for God's sake!'

'You're calling me a psycho?'

'Yes! You're a twenty-nine-year-old man who plays with puppets!'

'Mupp—'

'STOP!!!!' I scream, holding out my hand. 'Don't you *dare* correct me again, you freak!'

Wade takes a breath, stands up and walks toward the door. 'I think you should go now, Delilah,' he says, opening it. His nostrils are flaring.

'Gladly,' I say, putting Eva in her bag. She's still smacking her lips.

After I walk out the front door, I turn around to say goodbye to Wade, but he's already gone back into the apartment. Through the screen I see him kneeling on the floor, gathering up chunks of Muppet hair. It's such a sad sight. I pity him. Sensing that I haven't yet left, Wade turns around.

'What is it?' he asks rudely. 'What do you want?'

I was going to apologize for Eva's behavior, but by the look on his face, I can tell it won't do any good.

'*Ah . . . forget it,*' I say as I turn around and walk to my car.

* * *

'So what are you gonna do now?' Michelle asks, a little later that evening. I called her on my way home and told her what happened.

'I don't know. I was tired earlier, but like with Rod, the anger from what happened has given me energy, so I think I'm gonna start driving to New Orleans to see Abogado. It's only five hundred miles away or so. If I leave now, I should be able to get there around midnight.'

'That's a bad idea,' Michelle says, after hesitating a bit.

'Oh, don't worry. I was fine driving at night last time,' I say, assuming what she means by 'bad idea' is me driving at night.

'Sorry, that's not what I mean,' Michelle says. 'I think going to New Orleans in general is a bad idea. He doesn't want to see you.'

The 'he' she is referring to is #16, Diego Soto, also known as Abogado. I met him while on vacation with her in Barcelona. She hooked up with one of his friends and still keeps in touch with him, and because of it, she thinks she's little Miss Know-it-all.

'You don't know that.'

'I don't *know it* know it, but based on the way you two left things, I have a pretty good idea.'

'Oh, gimme a break. It happened two years ago. I'm sure he's over it by now.'

Michelle doesn't respond.

'How about this,' I offer, 'Colin e-mailed me the addresses of four more guys. How about I go see them first, and go to New Orleans only if they don't work out?

'Even then, I still think it's a mistake.'

'Well, I disagree.'

'Fine, whatever,' Michelle says, sounding aggravated. 'Do what you want – just leave me out of it.'

'Will do.'

After hanging up, I stare into space for a bit. Michelle's crazy to think Abogado still cares about what happened. There's no way he could. However, just in case he does, I'll put off seeing him until after I visit the next four. I don't have a very good feeling about things working out with any of them, but who knows – maybe I'll be surprised.

After packing my belongings and checking out of the hotel, I get in my car and head toward the highway. Since both Eva and I have had a stressful evening, I think soothing music is just what we need, so I tune my iPod to lovely tunes of John Denver. He brought us into Tennessee; he might as well take us out. Since we're heading to the Sunshine State, I tune to one of my favorite songs and begin to sing along. 'Sunshine on my shoulders.'

$3,526, 37 days, 14 guys left.

Chapter Six

#5 Tim the Townie
One half of the 'Thompson Twins' (not the 80s band);
rumored to have a big one, didn't.

#6 Ian Kesselman
Weirdly obsessed with his mom.

#9 Tom the Townie
Other half of the
'Thompson Twins'; rumored
to have a big one, did.

#12 Delaware Pepper
Yes, it's his real name.
Smelled like macaroni.

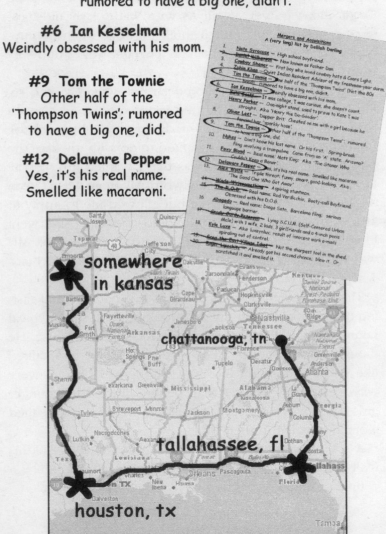

Four of a Kind

A week later, as I pull onto the highway in Kansas and head to New Orleans, I wonder how I'm going to break it to Michelle that I'm going to see Abogado. Suffice it to say, my reunions with Ian, Delaware and The Thompson Twins didn't go very well. As with Wade, I should have known better than to even think that one of these guys might be the one. People can change, yes, but really strange people usually don't.

The first disastrous reunion occurred when I visited #6, Ian Kesselman. I dated Ian ten years ago, when I was a sophomore in college. After graduating from high school, I didn't quite know what I wanted to do with my life. The only thing I knew *for sure* was that I wanted to go away to school. Away being the key word. My mom wasn't keen on me leaving the East Coast but allowed me to apply to Miami University in Oxford, Ohio, because she went to college there. Of all the schools that accepted me, MU was the farthest away, so that's where I went and that's where I met Ian.

The best way to describe Ian is to say that if central casting came knocking on my door looking for a stereotypical neurotic guy, I'd send them to Ian Kesselman's house. He thought he was Woody Allen – he walked like him, talked like him and thought like him. He copied him in every way except one. Rather than being attracted to younger girls, Ian was attracted to older women, mom-aged women, women in their fifties.

A lot of women in their fifties are attractive, so this really didn't bother me at first. However, after a while, a couple of things happened that creeped me out. For one, although he denied it after the fact, Ian hit on my mom when she came to visit for parents' weekend. Of course, she thought it was the coolest thing ever, that a college kid would hit on her, but when I told her he hit on her because he liked older women not because he thought she looked young, she didn't think it was so great.

'What does he think I am, like fifty or something?' my mom asked in a huff, acting all offended.

'You *are* fifty, Mom,' I reminded her.

'Yes, but I don't look it.'

'I agree, but apparently Ian thinks you do.'

A week after I said this, she ran out and got her first face-lift.

The second thing that turned me off about Ian had to do with the fact that he talked dirty to me while having sex. I was only nineteen years old at the time, and at that point in my life verbalizing naughty thoughts was something that happened only in Sharon Stone movies, not my dorm room. However, while this dirty talk caught me off guard, it alone wasn't what put me off. What did was that one time while we were having sex at his apartment, while he was saying something like 'Yeah, Mama, you know you want it!' I caught Ian looking at a picture of his mom on the nightstand. The first time it happened I thought it was a fluke. I thought maybe he was looking at something off in the distance and that the picture just happened to be in the way. But when it happened a second time, and then a third, I realized it was no fluke. That was it – three strikes, Ian was out.

Of all places for Ian to live today, it had to be Florida – the cottonhead capital of the country. (And I mean that in the kindest way.) Right then I should've figured out that Ian hadn't changed. But I didn't, no, not me, not dense Delilah. Singing 'I Saw the Sign!' by Ace of Base the whole way there to get myself back in the mood for Ian, I drove my cheap-ass, crappy little car to Tallahassee, staked him out, and learned that he was an aerobics instructor. Sure, the name of the gym he worked at was Fit 50, but the possibility of it being a fitness center for people over fifty years old never crossed my mind. No, I went shopping and bought myself a hot little leotard that was totally retro and totally cool. When I put it on, I looked just like Jane Fonda did in all those workout videos she made in the eighties – fierce. The very next day I trotted my twenty-nine-year-old tushy into Fit 50, only to find out that I was twenty-one years too early to be allowed past the front desk.

Any moron would have left at this point, knowing the kind of guy Ian was and all. But no, not me, not dense Delilah. No matter how many times I sang 'I Saw the Sign!' on the way down to Florida, I let all the signs go right over my head when I got there. I never put two and two together, never assumed that Ian worked at Fit 50 because he was . . . let's say . . . dating the owner or anything. (Which yes, he was, and yes, he is.) I thought it was a coincidence and threatened age discrimination, demanding to be allowed inside. My threats worked – they let me in.

When I walked into Ian's advanced aerobics class and looked around at my competition, I giggled, thinking, *I'll blow all these ladies right out of the water.* 'Thinking' being the key word there. Long story short, I passed out halfway

154

through the class. As if that wasn't bad enough, when I did some old man slipped me the tongue while giving me mouth-to-mouth. Yeah . . . *ewww*.

After leaving Florida, Eva and I moved on to #12, Delaware Pepper, who today lives in Houston, Texas. Although Delaware and I went to high school together, I didn't meet him until a year after we graduated from college, in 1998. I was answering phones at a design house in Manhattan at the time and was sitting outside on my lunch break one day, listening to the *Ally McBeal* soundtrack while trying not to eat and hiking up my skirt, when he walked over to me and said hello. He said it was good to see me, asked how I was doing, asked how my mom and Daisy were doing, and I had absolutely no idea who he was. For the twenty minutes Delaware talked to me, I sat there, searching my soul, wondering, *Who is this guy?* The look on my face must have been one of confusion, because the next thing I knew, Delaware was like, 'You don't know who I am, do you?' I shook my head and told him no – I was so embarrassed. 'Delaware Pepper,' he said, trying to jar my memory. 'We went to high school together.'

Even though I still didn't have a clue, I faked a moment of realization and exclaimed, 'Oh, Delaware, I'm so sorry! It's so nice to see you!'

Feeling bad about not remembering him, I invited Delaware to meet me and some friends for drinks that evening. When he arrived and joined the conversation, he started going on and on about how he graduated from Harvard and was hoping to go to M.I.T. to get his Master's degree. He was such a dork – a bore, actually – but for some reason I found myself oddly attracted to him. I think the reason had to do with the fact that he was a challenge. On the surface, Delaware was dull and strange, but underneath he was mysterious. I kept thinking if I could break through Delaware's shell and unearth his true potential, then I'd be better than all those people who wouldn't give him the time of day. Later that evening I ended up inviting him over and we ended up having sex – not very good sex. Because he was so inexperienced, Delaware had to stop every ten seconds to maintain stamina.

Anyway, that night was the only time we slept together. I broke things off with him a few days later because he smelled like macaroni. Seriously. I'm almost embarrassed to admit it because it's so stupid, but this is what happened. A few days after our night of passion, Delaware stopped by my apartment right after I had made a big pot of macaroni and cheese. It was the good kind, the kind with the powdered cheese packet, and I wanted to dig in. I didn't want company.

When Delaware walked through the front door, he immediately wanted action but I wanted . . . my macaroni and cheese. He started kissing me, and the whole time I kept thinking, *My macaroni and cheese is getting cold . . . it's not going to be creamy . . . it's going to get curdy.* When I couldn't wait any longer to eat, I pried myself away from Delaware and told him that I was hypoglycemic. While I ate, I gave him his own bowl to make him feel less rejected. It was only polite. As soon as we finished eating, Delaware went right back to kissing me and I got really grossed out. Not only was his mouth warm and sticky from the food, but he smelled like cheese, too. Just like that, it was over.

When I read that Delaware was living in Houston today, I wondered what on earth he was doing there. After waiting outside his house for three days and not seeing him, I was worried I might never find out, but then I read through the notes Colin gave me more thoroughly and found his work phone number, so I called it. When I did, I quickly learned Delaware wasn't doing anything in Houston – or on earth, for that matter. When his voicemail picked up, instead of getting the typical 'Hi, I'm not available to take your call' message, I got something a little more . . . out there.

'Hi, this is Dr Pepper.' Yes, Dr Pepper, that's been Delaware's name ever since he got his Ph.D. from M.I.T. 'I'm unavailable to take your call right now since I'm on the Space Shuttle Discovery servicing the Hubble Space Telescope. By the way . . . Hi, Mom!'

Yes, the Space Shuttle Discovery, the Hubble Space Telescope. Delaware Pepper, the guy I so foolishly broke up with because he smelled like macaroni, now works for NASA. Yes, in Houston we had a problem, and it was me realizing what an idiot I was seven years ago.

But Eva and I didn't give up, no. We got back in the car and drove all the way to a small rinky-dink town in the middle of Kansas to visit #5 and #9, The Thompson Twins. Obviously, these aren't the same Thompson Twins who sang the 'Hold Me Now' song that was so popular in the eighties, but twin brothers whose last name just happens to be Thompson. I'm not proud of it, but yes, I hooked up with brothers. I didn't do it at the same time or anything.

(I'm not *that* low-budget.) I hooked up with the second one almost two years after I had hooked up with the first, and in my defense, the only reason I did was because I thought he was the first. These guys were identical, they really were.

Well, almost.

I met Tim and Tom Thompson in college. They lived in Oxford, Ohio, but didn't go to Miami University. They were locals – local yokels – who grew up there. Seeing as though they were friendly guys, everyone on campus thought they were students, which they were, just not at Miami University.* They were cute in a skater boy kind of way, and both were tall and skinny with good, floppy, Hugh Grant-style hair.

The first twin I was with was Tim. We dated on and off for a few months at the beginning of my sophomore year in the fall of 1994. I don't remember why we broke up, but when we did, I remember that some girl asked me if the rumor was true, if Tim's penis was as large as everyone said it was. I had never heard such a thing, and unfortunately (for me) told her that there was no truth to it – Tim's penis was average.

I transferred to a different school my junior year and lost touch with The Thompson Twins. A year after leaving I went back to Oxford to visit a friend and go to a Barenaked Ladies concert that was being held on campus and ran into Tim at an after-hours party. Within minutes

* They took telecourses through the local community college and watched their classes on public-access television (or recorded them, if they happened to be on schedule at the local Piggly Wiggly grocery store where they worked).

of saying hello to each other the sparks between us flew, and before I knew what was happening, we were both barenaked in the bathroom having sex, which is when I figured out it was Tom and not Tim – his penis was enormous. Enormous. In fact, I didn't think penises could get as big as his was. The rumor was true; it was just being spread about the wrong brother. Anyway, back to the bathroom – by the time I realized my mistake, I was too late. Tom and I were already having sex. (And quite frankly, good sex.)

The fact that The Thompson Twins are almost thirty years old and still live together should've tipped me off that something wasn't right with them, but it didn't. I didn't realize just how wrong things were until I pulled up outside where they lived. It wasn't the double-wide trailer that turned me off – I don't like to criticize people who live in trailers because I'm still a renter and don't have a dollar in the bank, so who am I to judge? At least they own – it was more the overturned coolers and lawn chairs that littered the yard, the raw sewage smell that permeated the air, and the roasting spit with a charred old carcass on it that sat by the front door that I found undesirable.

Deciding I'd seen enough to officially take The Thompson Twins out of the running, I put my car in drive and pulled away. However, any hopes I had for an easy getaway were quickly halted when I ran over one of their kids. (I should say ran *into* one their kids, because I didn't actually flatten the child.)

Obviously it was an accident.

I'm still not sure whose kid it was because Tim and Tom have five between them – Nifty, Dandy, Thumper, Scooter and Bob. Thumper was the lucky one who met my bumper. He – I mean she – and her little butch haircut rode her bike into the middle of the street, right in front of my car. Although the collision could've been disastrous, thanks to my quick reflexes (and the four cans of Red Bull I drank to stay awake during the drive) my bumper ended up only lightly tapping Thumper's bike, a bike that stayed upright because of a set of training wheels she had affixed to the back wheel. She didn't fly over the handlebars, skid across the pavement or anything like that. All she did was slowly tip over the side.

When Tim and Tom heard the screech of my brakes, they both ran out of their trailer in all their glory. To say the least, the years have not treated these boys well. Since the last time I saw them, their hair, which was the one good thing they had going for themselves, had taken a tragic turn. I don't know who told them it's cool to shave lightning bolts into the sides of your head, but it's not. Ditto goes for the mullet cuts they were sporting. I don't care if you're Tim and Tom living in Kansas or a hipster living in Williamsburg, Brooklyn, the mullet is not, nor will it ever be, a cool haircut.

After examining Thumper, Tim, Tom and I found her to be fine. She didn't have an ounce of blood on her, just one little scrape. (So why all the tears? I don't know.) Because I'm an adult, I apologized to Thumper (even though it was she who rode her bike into the middle of the street), but Tim and Tom told me not to worry, saying accidents happen. It's funny, but with all the commotion, they never even asked why I was driving down their street in the first place. Once they realized it was me, they said it was

160

'damn good' to see my 'sweet ass', and then invited me inside their trailer for a 'brewski'. I passed on the beer (something about the way little Bob kept smacking gnats [fleas?] off his body freaked me out) and instead offered to take the whole family out to Thumper's favorite restaurant for dinner to say I'm sorry. (After you run over someone's child, it's best to keep them on your good side.) Had I known we'd end up at Long John Silver's, I might not have given her so much freedom in the choosing, but I'm sure the greasy fish smell will come out of my clothes eventually.

Since Tim's and Tom's wives were working (yes, both are married, but they told me it's a 'common law' thing, so Colin's off the hook for not finding this out), dinner ended up being just the eight of us. While we were eating, I found myself once again wishing, like I did with Wade, that there was a camera on my lapel. Tim and Tom kept comparing scars and tattoos, little Bob kept farting and asking me if I liked his tail, Nifty kept picking her nose and trying to pop the pimple on her cheek (I didn't even know little kids could get pimples), and Dandy and Scooter kept throwing ketchup-covered hush puppies, tartar-sauce-slathered fish sticks and buttery corn cobbettes at each other. As for Thumper, she was the only one who was pleasant. Maybe she was in shock, but she just sat quietly in her chair the whole night, staring (glaring?) at me, drinking her clam chowder.

Before getting back on the road that evening, I jotted down a short note on a napkin and had Tim and Tom sign it. Not that they read it, but they agreed to not sue me in exchange for a case of astronaut food. I'd picked up a box

161

of freeze-dried ice cream bars while I was in Houston and wow . . . those grubby little bastards went crazy for them. So did their kids.

After saying goodbye to everyone, I got in my car and was ready to pull away when little Thumper ran up to my door. I thought maybe she was going to thank me for dinner or perhaps say she wasn't angry at me for almost running her over, so I quickly rolled down my window. 'What is it, Thumper?' I asked with a smile.

Without hesitating, Thumper inhaled deeply through her nose and spit a big green loogey in my face. 'Watch where you're going next time, bitch,' she said, smiling right back. After politely nodding, I told her I would and then wiped my face clean.

Anyway, that happened last evening. As I drive down the highway today, heading back toward New Orleans, I do so in silence – No Ace of Base, no Ally McBeal, no Barenaked Ladies – and think about this idea of mine. Am I heartbroken that things haven't worked out with these last six guys? No. But am I a little freaked-out about it? Yes, and for a couple of reasons.

For one, I can't believe I've slept with such losers. I'm positive these guys weren't losers when we had sex, which leads me to wonder . . . did they turn into losers, or was my loser-radar just way off back then? Or are they *not* losers now, and have I just turned into a big bitch? Honestly, I can't figure it out. Where did things go wrong?

The second reason I'm worried is because I don't understand how my grandpa can run into just one woman from his past and have things click. Including the four guys I eliminated before I left, I'm batting zero for ten right now, which is not good, not good at all. Picking up my phone, I decide to call my grandpa to find out how things are going with Gloria. I'm not saying I hope things aren't working out between them, but if they aren't, I might feel slightly better. When my grandpa answers the phone, I cut to the chase. 'So, how's the love affair with Gloria' I ask.

'Oh, Darlin' . . . it couldn't be better!' he exclaims.

Shit! Oops! I mean, *great!* 'Really?' I ask. 'Are you sure?'

'Positive,' my grandpa says confidently. I can practically hear the smile on his face. 'I haven't felt the boom yet, but I really think it might happen.' After sighing heavily, I tell him that I'm happy for him.

'Hey, not to change the subject, but did I tell you I got a car?' he then asks.

'A car?' I'm confused. 'I thought you were gonna get a golf cart.'

'Well, I was,' he explains, 'but then I remembered that I'm living in Vegas not Florida, so I got myself a Camaro instead!'

'A Camaro?' *Oh Jesus.*

'Yep. It's orange,' he brags. 'You should see it.'

As images of my grandpa driving through Las Vegas in an orange Camaro while listening to Jefferson Starship fill my head, I shake my head. 'Well, have fun with it.'

'I will, Del,' he replies. 'I gotta run now, but I love you.'

'I love you, too.'

'Peace out, home fry.'

After hanging up the phone, I try to look on the bright side of things. Sure, ten are down, but I still have ten more to go. Ten good ones, too. In addition to Abogado, both

#7 and #13, Henry the Do-Gooder and Alex the Good One Who Got Away, are huge catches. Huge. All is not lost – I can still make this thing work.

After changing my tune, I turn my iPod on and play an Arlo Guthrie song that my grandpa used to sing to me when I was a little girl called 'The City of New Orleans'. Looking forward, I sing along and continue on my way.

$2,804, 31 days, 10 guys left.

Chapter Seven

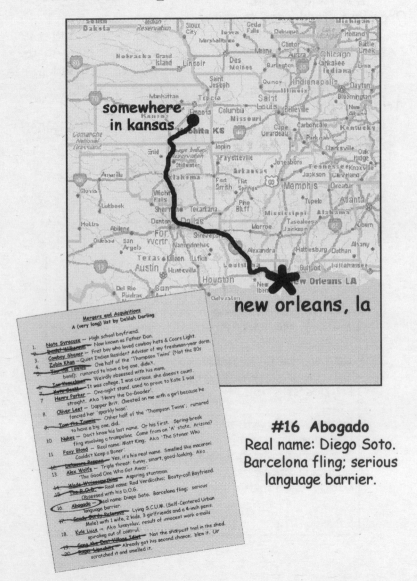

somewhere in kansas

new orleans, la

Mergers and Acquisitions
A (very long) list by Delilah Darling

1. Nate Syracuse — High school boyfriend.
2. ~~Daniel Wilkinson~~ — Now known as Father Dan.
3. Cowboy Shaner — Frat boy who loved cowboy hats & Coors Light.
4. Zubin Khan — Quiet Indian Resident Advisor of my freshman-year dorm.
5. ~~Tutwile Towne~~ — One half of the 'Thompson Twins' (Not the 80s band); rumored to have a big one...didn't.
6. ~~Tom Kesselman~~ — Weirdly obsessed with his mom.
7. Henry Parker — It was college. I was curious, she doesn't count. ~~Kate Grace~~ — One-night stand, used to prove to Kate I was straight. Aka 'Henry the Do-Gooder'.
8. Oliver Lest — Dapper Brit. Cheated on me with a girl because he fancied himself 'sparkly hose.'
9. ~~Tom-the-Tower~~ — Other half of the 'Thompson Twins', rumored to have a big one, did.
10. Nukes — Don't know his last name. Or his first. Spring break fling involving a trampoline. Came from an 'A' state. Arizona?
11. Foxy Blond — Real name: Matt King. Aka 'The Stoner Who Couldn't Keep a Boner'.
12. ~~Delaware Reagan~~ — Yes, it's his real name. Smelled like macaroni and cheese. Triple threat: funny, smart, good-looking. Aka 'The Good One Who Got Away'.
13. Alex Wolfs — Aspiring stuntman.
14. ~~Wade Worcestershire~~ — Real name: Rod Verdicchio; Booty-call Boyfriend.
15. The D.O.G. — Obsessed with his D.O.G.
16. Abogado — Real name: Diego Soto. Barcelona fling; serious language barrier.
17. ~~Cyclo-Barely Delaware~~ — Lying S.C.U.M. (Self-Centered Urban Male) with 1 wife, 2 kids, 3 girlfriends and a 4-inch penis.
18. Kyle Luca — Aka 'luxxynluv,' result of innocent work e-mails spiraling out of control.
19. ~~Cone the Ears-Village Idiot~~ — Not the sharpest tool in the shed.
20. ~~Roger Wessley~~ — Already got his second chance, blew it. Ur scratched it and smelled it.

#16 Abogado
Real name: Diego Soto.
Barcelona fling; serious
language barrier.

#7 Henry Parker
One-night stand, used to prove
to Kate I was straight.
Aka. 'Henry the Do-Gooder'.

#13 Alex Wolfe
Triple threat: funny, smart,
good-looking. Aka. 'The
Good One Who Got Away'.

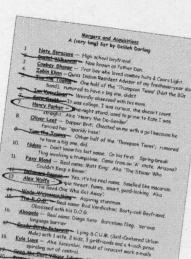

Mergers and Acquisitions
A (very long) list by Delilah Darling

1 ~~Nate Syracuse~~ — High school boyfriend.
2 ~~Daniel Wilkerson~~ — Now known as Father Dan.
3 ~~Cowboy Shaner~~ — Frat boy who loved cowboy hats & Coors Light.
4 ~~Zubin Khan~~ — Quiet Indian Resident Advisor of my freshman-year dorm
   (Not the 80s band), rumored to have a big one, didn't
5 ~~Wayne Towne~~ — One half of the 'Thompson Twins' (Not the 80s
   band), rumored to have a big one, didn't
6 ~~Ian Touchstone~~ — Weirdly obsessed with his mom.
   ~~Kate Tassel~~ — It was college. I was curious, she doesn't count
7 Henry Parker — One-night stand, used to prove to Kate I was
   straight. Aka 'Henry the Do-Gooder'.
8 ~~Oliver Leer~~ — Dapper Brit; Cheated on me with a girl because he
   fancied her 'sparkly nose'.
9 ~~Tam the Townie~~ — Other half of the 'Thompson Twins'; rumored
   to have a big one, did.
10 ~~Nukes~~ — Don't know his last name. Or his first. Spring-break
   fling involving a trampoline. Came from an 'A' state. Arizona?
11 ~~Foxy Blond~~ — Real name: Matt King; Aka 'The Stoner Who
   Couldn't Keep a Boner!'
12 ~~Delicious Raymond~~ — Yes, it's his real name. Smelled like macaroni.
13 Alex Wolfe — Triple threat: funny, smart, good-looking. Aka
   'The Good One Who Got Away'.
14 ~~Wade Witherspoon~~ — Aspiring stuntman.
15 ~~The B.C.B.~~ — Real name: Rod Verdicchio; Booty-call Boyfriend.
16 ~~Abagado~~ — Real name: Diego Soto Barcelona fling. serious
   language barrier.
17 ~~Condor-Jordy-Bazaroni~~ — Lying S.C.U.M. (Self-Centered Urban
   Male) with 1 wife, 2 kids, 3 girlfriends and a 4-inch penis.
18 Kyle Luxe — Aka luxeynluv, result of innocent work e-mails
   spiraling out of control.
19 ~~Greg the Fort Village Idiot~~ — Not the sharpest tool in the shed.
20 ~~Roger Langshire~~ — Already got his second chance. blew it. Or
   scratched it and smelled it.

TO: Delilah Darling
FR: Colin Brody
RE: Two married fellas

I found contact info on two more fellas:

• Henry Parker: Married; lives in Ohio.
• Alex Wolfe: Married w/2 kids; lives in Maine.

Do you want their addresses if they're married?
You said you were having a singles party, so
I'm guessing not.

By the way . . . where you been? Haven't
heard you singing in a while. Did you know I
can hear you sing through the walls? You do
a good Lionel Richie. Hey, jumbo jumbo.
Knock next time you're around. Or sing.

CB

Beep

Del, it's Mom. I don't know what's going on,
but I called your work number this morning
hoping to catch you between assignments
and was told by some guy named Roger that
you got 'laid off'. When I informed him he
was mistaken, he laughed and said he was
positive you were gone because he 'sent you
out with a bang' himself. Can you call me,
please to explain what's going on? Thanks.

Beep

Del, it's Daisy. Did you lose your job?
Mom's totally freaking out. Will you please
call her back?

I'm Flabbergasted

In my list of twenty, Abogado came after Rod, but almost two years after him. Although it was unintentional, I had a bit of a dry spell when I stopped going out every weekend. I didn't realize it at the time though. In fact, I didn't realize it until I made my list. It was during that time that I started working at ESD, and I guess I started to focus more on my career and less on my personal life.

In November of 2002, eight months after I started, Elisabeth gave the entire staff the week of Thanksgiving off as a paid vacation. She was always doing nice things like this for us. Michelle and I had become pretty good friends at this point, so we planned a trip to Barcelona together. Neither of us had been before, and both of us wanted to go. Although I don't speak a lick of Spanish, Michelle studied it for eight years and was positive she'd be able to get us around.

We got along great on the trip. We agreed on everything – where to go, what to see, what *not* to eat. Yes, although we loved Barcelona, we weren't crazy about the two foods that were served pretty much everywhere: fish and ham. Our problem with the fish was more of a preparation thing than anything else. The two times we ordered it, it was served to us whole, complete with its head and, yes, eyeballs. (In case you're wondering, the eyeballs were slightly shrunken but still intact from being cooked in hot oil.) It was like someone caught the fish, threw it into a fryer, and then slapped it on our plates. Maybe Michelle and I are high maintenance, but we couldn't eat it, not while it was staring at us. As for the ham, it had small white chunky things that were the consistency of cartilage in it. Whatever they were, they were gristly and unchewable, so we had to keep spitting them out into a napkin.

On our fourth day there Michelle and I started to get antsy, mostly because we were hungry. Seeing as though we needed to work off some of our energy, we called a guy we didn't know, a friend of a friend who lived in Barcelona, to see what he was up to that evening. After telling us that he was going to dinner with a group of his friends to a Chinese restaurant – yes, no ham, no fish – he invited us to come along. Needless to say, we eagerly accepted.

Spanish men go out in large groups, so dinner consisted of Michelle, me, and seven cute guys who were all around our age, if not a little bit older. They showered us with attention, and we loved every minute of it. Abogado was the friend of a friend. His real name was Diego Soto, but Michelle and I called him Abogado, which is the Spanish word for lawyer, because that's what he did for a living and because we couldn't keep everyone's name straight. He was gorgeous. He had beautiful flawless skin and shaggy almost-black hair. And his eyes . . . *wow*. Framed by a pair of black plastic-rimmed glasses that looked like they belonged to Clark Kent, Abogado's eyes were dark and mysterious.*

Despite the enormous language barrier that hampered us all (in addition to Michelle's weak Spanish, the guys spoke very broken English), Abogado and I hit it off right away, as did Michelle and a guy we called Dustin Hoffman. (He looked just like him; you should've seen

* Christopher Reeve, the world's best Superman, may you rest in peace.

him.) Abogado and Dustin Hoffman were so funny. They loved American movies and loved American culture. It was the year of *Star Wars Episode II: Attack of the Clones*, so they kept reciting lines from all the movies, like, 'May the force be with you!' For some reason they also loved the word *flabbergasted* and were under the impression that it was really popular in America. Rather than correct them and tell them it wasn't, Michelle and I decided that we'd start using it more, hoping it would catch on. It didn't.

By the end of dinner, Abogado and I were pretty much boyfriend/girlfriend, so he asked me to ride with him on his motorcycle to a discotheque that everyone was going to. There were so many reasons why I should've said no. For one, I had just met him; two, we had both been drinking heavily; three, I was in a foreign country where I didn't speak a lick of the language; and four, I was separating myself from my friend in said foreign country. However, for some odd reason I felt like living life on the edge, so I grabbed a helmet and hopped on. 'Hit the gas and drive me wild!' I told Abogado. 'Of course I do,' he responded (which really didn't make any sense).

Abogado gunned it and I held on for dear life as he sped down the street, wove in and out of traffic, ran red lights, and drove down sidewalks. His black hair flowed back at me in the breeze, and although it smelled a little bit like Chinese food, it was so sexy! The ride turned out to be both frightening and exhilarating.

After dancing the night (morning?) away, Michelle ended up going home with Dustin Hoffman, as did I with Abby, as I now affectionately called him. When we got back to his house, after some heavy petting, the two of us got naked. After copping a nice feel of Abby's *firme culo*, I reached around front and was flabbergasted to discover that he had an uncircumcised penis. Yepper. It was uncut, unaltered and unfuckingbelievable! It was the first uncircumcised penis I had come into contact with in my life, and wowie – it was amazing! Although Abby wanted to get down to business, I wanted to check it out so he had to be patient and wait. And turn on the lights. After exploring Abby's nether regions for a while, I looked up at him in awe and said, 'May the foreskin be with you'. Although he had no idea what I said, Abby kissed me passionately and then the two of us made sweet, sweet Spanish love.

The following evening Abby and Dustin Hoffman invited Michelle and me out to dinner again, and we graciously accepted. Although they took us to a place that served only ham, Michelle and I sucked up our dinner while Abby sucked his down . . . apparently a little too quickly. I'm not exactly sure what happened, but one minute he was fine and the next minute he was turning purple and grabbing at his throat. Dustin Hoffman was the first out of his chair.

For the next few minutes, Michelle and I watched in horror as Dustin Hoffman gave Abby the Heimlich maneuver, trying with all his might to dislodge the food from his friend's throat. After four or five futile attempts the outlook didn't look good, and tears began streaming down Abby's face. Seeing his friend cry got Dustin Hoffman's adrenaline pumping. After screaming '¡Yo te voy a salvar, amigo!' at the top of his lungs, he pulled his fists into Abby's ribcage so forcefully that he lifted him off the ground. Almost immediately, the offending piece of ham shot out of Abby's throat and landed – of all the places – directly on my cheek. Where it stayed. For a while. Seeing the result of his hard work so vulgarly displayed, Dustin Hoffman covered his mouth in horror while Michelle gasped and poor Abby fell back down into his chair, humiliated. Me? I calmly reached for a napkin and wiped my face clean. Trying to lighten the mood, Dustin Hoffman hit Abby on the back. 'You really should take smaller bites next time!' he said. Abby glared at him – now was no time for jokes – and then got up and left the table without saying a word. Dustin Hoffman followed.

Twenty minutes later, when the guys returned, Abby was quiet but better. Seeing as though Michelle was so turned on by Dustin Hoffman's act of heroism, she ended up going home with him again. When the two of them left, Abby invited me over as well. After what had just happened, I wasn't exactly 'in the mood', but knew that declining his invitation would make him feel worse. I ended up sleeping with him again, except this time, instead of thinking about his uncircumcised penis, I kept thinking of the choking incident – his purple face, Dustin Hoffman's blood-curdling scream, and of course the partially chewed piece of ham flying at my face. The night's main event was on instant replay, looped in my brain, and it was funny, so funny in fact that I accidentally let out a little laugh. When he heard it, Abby stopped what he was doing and looked at me, bewildered. 'Why come you laugh at me?' he asked.

'I didn't laugh,' I lied.

172

'Yes, you does,' Abby said, rolling off me. 'You laugh.'

Since I didn't want him to think that I was laughing at his ability to have sex, I told Abby the truth – that I was thinking about what happened and thought it was funny. I even did my best imitation of him and Dustin Hoffman, complete with sound effects, hoping to make him feel less self-conscious about what happened. I thought it would put him at ease, which it did in a way – his penis went limp, retreated into its foreskin and hid its head in shame. 'I think you should leave,' Abogado said. I tried to apologize, but he didn't want to hear it so I got dressed and left.

When I got back to New York, I sent Abogado an e-mail, apologizing again. In a reply he said it was no big deal, but the chilly tone of his words suggested otherwise. Michelle still keeps in touch with Dustin Hoffman, so I know that Abogado moved to New Orleans a year ago to open a cooking school. I probably could have come down here on my own without having Colin find him, but Michelle is always so secretive about him that part of me wondered if he was married. He's not. Regardless of Michelle's reasons, I hope Abogado's well, I hope he's happy, and I sure as hell hope he's teaching people to cook something other than ham.

Crescent City Cartwheels   Tuesday, 19 April

Eva and I got to New Orleans early yesterday morning and are now sitting outside Café du Monde in the French Quarter sharing beignets. I love beignets. My mom used to make them for Daisy and me when we were little girls.

173

She would let us help make the dough and cut it into squares, and we always used to argue over who got to sprinkle powdered sugar on top when they were done.

Last night Eva and I walked by Abogado's cooking school, which is also in the French Quarter. Located inside a tiny, yellow stucco town house with black shuttered windows and a fancy wrought-iron balcony covered with ferns and flowers, it's adorable. Peering through the windows, I could see that a class was in session and didn't want to go inside, so I took a pamphlet that was sitting in a little box near the door. I've decided that the best way to get to Abogado is to take a class and pretend that it's all one big coincidence when I see him.

While waiting to call the school when it opens, I look around the French Quarter and smile. While it's not quite back to the glory it once was before Hurricane Katrina hit, it warms my heart to see that many businesses are open and happy tourists are milling about.

At noon, I take my cell phone out of my purse to call the school when it suddenly rings. Looking at the caller ID, I see that it's Colin Brody, P.I., so I answer. He asks if I got his e-mail saying that Henry and Alex are married.

'Yeah, thanks,' I say, trying to hide my disappointment. It's a shame. They both had so much potential. 'Hey, by any chance do you know the name of the woman Alex married?' While Henry and I dated only briefly, Alex and I dated for five months. Just as things were getting serious, he broke up with me for another girl. I can't remember her name, but I think it was—

'Sarah,' Colin says. 'I think her name is Sarah.'

Yep, that was it. Sarah. I've always thought of Alex as the good one who got away. He was so sharp and mature – my mother loved him. When he broke up with me, he was honest about why he was doing it, honest about Sarah, and I always respected that. Oh well. I guess if a guy's going to leave you for another woman, it's better to have it be the woman he ends up marrying than some dime-store floozy.

'So how's it going?' Colin casually asks. 'Have you been finding these guys all right?' Still thinking about Alex and Sarah, I answer without thinking.

'Yeah, I found them fine but they've all been total busts so far. You should've seen them, they were total idiots. So I'm in New Orleans now, hoping things'll work—'

I suddenly realize what I'm saying and stop talking.

Oh my God . . . I just spilled the beans. Why did I spill the beans? How did I spill the beans? What did Colin ask to make me spill the beans? He asked if I found the guys all right.

'You totally tricked me into saying that!' I scream into the phone.

'Whoa, whoa, don't bite my head off!' Colin says defensively, letting out a chuckle. 'I did no such thing. All I did was ask you a question.'

'Yeah – a trick question,' I snap.

'It was no trick question. It was straightforward.'

'No it wasn't.' *Wait – was it?*

'Yes, it was. All I did was ask if you found the guys all right, like, did the invitations get to them.'

'If that's what you meant by your question, then that's what you should've asked. You specifically asked me if I *found them*, and you asked me casually, like we already talked about what I was doing.'

'And by "what you're doing" you mean tracking down old boyfriends, right?'

'Exactly.'

Shit! I did it again!

'Aha!' Colin exclaims. 'Got you twice!'

I don't say anything. I'm too angry.

'Oh, c'mon, Del,' he continues. 'Don't be mad. I'm just curious, that's all.'

I'm still too angry to speak.

'So, why *are* you tracking down old boyfriends? Is it like a twelve-step thing? Are you making peace with all your demons?'

'No, it's not a twelve-step thing, you moron!' I scream. 'And it's none of your business why I'm doing it!'

'I s'pose you're right,' Colin says. 'But if I knew, I might be able to help you out with a little more information.'

A little more information? My curiosity is piqued.

'What kind of a little more information?'

'Well, take your chef, for example,' Colin says. 'In addition to being single and straight, I found out that he's quite the catch down there in New Orleans.'

Piqued more.

'How so?'

'Well, while I was searching, I found an interesting article about him on Nexis, an article that was written a few months ago in the *New Orleans Times-Picayune*, an article that you can't find on Google.'

'And what did it say?'

'Hold on, let me get it.' I hear papers shuffling. 'Okay,

here it is. Let's see . . . it says that Diego Soto is a natural-born chef who never took a cooking class in his life. His new cooking school, which fuses Spanish, French and American cuisines, is all the rage in New Orleans right now. Quickly becoming one of the Crescent City's movers and shakers, he was recently spotted eating dinner with Emeril Lagasse. Diego Soto also just purchased a million-dollar loft in New Orleans' very trendy Warehouse District and is considered one of the city's most eligible bachelors.'

Emeril Lagasse? A million-dollar loft? A most eligible bachelor?

Bam!!!

I can't believe I hooked up with a most eligible bachelor! I know the *Times-Picayune* isn't exactly *People*, but it's still so exciting. This is it – this is it! Abogado is the one, I'm positive. All those others didn't happen for a reason.

Although I can barely contain my enthusiasm, I try to keep my cool. If Colin finds out just how keyed up I am about all this, then it'll mean he was right, that I should've told him what I was doing. With that said, after taking a deep breath, I clear my throat, and speak slowly. 'It's great to hear Diego's doing so well,' I say. The tone of my voice is low and serious.

'That's as excited as you're gonna get?' Colin asks, obviously surprised by my demeanor.

'Did you expect cartwheels?'

'Are you doing cartwheels?'

'No,' I say calmly. But I am pacing. I need to get off the phone and book myself into one of Abogado's classes immediately, before they fill up. 'Colin, is there a reason that you called?' I ask impatiently.

'A reason? Oh, yes, right,' he says, suddenly remembering that he called me. 'I can't find this guy Nukes, not without a proper first or last name.'

Nukes? Who in the hell is that?

Oh! Yes, right . . . Cabo San Lucas . . . Coco Locos . . . Trampoline.

'I did a search for people whose last name begins with the letters *N-u-k* and then narrowed the results down three times to include only men currently between the ages of twenty-seven and thirty-one, who lived in the state of Arizona or Arkansas or Alabama in 1997. I even looked in Alaska just for kicks. There were none.'

Okay, so he couldn't find him – I'm not surprised. And I really don't care, to be honest. Not with an eligible bachelor at my fingertips. 'Anything else?'

'No. Oh, wait – yes. Check your e-mail. I sent you another guy's information. Matt King.'

'Will do,' I quickly tell him. 'Do I owe you anything extra for finding the article?'

'Nah . . . it was my pleasure to get you as excited as I know you are, even though you're pretending not to be.'

I smile. He's good, this one.

'Well, all right then,' I say. 'Thanks and have a nice day.'

'Yes, you too, my dear. And good luck with the chef.'

As soon as I hang up the phone, I scream out loud. When I'm done, I look around and realize that not one person sitting around me has flinched. New Orleans rocks. I love this same thing about New York. I love that after a good date or a good meeting I can walk down the street screaming with joy if I want, and no one cares. No one calls the police or grabs their kids. If anything, they smile. You see, New York is filled with crazy people, so to everyone walking by me, I'm just one more crazy. It's a very freeing feeling.

After taking the pamphlet from Abogado's cooking school out of my purse, I dial the number on the front of it as quickly as I can. A woman answers the phone. When I ask her when the next available class is, she tells me it's my lucky day. Although everything is booked solid for the next three weeks, she just got a cancellation for a pastry class that evening.

Kick. Ass.

I tell her I'll take it.

After giving the woman my credit card number to hold the reservation, she tells me to arrive promptly at six o'clock that evening. 'It'll be a long class,' she says enthusiastically. 'You're going to explore the exciting world of the puff pastry!'

'Perfect!' I exclaim passionately.

Since I have a few hours to kill before class I decide to take a walk to the Warehouse District later that afternoon, to see where Abogado lives. My guidebook says it's considered the artsy area of New Orleans and is within walking distance from the French Quarter, so I decide to let Eva walk there on her leash for practice. Since being in Philadelphia, she's attempted to do so a few more times but hasn't gotten much better. She walks in circles and backtracks well but for some reason can't grasp the concept of going forward. However, that's all about to change because Mommy read *The Dog Whisperer* last night and has a pocket full of treats. Someone's going to get rewarded for walking forward today! While gearing her up, I check my home voicemail and hear two more messages from my mother. I haven't figured out what I'm going to tell her about losing my job yet, so I don't call her back.

Abogado's loft is located just off St Charles, a historic avenue in New Orleans (or so says my map), and although it takes Eva and me a little longer to get there than it would if I carried her, we get there and that's what's important. The treats seem to be working; she catches on quickly. (*Who's Mommy's little Miss Smarty Pants? Whooo? You are, dat's whooo!*')

Although I didn't bring my sunglasses/baseball hat disguise with me, I don't think it'll be a problem because it's the middle of a workday. I doubt Abogado's even home. After locating the correct building, I peek inside at the opulent lobby and am impressed at what I see. The old red brick façade seems to be all that's left of the original building. Everything else is shiny and new. Marble floors run throughout, and a doorman stands behind a big mahogany desk – it's fancy-schmancy. Curious as to what the lofts look like, I ask the doorman if they have any to show and he tells me no. After poking around a bit longer, I realize there's not much else to see and leave.

As we walk across the street, Eva squats to go potty. I've learned that she can't go when people are looking – she gets stage fright – so I look away. While waiting for her to finish, I glance back at Abogado's building and realize that I can see into the apartments from where I'm standing. Remembering that I have my binoculars in my purse, I pull them out to take a look, even though I know I shouldn't.

For the middle of a workday, there seems to be a lot of people out and about. Since I don't want any of them to think I'm a perv, I first pretend to look at the birds perched on top of Abogado's building and then shift my gaze down to the windows once I'm sure the coast is clear. I pan across the building. Hmm . . . ceiling, ceiling, wall, chandelier, and . . . that's it. How boring.

I put my binoculars down and let them hang around my neck just as Eva kicks her legs back like a bull, signaling she's done. After praising her for being such a good '*pooopy pooopy poo!*' I pull a tissue out of my purse for the clean-up. When I finish, I casually glance across the street to get one last look at Abogado's building and am horrified at what I see: Abogado himself is standing outside the front entrance, looking in my direction. My stomach drops as our eyes meet for a split second. Praying he doesn't recognize me, I quickly look away.

A few seconds later, I gather the courage to turn my head around, hoping that Abogado was looking at something just past me and has already gone on his way. As I slowly peer over my shoulder at his building, my stomach drops again when I see that he's not only still standing out front looking at me, he's now shaking his head in disgust as well.

Fuck.

I can't believe it – I've totally been busted.

I have to get out of here.

Turning around, I attempt to run down the street away from Abogado's building but am stopped short by Eva's leash. When I look down to see what the problem is, I find her sprawled out on the sidewalk, refusing to move. Of all the times! As I swoop down to pick her up, I see Abogado crossing the street, heading toward me.

Fuck. Fuck.

I can't believe this. I can't believe he's coming after me.

With Eva safely in my arms, I turn around once again and run as fast as I can down the sidewalk. I run and run and run, feeling like a criminal, like someone who just got caught shoplifting. I feel like Abogado is the fuzz, out to get me. The people I pass on the sidewalk stare at me, and I'm positive that, at any moment, someone is going to try and trip me so I don't get away. Hoping to prevent this from happening, I begin smiling at everyone I pass.

After running for what seems like one hundred blocks, I'm pretty sure I've lost Abogado and turn around. When I do, my heart begins beating faster. Not only is he still hot on my trail looking angrier than ever, but he's even closer to me than he was before.

Fuck. Fuck. Fuck.

I turn back around and pick up speed.

As Eva bounces up and down in my arms, small beads of sweat begin trickling down my forehead because not only is it warm outside, but I'm nervous and out of shape. Trying my hardest to lose Abogado, I quickly take a left down the first side street I see, then another quick right, and then another quick left. I have no idea where I am or where I'm going, but I don't care. I have to shake Abogado – I have to lose him! After one more block, I turn around again and—

Oh. My. God.

He's still there.

He's like the Terminator.

Fuck. Fuck. Fuck. Fuck.

Suddenly, I hear him call out to me: 'Delilah! Stop running!'

Fuck. Fuck. Fuck. Fuck. Fuck.

I don't know what to do! I don't know what to do! Do I stop? Do I pretend like this is all just a coincidence? Do I—

Suddenly a taxi drives by. *Yes!* After whistling the loudest whistle I've ever whistled, it stops. I'm in the backseat within seconds.

'The French Quarter please!' I yell up to the driver, as I crouch down on the floor. As the cab moves forward, a small sense of relief comes over me. I can't believe this. I can't believe I got caught. Of all the guys to catch me, why did it have to be Abogado? Why couldn't it have been someone like Wade? I know this is all my fault for not wearing my disguise, but—

Suddenly, the cab comes to a stop.

'What's going on?' I ask nervously. 'Why are you stopping?'

'Traffic.'

'Traffic? What do you mean traffic?'

'Traffic only means one thing.'

Lifting my head, I look out the front window and see dozens of cars stopped in front of us. Turning around, I look out the back window and see Abogado approaching the car.

Fuck. Fuck. Fuck. Fuck. Fuck. Fuck.

I hit the floor again.

I can't believe this is happening. He's going to call the police on me. I'm going to go to jail for stalking. Suddenly I hear knocking on the window.

Knock, knock, knock!

Eva begins to bark.

Ruff, ruff, ruff!

Abogado begins to yell.

'Delilah, I know you in there!'

Knock, knock, knock!

Ruff, ruff, ruff!

'Delilah! I see you! Open the door!'

Fuck ^{to the millionth degree}.

'Hey, lady – what's going on here?' the cab driver asks.

'Um . . . nothing, sir,' I say from the floor. 'How's that traffic looking?'

Before the cab driver has a chance to answer, I hear a *click* and feel a breeze. The back door next to me has just opened. I must have forgotten to lock it. Oops.

'Delilah, why are you following me?' Abogado asks.

Unsure of what to do or say, I pick up a crumpled piece of paper from the floor and hold it up. 'Here it is!' I exclaim, pretending I've been looking for whatever it is. I uncrumple it and read. 'It's my receipt from . . . Buddy's Bait Shop . . . for . . . five hundred night crawlers and an insulated worm container!'

Oh Jesus.

'Delilah, stop pretending you don't see me,' Abogado says. Looking up, I pretend to be shocked when I see him.

'Aboga – I mean Diego . . . is that you?'

'Yes, it is me, and you know it is me. Why is you run from mc?'

184

'Run from you? I wasn't running from you. I was running to catch up with this taxi. I left this very important receipt in the backseat.' I hold it up as evidence.

'Please, do not be lying,' Abogado says in a serious tone. 'You spy on me, I catch you, and now you run.'

'Spy on you?' I ask, my mouth dropping open. I pretend to be insulted. 'I would never do such a thing!'

Abogado shakes his head in disbelief. 'You know, I think it be coincidental when I see your name on the list for the baking class I teach tonight, but now I see it is not.'

The cab driver clears his throat. 'Hey, buddy,' he says to Abogado, 'you gonna get in or what?' Looking forward, I see that the traffic has started to move.

'Delilah, I insist you talk to me,' Abogado says, reaching in his pocket. Pulling out a five-dollar bill, he gives it to the cab driver. 'Please come out of the taxi.'

'I can't,' I say, shaking my head. 'I really can't. I'm late for a . . . *fishing* thing.'

Abogado gives me a look, a serious look, an intense look, a look that's just plain . . . well, *sexy*. His brow is furrowed and he's got a little wrinkle in the middle of his forehead. He's so cute. God, why did this have to happen? Looking away from him for a moment, I weigh my options. If I stay in this cab and leave, I will have blown any chance I might have with him. However, if I get out and talk to him, I might be able to save this situation. I turn back to him.

'I guess I have a few minutes to talk.'

After grabbing Eva and getting out of the taxi, I tell Abogado that I did sign up to take a baking class but didn't know that he was the teacher.

185

'So you aren't following me?' he asks.

'No, I swear.'

He gestures to my chest. 'Then why do you wear binoculars?' Looking down, I see them hanging from my neck. Oops. I forgot to put them away. 'And why do I see you look into the windows of my building?' Oops again. I was unaware that he actually saw me do this.

'Well,' I say, trying to think of an excuse, 'I'm scouting locations for a new Elisabeth Sterling Design store and think the Warehouse District is perfect and—'

'Michelle tells my friend you both lose your job.'

She did? *Damn her!* I try again.

'Well, there were some beautiful iridescent birds perched on the roof of your building and—'

'Those were pigeons.'

They were? *Damn them!* I rack my brain for another excuse.

'Delilah, stop lying,' Abogado says as he puts his hand on my shoulder. 'You only make this worse.' When I look up into his eyes, his sexy eyes that are still half-hidden behind a pair of Clark Kent glasses, my shoulders sink. Why am I even trying to lie my way out of this? I was caught in the act. Walking over to a nearby stoop, I plop down and hold my head in my hands.

'You're right,' I confess. 'I did stop by your place today to see where you lived, and I did sign up for the baking class knowing you were the teacher. I'm sorry but I just wanted to see you again and wasn't sure if you wanted to see me.'

Abogado clears his throat. 'Delilah, I am flattered you go to such great lengths to connect with me, but you are right. I do not want to see you and I do not want you to take my class tonight.' A pang of sadness shoots through my heart. I look up.

'But it all happened so long ago, why can't you just let it go? Why can't we pretend like we just met?'

'Because we did not just meet and I cannot let it go. Delilah, you laugh at me. Do you not understand? You knew that I was embarrassed about what happen that night and you laugh at me anyway.'

'No, you're wrong. I didn't laugh at you; I laughed at what happened. It might've been embarrassing, but it was still funny. You have to admit that.' Abogado doesn't respond. 'Look at it this way,' I continue, 'if *you're* embarrassed, imagine how *I* feel right now. You caught me spying on you. At least what you did – the choking – was an accident. What I just did was planned.' I hold my right hand up to my forehead and make the *L* sign. 'I'm a loser.'

After half-smiling for half a second, Abogado shakes his head. 'I'm sorry, Delilah,' he says. 'I appreciate you coming here, but I cannot stop thinking about what you do. I'd appreciate if you go home.'

'I understand,' I say quietly, accepting defeat.

After saying goodbye, Abogado walks away. When he disappears around the corner, I curse myself. I don't always think about the things I say and do, especially when I'm joking. I don't often think beyond the moment about how my words and actions affect people. I can't believe what happened has stuck with him for two years. Michelle was right.

After slowly standing up, I walk Eva back to the French

Quarter, back to the hotel. As we walk past a Red Cross donation box in the window of a store, I stop and put the same amount of money I was going to spend on the baking class inside. My relationship with Abogado might not be able to be revived, but I hope the great energy that once pumped through this city will be.

$2,284, 28 days, 6 guys left.

Chapter Eight

> ***Beep***
>
> **Del — it's Michelle. Why haven't you returned my phone calls? Also, your mom . . . she needs to be stopped. Will you call her back please? She somehow got into the building this morning and knocked on my door looking for you. I pretended not to be home. Call me. Bye.**

> ***Beep***
>
> **It's Daisy. I *really* need to talk to you. Call me.**

TO: Delilah Darling
FR: Colin Brody
RE: Nate Syracuse

Nate Syracuse is single and living in Colorado. In the attachment you'll find a number of addresses for him, including the most recent one in Boulder. If for some reason it doesn't open, you can get it off the internet... all you have to do is type 'Boulder County Jail' in the Google search bar, and it should pop right up. Hmmm... Jailbirds? I never would've guessed you liked criminals. You seem so innocent.

Seriously, he should be out in 30 days. If you want the address of where he'll be then, I can have one of the Jimmys call his parole officer and get it for you. Let me know.

CB

#1 Nate Syracuse
High school boyfriend.

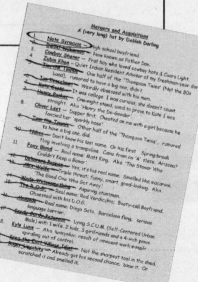

Mergers and Acquisitions
A (very long) list by Delilah Darling

1. Nate Syracuse — High school boyfriend.
2. Daniel Walker Jr. — now known as Father Dan.
3. Cowboy Shaner — First boy who loved cowboy hats & Coors Light.
4. Zubin Khan — Quiet Indian Resident Advisor of my freshman-year dorm.
5. Timmie Lawlor — One half of the 'Thompson Twins' (Not the 80s band). rumored to have a big one, didn't.
6. Tom Speakman — Weirdly obsessed with his mom.
7. Nate Syracuse — It was college. I was curious, she doesn't count straight. Aka 'Harry the Do-Gooder'.
8. Henry Porter — One-night stand, used to prove to Kate I was
   Oliver Lest — Dapper Brit. Cheated on me with a girl because he fancied her 'sparkly hose'.
9. Tom the Townie — Other half of the 'Thompson Twins', rumored to have a big one, did.
10. Nihhee — Don't know his last name. Or his first. Spring-break fling involving a trampoline. Came from an 'A' state. Arizona?
11. Foxy Blond — Real name: Matt King. Aka 'The Stoner Who Couldn't Keep a Bone'.
12. Delmonte Reposa — Yes, it's his real name. Smelled like macaroni.
    The Good One Who Got Away!
13. Alex Wolfe — Triple threat: funny, smart, good-looking. Aka
14. Wade Whitewater-thing — Aspiring stuntman.
15. The B.C.B. — Real name: Rod Verdicchio; Booty-call Boyfriend. Obsessed with his D.O.G.
16. Magico — Real name: Diego Soto. Barcelona fling. serious language barrier.
17. Cordy Barley Bezzington — Lying S.C.U.M. (Self-Centered Urban Male) with 1 wife, 2 kids, 3 girlfriends and a 4-inch penis.
18. Kyle Luxe — Aka 'luxeyhluv'. result of innocent work e-mails spinning out of control.
19. Greg the Cam Village 'Idiot' — Not the sharpest tool in the shed.
20. Roger Macchiato — Already got his second chance. blew it. Or scratched it and smelled it.

When Kitty Comes a Knockin'   Wednesday, 20 April

The next morning, as I wait in line to pay for gas while still in New Orleans, I feel sick to my stomach for a couple of reasons. For one, I'm not too eager to hit the road again because I hate, hate, hate my car. It blows. Literally. All over the road. It's a cheap little piece of shit that feels like it's made from an egg carton. And two, I can't believe the guy I shared my first time with is actually *doing time*. This is horrible – he was the first love of my life. He's where this all started. It's like a sign from God, saying, 'You've been doomed from the get-go. I don't even know why you're trying.'

Nate wasn't *the* love of my life, but he was my *first* love, and because of that, I've always held a special place for him in my heart. We went to high school together and dated on and off during our junior and senior years. I was crazy about him.

Nate had a private schoolboy look to him, very *Dead Poets Society*. He was a little bit of a hippy but in a privileged Connecticut sort of way. Like his sweaters might've had holes near the elbows, but they were made of cashmere. And he might've followed Phish around for a month, but he did so while driving a BMW. Nate was a spoiled rich kid all right, but he didn't act like one. He was quiet, kind and not at all arrogant.

On a beautiful spring day a couple weeks before we graduated, Nate came over after school. Since my mom and Victor were out of town, I offered him a beer and took one for myself. The two of us sat outside on the back deck and drank them. I'll never forget the way I felt that day. It was spring, so it felt alive outside, and I was getting ready to graduate and go out into the world, so I felt alive inside.

Nate and I looked at each other without saying much that day. I think the fact that we were going to different schools was sinking in and neither of us knew what to say. I can still see him sitting there, looking slightly disheveled in his navy blue school uniform. He was so cute – a loosened red tie hung around his neck and the top few buttons of his Oxford shirt were undone. A big mess of wavy brown hair sat on top of his head and his cheeks were slightly flushed.

After a while we both smiled at each other. I'm not sure what Nate was thinking when he did, but I knew that even if we lost touch, I'd always carry a part of him with me. Although I was so naïve, I was aware enough to know just how young and impressionable I was, aware enough to understand the influence Nate had on who I was and who I'd become. He instilled a free-spirited attitude in me, taught me to live life to the fullest, live life in the moment. And I've done that. Maybe a little too much in some respects, but still.

Later that afternoon a couple more friends came over. By that evening we were all buzzed, feeling melancholy and dancing to Cat Stevens. When the song 'Wild World' came on, Nate wrapped his arms around me and sang in my ear. He started kissing my shoulders, my neck, and then my lips.

The alcohol made the sex easier. It still hurt, but I was more relaxed, that's for sure. I remember it being awkward. I remember thinking Nate's penis was too big, that it wasn't going to work. But after trying for a while I was surprised when it did. Even though the sex didn't feel that good I still liked it. Despite the discomfort, I loved the closeness of it. I loved feeling all of Nate's weight on top of me. It was all so strange and new, and he looked into my eyes the entire time, telling me it would be okay. I loved that.

We spent every day together that summer. When we left for college, we decided not to break up but to take things as they came, to just see what would happen. We talked a few times the first week we got there but then not so much. A couple of months later I knew Nate had plans to come home for the weekend to go to a Santana concert, so I grabbed two friends, hopped on a train, and went as well. I wanted to surprise him, and well . . . I did. When I found him and some of our other high school friends, I saw him standing with a girl. I didn't know who she was. All I knew was that she was hanging all over him and he wasn't pushing her away. When I said hello to everyone, Nate nodded and then ignored me. At the time I felt like I didn't have a right to be angry because we said we'd take things as they came, but thinking back now, I had every right – I mean, we never officially broke up.

Daniel the priest was Nate's best friend back then and was at the concert that evening. Seeing that I was upset, he asked if I wanted to talk and I said yes. I remember thinking – hoping – that Nate would see me leave with Daniel, get jealous, realize he loved me, and come after me. He didn't.

Daniel and I started kissing in the parking lot, and the

next thing you know, were in the back of his mom's wood-paneled Wagoneer having sex. At the time I remember thinking Daniel's eyes were closed because he was thinking about Nate, feeling bad that he was having sex with his best friend's former girlfriend. Having learned how he ended up, however, I now know that wasn't the case; I now know that he was thinking about Jesus.

Nate found out about Daniel and called me a couple of times the following month to yell at me for it, which in a way made me happy – happy because he cared. (It's kind of screwed up to feel that way; but at the same time, it's kind of normal.) That winter, Nate's parents moved from Connecticut to Colorado so he stopped coming home for holiday breaks. I never saw him or talked to him again.

After paying for gas, string-cheese for Eva (she goes bananas for it), and a set of cab-driver beads for my back, I get back in my car and reread the attachment in Colin's e-mail with the details of what happened to Nate. Apparently he was arrested during some sort of environmental sit-in, along with a bunch of other people. Studying his file, I notice that there are two addresses listed for him. One is in Telluride and the other, oddly enough, is on Franklin Street in Manhattan. I think I would've heard if he moved back to the East Coast, especially New York, but maybe not – I don't talk to that many people from high school any more. Feeling bad about the way things ended with Abogado in New Orleans, feeling *desperate*, I pick up my cell phone and call the only phone number listed, which is in Colorado. Not

194

surprisingly, it goes right to voicemail. I decide to leave a message.

'Hey, Nate,' I say quietly. 'I'm sure this is kind of a weird phone call to get, but it's Delilah Darling. We haven't talked in ages and I was just thinking about you. I ran into Daniel not too long ago—'

Shit! Why did I mention Daniel? Way to bring up bad memories.

'Um . . . anyway,' I continue, 'I was just remembering how much fun we had back in the day and . . . I don't know . . . I kind of miss you sometimes.'

Okay, that was even more stupid – it's been eleven years!

'I mean I *think* of you sometimes,' I say, trying to cover. 'Anyway, give me a call.' After leaving my cell and home phone numbers, I hang up and hold my head in my hands.

Shit.

I should've rehearsed that.

Suddenly my cell phone rings, startling me. Knowing Nate wouldn't be calling me back this quickly (he's still locked up), I look at the caller ID. It's Colin.

'So how are things going with the chef?' he asks when I answer.

Going? I laugh at the thought – they *went*.

'None of your business,' I say. I'm still angry at him for tricking me yesterday.

'Fine, fine,' Colin says, sighing loudly. 'I don't know why you're so secretive. I mean, Kitty's so open.'

'You mean Kitty, like my mom?' I ask nervously. Please God, no.

'Yes, Kitty like your mom indeed.'

195

Oh no. A pit forms in my stomach.

'Uh . . . how do you know my mom's name?'

'Well, she introduced herself to me this morning after she woke me up, knocking on my door at eight o'clock.'

Michelle's message from this morning suddenly pops in my head. *Shit!* I should've done what she said; I should've called my mom.

'Why was my mom knocking on your door?' I ask, even though I really don't want to know.

'She knocked on everyone's door in the building. I was just the lucky one who answered. She was looking for you. She's worried. She said she left numerous messages for you at home but you didn't call her back so she tried you at work and heard that you got sacked. When I asked if she tried calling your mobile, she told me you didn't have one. Delilah . . . how could you not give your mother your mobile number?'

'You met her,' I say defensively. 'Would you, if you were me?'

'As a matter of fact, I did give her mine, after we finished our tea.'

'Oh, you'll regret it, mark my – wait – you had tea with my mother?'

'Yes, I did. She's got her knickers all up in a twist and needed someone to talk to.'

'Her knickers all up in a twist?' What in the hell? 'About what?'

'Well, Daisy's moved up her wedding.' Colin says this like he knows her. 'Instead of it happening in two years, it's gonna happen in two months, in the middle of June at the Waldorf-Astoria. They had a cancellation, and Edward, with all the connections he has being a big Wall Streeter and all, was able to snag the date.' He says this like he knows him, too. 'So anyway, Kitty was fine with everything until—' Colin stops talking.

'Until?' I push.

'Until she found out that Edward's Jewish.'

'Edward's Jewish?'

'Yep.'

Jewish? How could I not have known this? How could Daisy not have mentioned it to me? To anyone? 'Wait – he's black *and* Jewish?'

'It's been known to happen. You ever hear of Lenny Kravitz?'

'Yes, I know, it's just not very common.'

'Yes, I s'pose you're right.'

Wow, Edward's Jewish. Okay, I've processed it.

'I can understand my mom being caught off guard,' I tell Colin, 'but why is she upset?' She may be slightly crazy, but she's hardly anti-Semitic.

'Well, because Daisy and Edward aren't having the ceremony in a Catholic church, and she's heartbroken about it.'

'She's heartbroken about it? Oh please!' My mother is *so* dramatic. 'Colin, don't let my mom fool you into thinking she's a devout Catholic. When I was younger, she used to take Daisy and me to mass at the local hospital because the service in the chapel there was only twenty minutes long.' She did, I swear.

'I'm sure she had her reasons,' Colin says, defending her. 'She's a busy woman.'

'Yeah, yeah, whatever. So is she okay now?'

'Yeah, I think so. She seemed to calm down once the whiskey started working.'

'Whiskey? Colin! You gave my mom whiskey at eight o'clock in the morning?'

'Hey, don't jump down my throat! I didn't give it to her. She pulled a flask out of her purse and poured it in her tea herself.'

'No way,' I say incredulously.

'Seriously, she did. It was a small silver monogrammed flask.'

'Monogrammed?'

'Yep.'

'Oh my . . .' I can't believe my mother carries around a monogrammed flask. Oddly, I find myself having a little more respect for her knowing this.

'You should call her,' Colin says. 'But give her until at least three. She's got yoga today.'

'Yoga . . . right . . .'

After a long pause, Colin speaks somewhat reluctantly. 'You know, Delilah, I wasn't gonna say anything, but your mom asked me when the last time I saw you was because she was concerned. I told her it was last night because I didn't want her to worry. When I said that, her eyes lit up like a Christmas tree and she threw her arms around my neck and hugged the living daylights out of me. I think she thought I meant that we spent the night together.'

'You're joking . . . right?'

''Fraid not.'

Oh God, I'm so embarrassed.

'After that,' Colin continues, 'she started going on and

on about how worried she's been about you, with Daisy getting married first and all.'

Okay, I'm now more embarrassed. What was my mom thinking? To talk about me with her friends is one thing. To do it with some guy she thinks I'm dating is another.

'Colin, my mom can act kind of crazy sometimes,' I say, trying to explain, 'and I'm sorry you had to be on the receiving end of it.'

'Ah, don't worry,' he says quietly. 'Delilah, I know it's none of my business, but you're not tracking down old boyfriends because your sister's getting married, are you?'

I roll my eyes. I hate this – I hate having to defend myself.

'No, I'm sure it looks that way, but it's not.'

'Then I don't understand why you're doing what you're doing. I mean, are you trying to get back together with these guys you're having me find? Is that it?'

I hate this. I hate this, I hate this, I hate this.

'Colin, it's complicated and I don't feel like explaining. Please don't listen to my mom though. If any part of my life contradicts what she considers to be normal then she assumes I'm unhappy. It's like she's disappointed in me for not following the masses, for not following the same traditional path that her friends' daughters have followed. Do you understand?'

'Actually, I do. My father's pretty similar. Or he used to be, anyway.'

'In what way?'

'He's always thought I should pursue a more stable career. He'd do anything to get me interested in his business so that I can take it over one day and have what he calls a "normal life". While I don't mind helping him out here and there to pick up extra cash and what not, I've made it very clear that it's not what I want to do. Even if I spend the rest of my life struggling, getting bit parts here and there, I will never want what he has. This was hard for him to accept at first, but I'm my own person and he knows that.'

'I am too, but for some reason my mother doesn't see that.'

'Well, you need to tell her then, like I told my father. You don't have to be rude about it, but you gotta set her straight – otherwise, she'll never stop being disappointed. When you finally do meet someone and decide to get married, she'll find something wrong with the way you're planning your wedding – I mean, look at Daisy. After that she'll start in on your marriage, and after that she'll find something wrong with the way you're raising your kids. You gotta nip this thing in the bud or it'll never stop.'

I think about what Colin's saying; he's totally right. For as far back as I can remember, my mom's always been this way – from high school, to college, to getting my first job – and I've never dealt with it. I bitch and bitch and bitch about my mother, but I never tell her how I feel.

'Listen, if you're not ready to stand up for yourself yet, then at least throw your mom a bone for the moment, to keep your sanity.'

'Throw her a bone?' I'm confused.

'Yeah, tell her you're dating someone or something so she'll leave you alone.'

Although I laugh at Colin's suggestion, it isn't such a bad idea. My friend Julie has a pretend boyfriend named

Gary, and her mother – 'Smother' – thinks they've been dating for years. Every time she's supposed to meet him, Julie tells her that something's come up with Gary and he can't make it.*

'I guess you're right,' I tell Colin.

'Damn right I'm right. Now tell your mother how you feel or throw her a feckin' bone already so she'll leave you alone!'

'Okay, okay,' I say, laughing. 'I will.' I like Colin; he's funny.

'Excellent,' he exclaims. He then turns on the charm again. 'Now c'mon, tell me . . . how's it going with the chef?'

'You're very persistent, you know that?'

'I have to be. I'm an actor. Now fess up. I already know he's an old boyfriend; you might as well tell me how it went.'

'Okay fine,' I say, exhaling loudly. 'If you wanna know the truth, he caught me spying on him and thinks I'm a total loser.' I hear Colin stifle a laugh. 'It's not funny!'

'Oh, c'mon . . . yes, it is. A little bit, at least.'

'You weren't there.'

'No, I wasn't. Which sucks, to be honest, because I would've paid to see it.'

'Yeah, yeah – whatever.'

'So . . . how about the jailbird?' Colin asks. 'Who's he?'

'That's enough sharing for today,' I say quickly. Honestly, it's too painful to think about poor Nate behind bars.

---

* For example, the last time Smother was supposed to meet Gary, his private plane had mechanical problems and he got stuck in Miami. The time before that he was invited to attend J. Lo and Marc's impromptu wedding and had to fly to LA for the weekend.

'A story for another time, I s'pose. Until then, be careful out there, will ya?'

'I will. And thanks for everything – you know, with my mom.'

'Ah . . . 'twas nothin',' Colin says softly and sweetly.

After hanging up, once I'm safely on the highway, I call Daisy and find out that everything Colin said was true. She and Edward are indeed moving their wedding up. The only reason they were waiting two years in the first place was because they wanted to have it at the Starlight Roof, a legendary art deco nightclub in the Waldorf that was all the rage in the thirties and that's how long the wait was – two years. Despite the short notice, my mom was fine with the date change and didn't freak out until she found out Edward was Jewish.

'Mom, don't worry,' Daisy said, trying to calm her down. 'It's not like I'm converting or anything.'

'What about your kids?' she asked. 'How are you going to raise them?'

'They'll be aware of both religions,' Daisy explained. 'They'll have a Christmas tree and a menorah. They'll get the best of both worlds; it'll be great.'

'It won't be great, it'll be confusing,' my mom argued. She then sarcastically suggested to Daisy that she throw a Kwanzaa bush into the mix to really fuck them up.

'Every time I call her now she won't stop crying,' Daisy explains to me. 'Can you please call her and help smooth things over?'

'Absolutely,' I say.

After filling me in on the rush wedding plans, Daisy tells me that she and Edward have decided not to have a bridal party except for a maid of honor and a best man. After asking me to stand up for her (I of course say yes) Daisy tells me that she's already ordered not only *her* dress, but my dress, too. I'm horrified.

'Wait, what? You ordered my dress? Why? I mean, I didn't even try it on!'

'Oh, relax. It's a floor-length satin strapless gown and you'll look gorgeous in it.'

'What color is it?'

'Scarlet.'

'Scarlet? You mean like *red*?'

'Yep.'

Oh, great. This is perfect, just perfect. While Daisy will be a vision of white virginal beauty on her wedding day, I'll be the tramp in the red dress.

'Trust me, Del,' Daisy says, sensing my worry. 'I work in retail. I know what I'm doing.'

'You sell wallets, not dresses,' I point out.

'Not yet I don't,' she explains, 'but I'm working my way up the Saks ladder and will soon. By the way, this is ultimately your own fault. I thought you were on a business trip and didn't want the fact that I moved my wedding up to stress you out. Speaking of which, why did you lie about losing your job?'

'You saw how happy Mom was when I told her I didn't.'

'Yeah, I did, but I'm not Mom. You could've at least told me.'

'Yes, you're right, but it's a two-way street. You could've told me about Edward, too. Wait – why didn't you tell me about Edward?'

'I don't know,' Daisy says, sighing. 'I guess I didn't want Mom finding out about it from anyone other than me. You know how she is. When things turn out differently than how she expects, she doesn't exactly take it well.'

I laugh. 'You don't say?'

'But you know,' Daisy continues, 'call me crazy, but I think she's getting better, which is why her being upset over this religion thing surprised me.'

'Better?' I don't believe it. 'How so?'

'Well, since the engagement party, for example, she keeps telling me that she can't wait until February, black history month, because she went out and bought a book on Rosa Parks and is looking forward to wowing people with her knowledge.'

'She did?' I'm impressed.

'Yep. I think that once she gets over the initial shock of whatever it is that's different – she's gung-ho about it.'

Hmm. Good to know.

Before hanging up, Daisy tells me that the tasting at the Waldorf is set to take place in three weeks. She expects me to be there; I write down the date.

Later that afternoon when I'm sure my mom is home from yoga, I give her a call like Daisy asked to help smooth things over. (I make sure to hit *67 to block my cell phone number before I do. I don't care what Colin says; she does not need to know I have a cell phone.) After a twenty-minute conversation I'm able to convince her that it's not that big a deal that Edward's Jewish.

'Things could be much worse,' I tell her. 'He could be a member of one of those freaky religions out in Utah that condone polygamy. I saw a special on TV about it once, and the men believe they have to have three wives in order to get into heaven.'

'Maybe you're right,' she says with a sigh, still sounding somewhat disappointed. 'I was just really looking forward to hearing someone sing "Ave Maria".'

'Maybe someone still can,' I suggest.

My mom perks up. 'Do you think?'

'Yeah, ask Daisy. A little "Ave Maria" never hurt anyone.'

'You know, you're absolutely right! A little "Ave Maria" never did hurt anyone!'

'Great!' I exclaim proudly. I'm so happy to have helped! 'Now go call Daisy!'

'I will, but before I go' – the tone of my mom's voice changes – 'why didn't you tell me that you lost your job?'

Damn! I was hoping to hang up before she remembered to ask. 'Well, I was going to,' I say slowly, 'but I've been so busy lately and—'

'I've heard!' she screeches. The tone of her voice changes yet again. 'And he's so cute!'

For the next few minutes I listen to my mom gush about Colin, except she calls him *Cohlin*, like Colin Powell. When she finally stops talking to take a breath, I break it to her that we're not a couple. Although she sounds crushed at first, she tells me that she's going to remain optimistic because . . .

'Not only is he single, charming and sexy, but he lives right across the hall from you. It's so perfect! I was just reading an article about how men and women in Manhattan tend to date people who live in a location that's geographically desirable to them. For instance, if they live on the same subway line, then that's good. They

205

called it having a locationship instead of a relationship. Maybe you and *Cohlin* can have that.'

'*Cahlin*, Mom.'

'Oh right, sorry. Maybe you and *Cahlin* can have that.'

'Mom, I already told you – we're just friends. Actually, we're not even that – we're acquaintances. We're neighbors. We've met only twice. I barely know him.'

'Well, now's the perfect time to change that, seeing as though you don't have a job to get in the way, right?'

Before answering, I weigh my options.

If I tell my mom she's right, then she'll never leave me alone and she'll drive me crazy calling for updates. However, if I tell her that I'm not interested in getting to know Colin better, then she'll assume I'm a lesbian because how could any single woman not find him attractive – he's perfect. I suddenly remember his advice: throw her a bone.

'Actually, Mom, now's not the time because . . . because . . . because I've been dating someone else.'

'Dating someone?' My mother gasps with excitement. 'You have?'

'Yes, and I don't want to jinx it so I'd rather not talk about it.'

'Oh, I completely understand! But can you at least tell me his name? I'm just so excited!'

His name? Hmm. Oh heck, if Daisy can get a black Jewish guy . . .

'His name is Yoshi and he's a Japanese Buddhist,' I proudly exclaim.

'Yoshi?' my mom booms. 'A Buddhist? How exciting!'

'Yes, Mom. How exciting. Now no more questions.'

'I promise! Oh, wait – can I tell the ladies in my yoga class though? They'll be so impressed!'

'Sure, whatever.'

'Great! Oh dear, look at the time. I've gotta run. I'm meeting Sally Epstein out for an afternoon coffee. She's gonna teach me some hebonics.'

'Hebonics?'

'Yes, I'm gonna learn a little Hebrew so I don't embarrass myself when I meet Edward's parents.'

'Hebrew? Wow. Well, good luck.'

After hanging up, I giggle to myself and Eva. Yoshi, a Japanese Buddhist? Where the heck did that come from?

Chapter Nine

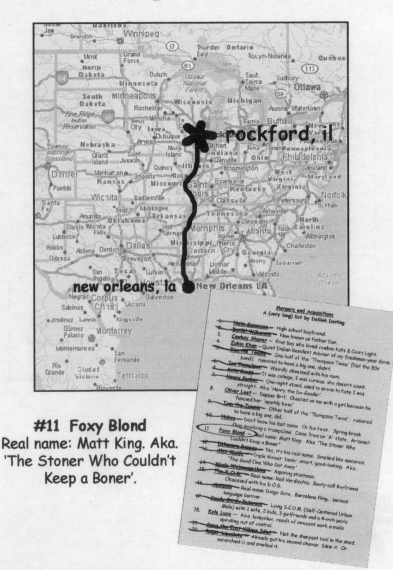

#11 Foxy Blond
Real name: Matt King. Aka.
'The Stoner Who Couldn't
Keep a Boner'.

> *Beep*
>
> It's Daisy. Thanks for telling Mom someone can sing 'Ave Maria' at the wedding, now Edward's mom is insisting we do that whole Jewish breaking of the glass thing – whatever it's called.
> *Heavy Sigh*
> I'm sorry, I'm not mad at you, it's just that everyone's just driving me crazy. You have no idea how lucky you are to be single!

> *Beep*
>
> Del – it's Michelle. I just got off the phone with Dustin Hoffman. You're such an idiot! I told you not to go! Call me. Bye.

Foxy Blond

I met #11 on my list, Matt King, also known as Foxy Blond, the summer after I graduated from college, when I was living in Chicago. After two years of majoring in Liberal Arts (the 'I have no idea what I want to do with my life' major) at Miami University, I realized I wanted to work in the design field. Even though it would have made more sense for me to attend a design school in New York, I transferred to the School of the Art Institute of Chicago. Two years after doing so, I ended up graduating with a bachelor's degree in Fiber and Material Studies. It might sound like a funny major, but knowing all about fibers and fabrics was extremely beneficial to my job at ESD.

The summer after I graduated, I worked as an intern in the marketing department of the Merchandise Mart, an enormous building that houses furniture showrooms for design professionals. Although I didn't get any hands-on design experience there, I was able to see how the industry worked, as well as network at design events they held that professionals from all over the world came to attend. In fact, I met the woman who later helped me get my job at Elisabeth Sterling Design at one of these events.

Although I met Matt while working at the Mart, he didn't exactly work in the building – he worked on the street in front of one of the entrances. He was a twenty-one-year-old construction worker. His dad made him get the job since he decided not to go to college. In the looks department, Matt was tall and lean with a surfer-boy look. Working all day in the sun dropped beautiful honey highlights in his dirty-blond hair and gave his skin a delicious golden glow. Oh, and his smile . . . Matt had a gorgeous smile that put Matthew McConaughey's to shame.

I noticed Matt's good looks right away, as did many of my female (and some male) co-workers. Since none of us knew his name, we referred to him as Foxy Blond. Everyone was gaga over him; he was the talk of the office.

After admiring Foxy from afar for a couple of weeks, I decided to take action one hot summer day when I was feeling sexy. Not only was I dressed sparingly in a tight black tank top, an even tighter black miniskirt, and huge black platform sandals, I was also covered in glitter.* (It was the summer of the Spice Girls and I had christened myself Glitter Spice.)† There was no way he could deny me.

During an iced-coffee run to a White Hen Pantry across the street, I decided to get Foxy a bottle of water and some ice. After all, he was working hard to make the street in front of my workplace a more enjoyable throughway, it was the least I could do. After paying, I embraced my inner Spice Girl and approached him.

'Hi,' I said, nervously. Foxy stopped digging and looked up. A blue bandanna was tied around his head – I assume to keep the sweat out of his eyes, which were a beautiful icy blue. I had never been this close to him before and never realized how gorgeous he really was. 'You look *hot*, you know, with the *heat* and all.' Unsure of what else I should say, I stopped talking.

---

* This was long before Carrie Bradshaw made the stiletto so popular; clunky shoes were in style, I swear.
† Nowadays, I'd be Tarragon Spice. Tarragon, what I like to refer to as the Forgotten Spice, is wonderfully delicious and terribly overlooked. I highly suggest that everyone start using more of it.

'And?' Foxy asked, after a bit.

'And well,' I continued, 'I thought you might need to cool down, so I bought these for you.' I held out the water and ice.

'For me?' Foxy asked, smiling. He took them from me. 'Wow, thank you.'

'You're welcome.'

After taking a swig of the water, Foxy took a piece of ice from the cup and ran it across his brow. As he did, it melted, sending little water droplets through the stubble on his face. Gosh, he was sexy! 'I'm Matt King,' he said. 'I'd shake your hand, but mine's dirty and now wet, too.'

Dirty and wet. How exciting!

'I'm Delilah Darling,' I said, extending my hand anyway. 'And I don't mind dirty and wet.'

Bad, Delilah! Bad, bad!

Smirking, Foxy took my hand and lightly shook it until I pulled it away.* 'I have to get going,' I said. 'But I'll see ya around.'

'I'm sure you will, Delilah Darling,' Foxy said, smiling. 'The girl who doesn't mind dirty and wet.' Laughing, I turned and walked away.

As I headed toward the entrance of the building, I could feel Foxy's eyes on me so I swung my hips something fierce. 'Foxy's gonna be my luvah!' I sang out to the tune of the Spice Girls' 'If you wanna be my lover!' as I walked through the front door. Glitter Spice had arrived.

The very next day Foxy asked me out, and within a week, we were in the throes of a full-blown love affair. I

---

* *Cosmo* says it's always best to end the first conversation with a man yourself. You gotta leave them wanting more.

was in love – in love! Connecticut didn't breed guys like Foxy (at least New Canaan didn't), and I had never met anyone like him before. He was rough, rugged and cool. Everyone wanted to be his friend.

I think part of the reason I was so head over heels for Foxy had to do with my age. I was twenty-one years old and had just graduated from college when I met him – the world was at my fingertips. I was hungry for life, for experiences. An optimistic 'I can do anything' feeling was running through my mind and gave me confidence, a confidence that translated in the bedroom. Even though Foxy was #11 on my list, I felt like sex was new with him. For the first time I started taking ownership over it. I was a girl on the brink of womanhood. Sex with Foxy was playful and thrilling. Every night after having it, we'd wrap our arms and legs around each other, talk, laugh and eventually fall asleep. The next morning we'd wake up still intertwined.

Since my summer internship didn't pay, I took a job as a cocktail waitress on the weekends to pay my rent. In addition to his construction job, Foxy played drums in a band. Because of these two things, our weekend nights out didn't begin until two o'clock in the morning, when we were both done working, and didn't end until the sun came up. We lived a fun, fast lifestyle, Foxy and I. We were young and poor, as were all of our friends, with nothing more than the wad of cash in our pockets we'd made that night. Having nothing gave us freedom – we didn't have anything to lose. I loved that summer. I loved, loved, loved that summer.

Then came fall.

It's funny how quickly things can change. Feelings, no matter how intense they are, can be fleeting. With the snap of a finger, happiness can turn to sadness, hope can turn to despair, and one day your past can catch up with you and make you realize you need to hit the brakes.

The moment I knew things were going to change was when Foxy lost his job. It caused a domino effect. Not only did he lose his income, he lost his tan, he lost his six-pack – basically, he lost his *foxy*. In the blink of an eye, Foxy Blond turned into Matt King, my unemployed boyfriend with a beer gut.

This alone didn't bother me – I'm not that shallow. I can deal with someone losing a job and gaining weight. (I mean, hello?) What bothered me was that he lost his zest for life; he lost his free-spirited personality. Since he was unemployed, Matt's harmless weekend partying started to spiral out of control and turned into daily occurrences. He was always either drunk or high and would frequently start arguments with me over stupid stuff. Initially these arguments led to some good 'love at first fight' make-up sex, but eventually Matt's chronic pot smoking negatively affected that area of our relationship as well. Yes, leaves weren't the only things falling in Chicago that autumn.

Matt didn't just lose a little wind in his sail – the thing couldn't even fly at half-mast. He couldn't get it up ever. Initially when it started happening, he would ask me to turn on Guns N' Roses music – I swear – as if listening to Axl Rose was the cure-all for drug-induced impotence. I did it though, of course I did. I was willing to try anything. Before every attempt at sex, I'd jump out of bed naked to throw on the CD, then I'd jump back in, lay there and wait while 'Paradise City' blared through the speakers and my boyfriend tried to psych himself into getting it up. I wish I could say it worked, but the best it ever did was get Matt's penis to the point of resembling an *al dente* noodle – mostly soft with a hint of firmness.

Things only got worse. Because of his healthy party habits, Matt fell two months behind in paying his rent, so I lent him eight hundred dollars. Stupid, I know. In order to pay me back, he started selling pot. When I asked him to stop, he refused, saying he was doing it for me. What was I supposed to say to that? 'How romantic?' What kind of bad music video was I living in?

Any idiot would've broken up with Matt, however, I wasn't just any idiot – I was an optimistic idiot. I thought I could help him. But his behavior soon became erratic. He was up and down, happy and sad – he was manic. In a matter of a few weeks, a glassy haze slowly replaced the sparkle in those beautiful, icy-blue eyes. Likewise, dirt replaced the highlights in his dirty-blond hair. Matt's instability soon made me feel out of control as well and I realized that for my own sanity, I had to get out of there. The wild, carefree days of summer had finally caught up with me. The world was still out there and I was still hungry, so I decided to go back to the East Coast.

I didn't tell any of my friends that I was leaving, not even Matt. I just planned one last night out to say good-bye without really saying goodbye. The night we all went out, about halfway through the evening, I looked around the bar that we were at and didn't see Matt. He didn't say he was leaving or going home, so I called his cell phone to see where he was. After two rings, he picked up. 'I'll be right in,' he said shortly, then hung up.

Thinking it was rude that he ended the call so abruptly, I went outside where it was quieter to call him back. After dialing his number, I held my ringing cell phone to my ear and the strangest thing happened: I heard the ringing in stereo. I heard it through the phone in one ear and from across the street in the other. When I looked over to where the live ring was coming from, I saw Matt standing on the corner, kissing another girl. With their arms wrapped around each other, the two of them talked and laughed just like we had done so many nights in bed. Since I hadn't hung up my phone, Matt's was still ringing. I watched him answer. 'I said I'll be right in!'

'Don't bother,' I said aloud. When Matt looked up and saw me, the smile disappeared from his face. He didn't know what to say. What was there to say? He cheated on me while he was out with me. What kind of person does that?

Deciding to leave, I turned around and went back inside the bar. As I gathered my belongings, my friends sensed something was wrong, but before anyone had a chance to ask what it was, Matt walked inside. 'You're leaving?' he asked.

'Yes,' I huffed, frantically grabbing my things.

'Oh, come on,' he sighed. 'Don't be so crazy.'

Don't be so crazy? Hearing those words come from his mouth filled me with anger. I couldn't believe that he of all people had the nerve to call me crazy. Unable to control my feelings, I began yelling at Matt, telling him what a loser he was. The entire time I did so, he stood in silence, staring at me. When I was finished, when I didn't have anything left to say, I waited for a response, waited for a reply, waited for an apology, but I didn't get one. Instead of telling me that he was sorry, Matt simply looked at me . . . and laughed. He laughed the biggest, loudest laugh I'd ever heard in my life. He laughed and laughed and laughed. To have someone laugh at you when you're angry is infuriating. After telling Matt that I never wanted to see him again, I walked out the door.

Eventually I got over Matt, but I never got over being *angry* at Matt because I never got an apology. Through the years, I always thought that maybe one day my phone would ring, and it would be him calling to say he was sorry, but that didn't happen. To be honest, when I made my list, even writing his name made me so upset that I thought about taking him out of the running completely. However, remembering the bad times soon got me thinking about the good. I remembered the day I met him and the nights I loved him. The more I remembered Foxy Blond, the more I forgot Matt King and decided he was worth another shot.

MMMail!   Monday, 25 April

Despite the fact that I left New Orleans with a negative attitude, the drive to Illinois was rather enjoyable because, after I hung up from my mom, I called Colin back to tell him about Yoshi and the two of us laughed and laughed and ended up talking for an hour. You'll never believe it, but I think talking on the phone actually helps me drive better. I'm still overly cautious, but since I'm gabbing I don't obsess as much over the clicks, hums and rattles and therefore drive a little bit faster. Don't get too excited, I didn't quite break fifty miles per hour, but I got close. Yes, my cell phone is a rock star, if that's possible.

Although Foxy lived in Chicago when I met him, he now lives with his parents in Rockford, a city about ninety miles west of Chicago. Okay, fine – WITH HIS PARENTS – are you happy? Yes, I know this is a possible sign that he's a loser (he is almost thirty years old by now, after all), but I have to give him the benefit of the doubt.

Rockford is located in Winnebago County, a county people claim is named after the Winnebago Indian tribe. I say claim because since I've been here, I've counted twenty-two recreational vehicles and zero Indians. My hotel, the Clock Tower Resort, even has a special RV parking lot. I'm not calling anyone a liar, but I think the possibility of the county being named after the motor vehicle is worth looking into.

Don't let the name of my hotel fool you into think I splurged – the place is less a resort and more a theme park. It's actually a Best Western hotel located right off the expressway whose main selling point is an indoor family water playland, complete with a corkscrew slide. Yesterday, while walking through the lobby, Eva and I had a run-in with a twenty-one-foot floating snake. When Eva saw it, she snarled and tried to jump out of her bag and attack, much like she did with Wade's puppet – I mean *Muppet* – but I stopped her. I'm a little worried and have started to feel badly for raising her in a car. I feel like one of those women you see on Lifetime, Television for

Women, one of those women played by Swoosie Kurtz or Meredith Baxter Birney who raises her children on the street. I know Eva's just a dog, but she still needs stability in her life, especially after everything she's been through.

But back to the hotel.

It's not too expensive, only eighty dollars a night. However, when you multiply this by four nights, it can get a little pricey. I got in late Thursday night and have been sitting outside Foxy's parents' house ever since. It's Monday now and still no Foxy. The only life inside are his mom and dad, or two old people who look an awful lot like him. I'm beginning to go stir-crazy and don't know what to do with myself. I've listened to my 1997 playlist – songs that remind me of Foxy – more times than I can count. Believe me, despite how much I used to love them, one can take only so much Spice Girls. They keep asking me what I want, what I really, really want. I don't ever want them to get back together, that's what I want. And then I want someone to tell me what happened to Chumbawamba.

After waiting a bit longer, I decide to call Colin to make sure he gave me the right address. When he answers, I greet him with song.

'MMMBop! Bop, bop, MMMBop! Yada ya-daaa! Bomb pops! Rock, rock, yeah-eah . . .' I don't really know the words.

'You really should stick with Lionel Richie,' he says. I laugh.

'Yes, maybe so. Hey, I have a question. The address you gave me for Matt King – are you positive it's the right one?'

'Yep,' Colin answers quickly and confidently. 'One hundred per cent.'

I let out a frustrated sigh. Where could Foxy be? Could he be in a boat? Could he be with a goat? Could he be on a plane? Could he be on a train? Could he be in a car? Could he be in a bar?

Oh . . . that hits a little too close to home. Actually . . .

Where is Foxy?
A poem by Delilah Darling

Could he be in a tree?
Tripping out or taking E?
Could he be drinking wine?
Shooting up? Doing a line?
Could he be smoking grass?
Eating shrooms or sniffing gas?
I will not leave, I'll find this man.
I will not leave, the tramp I am.

Damn, I'm talented.

I suddenly hear a grunt and a click come from the phone. 'What are you doing?'

'Sit-ups,' Colin says. His voice cuts out at the end. I think I've been put on speakerphone.

'Sit-ups? You don't need to do sit-ups; your abs look fine.'

'Aha! So you *were* looking at my abs that one day!'

'I might've caught a glimpse, but they were right in front of my face. I couldn't help it.'

'Uh huh . . . right.' Colin clearly doesn't believe my excuse. 'And how about my legs?'

'I plead the fifth on that one,' I giggle. 'So are you like a big workout fiend?'

'Not at all, but I gotta get serious about it because, well, I don't want to jinx it but I got an audition for *One Life to Live* later in the week.'

I gasp with excitement. '*One Life to Live* the soap opera?'

'Yes, *One Life to Live* the soap opera. Do you watch it?'

'No, it's just that . . . well, I knew you were an actor, but I wasn't sure if you were any good.'

'Gee, thanks.'

'I'm only teasing. Well, you sound busy, so I'll let you go.'

'Okay, I have to start doing lunges now anyway.'

'Well, good luck.' I almost hang up, but then . . . 'Oh wait – Colin?'

'Yes?'

'You don't need to do lunges. Your legs look just fine.'

I can practically hear him smile through the phone. 'I knew you were lookin'!'

I hang up with a smile on my face. A little harmless flirting after so many strike-outs is just what the doctor ordered. Feeling re-energized, I put my thinking cap on and look out the window at Foxy's parents' house. The mailman is parked out front. A few seconds later when he pulls away, I see a package sitting next to their mailbox. A package. I suddenly get an idea.

Now, I know it's wrong to steal someone's mail – it's a federal offense, an invasion of privacy – and I'd be pissed off if someone stole mine, but I need leads. I need that package.

Within seconds I'm running like a bat out of hell from the scene of the crime, holding not only the stolen package, but also a stack of mail. When I arrive back at my car, I jump in and lock the doors. After looking around to make sure no one saw me, I put on a pair of rubber gloves (in case the Feds dust for fingerprints) and start with the package. Addressed to Foxy's mom, it's from the Home Shopping Network. After tearing it open, I look inside and find six terrycloth hair turbans – Turbie Twists – that the enclosed pamphlet says are 'not as bulky as normal towels'. Holding one up, I cringe. It might not be as bulky, but it sure is ugly. I toss it aside and move on to the mail.

Bills, bills, more bills, and then . . . a small envelope from a place called Lily Pond. I tear it open. Inside is a note:

🌲 LILY POND

Dear John & Sylvia,

We had a nice breakthrough the other day. You did the right thing. Matt's in good hands. Keep your spirits up.

Dr Trudy Jacobs

98543 Lily Street – Rockford, IL 61101

Matt's in good hands? Hmm. Since I have my laptop with me, I begin driving around the neighborhood until I'm able to pick up a wireless Internet signal from someone's house. Parked out front, I Google Lily Pond. After 0.29 seconds, the results appear before me:

Lily Pond Substance Abuse Treatment Center
Alcohol and drug treatment center located in Rockford, Illinois.
www.**lilypond**treatment.org/ – 10k – Cached – Similar pages

Alcohol and drug treatment center? My heart sinks. Foxy's in rehab? Oh my God! An overwhelming feeling of guilt engulfs me. I feel partly responsible. Not only did his drug problem start when we were dating, but when things got bad I left him. I should've stayed and helped him get straight. I should've stayed!

After getting directions from MapQuest, I drive to Lily Pond as quickly as I can. When I arrive, I feel slightly relieved as I head down the long driveway. Lily Pond is a beautiful place, not at all what I expected. It looks like a resort – a *real* resort, not a Clock Tower Resort. Located on what appears to be a dozen acres, the heavily wooded grounds are filled with gardens and ponds. It's calming; it's serene.

After parking my car, I head inside and see a skinny, balding man standing behind the front desk. I walk up to him. He's wearing a name tag that reads CARL.

'Hi, Carl,' I say. 'I'm wondering if you can help me with something.' Carl gives me a fake smile and nods. 'I'm here to visit someone. Matt King.'

When Carl hears Foxy's name, he purses his lips

together. 'Mr King's not allowed to have visitors,' he says. He has a whiny, high-pitched voice.

'Really? Am I here on the wrong day? Is there a special "visitors' day" or something when I can come back?'

Carl shakes his head. 'No, Mr King's *never* allowed to have visitors, not unless they're doctor-approved.'

Oh dear . . . this doesn't sound good. Foxy must be in bad shape. I need to get in there and see him. I might be able to save him! I take a moment to study Carl. Although he appears to be a tough cookie, I think I can break him.

'Listen, Carl,' I say, batting my eyelashes, 'I've come a looooong way to see him. Can't you bend the rules just a little bit? Just for me? Pretty please?'

Bat, bat, bat.

Maybe it's the 'pretty please' that pisses Carl off, I'm not sure. All I'm sure of is that he's angry.

'Listen here, young lady,' he says quietly, leaning over the counter. He glares at me with his beady little eyes. 'I don't bend the rules for no one. So why don't you turn around, walk your pretty little ass right out that front door, and go home? Got it?'

Got it? Oh, I got it all right. I got myself another good idea. When I was a little girl, I watched a lot of *Charlie's Angels*, and because of that, I know how to get what I want. Without giving Carl the pleasure of a reply, I turn around and leave, but I'm not going home – I'm going undercover. I'm going . . . to rehab.

Undercover Angel

That evening I devise my plan. I have to flesh out three

things for my idea to work. For one, I can't just check into rehab with a dog, so I need to find a place for Eva to go. Two, I'd hate to be turned down for admission simply because I'm not addicted to drugs, so I need to get some drugs in my system in case they give me a blood test or something. And three, I need to find a hard-luck addict story, a story I can call my own. The experts that run that joint are going to ask questions when I get there, and I'm going to need to know how to answer. Yes, I'm completely aware of the fact that I'm beginning to lose it, but I'm running out of men, I'm running out of options. I need this thing to work with Foxy, I really do!

With regard to Eva, after doing a bit of research, I find a well-respected neighborhood veterinarian and make an appointment for her to get spayed. The kid at the pet store in Philly recommended that I do so before she turned seven months old; otherwise, she'll go into heat and get dog boobies, like five of them or something. The receptionist at the office tells me they keep dogs for two nights following a spay, which should give me enough time to get in and out of rehab – all I need to do while I'm in there is make contact.

Now, on to the drugs. While the idea of numbing the pain of rejection with a handful of dolls is somewhat appealing, I need to be of sound mind to pull this thing off.* I once watched a special on MTV that said if you eat a lot of poppy seeds before taking a drug test, the results

* Dolls (n): Slang term for pills made popular by a fine piece of American literature, *Valley of the Dolls*. God bless you, Jacqueline Susann, for writing one hell of a book that became one hell of a movie. May you rest in peace.

will come back positive for opiates. With that said, I reluctantly scarf down not one but six poppy-seed bagels. I say reluctantly because I don't eat bagels, not since my gynecologist told me that my cervix looked like one.

Finally, on to the hard-luck story. What are opiates? How does one feel when one takes opiates? Truth be told, I had no idea ... that is until I read a special edition of *Star* magazine dedicated to celebrities and their addictions. Yes, if the *E! True Hollywood Story* came in print form, it would be *Star*. After reading through the issue at least twelve times, I'm pretty confident I know my drugs, so I slam it shut and get a good night's sleep.

The next morning, after tearfully dropping off Eva at the vet (I felt so bad leaving her), I drive down Lily Pond's long driveway once again. Since it's so much nicer than any of the hotels I've stayed at so far (The Ritz doesn't count because I didn't stay the night), I'm somewhat excited to be here. After parking my car, I walk to the front door and do a quick check to see if Carl is on duty. If he is, my plan is to wait and check in when he goes to lunch. Not seeing hide nor hair of him, I walk inside and up to the counter. Standing in his place is a large black woman. Her name tag says LUCILLE. Looking up, she smiles when she sees me. 'Can I help you?'

'Yes, Lucille. I'd like to check myself in today.'

'Did you come all by yourself?' Lucille asks, glancing behind me. She looks concerned.

I nod pathetically. 'Yes.'

'You got an appointment?'

Oops. I didn't know I needed one. I nod pathetically again. 'Yes.'

After giving Lucille my name, I wait patiently as she begins flipping through pages of an appointment book. After searching and coming up empty, she looks up. 'I don't have anything here.'

Not wanting to be turned away, I lean my body against the counter for support and begin to do my best Anna Nicole Smith impression. 'Thaaaaattttttzzzz tooooo baddddd,' I say, slurring my words together.

'Oh dear,' Lucille says in a concerned tone. She can tell I need help. 'Why don't you go have a seat over there?' She motions to a fluffy white sofa in the corner.

'Thanks,' I say softly.

After a few minutes of waiting a woman named Jan comes to get me and takes me to her office. She has chipmunk cheeks – jowls – and crazy curly hair that somewhat resembles Michelle's, except it's black not red. The only piece of flair she's wearing to accessorize her all-black suit is a hot-pink leopard-print scarf. After apologizing for not having my appointment in the book, Jan asks if I remember who it was I spoke to when I called.

'I'm not sure,' I say. 'But I think his name was Carl.'

I hope that asshole gets in trouble.

For the next two hours I'm assessed by Jan, a doctor and a psychiatrist. I know what they want to hear because, in addition to watching a lot of *Charlie's Angels* as a kid, I also watched a lot of after-school specials, particularly the ones on addictions (those were always the best).

'I'm here because I want to be here, not because anyone's making me,' I tell them. 'Not only do I want to stop hurting others,' I then add, 'I want to stop hurting myself as well.'

'Attagirl,' Jan says. 'Admitting you need help is the first step to recovery.'

Needless to say, I pass my assessment with flying colors and am admitted to Lily Pond. I know it sounds crazy, but I feel oddly accomplished when I'm accepted – I never test well on things. Since my insurance from Elisabeth Sterling Design is still good for a couple more weeks, I pass my card over to take care of the thousand-dollars-a-day cost of Lily Pond and quickly sign the papers they give me. I don't have time to read them – I need to get inside now; I need to help Foxy!

My room is a special room, they tell me, one for detox. Located right off the nurse's station, it's not very private but it does have its own bathroom. Although there are twin beds inside, I'm the only new recruit right now so it's all mine. While I unpack a nurse stands with me, taking my cell phone (I should be focusing on getting better and nothing else) and anything else she deems harmful to my recovery.

Around noon someone rings a loud cowbell signaling it's time to eat, so I head toward the cafeteria. Unlike the beautiful grounds, the food at Lily Pond is exactly what I would expect to be served in rehab: over-processed, over-cooked, oversaturated. Soft vegetables, tough meat – it's disgusting. After taking the one apple I see, I take a seat alone and begin to look around for Foxy. Not seeing him anywhere, I check out everyone else. I'm not sure what I expected, but most of the people here look normal. Some of the guys are even hot, which is somewhat exciting. I

229

mean, it's a whole room of emotionally unstable men, looking for fulfillment, looking for a strong woman. I might be able to help not only Foxy but all of them.

Someone suddenly sits next to me, interrupting my people-watching. It's a man, but not one of the cute ones. He's shorter, fatter and balder than most of the others. 'What are you in for?' he asks. A pair of Playboy sunglasses hang from his shirt pocket.

'Three to five,' I say, pretending I'm in the slammer. He smiles.

For the next few minutes, The Playboy tells me all about his Oxycontin addiction. He tells me that rehab is working for him so far, but he's worried about getting out. You see, he's a thrill-seeker who is always looking for a rush. After telling The Playboy that he needs to find a hobby, something that can give him the same rush as Oxycontin, I tell him about a TV special I watched recently about roller-coaster enthusiasts, people who drove all over the country to ride on different coasters. The Playboy likes my idea and says he'll look into it when he leaves. Gosh, I haven't even been here for one day yet and I'm already helping people. Where is Foxy?

Therapy doesn't start until I'm done with detox, so for the remainder of the day I take a nap and then go to dinner. It's 'build your own potato' night, complete with bacon bits and nacho cheese. Barf. After grabbing another apple, I find a seat and look around for Foxy. Like this morning, I don't see him anywhere. After eating and people-watching, The Playboy stops by to talk to me once again about being a thrill-seeker.

The next day the same thing happens – sleep, eat, no

Foxy, The Playboy is a thrill-seeker. The only change is that a new woman has moved into the detox room with me. Although she seems nice enough, she's covered her bed with Beanie Babies, which frightens me.

On my third day in rehab, I wake up and realize that I have to leave in the afternoon to pick up Eva. The vet said she'd be ready to go around three o'clock so my plan is to leave right after lunch. Even though I miss her, I'm not happy about leaving. In addition to being upset about not connecting with Foxy, I'm peeved that I haven't gotten any therapy. I mean, I was looking forward to being analyzed by a real doctor, by someone other than an audiobook. (No offense, Tony Robbins, I still love you and your white teeth.) I know I'm not paying for any of this, but for what exactly have they been charging me a thousand dollars a day? It surely isn't the gourmet food. Nor is it the activities. Last evening I took an art therapy class hoping I'd get to throw down a slab of clay and make a pot like Demi Moore did in *Ghost* (because there's this one table in my apartment that just needs *something*), but all I got was some paper and pastels. Bottom line – rehab's a rip-off.

When I hear the cowbell ring, I head to the cafeteria one last time, praying I'll see Foxy. While waiting in line to see what I'm once again not going to eat, I look up and gasp when I see Foxy sitting in the corner eating alone. I can't believe it – I can't believe it's really him. He looks older and puffier. His strong jaw line isn't as chiseled as it once was. After staring at him for a minute, I snap out of it and realize this is my one and only chance to talk to him. I take a deep breath and then once again embrace my inner Spice Girl and go for it.

'Matt,' I say, when I arrive at where he's sitting. 'Hi.'

Foxy looks up. His icy-blue eyes are still hazy. He doesn't say anything. By the look in his eyes I can tell my face isn't registering, but I'm not offended, not like I was with Rod. Instead, I'm saddened. Foxy seems cloudy. Either he's on some heavy meds or his brain is fried – maybe both.

'It's me, Delilah,' I explain. 'Delilah, from Chicago.'

After a few seconds of silence, Foxy's mouth slowly widens revealing the beautiful smile he's always had. I melt – it's still blinding. 'Delilah Darling,' he says slowly, 'how in the hell are ya?'

'I'm good,' I say in a shaky voice as tears fill my eyes. Even though he remembers me, he seems so lost. 'How are you?'

He shrugs. 'Been better.' He pats the seat next to him. 'Here, have a seat.'

For the next ten minutes or so Foxy and I talk about what we've been doing since the last time we saw each other without going into too much detail. Oddly, he never asks why I'm in rehab, which makes me feel uncomfortable asking him. The whole conversation is very surface-level. Hoping to get him to open up more, I ask what he thinks of Lily Pond.

'Not a fan,' Foxy says, making a face. 'I hate how the sun pours into my room early in the morning. I hate how my bed is lumpy.' He looks down at his plate. 'I also hate the food.'

'No kidding,' I say, reaching over to pick up a piece of orange-tinged lettuce. 'I can't remember the last time I ate *iceberg* lettuce.'

Matt's face suddenly turns completely white. Was it something I said? He begins staring off into space. I become worried.

'Hey, are you okay?' I ask.

Matt doesn't answer. In fact, it's like he can't even hear me. I wave my hands in front of his face. 'Hellllllo? Anyone home?'

Suddenly Matt bolts from his seat and jumps on top of the cafeteria table. As he begins pointing at *nothing* in the distance, people around us start to whisper.

'Uh . . . are you okay?' I ask again.

He still doesn't answer.

Oh no . . . what have I done to him?

As Matt's breathing becomes heavier, the whispers become louder. Just as I'm about to stand up and try to convince him to come down, Matt suddenly screams at the top of his lungs.

'Iceberg, right ahead!'

Iceberg? What in the hell?

Before I have a chance to ask him what he means (or even get the hell out of here, for that matter), Matt turns to face me and backs up. Getting a running start, he then leaps off the table in my direction. As his body flies through the air above me in what seems like slow motion, I begin to panic. He's going to land on me, there's no doubt about it. I duck for cover.

Just as I anticipated, not more than two seconds later, Matt's body slams into mine, bringing us both to the floor. As food and drinks go flying, people begin screaming and complete chaos erupts. Lying on the floor, I try to get out from underneath him but I'm unable to do so. Likewise, I try to scream for help but I can't speak. Matt's body is completely covering mine; it's like he's trying to protect me from something.

I can't move.

I can't breathe.

Suddenly everything goes black.

A little while later I wake up. After focusing my eyes, I realize I'm lying on a bed in an examination room. Jan is standing over me wearing the same black suit she wore when I met her, except that her piece of flair has changed from the pink scarf to a rhinestone bird pin. Her arms are folded; she looks angry. Quickly sitting up, I look down and realize that I'm covered in food and soda.

'You just couldn't help yourself, could ya?' Jan asks in a hard voice. 'You couldn't let your boyfriend get better by himself – you had to come in here and mess with his emotions.'

Boyfriend? Mess with his emotions? Oh, no. Jan has it all wrong.

'Matt's not my boyfriend,' I say quickly. 'Really, he's not.'

Jan rolls her eyes. 'Don't lie to me, Delilah. Carl told me you came here a few days ago looking for him.'

Looking up, I see Carl's beady little eyes peering at me through a window in the door. *Tattle-tale.* Glaring, I give him the finger when Jan's not looking.

'Were you with him in Mexico when he ate the peyote?' Jan asks. I look back at her. I'm confused.

'Who? Carl?'

Jan gives me a look. 'No. *Matt.* Were you with Matt in Mexico when he ate the bad peyote?'

'Uh . . . *no.*'

Jan studies me for a moment. I think she can tell that I have absolutely no idea what she's talking about. Sighing loudly, she sits down next to me.

'Listen, Delilah, Matt's a very special patient here,' she says. Her voice is softer.

'Special how?'

'He has peyote-induced psychosis. The symptoms are similar to schizophrenia. He suffers from paranoid delusions, personality shifts and hallucinations, the most common being that he's on the *Titanic* when it's sinking. We think he was watching the movie when he was tripping.'

'Peyote-induced psychosis?' Oh no. 'You mean like . . . he's crazy?'

'Well, yes, kind of,' Jan says. 'We're hoping the delusions will go away though or at least wane as the drugs work their way out of his system, but it's hard to say. Lately things haven't been looking good. Certain trigger words – like in your case, *iceberg* – have been causing him to break into full-on re-enactments from the movie. Today's outburst wasn't bad, but last week . . . *sheesh!* After one of the other patients called him a *jackass* he took off all his clothes and started running around naked screaming, "Put your hands on me, Jack! Put your hands on me, Jack!" It wasn't pretty.'

Jan's words hit me like a ton of bricks.

Wow. I mean, *wow.*

There's no way I can spend the rest of my life with this guy. I need to get out of here. Realizing I'm in way over my head, I decide to come clean.

'Jan, I shouldn't be here. I don't really have a drug problem.'

Jan gives me a 'That's what they all say' look.

'Seriously,' I continue, 'I lied to get in here.'

'Delilah, you failed a drug test.'

'Yeah, I know. I planned that. I ate a lot of poppy-seed bagels before I got here.'

Jan looks confused, so I decide to tell her everything. I tell her how Matt and I dated eight years ago and how I was hoping to work things out with him. I tell her how I came to visit, but Carl was an asshole, so I went home and devised a plan. I tell her about the bagels again, about *Star* magazine and how I dropped my dog off at the vet to get spayed because I didn't want her getting dog boobies.

'Dog boobies?' she asks.

'Yep. And I have to leave now to go pick her up because she's supposed to come home today.'

'And by home you mean . . .?'

'A blue Ford Focus out in the parking lot.'

Jan stands up. 'You know I've heard every excuse in the book before, but never this one.' For some reason this makes me feel clever, so I smile. 'If what you're saying is true, though, if you did all this just to reconnect with an old boyfriend, then you, my dear, are—'

'Smart? Loving? Dedicated?' I interject.

Jan shakes her head. 'No. You, my dear, are crazier than Matt is.'

Crazier? Wait, huh?

After informing me that I signed a release form when I got here surrendering the right to check myself out (it was in the middle of all the insurance forms I didn't read), Jan leaves the room and tells me to go back to mine. When

236

she does, I immediately feel sorry for drug addicts – even when you tell the truth, no one believes you.

As I pass by a room on my way out of the examination wing, I glance inside and see Matt sitting on a bed alone. He looks confused; a pang of sadness shoots through my heart. What a waste of a life. I open the door and walk inside. When he looks up and sees that it's me, he looks back down, embarrassed. I walk over and sit down next to him.

'I hope you still don't mind dirty and wet,' he says, seeing my clothes covered in food. I let out a little laugh.

'I can't believe you remember that.'

'I can't believe you thought I'd forget that.'

Reaching over, I take his hand in mine. After the two of us sit in silence for a while, he turns to me. 'I'm sorry, Delilah,' he says.

Thinking he's talking about my clothes, I tell him not to worry. 'It'll wash out.'

'No, not for that,' he says. 'I'm sorry for everything, everything I ever did to you.'

Seeing the sad look on Matt's face, tears once again fill my eyes.

'I'm sorry for treating you the way I did when we were together,' he continues. 'I'm sorry for taking advantage of you. I'm sorry for cheating on you. I'm sorry for laughing at you. I'm sorry for . . .'

As Matt continues to apologize for everything he's ever done to me, I'm filled with sorrow. Although I've waited eight years for this apology, rather than make me feel better, all it does is break my heart. It breaks my heart because it reminds me of the good person he once was, it reminds me of all that's been lost and it makes me realize that I never would've been able to help him. Finally forgiving Matt, I wrap my arms around him. When I do, he wraps his around me as well. For the next few minutes, the two of us hold each other like we did all those nights in bed, except this time we cry.

'I'm scared,' Matt whispers in my ear, after a while. It's not going to be easy undoing what he's done to himself, and I think he knows it.

'I know you are,' I say. 'But it'll be okay.' I'm not sure if it will, but I don't know what else to say and I don't want him giving up hope.

When our eyes eventually run dry, I stand and walk to the door. Before leaving, I turn around and give Matt one last wave goodbye. For a split second, a glimmer of light replaces the haze in his icy-blue eyes. I think it's Foxy saying goodbye, so I blow him a kiss. I then turn around and walk out of the room, walk out of his life.

Chapter Ten

I'm still in rehab.

Chapter Eleven

I'm still in rehab.

Chapter Twelve

A Ferocious Bark   **Sunday, 1 May**

I'm finally out of rehab.

'Read before you sign next time,' Lucille says as she bids me farewell.

After leaving Lily Pond, I go to a bookstore and buy Matt a copy of *Chicken Soup for the Unsinkable Soul*. Lucille promised me that she'd get it to him. I adore and will forever be indebted to her. Not only did she convince Jan to call Michelle who verified I'm not a drug addict, she also took care of Eva. In addition to calling the vet to make sure she had come out of the surgery okay, she picked her up and took her home to recuperate.

I feel so irresponsible. I shouldn't have gotten a dog, and not just because I'm on a road trip. Don't get me wrong, I love Eva and am glad to have saved her, but what if there was no Lucille? What if it took me longer to get out of rehab? What would I have done then? Just leave her at the vet until I was ready to pick her up? Until I was done trying to sort out my own disastrous life?

Also, I didn't tell Michelle or Colin – the only two people who know I'm on a road trip – that I was checking myself into rehab. I thought I'd be out before they even realized I was gone, but I was wrong. I was unreachable for six days and all their phone calls went straight to voicemail. Thinking something bad happened to me, they both freaked out. All in all, Michelle left over twenty messages, each one sounding more panicked than the last.

As for Colin, he wasn't *quite* as worried as Michelle was until she came knocking on his door in hysterics, asking if he knew where I was. After calming her down, he told her that I was in Rockford visiting some guy named Matt King. I'd previously told Michelle about Matt, and the only thing she remembered about him was that he was my drug-dealing ex-boyfriend. In total, Colin left me about fifteen messages. I owe them both an apology.

Before getting on the highway, I find a quiet spot in a parking lot and pull out my phone. I take a deep breath and dial Michelle's number. She answers after two rings.

'Hi, it's me,' I say softly.

She doesn't respond.

'Listen, I'm really sorry for disappearing.'

'You're sorry?' Her voice is loud and sharp. 'That's all you can say?'

'I don't know what else to say. It was stupid of me to do what I did and I'm sorry.'

'You didn't think it was necessary to tell me or anyone else that you were checking yourself into rehab? You thought it was okay to just disappear?'

'No, but I didn't think I'd be in there for as long as I was and—'

'That's your problem, Delilah,' she yells. 'You don't think.'

I realize I don't have a right to be angry at Michelle, especially now, but I hate that she always makes my life her business. 'Michelle, why do you care so much about what I do?'

'Why do you care so much about what other people think?'

'I don't.'

'Yes, you do. If you didn't, then you wouldn't be so pre-occupied with some stupid *number* average, with fitting in with the rest of society.'

I sigh loudly. I don't know what to say.

'Your actions affect other people, Delilah,' Michelle continues, 'and that's why I care. I mean, imagine how Colin and I felt – we were worried. I had an interview at Vintage Vogue, and while I was there, during the entire thing, all I could think about was the possibility of you being dead. I couldn't concentrate and almost screwed the whole thing up.'

'I'm sorry, Michelle, really,' I say again. 'So, did you . . . get the job?' I'm almost afraid to ask.

'I don't know yet,' she says, sighing loudly, 'they haven't said. Listen, I don't mean for this to sound rude, but do me a favor and don't call until you're home, okay? I need to focus on job hunting and I don't want to be worrying about what you're doing every second of the day.'

'Okay,' I say softly. 'I won't.'

When I hang up from Michelle, I feel a little like the wind's been knocked out of me but I don't allow myself to crack; I have another call to make. I dial Colin's number. From his messages, it's clear that Michelle didn't tell him the reason I'm doing what I'm doing (thank God), but still, I'm embarrassed. After two rings, he picks up but doesn't say anything. No 'hello'. No 'how are you?' Just silence.

'Please don't be angry with me,' I say in a little voice. 'I just wanna let you know I'm okay.'

'Well, thanks for calling,' Colin says quietly, calmly, after a long pause. 'Thanks for being so *fecking* considerate.' The tone of his voice, although softer than Michelle's, is more frightening. 'You know, I'm not one to judge, I do stupid things all the time, but when some girl I don't even know comes knocking on my door, crying to me, saying you're dead, what am I to think?'

I don't say anything.

'I mean, put yourself in my position. When she told me this guy was some sorta drug dealer, not only did I worry something might've happened to you, but I felt responsible because I'm the one who gave you his address.'

'I'm sorry. I never thought about it that way.'

'Yeah? Well, think about it that way in the future, will ya? I'm not trying to be a dick, but I was really worried.'

'You were?' I ask. I'm somewhat surprised he seems so genuinely concerned.

'For fuck's sake, yes!' he yells. 'Of course I was! What kind of question is that? I don't want anything to happen to you!'

'I'm sorry, Colin. I really am.'

''Sokay,' he says, his voice becoming softer. 'I forgive you, but if you disappear again, I'll never speak to you for as long as I live. Do you understand?'

'Yes.'

'So where to next?' he asks after a long pause.

'Los Angeles,' I mumble. 'Unless you found someone else between here and there.'

'To be honest, I stopped looking when I thought you were napped by the druggie,' he explains. 'But I'll start again if that's what you want.'

'I do,' I say quietly.

'Okay then. But Jaysus, be careful out there, will ya?'

'I promise.'

After hanging up from Colin, I shut off my phone, lay my seat back and think. I think. Michelle was partially right in saying that I care about what other people think – that is partly the reason why I'm doing this. As for the other part, seeing Matt stirred up a lot of feelings, a lot of memories. So did hearing about Nate. Both of them got me thinking about connections that you have with people, *real* connections. I'm lonely; I really am.

As I realize this, tears begin to fall from my eyes. I cry because I don't want Michelle to be angry and I hate that Colin was. I cry because Nate's in jail and I couldn't help Foxy. I cry because I'm not jealous of Daisy, but I do envy what she has. I cry because I'm happy that my grandpa found love, but don't understand why I can't. I cry because I don't want to disappoint my mother, but I've already disappointed myself. I cry for all these things, but mostly, I cry because I'm afraid I'll be alone for ever.

Sitting on my lap, Eva peers up at me with her big brown eyes. She looks exhausted. After slowly lifting her leg, I look at her belly, look at her wound, look at the thin piece of thread that's holding her together. Ever so gently, I run my finger along the pink edges of her skin – her insides are slightly exposed.

'I'm sorry for leaving you,' I tell her as I put her leg back down. She scoots up my chest and licks tears off my face.

As I wrap my arms around Eva and hold her close to my heart, I can feel every bone in her body. Beneath her fluffy hair, despite her ferocious bark, beyond her low grumble . . . she's fragile.

We're more alike that I thought.

$1,984, 17 days, 4 guys left.

Chapter Thirteen

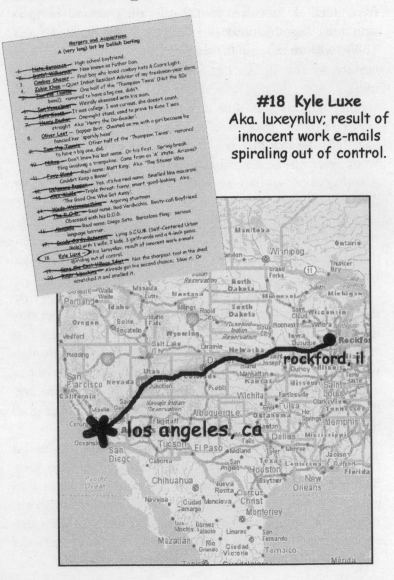

Mergers and Acquisitions
A (very long) list by Delilah Darling

1. ~~Nate Syracuse~~ – High school boyfriend.
2. ~~Daniel Wilkerson~~ – Now known as Father Dan.
3. ~~Cowboy Shaner~~ – Frat boy who loved cowboy hats & Coors Light.
4. ~~Zubin Khan~~ – Quiet Indian Resident Advisor of my freshman-year dorm.
5. ~~Timmie Towne~~ – One half of the 'Thompson Twins' (Not the 80s band); rumored to have a big one, didn't.
6. ~~Tad Kesselman~~ – Weirdly obsessed with his mom.
7. ~~Kate Goode~~ – It was college. I was curious, she doesn't count.
8. ~~Henry Packer~~ – One-night stand, used to prove to Kate I was straight. Aka 'Henry the Do-Gooder'.
9. ~~Oliver Leet~~ – Dapper Brit. Cheated on me with a girl because he fancied her 'sparkly nose'.
10. ~~Tom the Trevor~~ – Other half of the 'Thompson Twins'; rumored to have a big one, did.
11. ~~Nakos~~ – Don't know his last name. Or his first. Spring-break fling involving a trampoline. Came from an 'A' state. Arizona?
12. ~~Foxy Blond~~ – Real name: Matt King; Aka 'The Stoner Who Couldn't Keep a Boner'.
13. ~~Johannes Repper~~ – Yes, it's his real name. Smelled like macaroni.
14. ~~Alex Wells~~ – Triple threat: funny, smart, good-looking. Aka 'The Good One Who Got Away'.
15. ~~Wade Worthington~~ – Aspiring stuntman.
16. ~~The D.O.B.~~ – Real name: Rod Verdacchia. Booty-call Boyfriend. Obsessed with his D.O.B.
17. ~~Abrizzo~~ – Real name: Diego Soto. Barcelona fling; serious language barrier.
18. Kyle Luxe – Lying S.C.U.M. (Self-Centered Urban Male) with 1 wife, 2 kids, 3 girlfriends and a 4-inch penis. Aka. luxeynluv; result of innocent work e-mails spiraling out of control.
19. ~~Greg the Grease Village Idiot~~ – Not the sharpest tool in the shed.
20. ~~Roger Lipscher~~ – Already got his second chance; blew it. Or scratched it and smelled it.

#18 Kyle Luxe
Aka. luxeynluv; result of
innocent work e-mails
spiraling out of control.

rockford, il

los angeles, ca

It's amazing how quickly we heal. In the three and a half days it takes to drive to LA, the pink edges of Eva's skin melt together and her stitches begin to disappear. There will be a scar, of course, but you'll have to look closely to see it. As her spunk comes back, so does mine.

Since the drive takes us directly through Las Vegas, I call my grandpa but get Gloria's answering machine. Her message tells me that the two of them are out of town for the week, visiting the Grand Canyon. I look over at Eva. My grandpa goes on road trips with his girlfriend and I go on them with my dog. When did I become so pathetic? Choosing not to pinpoint a date, I crank up my 2003 playlist and sing along to Kelis and 'Milkshake' while thinking about the reason I'm going to LA, #18, Kyle Luxe.

Kyle and I met two years ago when he got a job working as a production assistant for Elisabeth's weekly television show, *Elisabeth Sterling Style*. It was Kyle's first real job; he had just graduated from college. Yes, he was young, but that's why I liked him. I had just come out of a pathetic relationship with Grody Gordy Peterson, and the chances of a twenty-one-year-old recent college grad being married were slim to none.

One week after we started working together, Kyle and I had both mastered water-cooler rendezvous and long lingers by the copy machine. I'm not sure what he saw in good OLD me, but I thought he was a breath of fresh air. Being so young, he hadn't experienced many of life's disappointments – no real broken hearts, no career setbacks

– so he wasn't jaded. He had an enthusiasm about life that was infectious. I felt young when I was around him.

Well, most of the time I did.

Sometimes, through the course of conversation, Kyle would say things that reminded me of our age difference. For example, the first time he came over to my apartment he looked around and said, 'Wow ... you have real furniture.' Another time I told him about an old Walkman tape player I had that used to eat cassettes. I was reluctant to throw it away because I was usually able to save the tapes by sticking a pencil in one of the holes and winding them back up. But the day it shredded my favorite Debbie Gibson cassingle beyond repair was the day it hit the can. After I told Kyle this, he stared at me blankly.

'You remember cassingles, right?' I asked.

Kyle shook his head. 'No.'

'They were cassette singles,' I explained.

Kyle looked confused.

'You remember cassettes, right?'

Kyle shook his head again. 'No.'

'Walkmans?'

'Nope.'

'Debbie Gibson?'

'Sorry.'

Seeing the worried look on my face (no doubt accompanied by a few fines lines and a forehead wrinkle), Kyle tried to make me feel better by telling me that he knew what they all were (except for cassingles and Debbie Gibson), he just didn't remember the time they were actually being used. Kyle didn't remember the time before CDs or digital downloads.

'How about Atari, do you remember that?' *No. Sega.*
'Busy signals?' *No. Call waiting.*

'Do you remember a time when getting up to change the TV channel didn't only happen because you lost the remote control?' *You mean it actually had a knob?*

While I shrugged Kyle's answers off and pretended they didn't bother me, I silently cursed the rapid advance of technology for emphasizing our age difference.

Within two weeks of meeting each other Kyle and I had gone on a couple of dates and kissed, but our relationship was still very innocent. Just as things were beginning to heat up the television department was moved to another floor in the building, another floor with its own copy machine and its own water cooler. Just like that, Kyle and I went from seeing each other ten times a day to seeing each other once a week. For most budding relationships this would be the end, but for Kyle and me it was just the beginning.

Enter e-mail and instant messaging.

For the first time since I met him, I was happy technology had been progressing at such a rapid pace. Within days of Kyle's moving, the two of us found ourselves in the middle of a hot and heavy Internet romance. Each day hundreds of e-mails and instant messages between us zipped through cyberspace, messages that at first outlined every detail of our monotonous workdays . . .

> DARLING: I hate the copier and I want to kill
> it.
> luxeynluv: did it jam again?
> DARLING: Yes. I want to bash it in with a hammer.

252

```
luxeynluv: do it.
luxeynluv: i'm gonna eat an apple now.
DARLING: Cool.
```

... ended up outlining every detail of our vivid imagin-
ations as telling each other what we were doing and
thinking turned into telling each other what we were
wearing ... and what we weren't.

```
DARLING: What are you wearing?
luxeynluv: a black izod shirt and khakis. you?
DARLING: A black and white wrap dress.
luxeynluv: and?
DARLING: Heels.
luxeynluv: and?
DARLING: Panties.
luxeynluv: what do they look like?
DARLING: Black. Lacy. Tiny.
luxeynluv: tiny like a thong tiny?
DARLING: Yep.
luxeynluv: what kind of panties were you wear-
ing yesterday?
DARLING: I wasn't.*
```

As Kyle and I began having no-holds-barred discussions
about everything, not just sex, our relationship went from
zero to sixty over the period of a week. Looking back
now, I can clearly see that e-mail distorted my perception
of our relationship, but at the time I didn't know it.

* I was, but they were big white cotton briefs and I didn't want to tell
him.

Speaking from experience, it is my belief that e-mail moves relationships along at an unnaturally fast pace. Because they're simply typing words into a computer, people aren't as guarded with their feelings and usually end up revealing way too much about themselves, way too soon. My relationship with Kyle out there in www land couldn't have been stronger, but my relationship with him in person was practically non-existent. I knew so much about him and yet I knew nothing. I didn't know his quirks, his mannerisms, his habits – I knew words on a screen. I barely knew Kyle, but at the time I really thought I did.

Whereas in real life all Kyle and I did was kiss, out there in cyberia we did much more. All our intimate talks, I mean *typing*, soon led to a rendezvous that wasn't beside the water cooler but in a downtown hotel room in the middle of a workday. I don't know what I was thinking. It was a Friday afternoon when it happened, and I was sitting alone in my office watching a special on cool hotels when I sent Kyle a message telling him to turn it on.

> DARLING: Hotel rooms are sexy.
> luxeynluv: yeah. they make me horny.
> DARLING: Me too. Have you ever been to The Mercer in SoHo? Just walking through the lobby gives me multiple orgasms.
> luxeynluv: multiple?
> DARLING: Yes. Multiple.
> luxeynluv: soho's only a five-minute cab ride from here you know . . .

```
DARLING: It is, isn't it . . . ?
luxeynluv: yeah.
luxeynluv: meet me there in an hour?
DARLING: Make it a half.
```

As soon as I agreed to meet Kyle, I started to worry. I was afraid that I wouldn't live up to his expectation of me, an expectation that I myself created in the e-mails I sent him. Seeing as though I'd always had a backspace button at my fingertips, I was able to edit what I said, I mean *typed*, and knew that I had come across sounding much more put-together than I actually was. I was terrified that Kyle would expect me to be a suave sophisticated woman because I'm really anything but.

Oh, but why was I worrying? We weren't going to be talking.

Seeing as though I was nervous already, what I now refer to as 'the underwear fiasco of 2003' only made matters worse. Let me start by saying that, with regard to sexy underwear, I prefer wearing lacy boyshorts and hipsters to thongs. I hate thongs, I do. Every time I wear one, I find myself picking it out of my ass all day. I find them uncomfortable, which is why I rarely wear them.* With that said, earlier that day in an e-mail I told Kyle that I was wearing a thong even though I wasn't because I knew that he liked them. Because of that, I had to run out and buy one before going to the hotel.

Lucky for me I knew of a lingerie store near The Mercer,

---

* I mentioned this to my mother one day, that I find thongs uncomfortable, and do you want to know what she said to me? She said, 'Maybe you need a bigger size.' Seriously.

so I stopped there quickly before checking in. Problem solved? Not quite. You see, my mother raised me right (okay fine, maybe not), so I don't wear new underwear unless it's been washed. Because of this, before Kyle arrived I tried to wash my new undies with the complimentary shampoo in the bathroom sink and then dry them with the blow dryer but I didn't finish in time. When he arrived and knocked on the door, even though the undies were still slightly damp, I put them on anyway.

When I opened the door to greet Kyle, I didn't feel much of a connection between us. To be honest, I felt more of a bond with Abogado, a two-night stand, than I did with him. However, I didn't turn back. Chalking up what I perceived to be a lack of chemistry to nerves, I ended up having sex with him. We were ready to take this plunge in our cyber relationship; we just weren't ready to take it in our real one. It was so awkward. I remember lying in bed afterward, trying to cuddle, but I couldn't get comfortable. I rested my head on his arm and felt like I was squishing him.

Kyle had to leave town early the next morning for a weekend wedding in Los Angeles, so I stayed in the room alone that night. The next day, during a bad case of post-sex regret, I decided that I was going to make things work with Kyle even though we didn't have any chemistry. After going back to the same lingerie store, I bought a sexy pair of lacy boyshorts thinking that maybe if I was more comfortable next time – more relaxed – the connection between us might be stronger. That Monday, using inter-office mail just for fun, I sent him the boyshorts with a note that said, 'How about I wear these next time?'

Long story short, there was no next time. Kyle never came back from LA. Ever. He didn't even come back to quit his job in person or pack up his apartment. He was just gone. Six days after our hotel-room rendezvous, when he finally called me to explain his sudden departure, he said that he didn't go to LA for a wedding but for an interview, and didn't tell me before he left because he didn't want word getting around the office. I was so insulted. 'You'll tell me how hard your dick is, but you won't tell me about a job interview?' I snapped. 'That's kind of fucked up, don't you think?'

'I'm sorry,' Kyle apologized, 'but it's my career and I take it very seriously.'

I hung up on him.

After a couple of futile attempts, I gave up trying to track down the envelope with my underwear inside. I thankfully never signed the note so if someone opened it they wouldn't know it was from me, but still, I would've liked to get it back; the undies were so cute. Two weeks later I had all but forgotten about them, when I got a phone call from the executive producer of *Elisabeth Sterling Style*, a woman named Margaret, saying she wanted to talk to me about something. I immediately began to worry. Even though she's not my boss, she's known for being as tough as nails and is definitely above me on the totem pole. I was positive she had found the underwear; I was positive I was going to be fired.

As I sat in her office later that afternoon, Margaret got right to the point. She was so angry that Kyle left without giving her notice that she personally went through his e-mail, hoping to find an instance of him violating his confidentiality agreement just so she could fuck with him. Unfortunately for her, she didn't find any such instances, but unfortunately for me, she did find something else: my e-mails. Kyle deleted them but didn't empty his trash. Dumb ass.

Although she could've been a bitch, Margaret was cool about things and said that she wasn't going to tell Roger because she knew he was an asshole. After advising me not to make the same mistake in the future, she dismissed me. Instantly feeling relieved that the only thing she found was a few sexy e-mails, I got up to leave her office. On my way out the door, she called out to me. 'Oh, Delilah?' I turned around.

'Yes?'

'You forgot your undies,' she said casually, sling-shooting them to me.

I caught them; my face turned beet red. 'Oh, uh . . . thanks,' I muttered. I then backed out of her office and made it my business never to run into her again.

Another One Bites the Dust　　　Thursday, 5 May

When I arrived in LA last night, I decided not to stay in another budget hotel (every room I've stayed in so far has looked like the setting for a bad porno movie), and instead treated myself to a room at the Viceroy, a luxury ocean-front hotel in Santa Monica. Yes, it's totally out of my price range, but I have a credit card for life's little emergencies, so I decided to splurge.

While in New York, I was able to find out on the Internet where Kyle lives and works – his name is listed in the credits for a home show that airs on NBC. I doubt that he's married – he's still too young – so I didn't think it was necessary to have Colin look into it. After unpacking my bag and taking a dip in the pool, I decided to call NBC late last night. I navigated my way through their phone system, and ended up in Kyle's voicemail. Since I wasted so much time in rehab, I had decided to cut to the chase and leave a message telling him I was in town, but after hearing his outgoing message I changed my mind. Kyle said he'd be out of the office on personal business until Monday, which is five days away. Since there's no way I'm staying in LA for five days (I can't afford it; my room at the Viceroy is $400 a night), I've decided to drive by his house this morning to see what I can find out. Maybe he went out of town.

Kyle lives on a curvy road in the Hollywood Hills, right under the D of the Hollywood sign, as a matter of fact. His house, like most in the neighborhood, looks small from the front but goes halfway down the mountain in the back. In short, it's enormous. Kyle must be doing well. I bet he has some real furniture by now.

After parking across the street, I put on my disguise and begin to look for signs of life in the house. The blinds are open, which is good, and . . . oh!

As a car pulls into the driveway, I duck. Peering up ever so slowly, I watch closely as three people get out. As they walk to the front door, I see that one of them is holding . . . a pie? Yes, it's a pie. They ring the bell and then wait for a few seconds until a woman opens the door and lets them inside. Twenty minutes later they emerge, get back in their car and drive away. Hmm.

Over the next couple of hours, this same thing happens over and over again. Random groups of people stop by with food and/or flowers and stay for a half-hour, tops. Since I can't see inside the house, I can't tell what's going on. I suppose I could hike down the side of the mountain and look in the back, but with my luck I'd have a run-in with a pack of rabid coyotes or a couple of hungry mountain lions. After thinking about what to do, I make a plan.

Pulling my car up as close to Kyle's driveway as I can get, I roll the windows partly down and hide on the floor of the backseat. My hope is that I'll be able to hear people talking as they get in and out of their cars and figure out what's going on. To cover myself so no one can see me, I pull a bunch of clothes out of one of my bags. As I bury myself underneath them, I'm thankful that I left Eva at the Viceroy because she'd make this very difficult to do.

After about ten minutes I hear a car pull up. Unfortunately, however, the people inside don't say much as they come and go so I don't learn anything. A little while later a second car arrives, and then a third, but just like the first, the passengers inside are quiet. Just as I'm getting antsy, a fourth car pulls up. When the people get out, I finally hear voices. As someone shuts the door, I hear them say, 'It's such a shame. He was so young.'

Instantly, everything makes sense. The visitors, the food, the flowers – someone must've died. Having listened to Kyle's voicemail message, I'm sure it's not him so I don't freak out, but I begin to wonder. Was it a family member? A friend? A roommate? I need to find out. As quietly as I can I pull out my laptop. Lucky for me, I'm close enough to Kyle's house to pick up his wireless Internet signal, so after logging on, I type his address into a reverse address search bar and hit enter. Hmm. The house has two phone lines. One is listed as Kyle's; the other belongs to someone named Zach Holden. I Google Zach Holden and—

Yep, just as I suspected. The first thing that pops up is an obituary in the *LA Times*. I read it. Although it doesn't say how or why, Zach Holden has definitely died. He was young, only twenty-five years old. My heart goes out to Kyle. Poor, poor Kyle; his roommate died. A memorial service is being held tonight, beginning at six o'clock, at a place called the Hollywood Forever Cemetery. After closing my laptop, I think about my next step. My first instinct is not to go to the memorial service, but the more I think about it, the more I think going's not such a bad idea. I mean, Zach and Kyle might not have even been friends; they might've just been roommates. If I were to show up, Kyle might be happy to see me, an old friend. It wouldn't hurt to just check things out I suppose.

Later that evening, after showering and changing at the hotel, Eva and I hit the road. (I felt bad about leaving her alone all day.) While we're driving, I tell her my plan. If Kyle looks devastated when I see him, then I'm going to turn around and leave. If he looks devastated but like he needs comforting, or if he looks bored like he's there out of obligation or loyalty, then I'm going to stay.

Unfortunately for Eva and me, owing to a bad traffic jam on Interstate 10, we don't get to the front gate of Hollywood Forever Cemetery until almost 7.30 p.m. Afraid

I might've missed the service, I haul-ass down the long driveway and quickly park my car. After cracking a window and leaving Eva in the car, I head to where the service is being held.

Holding my head down, I enter the chapel and begin looking around for Kyle. Since it's already so late, I'm surprised to find the place still crowded. I would've guessed most people would've gone home already, but apparently not. Because of this, it's not as easy finding Kyle as I thought it would be; I don't see him anywhere. While studying the crowd, I realize that it's made up of mostly men. Sad men, somber men, and well, to be honest . . . *hot* men. Seriously, the place is filled with babes. Young cute babes. Well-dressed babes. Babes who smell good. Damn . . . if the crowd here tonight is a random sample of men in LA, then I need to come out to the left coast more often.

After looking around for a few more minutes, I don't spot Kyle anywhere and decide to stop searching. Assuming he's gone home, I head over to where some pictures are hanging in the distance, curious to see what Zach looked like. When I arrive to the display, I gasp. Zach Holden wasn't just gorgeous, he was Orlando Bloom gorgeous. He really was. My eyes dart from photo to photo. What a looker. What a hunk. What a shame. He seems so happy and fun-loving. In many of the pictures he's whitewater rafting, bungee jumping, skydiving – he's so adventurous! You know, I have to be honest . . . I don't like wakes, I don't like caskets, and I don't like dead people – but I gotta see Zach Holden in person. Turning around, I begin to look around for a coffin.

After scanning the room for a few moments, I don't see one, so I nudge a man standing next to me. 'Excuse me, sir? Where's the casket?'

Turning to me, he gives me an angry stare.

'The casket?' he shrieks. I nod.

'Yeah, is it an open casket?'

The man shakes his head in disgust. 'What kind of a sick person are you?' he asks. 'After what happened to Zach, after the accident, do you really think they'd have an open casket?'

The accident? What accident? Before I have a chance to ask, the man storms away. When he does, I see something in the distance: an urn.

Oh no. Poor Zach Holden. Poor hot sexy Zach Holden. He was cremated.

Suddenly, I hear my name. 'Delilah?'

Recognizing Kyle's voice, I turn around. Looking into his eyes, I'm more taken aback than I was when I saw Zach for the first time – Kyle looks good. He looks really, really good. LA has treated him well. 'Kyle,' I say slowly, pretending to be surprised, 'hi.'

'Hi.' He leans in to give me a hug. 'This is odd.' As we embrace, I think, *There's nothing odd about this at all.* Kyle feels good. His body is so young, so solid, and so perfect that I don't want to let go. So I don't.

Shit. I've turned into my mother.

'What are you doing here?' Kyle asks, trying to pry himself away from me.

'I'm here to say goodbye to Zach,' I say, squeezing the living daylights out of him.

'You are?' Pulling away from me with all his might, Kyle

finally frees himself. He backs away. 'I didn't know you knew him.'

Nodding, I look over at the urn. 'Yeah, poor guy. He was so young.'

Kyle sighs. 'Yeah, I can't believe he's actually gone.'

'Me neither,' I say, shaking my head. 'And the accident ... what a horrible way to go.' Poor Zach Holden. Poor hot sexy Zach Holden.

'I told him not to go,' Kyle says. I look back at him. 'But did he listen? No.'

'Well, he never was a good listener,' I say quickly, like I know him.

'You got that right. The whole thing is so stupid, really.' Kyle rolls his eyes. 'I mean, it's stupid that he was even there. But that's Zach for you; always doing crazy things.'

'Yep ...' I say, even though I have absolutely no idea what he's talking about.

'He sure did go out in a blaze of glory though!'

Blaze of glory? What happened to Zach Holden? Poor hot sexy Zach Holden?

'Hallelujah, Zach,' Kyle whispers.

'Yeah,' I say softly, 'hallelujah, Zach ... you crazy son of a bitch, you.'

Giving me a funny look, Kyle cocks his head.

Oops. Perhaps I've overdone it.

'How did you know Zach?' he asks. His tone changes. He seems suspicious.

'Oh, well ...' Oh, well I never thought about this. Looking over at the pictures again, I try to think of something to say. 'We were ...' The word 'gym-buddies' comes to mind, but part of me wishes that Zach and I were more than that. 'Zach and I were . . .' Although I'd give anything to say 'lovers' right now, I have to keep in mind that I'm trying to get Kyle to like me, not hate me.

'You and Zach were what?' Kyle asks, pressing me to continue.

Looking over at him, I suddenly remember that guys his age are fueled by competition. I wonder what would happen if I did tell him Zach and I were lovers. Would he get jealous? Let's see.

'Zach and I were . . . *very close*,' I say warmly, suggesting we might've been romantically involved. Kyle's eyes widen; that's a good sign.

'Very close?' he asks. He seems surprised. 'In what way?'

'You know, I don't think this is the appropriate time or place to talk about it,' I say quietly, glancing around. 'I mean a memorial service is hardly a place to gush about your love life – oops!' I quickly cover my mouth with my hand, pretending I didn't mean for that to slip out.

'Love life?' Kyle shrieks. His face turns slightly white. Clearly I've struck a nerve; I just hope it's the competitive jealous one, not the hateful one.

'You know, Kyle, I didn't want to talk about this today,' I say softly, looking around. 'The only reason I came here tonight is because, because—'

'Because what?' Kyle interrupts. His voice is loud and sharp.

'Because I miss Zach.'

Kyle doesn't say anything. He simply looks me up and down while furrowing his brow. I think he's jealous. Yes, he's jealous! I bet right now at this very moment he's regretting leaving me high and dry in New York.

'How long ago were you and Zach . . .? I mean, how long ago did you and he . . . When was the last time you saw him?'

'Gosh . . .' I pretend to be thinking. 'It had to be just a few months ago.'

Kyle begins breathing heavily. Oh, he's jealous. He's so jealous!

Turning back to the pictures, I look at one of him and Kyle whitewater rafting and begin to ramble. 'Gosh, I remember a time when Zach and I went rafting and he refused to hold on. I kept saying, hold on, hold on, Zach! But did he listen? No. Of course he ended up falling over the side. He was such a daredevil.' After glancing over at another picture, I'm just about to tell Kyle about the time Zach's parachute almost didn't open when we went skydiving, when suddenly I hear a racket behind me. I turn around. Something comes flying at my head.

'Ouch!' I scream as it slams into my forehead. I hear people gasp.

Reaching up, I realize that I'm covered in a gritty substance. It's all over my face and in my hair. What in the hell just happened? Was there an earthquake? Did something fall from the ceiling and land on top of me? As I try to wipe my eyes clean, they sting and tear. Turning to where Kyle was standing, I open them as best I can and look at him. Although I can't be certain, I think he looks a little . . . angry.

'I knew it!' he screams at me. There's hatred in his voice. 'I knew it!'

Yep, he's angry. And I'm confused.

'You knew what?' I ask. 'Wait – did you throw something at me?'

'I knew he was cheating!' Kyle screams.

Cheating? Just as I'm about to ask Kyle what in the hell he's talking about, something dawns on me. Slowly turning back to the pictures, I look at them again more closely and realize that Kyle's in almost every one of them.

Oh my God.

Was Kyle dating—

'Zach!' he screams. 'That's who! Zach's nothing but a cheat!'

Oh my God, he was!

I cover my face in horror. Kyle's . . . gay?

After taking a moment to process this, I uncover my face and turn back around. Kyle's staring at me. The look on his face is so hateful. Suddenly a morbid thought crosses my mind . . . Kyle thought Zach was cheating on him with me. He threw something hard at my head. Now I'm covered in grit. Oh my God . . . could the grit possibly be . . . ashes?

Oh my God, it could be!

Completely losing all sense of reality, I begin jumping up and down wildly. 'Get it off me!' I scream hysterically. Grit flies out of my mouth as I do. 'Get it off me now!' Bending over, I violently shake my head from side to side. My arms are flailing in every direction. 'Please! Somebody! Help!' As I begin sobbing uncontrollably, tears gush from my eyes, washing them clean.

Suddenly someone grabs hold of me. It's a woman – the same woman who answered Kyle's door. 'Calm down,' she says, trying to shake me still. 'It'll wash off – calm down!'

'I can't calm down! I have death on me! Death!'

'Death?' She's confused. Suddenly she has a moment of realization and gasps. 'Oh no – you have it all wrong! It's not death. It's just dirt!'

Dirt? Wait, huh?

The woman bends down and picks up an empty ceramic planter and chunk of soil from the ground. As she hold them out to me, I slowly stop shaking.

'See?' she says. 'Kyle threw a plant at you.' After looking at the chunk of soil – roots are coming out one end, green foliage the other – I look over to where the urn was sitting and see that it's still there, in one piece. I let out a sigh of relief and then look back at Kyle. He's crying. Oh my God . . . I can't believe this. I can't believe what I've done.

'Kyle, I lied,' I quickly say. 'Zach and I were never lovers.' Kyle doesn't react. All he does is blink. More tears slide down his cheeks. 'Seriously,' I continue. 'I didn't even know him.'

'Why would you lie about something like that?' he asks, his voice cracking.

'I wanted to make you jealous. Obviously I didn't know you were dating him.'

'If you didn't know that I was dating him, then how would that make me jealous?'

'I thought you'd be jealous because *I* was with one of your friends, not jealous because your *boyfriend* was with one of your friends.' Kyle looks at me blankly. 'Kyle, I didn't know you were gay!' I blurt out. Hearing myself say it aloud suddenly makes it real. 'Wait, you're gay? When did you become gay?'

Kyle looks around the room self-consciously, prompting me to do so as well. Everyone's staring at us. Kyle looks back at me. 'Delilah, we should probably go talk.'

'Wait, is this *Delilah* Delilah?' the woman holding the ceramic planter asks Kyle. I turn to her.

'How do you know my name?' I ask. She looks to Kyle.

'Delilah, come on,' he says, motioning to the front door. 'Let's go outside.'

For the next hour I sit in my car eating a bag of Cheetos while Kyle explains himself. He says that he always knew he was gay but was afraid to admit it. He thought that if he ignored it, it would go away. He had girlfriends all through high school and college, and then I came along. He wanted to like me, he did, but told himself that if he didn't feel a connection when we were physically together, that he'd stop fighting it. The lack of chemistry between us that day at The Mercer wasn't just in my head, it wasn't just because I was nervous – he didn't feel anything for me either. Having admitted this, Kyle looks to me for a response, but I can't speak. I can't say anything because I'm in shock. I can't believe Kyle's gay. I eat a Cheeto and then give one to Eva.

Kyle tells me that the weekend he went to LA, he really did go for a wedding. Telling everyone in New York that he got a job in LA was just an easier way for him to explain why he moved so suddenly. He really just wanted to start fresh, start anew and start immediately. Having admitted this, Kyle once again looks to me for a response, but I can't speak. I can't say anything because I'm still in shock. I can't believe Kyle's gay. I eat another Cheeto and then give one to Eva.

The woman inside holding the planter is his sister. She knows all about Kyle's and my day of passion at the Mercer because he told her – and his whole family – when he came out of the closet. I'd like to ask if he left out the damp underwear when recounting the details of our hotel rendezvous to his entire family, but I can't speak. I can't say anything because I'm still in shock. I can't believe Kyle's gay. I eat another—

Oh, shit. I'm out of Cheetos.

For the next twenty minutes Kyle and I sit in my car in silence. While licking cheese off my fingers, I watch as Kyle samples the small bottles of liquor I took from the minibar at the Ritz. They were in the bag I opened this morning, the bag filled with clothes, the clothes that I hid under while spying on him. As Kyle holds each bottle up one by one, I watch in awe as he systematically reads the label, cracks the top, takes a swig, swishes it around in his mouth, swallows, replaces the cap and then moves on to the next. It's fascinating to me for some reason. After taking God knows how many swigs, Kyle suddenly bursts into laughter – uncontrollable laughter – that sends more tears down his cheeks.

'What's so funny?' I ask.

'I threw a plant at your head,' he says, wiping his face dry. 'And you thought it was an urn filled with ashes!' As he bursts into laughter yet again, I glare at him.

'Oh, come on,' Kyle says, off my look. 'You lied about sleeping with my dead boyfriend – it's funny.'

'No, it's not,' I snap. 'Nothing about this is funny.'

'Yes it is, Delilah. All of this is.'

'All of what is?'

'Life,' he says, looking around. 'Life is funny.'

Irritated, I look away from Kyle, away from the mirror, away from myself and stare out the window.

'I'm not mad at you, Delilah,' Kyle says after a bit. 'I don't care. In fact, I'm happy you got me out of that place.' I look over at him. The fact that he's trying to make me feel better on a day like today is just plain wrong.

'Kyle, I should go,' I say. And I should – I should go home. I should go back to New York. This was all a big mistake. I mean, what am I doing, really? Every re-meet has been more disastrous than the previous one.

'Okay,' Kyle says softly. 'I understand.' He reaches over and squeezes my hand. 'Do you have my phone number?'

'Yeah,' I say. I have your home number and your work number and your address – I have it all.

'Call me sometime, okay?' he says. 'Really, I mean it.'

'Yeah, okay,' I say, but I know I won't.

I drive down Interstate 10 heading back to my hotel in a daze. I'm not aware of the cars around me or that Eva's sitting on my lap licking cheese dust off my skirt. I suppose that out of twenty guys, this was bound to be the case for one of them, but Kyle? No way. Hearing the beep of my cell phone signaling I have a message, I pick it up and check my voicemail.

'Hey . . . it's me.' It's Colin. 'I have a couple of updates for you.' Even though I've decided to go home I sigh with relief; I need something to take my mind off all this.

'I found Oliver Leet and Shane Murphy,' he says. 'Oliver lives in London, Shane in Minneapolis. Both are single, but – I hate to break this to ya, babe – both are gay.'

Gay? GAY? Both of them? WHAT???????

Suddenly everything happens at once. Just as I drop the phone, my hand slips on the wheel and I veer into the dreaded left lane. As cars begin to honk, I begin to scream and then begin to smell something rotten. Looking down, I realize that Eva is pooping on me. Cars continue to honk and I continue to scream and Eva continues to poop, and I look in the rear-view mirror, begin to change lanes and then reach for a tissue. The next thing you know I'm veering back over to the right while picking up poop and rolling down the window. What happens next is like slow motion. With my hand out the window, I let go of the poop-filled tissue. After fluttering through the air like a bird for a few seconds, it smacks against the front windshield of a police car behind me. Instantly, his lights go on.

Oh. My. God.

I'm going down, there's no doubt about it.

After quickly pulling over, I sit in my car and watch the policeman get out of his. While doing so, I pray to Zach Holden to help me, poor Zach Holden, poor hot sexy Zach Holden. The policeman, a big guy with a buzz cut, looks like a real asshole. Sporting mirrored sunglasses and a tan uniform, much like the one Ponch wore on *CHiPs*, he walks over to his windshield. Pulling a pen out of his pocket, he pokes for a few seconds at the tissue, which exploded upon impact. To say the least, it's not a pretty sight. Eva's poop, which usually resembles a small brown Tootsie Roll, now looks like . . . well, it looks like any piece of poop would look after hitting a car going fifty miles per hour. It's splattered all over the place. Shaking his head in disgust, he walks toward my car. Although I can't see his eyes, I can tell he's angry. This is not good; this is not good at all.

'What in God's name do you call that?' he screams, pointing back to his car with the pen. Okay, he's not just angry – he's pissed. Sticking my head out the window, I look back toward his car and decide to play dumb.

'Well, I'm not sure,' I say coyly, 'but it looks like it could be . . . a piece of dog poop.'

The policeman gives me a look that says, 'No shit, Sherlock.' He's not buying my innocent act for one minute. 'Oh, it looks like it, huh?' he says. 'Well, what's it doing on my windshield?'

I try to think of something to say. 'Well, sir . . .' Catching a glimpse of my reflection in his mirrored sunglasses, I see the guilty look on my face. He saw me throw it; he knows I did it. Why am I even trying to lie about it? I sink into my seat. 'I'm sorry, but my dog pooped on me,' I confess, 'so I picked it up and threw it out the window without thinking because I didn't know what else to do.'

Reaching over, I grab Eva and hold her up like she's a piece of evidence. While doing so, I try to send subliminal messages to her, asking her to smile for him like she did for me when I got her. But she doesn't receive them, she doesn't pick up on it. After staring at the policeman blankly for a few seconds, all she does is fart. Hearing it, the policeman shakes his head in disgust. Suddenly I feel her stomach gurgle – I think someone ate too many Cheetos.

'I'm sorry, sir, please forgive me,' I beg, putting Eva

back down. 'It was just really smelly and I didn't want it in my car.'

'Oh yeah? Well, I didn't want it on my windshield!'

Changing his gaze from me to the floor of the front passenger seat, the policeman suddenly gets a funny look in his eye. When I turn to my right and see what he's looking at, my stomach drops as I spot a few empty small liquor bottles laying on the floor in plain view. Kyle . . . Fuck!

I turn back to the policeman. 'I can explain that,' I say, pointing. He shakes his head.

'Ma'am, I'm gonna need you to step out of the car.'

Chapter Fourteen

A Little Bit Sweet   **Sunday, 8 May**

I've been lying in bed at the Viceroy for two days, waiting for a giant earthquake to rock California, break off the little bit of beach that this hotel sits on, and send me surfing out to sea. It's bound to happen, with my luck. In addition to the $1,000 ticket I got for having an open container of alcohol in the car, I got a $500 ticket for littering, a $1,000 ticket for improper disposal of dog waste, a $150 ticket for improper lane usage, and a $150 ticket for speeding. Yes, speeding. Me. Apparently, as well as talking on the phone, learning that three of my exes are gay also helps me drive a little bit faster. I didn't just break fifty – I broke eighty. I got a ticket for going eight-one miles per hour.

Considering that the room costs four hundred dollars a night, I probably should've checked out and had my breakdown at a more affordable hotel. But after giving it some thought, I decided it was better to stay put. My thinking is this: if you're teetering on the edge of sanity, staying at a HoJo Inn by the airport will surely do you in. I mean, the only thing that's really keeping me sane right now is the thread count. Okay fine – the marijuana I bought from some kid by the pool is helping, too, as are the PlayStation video games the concierge gave me, and of course the sweet sounds of one Lionel Richie. The four of them together are like two sets of Wonder Twins powers, activating . . . in the form of . . . a very, very fucked-up tramp that's too comfortable, too entertained and too stoned to jump off the balcony.

I feel numb, and not just because of the pot. I'm in shock. I can't believe Kyle's gay. I can't believe Shane's gay. And I can't believe Oliver's gay. I take a hit of my joint and then cover Eva's face so she doesn't get a contact buzz.

Shane, #3, was a year older than me and my first college crush. I met him at an after-hours party at his fraternity house and dated him for one whole week. Everyone called him Cowboy Shaner because he was really into cowboy gear. He didn't grow up on a ranch or anything, so I'm not sure where the fascination came from, but he was always wearing cowboy hats and boleros. You know, stuff like that. If you told me back then that he would've turned out gay, I would've laughed in your face. Shane was a stud. I mean, gosh, he had this one pair of angora chaps that he wore everywhere. He was macho.

Thinking back now, Shane did say something once that might've been a sign he'd turn out gay, had I read it properly. He told me that he had a 'boy crush' on one of his frat brothers. Yes, a 'boy crush'. Do straight guys have boy crushes? I always thought they did, but perhaps I'm wrong.

As for Oliver, #8, I'll admit that I've always had a feeling that he might've been slightly gay, if that's possible. The main reason for this is because right before we broke up, he went to a wedding and—

Suddenly my phone rings. I look at the ID. It's Colin. I

don't feel like talking but by the time my brain sends the message to my hands to not pick up the phone, they already have. The T.H.C. in the P.O.T. is making me S.L.O. (I wonder what The R.O.D. would think of that?)

'Top of the morning to ya,' I say.

'Ehm . . . you know Irish people really don't say that, don't ya?'

'No? Bummer.' I feel let down.

'And you know it's the afternoon, don't ya?'

'Really? Bummer.' I feel let down again.

Colin senses something's wrong. 'Hey, you okay?'

'Depends what you mean by "okay".'

'Well, for starters your voice sounds a little hoarse.'

'Well, that's because I've been singing—' I break into Lionel Richie – 'All night long!'

'Oh my . . . '

'Hey, let me ask you something. Have you ever had a boy crush?'

'A boy crush? What the fuck is that?'

'A crush. On a guy. A boy crush.'

'Delilah, I'm not gay.'

'Yeah, I know that. I'm just wondering if straight guys ever have crushes on other guys.'

'Ahhh . . . that'd be a big fat no.'

'Hmpf. Interesting. Okay, let me ask you this then: would you know what brand of hose a woman is wearing just by looking?'

'Oh, I get it now,' Colin says knowingly. 'Which one had a boy crush?'

'The cowboy,' I confess.

'And which one was into hose?'

'The Brit. He cheated on me with a woman because he said he fancied her sparkly hose.'

I dated Oliver when I moved to Chicago, right when I started at the School of the Art Institute of Chicago. He was from London and had the greatest British accent. No matter what he said, he sounded smart. Gosh, how I loved listening to him talk. Sometimes, when he told me stories, I'd close my eyes and pretend like he was Huge Grant.* His sweet voice was music to my ears. And he was such a good dresser, too, so dapper and stylish. He always wore these adorable tailored pinstriped suits that looked like they came right off Savile Row. We had so much fun together, Oliver and I. We'd go shopping, go on garden walks. He was a great boyfriend. But then he cheated on me with a woman he met at a wedding.

'He didn't say he fancied her *legs* in her sparkly hose?' Colin asks.

'No. I remember his exact words. He said, and I quote, "Her Givenchy hose were scrumptious! I fancied them so much that I wanted to eat them right off her!"'

'He used the word scrumptious?'

'Yep.'

'And that wasn't a little weird to you?'

'No, just the fact that he knew the brand was.'

'If you didn't pick up on the word scrumptious being a sign, then something's telling me you probably let a few others go right over your head.'

---

* Nowadays I'd pretend he was Prince William. Actually, maybe Prince Harry. He seems like he'd be so much more fun to hang out with.

'I didn't, I swear. The hose was the only sign, I promise.'

'Okay, let me ask then . . . where'd you meet him?'

'The tanning spa.'

'Delilah . . .'

'No, no, it wasn't like that! He didn't go there to tan – he worked there.'

'Delilah!' Colin's voice is louder. 'You actually paid me to confirm this for you? You couldn't figure this out on your own?'

'Like I said, there were no other signs.'

'Oh yeah? What'd you do on your first date?'

'He invited me over for dinner and a movie.'

'What movie?'

'*Beaches*.'

'I rest my case.'

Since Colin seems to be reveling in the fact that he's a tad more perceptive than me, I decide to keep to myself that the date was on Super Bowl Sunday, that it was Oliver's second time seeing *Beaches*, and that we both went out and bought the Bette Midler soundtrack the very next day. 'Why are you calling me?' I ask grumpily. I don't want to talk any more.

Well, I have more news for you, and it might be kind of upsetting.'

'I'm pretty sure I can take it.'

'Okay, well,' Colin says, his voice taking on a more serious tone, 'I found Zubin Khan, and—'

'Oh, wait, let me guess – he's gay!' I say sarcastically.

'No, he's not gay,' Colin says slowly, cautiously. 'He's—'

'Oh wait, wait, I got it – he's in jail!'

'No, he's not in jail either. Listen, Delilah—'

'Well then he must be dead!'

Colin doesn't say anything.

'He's dead?' I ask slowly.

'Yeah, sorry,' Colin says delicately. 'But he went quickly, didn't feel a thing.' There's an awkward pause. 'Uh . . . were you close to him?' he asks.

'No, not really . . .'

Zubin Khan, #4, came right after Cowboy Shaner, which is kind of funny if you think about it because he was Indian. He was both my resident advisor and my anthropology tutor during my freshman year in college. My mom met him the weekend I moved in and wanted me to become friends with him because he was really smart, and she was hoping some of his brilliance would rub off on me. In a way, she got her wish – something of Zubin's did end up rubbing off on me all right. It just wasn't his brilliance.

And now he's dead. Wow . . . I'm speechless.

'So uh, that's it, I guess,' Colin says, after a bit. 'I'm done.'

I'm confused. 'What do you mean done?'

'Done, like I found all your guys.'

Found all my guys? All fifteen of them? He couldn't have. 'No you didn't, did you?'

'Yeah. Well, except for that Nukes guy, but I told you that wasn't gonna happen.'

I add up everyone in my head. Nate's in jail, Daniel's a priest, Shane's gay, Zubin's dead, Tim's a townie, Ian prefers sweatin' with the oldies, Henry's married, Oliver Leet's a little bit sweet, Nukes is not a nickname based on a last name, Tom's a townie, Foxy's in rehab, Dr Pepper's in space, Alex is married, Wade's a puppeteer – I mean *Muppeteer* – Rod sells beauty products, Abogado doesn't forgive and forget, Gordy's still grody, Kyle's gay, Greg's still an idiot and Roger likes to scratch and sniff.

Oh my God . . . that's twenty.

I can't believe it. I can't believe this is over.

I didn't expect it to end so abruptly. I'm in shock.

Suddenly I let out a little laugh. By God, Kyle is right.

'What's so funny?' Colin asks.

'Life,' I say. 'Just life.'

With that, I begin laughing hysterically. I laugh about Muppets and puppets, bitches and studs, macaroni and cheese, cowboys and Indians, Thumper and my bumper, and Nifty and her pimple. I laugh and laugh and laugh. I actually may die laughing.

'Del, are you okay?' Colin sounds concerned.

'Yes – I'll – be – fine,' I manage between guffaws, giggles, chuckles and chortles. 'Really – I'll – be – fine . . .'

$65, 11 days, 0 guys left.

Chapter Fifteen

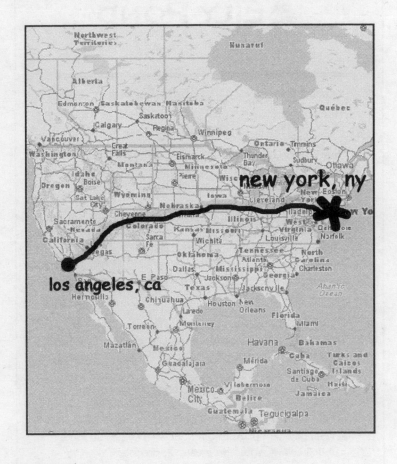

LILY POND

Substance Abuse Treatment Center
98543 Lily Street - Rockford, IL 61101

Monday, 9 May   BALANCE DUE: $5,324.54

Kitty Cannon
1632 Bluebird Drive
New Canaan, CT 06840

Dear Ms Cannon:

Delilah Darling checked into Lily Pond Substance Abuse Treatment Center on 26 April of this year for a horrible addiction to what she called 'the dolls'.

For reasons known to Ms Darling, we were unable to submit a claim to her insurance company for the five days of in-patient care she received. We've attempted to contact her to resolve this matter but keep reaching a woman who claims to speak only hebonics ... whatever that is.

Since you're listed as the emergency contact person on the back of her insurance card, which we copied, we're asking for your help in locating Ms Darling. We have several payment plans to offer her, so if she could kindly call us back, it would be greatly appreciated.

Yours truly,

Jan Moran (815) 555-HELP

Beep

Del, Michelle . . . I got it! I got the job at Vintage Vogue! I can't believe it – I'm so excited! Listen, I'm glad you're home safely and I'm not angry any more, so call me, okay?

Beep

Hey, Darlin' . . . it's Grandpa. Just got your message. Darnit! I can't believe I missed you! If I knew you were coming out, I would've rescheduled our trip.

Listen . . . sorry to whisper, but I gotta talk to you about something private. I feel silly asking, but I don't know who else to turn to — I'm thinking about waxing my chest and have a couple of questions. Can you call me? Love you. Bye.

Beep

Delilah, this is Patsy calling on your mother's behalf. She's a little fragile right now due to a letter she received – I'm sure you're aware of it. She wanted me to remind you that you have an appointment at Saks to have your dress tailored after the tasting today. I sure hope it fits. Daisy insisted on ordering you a size eight, even though both your mom and I told her to get you a twelve. Bye!

A Taste of Things to Come   Monday, 16 May

I'm still in bed, but I'm home. I tried to drop my car off in LA and fly back, but doing so would've cost me close to two thousand dollars, so I drove. I don't have two thousand dollars. I don't have anything, actually. I don't own my own company. I don't even have a job. I don't own a loft in TriBeCa. I can't even pay my rent. I don't have a husband or a family. I don't even have a boyfriend.

The only thing I have is a dog.

But she's a good dog, the best, in fact. On the way home from LA, I told Eva Gabor she was my best friend. We were somewhere in Oklahoma at the time, listening to 'Mandy' by Barry Manilow, the song that is rumored to have been written for someone's dog who died or something. As Barry came through my speakers, I wondered what I'd do if I didn't have her. By the time the song ended, tears were streaming down my face. I turned to Eva Gabor and told her how special she was, and she blinked, like she always does, and then smiled, which she hasn't done since the day I got her. That's when I told her the good news about being my best friend. To celebrate her new title, I sang a Cat Stevens song to her called 'I Love My Dog' and fed her string cheese. It made her constipated.

Singing Cat Stevens got me thinking about Nate again, which made me more depressed than I already was because he never called me back. I'm so pathetic. I can't even get a guy who was in jail to return a phone call.

I thought I was so clever in doing this. I thought I was getting around Daniel's advice to analyze each guy by tracking them all down, but I wasn't. In fact, I ended up doing just what he wanted me do, only in more depth. Rather than skimming the surface of each relationship while sitting at home, I dove in headfirst by finding them all. What was I thinking? Daniel thought doing this would bring me clarity, but it didn't. If anything, it's made me more confused and depressed than I was before I started. Depressed because every guy on my list was a mistake. I regret them all. Confused because there's no one reason why I ended up sleeping with each one, nor is there one reason why each relationship ended. How can I learn from my mistakes if I can't pinpoint what they are?

I haven't seen Michelle or Colin since I've been home. I called Michelle to congratulate her on her new job, and we talked for a second, but then she had to go. She's already started at Vintage Vogue and has been swamped. As for Colin, he's knocked on my door a couple of times and even called, but I didn't answer. I don't want to see him. I'm too embarrassed about everything. I shouldn't have hired him, a neighbor. What was I thinking?

When my mom got the Lily Pond letter last week (which I can't believe Jan sent – where does she get off doing that? I bet Carl put her up to it), she rushed over to his apartment in tears, sobbing, '*Cohlin*, what are we gonna do about our girl?' Apparently, Patsy advised her not to confront me, saying any undue stress might cause a relapse. Although I can't stand her, I'm actually happy for once she stuck her nose in my business. Colin said he was so caught off guard when my mom showed up that he panicked and blamed everything on Yoshi, my make-believe boyfriend, saying he got me into drugs.

'Couldn't you have told her it was a mistake?' I asked.

'I s'pose,' he said. 'But once I started tellin' her what a wanker Yoshi was, I got really into it and I told her I beat him up. Instead of complaining, you should thank me.'

'He was imaginary,' I pointed out.

'That's not important,' Colin said. 'What's important is that I defended your honor, which I will always do.'

Even though I was touched by Colin saying this, I was also irritated because now I don't have a make-believe boyfriend and I have to see my mom at the tasting today.

After climbing out of bed and taking a shower, I make my way to the closet and pull out a black jersey-knit wrap dress and black heels to wear. I'm in mourning. While getting dressed, I realize the dress is big on me. Aside from the Cheetos in LA, I didn't eat much while I was away and must've lost weight. In addition to Eva, at least one other good thing came out this trip.

The Waldorf-Astoria is an enormous hotel located just north of Grand Central Station on Park Avenue. After asking a bellman to point me in the right direction, I make my way through the elegant lobby to the wedding salon, where I find Daisy and Edward already waiting. Daisy, looking fabulous as always in a simple yellow dress, smiles big when she sees me and bigger when she sees Eva. I didn't want her to be angry about the 'Ave Maria' thing, so I dressed Eva up in a pink taffeta doggie brides-maid dress, doggie shoes that look like Mary Janes, a faux pearl necklace, and a rhinestone tiara to say I'm sorry.* Even though I can barely see her under the accessories, I can tell she's glaring at me, angry that I've pimped her out like this. When I telepathically tell her that the outfit was necessary, she perks up and showers Daisy with kisses.

'Heaven help me!' Daisy squeals, as she holds Eva up. 'I want one!' Turning to Edward, she bats her eyelashes at him. '*Pleeeeeze?*'

Instead of answering her, Edward turns to me, thin-lipped. 'Thanks, Delilah, thanks a lot.'

I tell Daisy a modified story of Eva (I got her in New York not Philly, one week ago not five weeks ago), and she curses the make-believe pet store I said I bought her from, and asks me to write down the address so she can yell at the ornery old lady who put her in the basement.

'I will later,' I say, suddenly hearing a breathy voice from behind me.

'Delilah . . . '

Oh no, it's my mom. Reluctantly I turn around and find her staring at me pathetically. Her hair is perfectly coiffed and colored, her head slightly lowered. Standing next to her is Patsy.

'Mom!' I exclaim, raising my voice an octave, trying to sound excited to see her. 'How are you?'

'Never mind me,' she says, patting down the wrinkles in my dress. '*You*. How are *you?*'

'I'm—'

'Come,' she says, not letting me finish, 'come to Mama.' My mom hugs me hard like she always does, squeezing

---

* The outfit was another one of life's little emergencies.

me so intensely that I can barely breathe. Although I try to pull away, I can't, so for the next minute, I find myself gasping for air as she silently rocks me back and forth. When she finally (thankfully) releases her hold on me, she whispers in my ear, 'You gotta feel it to heal it, Delilah!' Although I have no idea what she's talking about, the fact that Patsy gives my mom a thumbs-up when she says this makes me think it's some kind of rehab saying.

After turning around to say hello to Daisy, my mom jumps back when she sees Eva in her arms. 'Oh my!' she says, clearly startled. 'Who's this?'

'Delilah got a dog!' Daisy cheerfully explains. Holding Eva up, she introduces the two of them. 'Mom, say hello to Eva, and Eva, say hello to Grandma.'

'Grandma?' The look on my mother's face instantly changes. 'I'd prefer it if she'd call me Lola.'

'Lola?' Daisy asks, confused.

'Yes, it means *grandma* in Tagalog, a language they speak in the Philippines.'

Daisy and I exchange odd glances. 'Um . . . that's great, Mom,' Daisy says, turning back to her. 'But we're not Filipino.'

'And *we're* not a grandma yet either,' my mom snaps, clearly annoyed she's been called one, 'so watch your mouth!' As Saul, the wedding coordinator, suddenly enters the room the smile on her face instantly reappears. 'Saul!' she booms, turning to him. 'It's so good to see you!'

'Oh, you too, Ms Kitty!' he screeches, taking hold of her hands. As the two of them exchange air kisses, Daisy elbows me.

'Lola?' she mouths.

Having no explanation, I simply shrug.

After greeting everyone else with the same fanfare, Saul freezes when he sees Eva. 'Oh no . . .' he says to Daisy, who's still holding her. 'We don't allow dogs in the kitchen, which is where the tasting takes place. It's a health code violation.'

A health code violation? *Oops*. I didn't think of this.

Although Saul offers to put Eva in his office, I tell him it's not a good idea (she has a history of chewing corners off end tables and desks) and instead offer to run her home. We're still waiting for Edward's mother to arrive and it shouldn't take me long.

'No, no, that's nonsense,' my mom says, pulling out her cell phone. 'Call Michelle and see if she'll come pick her up.'

'I would, but she's working,' I explain. 'There's no way she'll be able to come. She's been so busy.'

'How about *Cohlin*?' she then asks.

'I don't have his number,' I lie.

'Where did Michelle get a job?' Daisy asks, interrupting us. I begin telling Daisy about Vintage Vogue when, out of the corner of my eye, I see my mother hold her cell phone to her ear. Thinking nothing of it, I continue talking until I hear my mom say, '*Cohlin*? Is that you?' I whip back around.

'Mom!' I yell, trying to grab the phone from her. 'Give me that!'

After waving me away, my mom puts a finger in her free ear to drown out my yelling. As she walks away, I begin to feel sick to my stomach. I don't want to see Colin. Damn it!

While I wait in agony for my mother's return, praying she'll tell me he's too busy to come, Edward's mom, Ruth, arrives. Since she was recuperating from a face-lift at the time of the engagement party, she didn't attend, so neither my mom nor I have met her. After introducing myself and saying hello, my mom returns.

'*Cohlin*'s on his way,' she says with a smile. She then turns to Ruth. After admiring her flawless, tawny skin, she attempts a joke. 'I thought Edward said his *mother* was coming . . . not his *sister*!' My mom smiles and Ruth laughs, and just like that the two of them are buddy-buddy.

'Since we have to wait for *Cohlin*,' Saul says, getting everyone's attention, 'why don't I take you all on a quick tour of the hotel and show you the Starlight Roof?'

'Well, *matzoh tov* to that!' my mom proudly exclaims. Even though she's butchered the word *mazel*, Daisy, Edward and Ruth all smile at one another, happy she's at least trying. As they file in behind Saul, excited for the tour, my mom lingers back for a bit. Once she's sure everyone's out of an earshot, she turns to me.

'Delilah, quick!' she says frantically, undoing the top three buttons on her blouse. She gestures to her necklace. 'Do you think it's too big?' Looking down, my eyes widen when I see what is quite possibly the largest diamond-crusted gold crucifix I've ever seen.

'Not if you can beatbox,' I joke.

She swats my arm. 'Be serious!'

'It's fine, Mother,' I say, rolling my eyes, 'just fine.'

For the next twenty minutes or so, with every silk curtain and allegory mural I pass, I worry about seeing

Colin. Even though he doesn't know the reason behind it, I'm still embarrassed that he knows what I've done. Also, a part of me is afraid that what happened with Kyle and e-mail will happen with Colin and the phone, minus the romance part, of course. After I left Lily Pond, he called me every few hours while I drove to LA to make sure I got there safely. He did the same thing while I drove back to New York, too. We've talked on the phone a lot, particularly in the last two weeks, and I'm afraid that things will be awkward when we see each other. We know each other but don't really know each other. I consider him my friend, but he's not really.

Thankfully, watching my mom try to impress Ruth takes my mind off things. Every time I feel weak in the knees, she says something that makes me laugh. For example, when Saul explains to us that a large mosaic floor in the lobby is made of 148,000 tile pieces, she exclaims, '*Soy vay!*' After that, she proceeds to describe our grandpa to Ruth as a man with a lot of *shitspah*. The only word she actually gets right is when, after I jokingly ask why she isn't speaking Tagalog, she quietly tells me to stop being such a *schmuck*.

The Starlight Roof is located on the eighteenth floor in a separate, more exclusive part of the hotel made up of suites and apartments called the Waldorf Towers. When we walk inside the exquisite art deco ballroom, we collectively gasp – it's breathtaking. Cream-colored silk damask curtains cascade down a wall of floor-to-ceiling windows that overlook Park Avenue. Austrian crystal chandeliers hang from either end of a gilt-trimmed ceiling, a ceiling that at one time opened to the stars.

'It doesn't open any more,' Saul says, as everyone looks up, 'but you'd never know it.' As he flips a switch on the wall, thousands of tiny blinking lights turn on, illuminating the ceiling. As they twinkle high above our heads, they resemble stars. When I look over at Daisy and Edward and see them gazing up at this man-made moonlight, I become melancholy. They look so happy. This is all so perfect.

After taking the elevator down to the lobby, everyone walks back to the wedding salon. In the distance, I see Colin standing by the door, wearing a thin navy-blue T-shirt, a beat-up pair of old Levi's, and Converse sneakers. '*Cohlin!*' my mother exclaims when she's sees him. 'Thank you, thank you, thank you for coming!' We all arrive to where he's standing.

'Ah, 'twasn't a problem,' he says, smiling. He then looks at me. I instantly blush.

Shit! I forgot how cute he was. Hoping he didn't see, I quickly look away.

'Mom, it's *Cahlin*,' I say, turning to her.

'Oh, I know. *Cohlin*'s just my little pet name for him.'

As my mom winks at Colin, I look up and shake my head in embarrassment. *Why, God? Just why?*

After quickly saying hello to everyone, Colin looks down at Eva, who's half in and half out of her bag. 'This must be the Hungarian import,' he says, crouching down. When he sees her outfit, a puzzled look comes over his face. 'What's she wearing?'

'A bridesmaid dress,' I say.

'And shoes,' Daisy adds.

'And a necklace,' Edward adds.

'And a tiara,' Saul adds.

Colin looks at me pathetically.

'I got kinda carried away,' I mumble.

Saul claps loudly. 'Come on, everyone! We need to get moving!' As everyone files out of the salon, he turns to me. 'Delilah, we'll be waiting for you by the elevators.' I nod.

With everyone gone, Colin and I are alone. Afraid I might blush again, I quickly hand Eva over without making eye contact with him. 'Sorry it's so girly-looking,' I say, apologizing for the pink and green argyle. 'Do you wanna just take her home and I can pick her up later?'

Instead of answering, Colin moves his head up, down and around, trying to make eye contact, and I move my head up, down and around, trying to avoid it. It's like a game of keep-away. After a few seconds, I end up losing.

'That's better,' Colin says when our eyes meet. He then smiles. And I then blush again.

Damn it.

'Actually, I've got some things to do,' he continues. 'So how 'bout I meet you back here in a couple hours instead?'

I nod. 'Sounds good.' After saying goodbye, I join the rest of the group by the elevators.

Like the rest of the hotel, the kitchen is enormous, which thrills my mother beyond belief. Seeing ovens large enough to bake racks of meat and fryers large enough to cook crates of vegetables gets her so worked up that she needs a drink to settle down. Lucky for her, the wine flows freely when we finally sit, and everyone joins her in drinking excessively except Daisy and me. I feel some-what sick. I must still be nervous.

For the next two hours, everyone helps Daisy and Edward not only decide the menu but also pick out the china, crystal and linens that will be used on their big day. We all eat like kings and queens as servers bring trays of food – trays filled with lobster, steak, chicken, and foie gras; with mushrooms, potatoes, onions and asparagus; and with yellow cake, white cake, chocolate cake and red devil cake. Everything is so delicious that we have a problem deciding what to have. By the time the tasting is over, so many bars have been added to the big day – from martini bars to oyster bars to ceviche bars to coffee bars – that I lose track.

Before leaving, while waiting for Saul to go over an official list of things with Daisy and Edward, Ruth asks me if *Cohlin* is my boyfriend. Hearing this question makes my mother sink in her seat. Seeing as though I'm single again because my make-believe ex-boyfriend was a drug addict, she's not sure what to say. Usually she'd tell whoever's asking that I work too much, but since I currently don't have a job, she can't do that.

'No, we're just friends,' I say. 'Actually, not even friends – we're neighbors.'

'Oh, I see,' Ruth says. 'Do you have a boyfriend?'

'Delilah doesn't have much luck in the men depart-ment,' Patsy pipes in, deciding to answer for me. Ruth turns to her.

'Oh no? And why's that?'

'Because either she dates losers or she doesn't date at all!' Patsy laughs after she says this, like she's joking, but both she and I know she believes every word she said.

'For your information, Patsy,' I say, sitting high in my chair, 'I don't need a man.' While I try to convince myself that I believe this, I glance over at my mother. She seems horrified by my comments. I mean, what kind of woman doesn't need a man? A lesbian, that's what kind.

Just then, thankfully, Saul, Daisy and Edward return with the paperwork. After announcing it's time to leave for my fitting at Saks, I quickly say goodbye to everyone and race toward the elevator bank, hoping to get a car by myself. I want to get out of here. After pressing the button, I wait for a car.

And wait.

And wait.

A few minutes later, an elevator finally arrives. Just as I step inside, the rest of the group turns the corner and Edward asks me to hold the doors. Reluctantly I do. As we all ride back to the lobby together, I can't help but notice that my mother is staring at me. She looks like she's biting her tongue. She's had one too many glasses of wine and I can tell she's dying to say something to me. Looking away, I ignore her.

While walking toward the wedding salon, I feel relieved when I see Colin waiting in the distance and pick up my pace. When Eva spots me and sticks her head out of her bag, I notice that she's not wearing any of her clothes. Then I notice something else. Then I notice . . . bangs.

Arriving to where Colin is standing, I pull Eva out of her bag and am horrified at what I see: all her hair's been cut off, including her handlebar mustache and topknot. As the rest of the group approaches, I hear a collective gasp from behind me.

'What did you do to her?' I shriek, looking up at Colin.

'I got her a proper haircut,' he replies innocently. He's smiling from ear to ear, thinking he's done a nice thing.

'And what would possess you to do that?'

Sensing my unhappiness, Colin's smile slowly disappears. 'Well, uh . . . it's warm outside today . . . and you had her stuffed in this bag all dressed up like a—'

'Baby,' Patsy blurts out from behind me.

Turning around, I shoot her a dirty look.

'Well sorry, but it's true,' she says in defense. 'That's why a single woman your age gets a puppy, to satisfy your ticking biological clock.'

'That's not why I got her.'

'Oh, please,' Patsy says, rolling her eyes. 'Clothes aside, look at that bag – you might as well get her a stroller.'

Looking over at Daisy and Edward, I see that they're laughing. Ruth is laughing, too. The only person who seems as horrified as me is my mother, but she's not looking at Eva. She's looking at me. She's biting her tongue still, too. After sending Patsy a subliminal message to BURN IN HELL, I turn back around to Colin.

'I'm sorry, Del,' he says, 'but she looked hot, so I took her to get a haircut.'

'Where? Supercuts?'

'No, someplace down the street,' he says, not picking up on the fact that I was being sarcastic. He looks down at Eva. 'What, don't you like it? I think she looks cute.'

'She doesn't look cute,' I say, shaking my head, 'she looks like a, a—'

'Lesbian!' my mom suddenly screams.

A lesbian? *Lovely, just lovely.* Ever so slowly, I turn around and look at her. Although she still looks upset, she seems somewhat relieved to have gotten that out.

'Mom, she's *not* a lesbian,' I say slowly.

'Well, then, I don't understand – why is she still single?'

'Maybe she *wants* to be single – have you ever thought about that?'

'Nobody *wants* to be single, not for ever, not for as long as she has.'

'Well, then, maybe she can't figure out what the reason is, and maybe your harping and worrying only makes things worse.'

'I only harp and worry because I care,' my mom says, her voice softening. 'I don't like seeing her lonely.'

'She's not lonely,' I reply, my voice softening as well.

'Yes, she is.'

I hold my mom's gaze for a few seconds and then look away. As I turn back to Colin and Eva, I catch a glimpse of Daisy, Edward, Ruth and Patsy, all looking very confused. Taking Eva's bag from Colin, I turn and walk toward the front door. As I do, I hear Daisy mumble: 'All that about a dog?'

Sizing Up

A minute later, I'm walking down the street holding my dog, which looks like a Chihuahua – which is what I was going to say. Colin trots next to me, apologizing for the one hundredth time. The thing is, I'm not mad about the buzz cut any more. Eva is cute no matter what her hair

299

looks like. I'm just frustrated about everything. I feel aimless, useless. What am I doing with my life? Moreover, what is Colin doing and why is he following me?

Once I get to Saks, a wedding associate hands me my dress, shows me to a fitting room, and tells me she'll be back. The dress, a strapless Vera Wang design, is simple and elegant. As I get undressed to slip it on, my cell phone beeps, signaling a message. I stop what I'm doing to listen. 'Hi Del, it's Mom . . .'

Oh, great. I can hardly wait to hear this.

'I'm sorry about my outburst at the hotel,' she says. 'I guess I'm just looking for an excuse because I don't understand why you haven't met anyone yet, and I don't like seeing you alone. Honey, I worry about you because I think you're too much like your grandpa when it comes to love. It's not like it is in the movies. There is no boom. You're being unrealistic and waiting for a perfect guy to come along, a perfect guy that doesn't exist. You keep getting caught up in things that are larger than life – ideas, men – things that sweep you off your feet. But easy come, easy go. I'm not telling you to settle, but you need to *settle down.* In life, in love. Quit making things so difficult for yourself. Quit fighting everything in your life, Delilah, from imperfect men to my hugs. If you relax and give in, you'll find that it's much easier to breathe.'

When my mom's message ends, I click my phone shut, sit down and think about what she said. Maybe I do make life more difficult than it needs to be. Maybe I am holding out for a perfect man; maybe that's my problem. Twenty men – it's like I wasn't too picky in having slept with them all, but I was too picky in eliminating them all from being the one, you know? I realize I didn't walk out on every relationship, but I did walk out on a lot of them. Either way, I didn't care enough to try and make things work with any of them.

Damn it! I'm more confused now than I was before I left.

I stand back up and slip the dress over my head. When I look in the mirror, I'm relieved at what I see – the dress is beautiful. Daisy got it right, all of it – the color, the style, everything – it's perfect. The back resembles a corset and both zips and laces closed. Although I try, I can't reach to fasten it, so I peek my head outside the door and look for the bridal associate.

'She ran out for a minute,' Colin says when he sees me. He's sitting on a chair outside the fitting room, holding Eva on his lap. 'Do you need help with something?'

'I need to be zipped and laced,' I say quietly.

'I can do it,' he offers.

Hesitating for a moment, I glance down at Eva. Colin's dressed her back up in her dress and tiara, no doubt trying to make up for the bad haircut. Oh my God. He's such a nice guy. Why am I such a bitch? I look back up.

'Okay,' I say, and then I let him in the fitting room.

After putting Eva down on a chair, Colin walks over to where I'm standing on a little pedestal in front of the mirror. Standing behind me, he slowly pulls up the zipper and then begins to tighten the laces, one row at a time. As he does, I can't help but feel nervous – I feel so exposed. When he finally finishes, he ties a bow at the top and then gently moves his hands up across the top of my back, resting them on my bare shoulders.

301

'Why've you been avoiding me?' he asks, as our eyes meet in the mirror. I feel a flash of heat in my face.

'I haven't been avoiding you.'

Colin raises a brow. 'Yes, you have.'

'No, really, I haven't.'

Taking me by the shoulders, Colin turns me around so that the two of us are face to face. Standing on the pedestal, I'm almost as tall as he is. 'Yes, you have,' he repeats slowly. 'You've been avoiding me and I wanna know why.'

Looking at him closely, I don't say anything right away and instead study his face. In addition to his big brown eyes and chiseled jaw, he has thick, almost unruly eyebrows and a slight five o'clock shadow. He's so perfect yet so messy. He's clearly not vain.

'Come on,' he says again. 'Tell me.'

I look down. Although I want to stay strong, his good looks make me weak in the knees. 'I don't know,' I say, instantly letting my guard down. 'I'm embarrassed, I guess.'

'Why? Because three of your ex-boyfriends are gay?'

'No,' I say shaking my head, 'it's more than that.'

Colin lets out a sigh. 'Del, why won't you tell me what you were doing? Maybe I can help.'

Looking back at him, I don't say anything.

'How 'bout if I tell you something embarrassing about myself?' he offers. 'Will that make it easier?'

'Depends what it is,' I say. 'It has to be *big* embarrassing.'

'I can do that.'

I think about it for a bit. 'Okay,' I say eventually, giving in. 'If you tell me something embarrassing, then I'll tell you.'

'Deal.' Colin's face turns serious as he gets ready to fess

up. 'Okay, I've never told anyone this, but . . .' He pauses, obviously nervous. 'I can play the button accordion,' he blurts out. 'I can. My mom made me take lessons when I was a little boy, and I can still play to this day.' Looking down, Colin shakes his head, pretending to be beside himself with embarrassment having admitted this. I hit him in the arm.

'Colin, be serious!'

He looks up, laughing. 'I'm sorry,' he says, 'really. It's just that, after the whole your-dog-is-a-lesbian conversation at the hotel, you've been so tense and I wanted to loosen you up.'

'I'm fine,' I say, even though I'm irritated. 'Now, come on. Be serious.'

'Okay, fine. I will. Sorry, no more jokes, I promise.' The look on Colin's face turns serious once again. 'Truthfully . . .' he then says slowly, 'I fucked up my soap opera audition. I screwed it up really badly, and it was horrible, the most embarrassing thing ever.' By the look on his face, I know he's telling the truth.

'How so?' I ask.

'I don't know.' He shrugs. 'I don't know what happened. I'm usually pretty confident, but for some reason when I got to the studio where the audition was, I started sizing myself up compared to the other actors in the waiting room. We were all up for the same part. I don't know why, but I started thinking, *That guy's taller than me* and, *That guy's better looking.* I started obsessing over stupid shit. Pretty soon I was questioning my acting ability, and by the time I got into the room with the producers, my confidence was shot. I forgot all my lines. I kept tripping over my words. They were smirking; it was horrible. I totally blew it.' Colin looks down. He looks genuinely disappointed and embarrassed. I feel bad for him.

'I'm sure it wasn't as bad as you think it was,' I say, trying to make him feel better. 'You're probably just being hard on yourself.'

He lets out a little laugh. 'Trust me – it was horrible.'

'Well, there'll be more auditions, right?'

'Yeah, but the reason I'm so upset about this is that, after I left, I started rethinking what I'm doing with my life. I started thinking that maybe my father is right, maybe I do need to have a back-up plan. This is the first time I've ever really doubted myself.'

Putting my hand on his shoulder, I speak honestly. 'Listen, Colin, I know I was excited when you told me about this audition, but the more I think about it now . . . do you really want to be on a soap opera anyway? I mean, I know it's a big deal and all, but—'

'No,' Colin says quickly, interrupting, 'I don't wanna be on a soap opera. I never have. When I got the call, I was kind of excited because there's something appealing about a steady job and paycheck, but I didn't really wanna do it. Do you know what I mean?'

I nod. 'Security is attractive.'

'I'm not saying I'm too good for a soap opera,' Colin continues, 'but there's other stuff I want to do, other stuff that pushes me and excites me, and this role didn't do that.'

'So don't let something that you never wanted make you feel like a failure,' I say. 'It happened for a reason.'

'Yeah, yeah . . .' Colin shrugs. 'That's easy to say, harder to do.'

'Do you have anything else on the horizon?'

Colin's eyes light up. 'Well, yeah, I met with a director about a role in an independent film he's trying to get funding for. It's an amazing script – it's like a modern-day Irish gangsta thug movie.'

'Irish gangsters?' I give Colin a funny look. 'Is there such a thing?'

'Absolutely,' he says, trying to act tough. We both laugh.

After we both compose ourselves, Colin moves my hand off his shoulder and holds it. 'Okay,' he says, looking me in the eye, 'I shared; now it's your turn. Why were you tracking down old boyfriends?'

Damn it. I don't want to tell him, but I said I would. With that, after taking a deep breath, I begin taking. 'Well, about seven months ago, I read a survey . . .'

For the next ten minutes or so, I tell Colin the truth. I tell him about Roger and Daniel, about Daisy and my mom – I tell him everything. He never laughs, smirks or rolls his eyes. He simply listens intently and nods.

'You think I'm crazy, don't you?' I ask when I finish telling him the whole story.

'No, I don't think you're crazy,' he says kindly. 'But I do think you're making a big deal out of something that's not.'

'Maybe for a guy this isn't a big deal, but for a woman it is.'

Colin shakes his head. 'Del, if you're eighteen years old and you've had sex with twenty guys, then yeah, sure, I can understand freaking about it, but not when you're our age. Also, you can't compare yourself to an average, or anyone else for that matter, without taking into consideration the quality of the relationship you've had with each guy.'

I laugh. 'Okay, Sally Jesse.'

'Hey, you wanted me to be serious and I am,' Colin says. 'Listen, I guarantee there's a woman out there somewhere who's had sex with ten men – half the number you had – yet never knew any of them for more than an hour, never got any of their phone numbers afterward, and never saw any of them again. On paper, her number would be lower than yours, but she's definitely a little more . . .' Colin searches for the right word.

'Trampy?' I propose.

'No, forget I even said that,' Colin says, waving off my suggestion. 'Labels aside, the bottom line is that how many people we've all slept with isn't a big deal.'

'Oh, right,' I say, rolling my eyes, 'like you wouldn't care if your girlfriend slept with twenty guys before you?'

'I wouldn't care because I'd never ask. Whether her number is twenty or one, how would me knowing that affect our relationship? Would it make me laugh harder at her jokes? Would it make us get along better? No. That has no bearing on a real relationship whatsoever. I mean, the fact that a woman is a prude might be exciting for a second – a chase is always fun – but it's more of a novelty, a wrapper, than anything else. Once you get into a relationship, it's the meat and potatoes that count, not the package it came in.'

I struggle with this. I want to agree with him. I want to believe that this is not a big deal, but I can't. 'I see your point, but it's still hard for me to let this go and pretend it doesn't matter. Sex aside, something must be wrong with me if I can't seal the deal. I've had twenty intimate relationships, twenty opportunities. And many more that weren't intimate. What's wrong with me?'

'Nothing's wrong with you. You just haven't met the right person yet.' Suddenly a knowing smile comes over Colin's face. 'You know what you're doing?' he asks, smiling. 'You're doing the same thing I did in that waiting room during the audition. You're sizing yourself up against your competition, the other women out there, and second-guessing yourself.'

'Yeah, you're right, but like you said, I can't help it.'

The two of us sit in silence for a bit.

'You know, to make all this worse, having gone back, I now feel like a bigger screw-up than before I started. I've dated nothing but losers. I have poor judgment.'

Colin lets out a little laugh. 'You're brave.'

'How so?'

'You wouldn't catch me revisiting the ghosts of girl-friends past.'

I smile. 'Oh, and why's that?'

'They just uh . . . well,' he stutters, 'some of them might not be too excited to see me.'

I give him a look. I know his type. 'You're a heart-breaker, aren't you?' I ask.

'No,' Colin says, defending himself. 'I just don't fall in love very easily.'

I nod. 'Yep, you're a heartbreaker.' As Colin laughs, I suddenly realize that I'm completely comfortable with him. I don't get the same awkward feeling I got with Kyle. Granted we haven't been having sex in this fitting room, but still. 'You know,' I tell him, 'I was worried about seeing you today.'

Colin looks at me funny. 'Worried? Why?'

'I thought it would be weird after talking so much on the phone, because we know each other but don't really know each other, you know? I mean, we haven't spent time together or anything.'

'Well,' he says, 'what's the verdict? Weird or not?'

'Not,' I say, smiling. 'How about for you?'

'All's good,' he says, winking. 'But, you know what? To make sure things don't become weird we should look at each other without talking, to make up for the times we talked on the phone without looking.'

I laugh. 'That'll take hours.'

'Well, I have all night. How about you?'

'Not only do I have all night, but I have all day tomorrow and the next day and the next day. I have no job, no life – I don't have anything. Except a dog.'

'Well, then let's get going.' Taking me by the shoulder once again, Colin turns me back around. The two of us then look in the mirror at my scarlet dress.

'I feel like Hester Prynne, standing up here in this dress,' I joke. 'I feel like there should be a big letter *A* on my chest or something. Or at least a *T* for *tramp*.'

'Nah,' Colin says softly. He slides his hands down the sides of my arms, giving me goose bumps. They land at my waist. 'There should be a tiara on your head because you look like a princess.' Suddenly remembering Eva's wearing one, Colin reaches over, plucks it from her head and puts it on mine. I laugh when he does. 'This is some dress, my dear,' he then says, gazing at it in the mirror. 'This is some dress.'

20 Times a Lady

After walking back to the Waldorf, Colin drives us to the apartment on his beat-up Vespa. As per my request, he doesn't go faster than fifteen miles per hour because Eva is pressed between the two of us in her bag and I don't think it's safe. By the time we get home, we both look wild and crazy from the ride. It's unusually humid outside, too humid for May. The air is getting thick. I think it might rain.

After I change into jeans and a T-shirt, I go over to Colin's. Neither of us have our air conditioners in yet and his apartment is slightly cooler than mine. For the remainder of the afternoon, the two of us hang out and do silly things. We draw caricatures of each other, watch his one appearance on *Law & Order* (he had one line and did a really good job), and have staring contests to balance out the phone calls. (He wins each time because I keep bursting into laughter.) After he calls the Jimmys to ask if they can help make my five tickets disappear (they can – kick ass), the two of us then watch Eva explore Colin's apartment. It's amazing the way she works the perimeter of a room, eating dust. She's like a Roomba.* Seriously, throw away your brooms, donate your vacuum cleaners, and fire the maid. All you need to keep a clean house is a Yorkie.

---

* One of those robotic vacuums that cleans the floor while you sit on the couch and do nothing.

As night falls, the air gets thicker, and although Colin's apartment is stuffy, it's nice to hear the hustle and bustle of New York City – the traffic, the people – instead of a buzzing air conditioner. For dinner we order in Korean food and, afterward, lay on the couch in the dark – each of us at an end – split a bottle of wine, and tell stories. I tell Colin about rehab, the twins, Muppets and puppets, and he tells me more about Dublin, acting and his family.

'No, no, no,' I say, as he's telling me. 'I want to know more about the ghosts of girlfriends past. I wanna hear some dirt.'

'Noooooo,' Colin says, laughing. 'Absolutely not.'

'Okay, then how about the ghosts of girlfriends present?'

'I don't have any girlfriends present.'

I roll my eyes. 'Oh, give me a break. Your cell phone's been ringing nonstop since Saks.' Just as I say this, the light of his cell phone glows yet again, signaling a call. Grinning, we both reach for it at the same time – I get it first. While flipping through the calls he's recently received, I read the names aloud. 'Britney, Lacy, Mark, Amy, Chrissy, Alison.' I put the phone down. 'That's five women in the last few hours!'

'Those women are not my girlfriends,' Colin says defensively.

'Do they know that?'

'Of course they do!' he exclaims. 'Listen, I'm no angel, but I'm no pig either. I don't sleep with multiple women at the same time and I've never treated a woman with anything but respect.'

'So you don't have a girlfriend, then?' I ask, doubting him.

Colin shakes his head. 'Nope. I have a friend who's a girl, but she's not my girlfriend, and it's basically over.'

'Why's it over?' I ask curiously.

Colin shrugs. 'It just wasn't there.'

'What's *it*? What are you looking for?'

'I don't have a list or anything. I just haven't met that person that I want to hold a boom box up for yet.'

Boom box . . . 'You mean like Lloyd Dobler? *Say Anything* . . .?'

Colin nods, smiling, thinking of it. 'Yep.'

'Great movie . . . '

'The best.'

In *Say Anything* . . . John Cusack plays Lloyd Dobler, a quirky guy who falls head over heels in love with a girl named Diane. When Diane breaks up with him, he's so determined to get her back that he goes to her house and stands outside her window holding up a boom box blasting the song 'In Your Eyes' by Peter Gabriel. He's not just heartbroken. He's positive that they're meant to be together, so he goes back for her.

'You know that excuse . . . it's not you, it's me?' Colin asks.

I nod. I've used it and I've had it used on me.

'I say that a lot,' he continues, 'when I break up with someone, but I don't really mean it when I do. I'm not the reason my relationships end but neither are the women. It's not me and it's not them – it's that we never had a *we*. There was no *us*. It's hard to say what makes two people have that, because it's something you can't put into words. It's a feeling. I know it's only a movie, but I want the feeling that Lloyd had, that no matter what, he had to do everything in his power to get Diane back.'

'My grandpa calls that the boom,' I tell him. 'He says it's different from love or lust; it's deeper. It's a feeling that hits you hard when you have a real connection with someone.'

'Exactly,' Colin says.

Remembering my mom's message, I can't help but wonder if thinking like this is crazy.

'Colin, do you ever think you're being an idealist?' I ask. 'Do you ever wonder if you're holding out for something that doesn't exist? I'm not being pessimistic, and although I'd like to believe that a *boom* or *we* or *us* exists, I'm not sure I do any more.' I mean, maybe my mom's right. Maybe I've been holding out for something that's unrealistic.

'Of course it exists,' Colin says ardently. 'But like I told you, it takes some of us longer to find it than others.'

As the two of us sit in silence, I think about Lloyd Dobler some more and then something suddenly dawns on me. I went looking for twenty guys, not one of which ever came looking for me. I can make fun of them all I want, like Wade or the twins, but the truth is that when I left, none of them called me or wrote me – let alone held up a boom box. No one really cared.

'What are you thinking about?' Colin asks after a bit.

'Nothing,' I say quietly. Then I look at him and smile. 'Who would've thought such a sweet-talking ladies' man like yourself would be such a romantic?' Colin throws a pillow at me.

As we sit in the dark and stare some more, Colin smokes a cigarette, which he says he normally doesn't do. Usually I think smoking is gross, but there's something sexy about Colin doing it tonight. Maybe it's the way the orange embers light up his face as he takes a drag or the way the smoke hangs in the air, illuminated by the streetlight coming in through the window. I don't know. It's just such a sexy New York moment, something you might see in a magazine or in a movie, or, if you're lucky, in person. It's the heat, the smoke, the noise, the wine, the dog, the tins of half-eaten food lying on the table, the hula hoop in the corner, and the grittiness that makes this city so fabulous. I like Colin. I don't know why I felt nervous about seeing him. For being so good-looking, he's surprisingly unpretentious. He puts me at ease.

'Tell me about your accordion.' I ask when he finishes his cigarette.

'Okay, I will,' he says, 'but you gotta come lie right here next to me while I do because I don't want to talk about it loudly. I don't want anyone to hear.'

Laughing, I get up and walk over to his side of the couch. When he scoots over, I lie down next to him and rest my head against his shoulder. Once we're comfortable, he begins.

'Well, it's about this big,' he whispers, holding his hands out a foot apart. 'But it can get this big,' he adds, spreading them apart another foot. 'And it's got buttons on both sides.' He begins to move his hands wildly up and down.

'It doesn't have a piano on one side?' I ask. I thought they all did.

'No, that's a *piano* accordion,' he explains. 'Mine is a *button* accordion. No piano – only buttons.'

I smile . . . got it. 'What color is it?'

'Red.'

'How does it sound?'

'It goes *bum ba ba, bum ba ba. Bum ba ba, bum ba ba*,' Colin says, doing his best accordion imitation. 'Wanna hear a song?' I nod enthusiastically. After clearing his throat, Colin starts to play his fake accordion and sing. 'Thaaanks for the tiiime that you've giiiven me. The memorieees are alllll in my miiind . . .'

I smile; it's Lionel Richie.

'And nowww that we've commme to the ennnd of our rainbowww, there's somethiiing I mussst say out louddd. You're once . . .'

'Once!' I add.

'Twice.'

'Twice!' I add again.

'TWENTY TIMES a laaaaaaaaaddyyyyyy!'

Twenty times? I playfully swat Colin's arm. Laughing, he continues to sing.

'And I lovvve youuu. I luh-huh-huvvv youuu!'

When Colin's done with his rendition of 'Three Times a Lady', I can't help but ask him what the song means. 'To be three times a lady? Or twenty times?'

'Beats me.'

I don't remember falling asleep, but the next morning I wake up still lying on Colin's couch. Sitting up, I look toward the kitchen and see him standing over the stove, spatula in hand. He's wearing a T-shirt and boxer briefs again, like he was the day I came home from Roger's. Eva is hovering around his feet, licking up spills and droppings – she's a mop today. Hearing me rise, Colin turns around. His hair is messy again; his eyes are sleepy.

'Top o' the mornin' to ya!' he says in jest. He then motions to a small kitchen table. 'Please, come sit yourself down.'

After standing up, I walk to the table and smile at what I see. On top of a place mat sits an empty plate, silverware, a glass of orange juice, and an empty beer bottle holding some kind of a leafy branch. 'I pulled it off the tree outside the window,' Colin explains when I reach out to touch it. I smile. I can't believe he made me breakfast; I'm impressed.

But then I get a whiff of what he's cooking.

'What are you making?' I ask uneasily. Whatever it is, it's a smell I've never smelled before.

'Oh, you're gonna like it,' Colin says as his grin widens. The look on his face resembles that of a little boy who's just built a bottle rocket and is eager to test it out. 'It's a very special fry, but I can't tell you what's in it. In fact, you have to close your eyes when you eat it.'

'Close my eyes? Why?'

'Because it's more fun to guess what's in it than to actually look at what's in it.'

Oh no. 'Is this one of those mixing-leftovers together kind of thing you were telling me about?' I ask. Colin nods. 'Okay,' I sigh. I mean, how bad can it be? Sitting down, I close my eyes. 'Bring it on.'

For the next half-hour or so, I try my best to guess the magical ingredients of Colin's fry. Aside from eggs, I taste pepperoni pizza, cheese, calamari, a cheeseburger (with bun), an onion, chicken tikka masala, and yes . . . an egg roll. While I am eating, Colin frequently takes the fork out of my hand to make sure I have a little bit of everything on each bite. He says doing this is necessary in order to fully appreciate what he's created.

When I finally finish eating, I open my eyes, look down at the plate and jump at what I see. The multi-colored concoction looks frightening. 'You're supposed to approach love and cooking with reckless abandon,' Colin says, attempting to explain.

'I've never heard that, but between the two of us, I think we've accomplished it.'

Colin laughs.

Looking back at the table, I can't help but feel touched. Breakfast was just like the tasting at the Waldorf, except it was just for me. When I turn back to Colin, I glance down at his perfect pink lips and suddenly get the urge to kiss him. I really do. I just want to lean over and plant my lips on his.

But I can't do that.

I can't kiss the first guy who's nice to me; I can't kiss Colin. I need to take something away from all this. I need to learn a lesson. My mom was right; I have an unrealistic idea about love. I get caught up in the moment too easily. New things are exciting. Colin is new. And I know guys like him. He's a heartbreaker; I don't care what he says. To allow myself to feel flattered by all of this would be a giant mistake. I'm not saying kissing him would end in sleeping with him, but if for some crazy reason it did – even down the line – he'd be just another number, just another name on my list. Easy come, easy go. I need to settle down; I need to back off.

When I look back up at Colin, I realize that he's not smiling. As I once again glance down at his perfect pink lips, he moves slightly closer to me, and then losing all sense of reality I move slightly closer to him, and then—

We both slightly jump back when we hear knocking come from the hallway.

'What was that?' I ask Colin.

'Uh . . . it sounds like someone's knocking on your door,' he guesses.

Standing up, I walk over to Colin's door. I open it. Peeking my head out into the hallway, I see the back of a guy standing in front of my door, dressed casually in tan corduroys, a blue long-sleeved T-shirt, and flip-flops. I can't tell who it is.

'Can I help you?' I ask. As soon as I do, before he turns around, I notice little holes in the elbows of his T-shirt.

Wait, holes in the elbows of his T-shirt? Could it be?

When the guy turns around, I'm shocked to see that it is.

'Hey,' Nate says warmly, Nate who was in jail, Nate my #1. His hair is still floppy and his cheeks are still flushed – he looks good. Holding flowers, he smiles and points to my door. 'I'm sorry, I thought this was your apartment.'

'Uh . . . it is,' I say nervously, stepping into the hallway. I close Colin's door behind me. 'Uh . . . what are you doing here?' I'm shocked to see him; I honestly can't believe my eyes.

'Well, I got your message and' – he walks over and hands me the flowers – 'I was just wondering if you'd like to go to dinner tonight.'

'Dinner?' I let out a nervous breath I've been holding and smile. 'That'd be great!'

I hear Colin's door open and turn around to find him standing in the doorway, holding Eva. He gives Nate a once-over but doesn't smile; he seems wary of him. I introduce the two of them. When Colin hears Nate's name, he raises an eyebrow, no doubt realizing who he is: he's the jailbird. After that, we all stare at one another uncomfortably for a few seconds.

'So, Delilah,' Nate eventually says, 'how about I come back around eight?'

'Eight sounds great.'

'Perfect,' Nate replies, 'I'll see you then.' After leaning in and giving me a kiss on the cheek, he turns and walks down the stairs. As soon as Colin and I hear the front door of the building open and close, he turns to me.

'The jailbird?' he says pathetically. 'You're gonna go to dinner with the jailbird?'

'Hmmm . . . is it my imagination or did the Jimmys – who are police officers – mention something to me about you keeping their hands full?'

'That,' Colin says, holding his pointer in the air for emphasis, 'has nothing to do with this situation right here.' He waits for me to respond, but I don't say anything. 'Delilah, did nothing I say yesterday register with you?'

'Yes it did, but you don't understand – this is different. Nate was my first love. I'm not going to dinner with him because he's one of the twenty and if things worked out between us my number wouldn't go up, I'm going to dinner with him because he's my first love and well . . . he came back for me! That has to mean something!' Suddenly

318

remembering the way I felt when Nate and I first dated makes me giddy with excitement. I feel like a teenager again!

Colin shakes his head. 'I'm sorry, I don't mean to be negative,' he says, running his hand through his hair, 'but I don't have a good feeling about this guy. Call it Irish intuition.'

'There's no such thing.'

'Sure there is,' he insists. 'My mum and my sister both have it.'

'They have women's intuition.'

'Whatever,' Colin says, waving me off. 'I have it too.'

'Well, I'm sorry, but I have a good feeling about this guy. Besides, what happened to "approach love and cooking with reckless abandon"? Huh?'

Realizing I have a point, Colin angrily grunts. 'Fine!' he grumbles, storming back into his apartment. 'But I'm gonna keep my Irish eyes on him, and if he screws up just once.' He stops talking for a second. 'Let's just say the Jimmys will have their hands full again.'

'Thank you,' I say with a giggle.

Chapter Sixteen

Beep

It's Michelle . . . I'm so sorry that I've been MIA and that we keep missing each other. I'm dying to hear how it's—

Click

Oh crap! That's my other line . . . I'm at work, I'll call you back.

Beep

Okay, it's me again. I can't believe things are working out. It's amazing. Who would've thought —

Loud Thump

Oops, sorry . . . dropped the phone. What was I saying? Oh, right . . . who would've thought that this idea of yours—

Click

FUCK . . . there it goes again! I'll call you back.

Beep

Sorry . . . this place is a zoo. It's so disorganized. Where was I? Oh right. I'm so happy things are working out with Nate. I'll try to catch up with you later tonight. I want to hear details. Bye.

Settling (Down)

Three weeks later I find myself settled into a comfortable relationship with the first love of my life. On the night of our dinner date, Nate took me to Nobu and the two of us talked over sushi for hours. We got along so well; it was like no time had passed since we had last seen each other. Nate told me that he's been living in Colorado since college. Three years ago he bought a place in Manhattan and, up until recently, was splitting his time between his place in Telluride and here. However, after spending ten days in the Boulder County Jail (they let him go early for good behavior), he decided that he had had enough of Colorado and has decided to move to New York permanently.

I knew Nate came from a wealthy family, but I guess I never knew just how wealthy. His grandparents set up a trust fund for him and he never has to worry about money – ever – which is why he can live wherever he wants. However, just because he's loaded doesn't mean he's a deadbeat. He's involved in many environmental organizations, which is how he ended up in trouble. He was arrested during a peaceful protest gone bad. He always was an earth-lover; I'm not surprised he ended up this way. Anyway, after what happened in Boulder, Nate told me that he's decided to take a break from all that for a while and maybe do some traveling.

Talking about where we've been soon had Nate and I talking about where we were the last time we saw each other. After he apologized to me for what happened at the Santana concert (the girl), I apologized to him for what happened at the Santana concert (the priest), and then the two of us started reminiscing about the good times before that. We talked about dating on and off during high school, we talked about how crazy we were for one another the summer before we left for college, and we talked about our first time.

Since Nate lives less than a block away from Nobu, he invited me over to his place for a drink after dinner and I, of course, said yes. Of all the places for him to live in New York, would you believe it's a loft in TriBeCa? Seriously, he lives in my dream home. It's amazing, too. It's enormous, like 4,000 square feet enormous, and beautifully decorated. Nate has style.

Having one drink on the sofa soon led to kissing on the sofa, which led to . . . well, I left the next morning. Yes, I slept with him on the first date, but it wasn't technically our first date, I guess. I wasn't sure what to do with regards to this, to be honest. I mean, if you've already slept with someone, do you have to play all the games again if you reunite years later? Do you have to wait three dates or however long it is women are waiting these days to sleep with them again? I decided the answer to that question is no.

Anyway, I felt like it was the first time all over again. The entire night I kept having flashbacks to the way things were. I kept feeling like I was seventeen years old again. The next morning, when I rolled over and saw Nate sleeping next to me, it was so weird. I couldn't believe I was actually with him again. I still can't believe it. I mean, first loves reuniting after years apart – I feel like my life has turned into all those movies I watch.

Since that evening, our relationship has moved at

whirlwind speeds. We've been out almost every night and have already fallen into a routine. Every night we go to dinner with any one of a half-a-dozen couples he runs around with, then go to someone's place for a few drinks, and then I stay over at Nate's. I feel as if I've all but moved in with him. As for Eva, she comes with me when I stay over at his place and loves it there. She runs around like it's a racetrack, sliding all over the polished wood floors. She likes Nate's place more than Nate, actually. For some reason she's afraid of him. I jokingly blame Colin for this, telling him that his negativity from the first meeting he had with Nate in the hallway rubbed off on her. He was holding her, after all, while he was giving Nate a once-over.

Speaking of Colin, he hasn't warmed up to Nate very much since their initial meeting, which can make things difficult. Since Michelle has been working so much, he's become kind of like my best friend. Basically, if I'm not with Nate, I'm with him. He keeps telling me that his 'Irish intuition' was right, that Nate has proved to be nothing but a 'snotty-nosed little bastard' who uses his money to get what he wants. 'I'm surprised he didn't buy his way out of the clink,' he said to me just last week. (Nate did, in fact, try to buy his way out of jail but was unsuccessful, however, I didn't tell Colin that.) What prompted this conversation was that Michelle got me an interview with Vintage Vogue to be a designer – which is what I've always wanted to do – and Nate asked me to postpone it until August because he's planning a vacation in July and wants me to go with him. When I told him that I can't afford to go two more months without a job, that I need to pay my rent, he paid it for me. I felt kind of weird letting him do that, but the more I thought about it, the more I thought it was okay. I mean, it's not like he worked for the money and it's not like there's not more where it came from.

The reason this made Colin angry is because he says Nate is stopping me from fulfilling my dreams. 'The fella you're with should encourage you and push you to be the best you can be,' he said, 'not encourage you to pass up opportunities so you can live life according to his schedule.' I see Colin's point and may still go to the interview, but I'm not sure yet. I blamed passing it up on the fact that I'm too overwhelmed with Daisy's wedding right now, which is a week away. As soon as it's over, I could always call Michelle and reschedule it, I guess. Things have really been heating up there, she said. Elisabeth's trial started this week and rumor has it she's going to get off. If and when she does, the two companies will be in direct competition with one another. Michelle said they'd do anything to keep Elisabeth's old staff members from going back to work for her if that happens.

Anyway, back to Colin and Nate. Nate hasn't exactly warmed up to Colin either. I think he can sense that Colin doesn't like him because he keeps saying things to him in jest about being Irish, things that come off as being rude. Last week, for example, he asked Colin if he's yet mastered being able to punch someone without spilling his pint. He also keeps making jokes about pink hearts, yellow moons, orange stars, green clovers and blue diamonds. I said something to him about stopping, because I can see Colin's blood boil every time Nate says something like this, but Nate told me that he's only kidding and says that Colin needs to lighten up. 'I wouldn't crack so many jokes if he'd get over his jealousy and be nice to me,' Nate then said, 'but he can't.'

'What jealousy?' I asked him. I don't think Colin disliking Nate has anything to do with the fact that he's dating me. I think if they randomly met in some bar that they'd detest each other as well.

'The guy's a struggling actor-slash-bartender who rents a box in the East Village and drives a beat-up Vespa,' Nate explained, 'and I own a huge loft and drive a Porsche.' (He does drive a Porsche, by the way.)

While there's a small chance Nate could be right, I don't think he is. Colin's not the jealous type – he's too sure of himself and comfortable in his own skin to be envious of Nate or anything that he has. Besides him telling me about the soap opera audition, I've never known him to lack self-confidence.

Anyway, tonight should be interesting. Nate and I are going to dinner with some of his friends at Spice Market, a hip Asian restaurant in the Meatpacking District owned by Jean-Georges. Afterward, I've made plans for all of us to visit the vodka bar where Colin bartends, so we'll see how they treat one another. I'm kind of worried, to be honest. Dealing with Colin and Nate alone is one thing. Dealing with Colin, Nate and a couple of Nate's rich friends egging him on is another.

About an hour before dinner, while I'm at Nate's getting ready, Daisy calls to tell me how good the food is at Spice Market. While I'm trying to remember her recommendations on what to order and what not to order, she begins to tell me something else, but then hesitates. I demand that she spits it out.

'Do you remember my friend from high school, Ally Hathaway?' she asks.

Remember? How could I forget? She and Daisy were inseparable. 'Yeah,' I say.

'Well, she's coming to the wedding,' she says, 'so I was talking to her on the phone. When I told her about you and Nate being together, she got really quiet and then admitted to me that she got together with him the summer you and he were so hot and heavy, the summer before you both left for college.' I sit down as Daisy continues. 'She said she's always felt so bad about it, and always wanted to fess up to me about it, but never did.'

'Daisy, I was with him almost every day that summer,' I say, not believing her. 'I'd know if he were with someone.'

'That's what I told her, but she insisted she was telling the truth. Delilah, I believe her. She'll be at the wedding, you can ask her' – Suddenly Daisy stops talking – 'uh oh . . . hold on!' After hearing a thud, like she's dropped the phone, I hear the sounds of . . . someone getting sick? About thirty seconds later Daisy returns. Her voice is weak. 'Sorry about that . . .'

'Daisy, are you okay?'

'Yeah, it's just stress. Don't worry.'

'Just stress?' Something's not right. 'You've never been sick from stress before.'

'I've also never planned a wedding before. Seriously, thanks for the concern, but I'll be fine.'

'Okay . . .' I say uneasily.

'Back to Nate though. Delilah, I'm not saying dump the guy – I mean, it happened years ago – but just be careful, will you?'

'Yeah,' I say quietly, 'I will. Thanks for telling me.' Just then I hear the beep of my call waiting and look to see who it is. 'Oh, that's Colin,' I tell Daisy, 'I need to take this. I haven't talked to him in days and need to make sure he's working tonight.'

'Colin the fox?' Daisy asks excitedly. 'The sexy Irishman?'

'Yep.'

'I know I'm engaged,' she says, 'but that boy made me weak at the knees.'

I laugh. 'Bye, Daisy.'

After hanging up, I click over. Although the only thing I can think about is Ally Hathaway, I try to put her out of my mind. 'Where in the hell have you been?' I ask Colin, only half-joking. He hasn't returned my calls for two days.

After apologizing, Colin shares big news with me: he got another soap opera audition, but this time for a role on *All My Children*. 'I just got back from LA,' he says. 'Everything happened so last minute, I'm sorry. I tried to call and tell you, but the cell reception out there is for shit; I could barely get a signal. Anyway, the audition went great – much better than the last one.' Colin sounds excited.

'I thought you didn't want to be on a soap opera,' I say, reminding him.

'I didn't – I don't – but, this role isn't that bad,' he tells me. 'The character's name is Holden Jessup and he's a long-lost cousin of the Cortlandts. After being held in a Bolivian jail for years, he breaks free and makes his way back to Pine Valley. While trying to resume a normal life, he struggles with terrifying flashbacks to when he was held captive. It's all very psychological.' Even though

Colin is trying to convince me of this, I can tell he doesn't quite believe it himself.

'Col, this doesn't sound psychological; it sounds typical. You're better than a Bolivian jailbird. What about the independent film? The Irish gangsta thug thing?'

'It hasn't happened yet, and I need to explore my options.'

'Well, I think you're selling out.'

'I should say the same to you,' Colin mumbles.

'What's that supposed to mean?' I ask.

'Nothing . . . forget it,' he says quickly. 'The thing is, Del, all actors wanna make movies like *Fight Club*, but we need to pay the bills.'

'I understand,' I say softly. 'Speaking of which, you're still working tonight, right? Because we're still planning on coming in around eleven or so.'

'Yepper, and I'm excited to see ya. It's been two whole days.'

I laugh. 'I'm excited to see you, too.'

After hanging up the phone, I finish getting ready and walk into the living room. Nate is sitting on the sofa, drinking a Martini and talking on the phone. I sneak up behind him.

'Boo,' I whisper quietly in his ear. He jumps, startled, turns around and smiles.

'Hey, uh . . . I'll call you back,' he says into the phone. He then hangs up. 'You scared me.'

'I know,' I say playfully. 'Who was that?'

'Who was who?'

'On the phone.'

'Oh, uh . . . Charlie,' Nate says. 'I wanted to make sure he and Cristin were going to be at dinner tonight. She wasn't feeling well earlier and he wasn't sure they were going to make it.' Nate leans over and gives me a kiss. 'We're running late,' he says, glancing at his watch. 'You ready?'

'Yeah,' I say.

As Nate and I ride down in the elevator of his building, I look over at him staring into space and once again think about what Daisy told me. Even if she's right, there's no use in bringing it up. I mean, we were seventeen years old at the time. All saying something would do is either start an argument or make things weird between us. My mom is right. I need to stop making things so difficult for myself. I need to settle down.

After arriving at Spice Market, Nate and I meet two couples – Charlie and Cristin and Teddy and Patty – at the bar downstairs. The restaurant, with its dim lighting, upbeat music, and softly carved teak wood furniture, makes me feel like I'm in some exotic locale in Southeast Asia somewhere. After one drink, not only have I forgotten that I'm in Manhattan, I've forgotten all about Ally Hathaway as well.

After heading upstairs to the dining room, the six of us take a seat at a small alcove table, and then proceed to dine on delicious lobster rolls, chili-rubbed beef tenderloin, and shrimp and noodles for the next two hours. Afterward, while the men settle the bill, the three of us women get to talking and I ask Cristin how she's feeling.

'Fine,' she says, looking at me funny. 'Why are you asking?'

'Well, Nate was talking to Charlie right before you guys came tonight,' I explain, 'and he said you weren't feeling well. He said you almost didn't come.'

'No,' Cristin says, shaking her head slowly. 'Everything's fine.'

'Oh, I must've misunderstood,' I say, looking over at Nate. He did say he was talking to Charlie and that something was wrong with Cristin, right? Yes, I'm sure he did. Suddenly he looks up at me and smiles.

'So, Del, did you call your pal and make sure he's going to be working tonight?'

'Yeah,' I say, snapping out of it. 'He was out of town, but he's back, so we're all set.'

'You mean he left town without telling you?' Nate jokes. I make a face at him. 'Where'd he go?'

'LA, for an audition.'

'Audition for what?'

'*All My Children.*' I see Nate, Charlie and Teddy exchange funny looks with one another. 'Stop it!' I say as they begin laughing.

Teddy elbows Nate. 'Hey, is this the guy who doesn't like you?'

'Yeah, he's a soap opera star,' Nate says, making fun. They all laugh again.

'He's not a soap opera star, Nate,' I say, defending Colin. 'And he probably won't ever be. He's just keeping his options open.'

'I know, I'm just kidding, babe,' Nate says. 'Don't be mad.'

'You better be nice tonight,' I warn.

'I will,' Nate says. He then mumbles, 'I don't want him to beat me up.' As all the guys laugh again, I shake my head. I was afraid of this. I was afraid that Nate would somehow feel empowered having his friends around.

'I'm serious,' I say again.

'Me too,' he replies.

Erin Go Brawl

After a short cab ride we arrive at the East Village bar where Colin works. It's a little after eleven when we walk inside. When I see Colin standing behind the bar giving a Martini shaker a good whirl, I smile and then cringe. He happens to be wearing a Kelly green T-shirt and I just know Nate's going to give him shit for it. When he finishes what he's doing, he looks in our direction and smiles when he sees me. As he makes his way over to us, three people sitting at the bar in front of us get up and leave, giving us their seats.

'I planned for that to happen,' Colin says as he arrives to where we're standing. He then leans over the bar and gives me a kiss. 'Welcome.'

As Cristin, Patty and I take our seats, I look over at the two of them and laugh. They're both staring at Colin with their jaws dropped open. 'Damn,' Cristin mumbles as I nudge her back to reality, 'I need to come to the East Village more often.'

'No shit,' Patty agrees.

Colin looks at Nate. 'Hey, mate,' he says politely, holding out his hand. 'How's it goin'?'

'Swell, mate,' Nate replies mockingly. After shaking Colin's hand, he looks around the bar. 'I'm impressed,' he says, nodding favorably. 'I'd expect an Irish bloke like yourself to be pulling pints in a grimy pub somewhere. This place is as clean as a whistle!'

Hearing Nate utter the line from the Irish Spring commercials amuses Charlie and Teddy. As they both look away to keep from laughing, I kick Nate in the shins and glare at him. He turns back to Colin. 'Hey, just kidding, man,' he says quickly. He then glances at his T-shirt. 'I see you got your colors on tonight, though.'

Unsure of what to make of Nate's comedy routine, Colin laughs. 'Do you do shows around the city?' he asks, in a cheeky sort of way. 'Or are you strictly an open mike kinda guy?'

'You're funny,' Nate says.

Colin raises an eyebrow. 'Not as funny as you.' He then turns to me. Leaning forward on the bar, he reaches over and takes my hands in his. 'Paired with the accent, the green T-shirt makes the ladies go crazy.' He winks. 'Right, Del?'

Since I can tell that Nate is none too pleased that Colin's holding my hands, I smile and nod. 'Right,' I say proudly. And then I laugh inside.

Serves Nate right.

Despite the uncomfortable beginning, the evening proceeds rather smoothly. The bar is hopping, the atmosphere is cozy, and the drinks are stiff. As the six of us chat and have a nice time, Colin works and pops by every once in a while to say hello. After about an hour, Nate, Charlie and Teddy begin chatting up two girls sitting next to us at the bar who have been drooling over Colin all evening. They keep asking them why they're wasting their time on a bartender when the place is filled with other single men. Much to Cristin's, Patty's and my amusement, the girls don't answer our guys and couldn't care less what they have to say. They keep staring in Colin's direction, watching him shake, pour, serve, shake, pour, serve. When Colin sees us laughing and realizes what's going on, he shrugs and looks at Nate. 'I told you, man,' he says, smirking, 'the T-shirt.' He points to it. 'You might want to get yourself one.'

By the time I finish my second Martini, the girls finally realize that Colin isn't interested in them and turn around to talk to Nate, Charlie and Teddy. After about a half-hour of this, Cristin and Patty dismiss themselves to go to the bathroom, leaving me alone at the bar. Looking around, I see that things have slowed down and glance over to where Colin's standing. When I do, I catch him looking at me. Instead of looking away from me, he winks and smiles. He then makes eyes at Nate and the two girls, hinting that he's flirting with them. After quickly assessing the situation, I wave it off. Colin walks over.

'Your boyfriend seems keen on those two,' he whispers, once again reaching out to hold my hands.

'No, he's just being friendly.'

'No, seriously, Del,' he insists, 'he's into the one on the left. I can tell. He keeps touching her knee.'

I turn around and look again. When I do, Nate looks up. Seeing that Colin is once again holding my hands, he gives him a funny look.

'How's the drink?' Colin asks when he does.

'Magically delicious,' Nate replies. He then shakes his head and goes back to the girls.

'He's almost laughable,' Colin says to me, as we both turn back to each other. 'I mean, can't the guy come up with something a little more clever?'

'I'm sorry,' I say, apologizing for Nate's behavior. 'I think he thinks he's being funny.'

'Funny?' Colin laughs. 'Is that what that is?' Colin shakes his head, shakes him off. 'Hey, listen,' he then says, changing the subject, 'I gotta talk to you about something.' The tone of his voice is serious. 'I got —'

Colin suddenly stops talking when another bartender accidentally bumps into him. Realizing this isn't the place for a serious talk, he looks over to where a curtain is hanging near the other end of the bar. 'Hey, come meet me back there, will you?' I look to see where he's motioning to and nod.

After telling Nate that I'm going to the bathroom, I make my way to the other end of the bar. When I arrive and begin looking around for Colin, I'm startled when an arm darts out from behind the curtain and pulls me behind it. 'Sorry,' Colin laughs, seeing me jump. Looking around, I that we're in some sort of small supply room. The curtain is the door.

'What's up?' I ask.

'Well, I got news,' he says, smiling. 'I got the part. *All My Children*. They called this evening right after I hung up with you.'

'Really?' I ask. I'm shocked that he seems so happy about it; I didn't think he wanted it that badly. 'So you're gonna take it, then?'

'Yeah,' Colin nods, 'but it starts really quickly. I'd have to leave Monday and—'

'Wait,' I say interrupting him. Leave? 'What do you mean *leave?*'

'It's in LA.'

LA? I'm speechless. I knew the audition was there, but it never crossed my mind that Colin would actually have to move.

'What's wrong?' Colin asks, sensing my unhappiness.

'Well—'

Suddenly a bartender walks through the curtain and squeezes behind Colin. After quickly grabbing the few things he needs, he walks back out. As he does, Colin steps in closer to me to give him more room. Looking down, I realize that his body is all but touching mine and can just make out the outline of his perfect six-pack abs through his T-shirt. Without thinking, a small smile creeps across my face. As soon as it does, I close my eyes and become embarrassed because I'm sure he saw me. Thinking I've been busted yet again for checking him out, I slowly look up. When I do I'm relieved, surprised and amused to see that Colin hasn't been paying attention to where my eyes have been looking because his own are staring at my clingy shirt, staring at the outline of my breasts. As I begin to giggle, Colin realizes that he's been caught looking for a change. As a tiny smile appears across his face, he looks up.

'So . . . what'd you think?' I ask as our eyes meet.

'Do you really wanna know?' he whispers, stepping in even closer to me. He puts his hands on my waist and, for a split second, both of us stop smiling. Suddenly becoming incredibly nervous, I look away.

'Actually, no,' I say quickly.

Colin's hands slowly fall from my waist. The two of us then stand in awkward silence for a moment until he clears his throat.

'So uh, about the job,' he says. 'I can tell you aren't too happy for me.'

'No, I am,' I say, looking back at him. 'I'm happy that you got it, but I just . . . I don't know . . . I don't want you to move. You've kind of become one of my best friends.'

Colin looks at me and smiles. Obviously touched by what I've said, he pulls me closer to him and wraps his arms around me. 'I don't want to move either,' he says quietly, 'but, Del, I'd be an idiot to pass this up.'

'Yeah, I know,' I say softly. 'Just think about what you're doing though, and remember, don't take the part if you think you're settling.'

'I will.'

'I better get back,' I say, pulling away. Without looking at him, I turn and walk away. While doing so, I feel an electricity come from behind me. It's like a pull, coming from Colin. I can't deny that I feel something for him, *from* him. We've gotten to know each other so well, and—

Oh, forget it. It's all so silly really.

I've had two Martinis, that's all. I can't think straight.

After making my way back to my seat, Colin makes his way back to the bar. Looking a bit more serious than he has all night, he gives me a half-smile and then looks away. Unsure of what that means, I turn back to Cristin and Patty and try not to think about it.

Around two o'clock or so, after we've all been generously served, the bar gets ready to close. As the place clears out and the guys settle up the bill, Cristin, Patty, and I go to the bathroom. On our way out, we're surprised to discover that Nate, Charlie and Teddy aren't around. Nor is Colin, for that matter. Assuming that they're waiting outside, we head toward the front door. As I pull the door open, I hear yelling and look up. When I see Colin and Nate being held back from each other by Teddy and Charlie, my heart drops. Nate's lip looks red and puffy, like it's been punched, and Colin looks angry but unharmed. Suddenly Colin yells at Nate, 'You're a fucking liar!' Nate doesn't respond. I quickly approach them.

'What's going on?' I ask nervously.

'What's going on,' Nate says, 'is that your idiot friend here is insane.' As a small drop of blood forms on his lip, I reach up and touch it.

'Oh my God,' I say, quickly turning to Colin, 'did you punch him?'

'You're damn right I did!' he answers angrily. His temper has gone wild. After explaining something about Nate walking one of the two girls who were sitting next to us all night outside, he says something about how he saw Nate kiss one of them so he came outside and punched him. I think. The truth is that I can barely understand what Colin's saying. He's so angry and talking so quickly and I'm in shock because he punched Nate.

He punched Nate.

Oh my God! Mortified, I cover my face with my hands.

'Del, he's crazy,' Nate says, after hearing Colin's explanation. 'I walked outside to get some fresh air and he followed me and started shit with me.'

'Yeah, I did follow you outside,' Colin says, 'but not to start shit with you. You brought this on yourself.'

'Listen, dude,' Nate says, pulling away from Charlie, 'the bottom line is that you don't like me and you never have because you wanna screw my girlfriend.'

Screw my girlfriend? What? I uncover my face and look at Nate, and then at Colin.

'No,' Colin says calmly as he pulls away from Teddy, 'I don't like you because I care about your girlfriend and I don't like seeing jackasses like you fuck with her.' As Colin stares at Nate and Nate stares at Colin I become worried.

'You guys – stop,' I say, walking in between the two of them. 'This is stupid.' I turn to Colin. 'I'm sure this was just a misunderstanding.'

''Twas no misunderstanding,' he says quickly. 'Del, your boy here's an asshole.'

Hearing this, Nate lets out a laugh. 'Yeah, *I'm* the asshole,' he then says sarcastically, 'not the maniacal import here.'

'Oh fuck off, man,' Colin says, narrowing his eyes.

'Stop it, both of you!' I demand. I then turn to Nate. 'Do you mind giving Colin and me a second?'

Nate looks at me for a moment, and then slowly shakes his head. 'Yeah, fine.' As he walks away, his friends follow. As soon as Colin and I are alone, I turn to him. I'm so angry that I can barely speak.

'You *punched* my boyfriend?' I yell. 'What are you, *twelve*?'

'No, but—'

'No, but nothing, Colin! You know, you hate it when Nate makes all those stupid jokes to you, yet you just went and backed up everything he says. You punched him. In a bar.'

'Outside a bar,' he mumbles.

'Oh what's the difference? Regardless of where it happened, what a great way to prove to him that you're not a drunk fighting Irishman!'

'Hey, I don't have anything to prove to that guy!' Colin huffs. After sighing heavily, he turns and walks away from me. I can tell that he's angry at me for being angry at him.

'Colin, wait,' I say, following him. I feel bad for yelling. 'I didn't mean that, but you just can't go punching people!'

'Gee, thanks for the advice, Delilah,' he yells without turning around. He won't even look at me. After turning the corner, he finally stops walking. 'Wait, why are you yelling at *me*? I'm not the bad guy here.' Turning around, Colin waits for my reply, but I don't say anything. The truth is, as much as I hate to admit it, I don't know if I believe him. Once he realizes I'm not going to answer him, he lets out a tiny sigh. 'Oh, I get it,' he says, as a knowing look comes across his face. 'You don't believe me, do you?'

'No ... I just ... well ... maybe you saw something you wanted to see.'

'What's that supposed to mean?'

'It means that I know there's a connection between us, Colin. I feel it and I'm assuming you do too.' Colin doesn't deny this, so I continue. 'I mean, Nate is right – you haven't liked him since you met him. I don't think you're giving—'

Suddenly out of nowhere Colin walks up and kisses me. There's no other way for me to explain it except to say just that. One minute I'm talking and the next minute he's kissing me. He simply walks over, takes my face in both of his hands, and starts kissing me.

Once it registers with me what's happening, my knees give out a little bit. As I fall backward, Colin slides his hands from my face around to my back and holds me up. As he pulls me in closer, as his kisses become deeper, I literally melt into his arms. His lips are so soft and so moist. And his body is so strong and so lean. This is all so perfect, and then I suddenly . . . I suddenly . . .

I suddenly realize how wrong this is.

'I can't do this,' I say, pulling myself away from Colin.

'I know . . . break up with him,' he says, pulling me back.

'No, not Nate,' I explain, 'you.' I back up again. 'I can't be with *you*. Colin, this is what I'm talking about. Me and you. What just happened. This is why I don't believe you. I'm sorry, but I think you saw what you wanted to see.'

'Del, if anyone is imagining things here, it's you, not me. You're imagining this Nate guy to be the one because he was your first love, because he's got what you dreamed you'd have one day, and because if he is, then you won't up some stupid limit you've set in your head.'

'That's not why I'm with him, not any more,' I explain. 'I mean, he came back for me, that has to mean some-thing.'

'Jaysus, Del! Are you that easy?'

Am I that easy? 'Pardon me?'

Colin shakes his head. 'That's not what I meant. I meant just because someone comes back for you is no reason to be with them; just because someone loves you is no reason to love them back.'

I look away; I'm so confused. 'Colin, even if there was no Nate, if something were to ever happen between us it would end miserably and you know it. You're not good at relationships. You admitted it to me.'

'Yeah, you're right, I did. I am bad at relationships. And maybe you and I would be a mistake, but maybe we wouldn't. If you don't try, you'll never know.' Colin stops talking and waits for a response, but I don't say anything.

Suddenly I realize I'm scared. I'm scared of him. I'm scared to take a chance. Even if Nate wasn't in the picture, I don't think I can do this again. It's not so much going to the number twenty-one that scares me; it's the thought of Colin breaking my heart. The thing about Colin is that, looks aside, he's a wonderful person and I'd fall head over heels in love with him if I haven't already, there's no doubt about it. And there's also no doubt that he'd eventually leave me. There's no way anything between us would go somewhere. I'm done with flings. I want the next thing – I want the *real* thing. There's a possibility that I can have that with Nate. I'm not going to throw that away and take a chance on something that might not work out.

'Listen, my timing might be bad,' Colin continues, 'but my intentions are good.'

'Good intentions aren't good enough, Colin,' I say quietly. 'I need more than that.'

Colin hesitates and then speaks slowly. 'If you don't want to take a chance on me then fine, I'll learn to live with it. But I can't stand by and watch you be with this guy.'

'Then don't,' I say. 'Go to LA. Leave. Now you have more of a reason.'

Hearing this, Colin slowly takes a step away from me.

'Sorry,' I say quietly. Then I turn and walk away.

Chapter Seventeen

Beep

Delilah, it's Mom. Wedding bells are ringing! Make sure you check in at the Waldorf by ten o'clock this morning. After that, meet all us ladies in the lobby at 10:30 for our spa day at Bliss. Don't be offended, but I booked you a little more time than the rest of us — your eyebrows really need a waxing, as does your upper lip. Hopefully, you'll be done with everything by the time rehearsal starts at six.

I was thinking . . . maybe you should tell Nate to skip dinner tonight and just join you tomorrow. You'll be red from being poked at all day and it's probably not a good idea if he sees you like that. Okay, see you in a jiffy!

Beep

Hey — it's Daisy. I can't believe it's wedding time! I'm dying!
Don't worry about picking up your dress from Saks — they're going to deliver it to the hotel along with mine. Can't wait to see you!

The night of the fight, when I walked away from Colin, I didn't know what to do. Well, I did in a way. I knew not to cry, but that was about it. I was fighting back tears. It was painful to walk away from him. It almost hurt, I swear. I've grown really close to him in the last few months, and the thought of possibly never talking to him again felt like a stake through my heart. To make it worse, when I turned the corner and saw Nate standing alone waiting for me, when I looked him in the eye, I felt a pit in my stomach. He looked guilty.

Neither of us said anything to each other in the taxi on the way home that night. We both just sat there in silence, holding hands but looking out opposite windows. Things have been awkward ever since. When we got back to Nate's, he fell asleep quickly while I stayed up, rehashing the night in my head. I kept trying to remember if I saw something odd between him and either of the two girls sitting next to us, but I couldn't. The truth is that I barely paid attention to them. I barely paid attention to Nate. The only person I paid attention to was Colin.

Going over the night in my head soon had me remembering what Daisy said about Ally, which soon had me thinking about the odd phone call Nate said he had with Charlie about Cristin being sick. After double-checking to make sure he was asleep, I found Nate's cell phone and, before I could stop myself, started going through all the calls he placed and received that day. I hated myself for doing this because I've never been a jealous girlfriend, but my gut told me something wasn't right. Although I prepared myself to find the worst, I didn't find anything, which in a way was worse. The entire call history on Nate's phone had been erased. Not a good sign. At that point I started to wonder if maybe I rushed back into things too quickly. Although I've known him for fifteen years, I don't really know Nate. Realizing this got me thinking about Colin again. I was so worried that I'd feel this way about him when I got back from my little trip, but the opposite proved to be true. I feel like I know Colin now better than I know Nate.

I fell asleep on the sofa that night. When I woke up the next morning, I felt slightly better. Things were still awkward between Nate and me, but without the Martinis to cloud our minds, everything was a little easier to deal with. We ended up going to a place around the corner for breakfast, a place called Bubby's. By the time the food came, we had started talking but still hadn't said anything to each other about the previous evening. On the way home, I decided to let it go and instead brought up something else. 'Hey, do you by any chance know a girl named Ally Hathaway?' I casually asked him.

Nate shook his head. 'No. Should I?'

'Not necessarily. She went to our high school, that's all. I was just thinking about her and was curious if you knew her.'

'No, sorry.' He seemed sincere; I believed him.

I finally ended up going home Monday night. When I did, I bravely knocked on Colin's door. I was hoping to tell him that I was sorry, but he didn't answer, so I left him a message asking him to call me. By Tuesday he hadn't called back, so I sent him an e-mail. Again, I got nothing. Wednesday evening I went to Michelle's for dinner – I hadn't seen her in what seemed like ages – and while I was there, I asked if she had seen Colin recently.

'Yeah, I saw him leaving early Monday morning with a suitcase,' she said.

'A suitcase?' I asked, and then I couldn't breathe.

I told Michelle everything. When I did, when I was done, she shook her head and told me she wasn't surprised. 'Going back to when you checked yourself into rehab, when I knocked on Colin's door freaking out, he was really concerned about you,' she explained, 'more concerned than a random neighbor would be.' She said she had a funny feeling about the two of us that day. Hearing this made me want to cry because the reality of the situation sunk in – what if I never see him again? I mean, assuming he took the soap opera job in LA. What if he moved away for good and we never talked to each other again?

After consoling me, Michelle encouraged me to reschedule my Vintage Vogue interview, saying that I needed to get some structure back in my life. She couldn't be more right. We ended up calling her boss that night and setting something up for next week. As much as I'd love to go on vacation and run around the world with Nate, I can't put my own dreams on hold to do so.

Anyway, while packing my bag for the Waldorf this morning, I begin to feel as if I've lived a hundred years in the last few months. Thinking back to when all this started, thinking back to Roger, it seems so long ago.

After Eva hops in her bag, the two of us make our way downstairs and try to flag down a taxi, which proves to be hell. It's been raining for a week straight, ever since Nate and I were walking back from Bubby's, actually. After waiting on the corner for a while, we eventually get one.

I arrive at the Waldorf safely, wait at the check-in counter and wonder what kind of room I'll have. I hope it's a nice one, one with a good view. I need to look out at this big beautiful city and clear my mind. When the man standing behind the counter is done pressing buttons, he hands me a keycard. 'Your room is five-D,' he says.

'Five-D?' This concerns me. 'Does that mean it's on the fifth floor?'

The man nods. 'Yes.'

I make a face. I'm disappointed. 'I was hoping for something higher, something with a nice view.'

'I'm sorry, but right now we don't have another room available. We're totally booked. But I assure you, you'll like the room.'

'Okay,' I say, reluctantly taking the keycard. 'Thanks.'

After a short elevator ride, I locate my room and unlock the heavy wooden door. When I push it open, I see that it's decorated in rich burgundy and burnt-mustard tones. It's warm and cozy, which, with all the rain, is actually kind of nice. I put Eva down and then walk over to the window and pull back the bulky curtains to see the view. I'm pleasantly surprised to find myself with a view of Park Avenue. Things definitely could be worse.

After meeting Daisy, my mom, Patsy and Ruth in the lobby for spa day, we all catch a cab to Bliss, a spa in SoHo. For the rest of the day, while being steamed, massaged, plucked, painted and waxed (which my upper lip did *not* need, for the record), I think about what to do. Things have been too weird with Nate and I need to make a decision. Either I need to put everything behind me, give him the benefit of the doubt and move on, or I need to confront him and possibly end things. Seeing me in deep thought, Daisy can tell something's wrong. She asks if it's about Nate. I tell her yes.

'Did you say something to him about Ally?' she asks.

'Kind of,' I say, 'and he denied even knowing her.'

Daisy gives me a compassionate smile. 'Del, when you're really in love, when it's the right guy, it's not this hard, you know? Things fall into place; they work. If it's meant to be, it'll work itself out.' I nod; I know it will. 'Is he coming to the rehearsal dinner tonight?'

'Yeah,' I say, 'against Mom's better judgment.' As I tell Daisy this, I make a decision. Sort of. I decide to make a decision at the end of Daisy's wedding weekend. If things between Nate and me go well, if they seem like they're going back to normal, then I'll forget about everything and concentrate on making it work. If not, then . . . well, we'll see.

That evening after the rehearsal, my family and Edward's family go to the Manhattan Ocean Club for dinner. When we arrive my low spirits perk up when I look across the room and see my grandpa (or a man who resembles the grandpa I remember) standing in front of me. Standing next to him is Gloria. They just drove in from Vegas and came straight here.

'Grandpa!' I scream, running toward him. I throw my arms around him. 'I'm so happy to see you!' After giving him the biggest hug ever, I let go, back up and give him a once-over. Oh, dear . . . I love my grandpa, but I don't know what to make of him. He's dyed his hair and eyebrows an unnatural dark-brown color, and he's wearing a white linen shirt unbuttoned down to his belly, three necklaces (leather, silver, turquoise), an oversized Western silver buckle on a carved brown leather belt (which I'm guessing is the one he made), and a scarf tied around his neck. He looks like a . . . a . . . a gigolo. Seeing me eye him, Gloria hits his chest with the back of her hand (which is, yes, waxed smooth).

'This one,' she says, 'thinks he's Warren Beatty in *Shampoo*.'

Or yes, he looks like him, too.

'The next thing you know,' she continues, 'he's gonna start carrying a blow dryer around in a holster and trade in his Camaro for a motorcycle.'

My grandpa rolls his eyes. 'Please, Gloria! Enough with those remarks already!' He sounds slightly irritated. When Gloria shakes her head and walks away, I turn to him.

'Grandpa, what's wrong?'

'Well . . .' he says, hesitating for a bit. 'Gloria and I broke up.'

Broke up? I'm thrown for a loop. 'Why?'

'To be completely honest, Darlin', I never realized how many fish there are in the sea.'

Come again?

'We haven't been getting along that well and I kept meeting all these other ladies – nice ladies – who made me realize that it was silly to force something that wasn't working.'

'Okay,' I say slowly. 'Then why is she here?'

'We already made the plans so she came with me

anyway. You know, we still get along, but she just wasn't it.' My grandpa looks sad as he says this.

'You're upset about this, I can tell.'

'Yeah.' My grandpa nods. 'You know, even if you know something doesn't have a chance in hell of surviving, it's still sad when it dies.'

Just then I look up and see Nate walking through the door. Dressed in a blue suit, he smiles when he sees me. As he walks in my direction, I look back to my grandpa. 'I'm sorry things didn't work out,' I say. 'So what are you gonna do? Are you going to go back to Vegas? Or stay here?'

'I'm not sure yet.' He shrugs. 'I've got some thinking to do.'

As Nate arrives to where the two of us are standing and takes my hand, I can't help but to think, *Me too*.

Dinner ends up going exactly as I suspected it would, but not as I hoped. While Nate and I talk to other people, we barely speak to each other. Every time we do say something to one another, I feel like it's forced. I feel like I'm pretending. I don't know what's happening and I don't know how to explain it. I just think some relationships can handle problems and some can't. I don't think this is going to work out. I need to tell him.

Arriving back at the hotel with Nate, I suggest we go for a drink in the hotel bar; he says yes. While racking my brain trying to think of what to say, fate steps in and makes things a whole lot easier. While walking through the lobby, we happen to bump into Ally Hathaway as she checks in.

'Delilah, hi,' she says, bouncing over to me with her

fluffy brown hair, hair that appears to go flat when she sees Nate standing next to me.

'Hi,' I say. After giving her a brief hug, I glance over at Nate and see that his face is beet red. The three of us stand in awkward silence for a few moments. 'Ally, do you know Nate?' I finally ask.

'Yeah,' she says coldly. 'Long time no see.'

'Yeah,' Nate mumbles uneasily.

Looking at Nate standing with the two of us fidgeting uncomfortably, I see the same guilty look I saw after I walked away from Colin that evening. Nate doesn't have a poker face, to say the least. He makes this easy for me to do. I turn to Ally. 'Ally, would you like to have a drink with us?' I do this simply to fuck with him.

After looking at Nate and then at me, Ally smiles. I think she realizes my intentions. 'I'd love to,' she says graciously. 'Just let me run to my room quickly, and I'll meet you back down here in a jiffy.' As Ally walks away, Nate turns to me.

'Why'd you do that?' he asks.

'I should be asking you that question.'

Looking away, Nate lets out a nervous laugh. 'Delilah, are you really mad at me for something that happened eleven years ago?' he asks.

'No, I'm mad at you for lying to me about it six days ago.'

'Well,' Nate says rudely, 'I'm not gonna stay here and have drinks with you two. I mean, if that's what you think, then you're crazy.'

'I'm not crazy,' I say, 'and I'm not average either. I don't know why I was so hung up on thinking I needed to be.'

351

Nate gives me a confused look. 'What are you talking about?'

'Nothing,' I say, shaking my head. 'Nate, I think you should go home. For good.'

He nods. 'Yeah,' he says quietly. 'I think that's a good idea.'

Nate doesn't kiss me goodbye, he simply turns around and leaves. And I let him. I don't press for the truth about the phone call or about what happened the night with Colin, because I already know. When he walks out the revolving door and disappears from my sight, I let out a sad sigh, then a glad one, and then another sad one. I'm sad things didn't work out with Nate, glad I wasted only a month on him, and sad I screwed things up with Colin in the process. I care about Colin; I can't deny it. I care about him more than I've cared about any man maybe ever. I can't believe it, but I think I might love him.

Oh, God.

When Ally walks back into the lobby a few moments later, she looks around for Nate. 'Where did he go?' she asks.

'Home,' I say.

'Thank God.' She sighs. 'He's such a lying dick.'

One Hell of a Ride   Saturday, 18 June

The next morning I put a smile on my face and, with Eva, head up to Daisy's suite on the twenty-ninth floor of the Towers, the fancier part of the hotel, to get ready for the big day. When I get to her room, I know I'm in for a treat when I see double doors. After I ring the doorbell (neat, huh?) and wait, Daisy answers, wearing a silk robe and a smile that stretches from ear to ear.

'*Vwelcome, madam*,' she says in a bad Russian accent. '*Vwelcome to my humble abode!*' As she playfully grabs my arm and whisks me into a lavish marble foyer, I'm speechless.

'Your room has a foyer?' I ask, looking up at a sparkling crystal chandelier.

'*Oui, oui!*' Daisy squeaks giddily, moving on to French. After closing the door behind me, she leads me into the living room and gives me a mini tour. Like my room, Daisy's suite also has a view of Park Avenue, but that's where the similarities end. Aside from being significantly larger, her suite is decorated in light blue and green hues, giving it a very serene feel. Soft cream-colored linen covers, cushioned wall panels, and layers upon layers of gold silk drapes cascade down windows. A fireplace dominates one end of the room, while a plush up-holstered sofa, settee and winged chair embellish the other. Gold candelabras and gilded mirrors hang from the walls, and fresh flower arrangements adorn every table. Off the living room sits a small kitchenette, currently over-flowing with gift baskets.

After we pass through a set of sliding wooden doors, Daisy shows me the bedroom, which, with its hand-woven needlepoint floral carpets and lavish king-sized bed, is just as lush as the rest of the place. Adjacent to this is an enormous dressing area and, of course, a whirlpool bath.

After heading back to the living room, we plop down on the sofa. I look at her, sitting there, surrounded by all this opulence. She looks blissful, but anyone would, right? Out of nowhere, she suddenly reaches over and grabs my arm. 'You ended it, didn't you?' she asks.

I let out a sigh and nod. 'Yeah.'

'But that's not why you're sad today, is it?' she asks. I give her a confused look. 'I'm going to take a wild guess at something; tell me if I'm right. You thought you loved Nate, realized you didn't, realized you loved Colin in the process, but lost him.'

I look at Daisy; I'm amazed. 'Wow, you're good.'

Daisy smiles. 'I know. I'm not as dense as I seem to be sometimes.' She scoots over and puts her arm around me. 'Remember what I said. If it's meant to be, it'll work itself out.'

I nod. 'I know.'

'Does Mom know yet?'

'No,' I say, rolling my eyes. 'She's gonna think I'm a lesbian once again.'

'Well, look on the bright side,' Daisy says as she pets Eva on the head. 'If she does then at least you'll match your dog.' I laugh, and then Daisy and I hug.

A few moments later, when my mom comes up to Daisy's room, she freezes when she sees both our faces, knowing something's up. 'The last time you two looked like this,' she says, 'was when you melted your Barbie doll onto my antique coffee table.'

I don't remember this; I look to Daisy.

'We were trying to give her a tan in the Easy-Bake oven,' she says, 'remember?'

'Oh, right,' I say, as it comes back to me. (Kids, don't try this at home.)

Mom takes a seat between us on the sofa and I tell her about Nate. I don't tell her about Colin though – I don't want her to give me grief for ruining things. When I finish, she sits in silence for a bit. After looking up and seeing my face, she reaches over and hugs me hard. Remembering what she said in her message about a month ago, I give in and don't fight it. When I do, I realize that, by God, she's right. It is easier to breathe.

'Delilah, you and Daisy are my angels,' she says, as she feels my body soften. 'I know I give you a hard time about being single and I don't mean to, but I just want you to be happy.'

'I want to be happy, too, Mom. But I'm not gonna be with someone just to be with someone. If I force it, I'm just going to end up unhappier.'

'I know,' she says, sighing loudly. 'You're right.'

'Yes, I am. I have to figure things out for myself on my own schedule. Just because I don't live life like the rest of your friends' kids do, doesn't mean something's wrong with me.'

'I know,' she says.

'Good, but I need you to know always, Mom, not just now because you're in a good mood because Daisy's getting married. If I'm still single in a year, you need to be fine with it then, too. And know that it doesn't mean I'm a lesbian.'

'I know you're not a lesbian, honey,' my mom says, 'and I'm sorry.'

After Daisy leans in and we all group-hug, I begin to feel better. Do I expect my mom's nagging to stop for ever? No, but it's nice to know that at least for today it will.

After letting go, Daisy looks at Mom and winks at me, signaling she's up to something. 'Delilah,' she then says, 'I know you're not a lesbian, but didn't you experiment once in college?'

I choke. Even though I know Daisy is saying this just to mess with my mom, she doesn't know how close to the truth it actually is.

'Uh . . . yeah, once,' I say, going along with her. 'But it was above the belt, so I don't count it as the real deal.'

After watching the blood drain from Mom's face, Daisy and I burst into laughter. After doing so, we both look at my mom, and in unison, say, 'Kidding!'

'Oh, thank heavens!' she exclaims as the color comes back to her face. She then leans into me. 'If you are a lesbian though, Delilah, please know that I'll be fine with it.'
I shake my head and look back at Daisy.

'C'mon,' she says to the two of us, 'let's get ready . . . I'm getting married!'

Daisy ends up being the most beautiful bride I've ever seen, not that I doubted she'd be anything but. She doesn't pull her hair back or put it up in a bun, as so many brides do, but leaves it wild and free, which makes her look more gorgeous than ever. Throughout her entire engagement, she's had a glow to her that I've never seen. Love agrees with her. Standing once again on a small platform in my scarlet dress, I watch my grandpa walk her down the aisle with tears in his eyes. I then think back to the last time I saw him cry, which was when Daisy and I were kids, when he came to school to kidnap us.

The only thing that prevents me from bawling and

brings a smile to my lips is the sight of my mother weeping in her chair, wearing the largest rhinestone-encrusted crucifix brooch I've ever seen. She makes me laugh, my mom. Before the ceremony, Daisy realized that she had spent all morning hiding rosaries everywhere and yelled at her. She found one in her bouquet, another sewn into the bottom hem of her dress, and more worked into the floral centerpieces on the tables. God knows where else my mother hid them. (Actually, he probably does.) Anyway, when someone begins to sing 'Ave Maria' at the end of the ceremony, she breaks into a full sob and sings along, at which point both Daisy and I burst into laughter. Equally pathetic, Edward's mother also loses it when Edward does the whole 'stepping-on-the-glass-thing', as Daisy puts it. (Thank God – at least they're both wacky.) When the judge who's presiding over the ceremony finally announces Mr and Mrs Edward Barnett for the first time, an equal mix of 'Amens' and 'Mazel tovs' ring through the air, and then everyone begins to party.

The reception goes off without a hitch. The drinks flow freely, the food goes down smoothly, and the Starlight Roof couldn't look more festive with the flowers blooming, candles flickering and ceiling twinkling. Despite all this joy, however, I still find myself a bit melancholy. After Daisy and Edward cut the cake, I head over to a window and look out at the city. When I do, I realize that it's finally stopped raining.

When I think of last time I wore this red dress, with Colin in the fitting room at Saks, I get sad. Remembering the way his strong hands felt as he zipped and laced me up, remembering the way he gave me goose bumps, brings a tear to my eye. It also gets me thinking about my twenty guys again. Even though I've just about come to terms with it and realize that it's no reason to settle down with someone you don't love, I still believe that most of them were mistakes.

And then I hear a voice.

'I've never seen anything so lovely.'

When I turn around, I see my grandpa. Even though he's too tan and his hair is too dark, he's still handsome. As he walks up to me, he looks out the window as well.

'I know, it's a beautiful view, isn't it?'

'I was talking about you,' he says, putting his arm around me. 'But it is too, yes.'

'Thanks,' I say, hugging him.

'You're gonna be okay,' he says, squeezing me tight. 'You know that?'

'Yes, I do. I just have a lot of regrets, that's all. I've made a lot of mistakes.'

'Ah . . . there's no such thing! There are the choices that we make and the consequences, that's all.'

'I know, but I keep thinking that maybe if I did things differently, then the consequences wouldn't have been the same.'

'Of course they wouldn't be, but then neither would you. Everything you do in life, whether it's good or bad, makes you who you are. Don't *maybe* your decisions to death because you can't change them.'

'That's easier said than done.'

'You're right,' he says, patting my shoulder. 'But if you're going to think about your past rather than dwell on the reasons you shouldn't have done something, remember the reasons you did.'

I look up. 'What do you mean?'

'I mean everything we do in life has some element of right and wrong to it.'

'Like?'

My grandpa thinks. 'Give me an example of something really silly that you've done in your life – something that looking back now doesn't seem so smart.'

I laugh – where do I even begin?

'And don't hold back,' he adds, 'just because I'm your grandpa. Give me a good example.'

'Okay,' I say, after thinking about it. 'One time I rode on the back of a motorcycle with a strange man through the streets of Barcelona at two o'clock in the morning.'

My grandpa breathes in and out heavily for a few seconds. Once he seems calm, he turns to me. 'Don't ever do that again!'

'You said don't hold back!' (And even so, I still did – I left out the drinking part.)

'I know, I know, you're right,' he says, regaining his composure. 'And forgetting that you're my granddaughter for a moment, it's a good example. With that in mind, forget all the reasons why you shouldn't have done it.'

'Okay, forgotten.'

'I bet it was one hell of a ride . . .'

Instantly, I smile. 'Oh, it *was*, Grandpa,' I say, turning to him. 'It was exhilarating!'

'Exactly!' he says, pointing at me for emphasis. 'If you're going to remember anything from your past, then do so fondly because you can't change a thing about it.'

Wow.

I mean, *wow.*

This simple idea is the most freeing thing I've ever heard in my life. It's better than any self-help book I've read or any audio program I've listened to.

'Delilah, life is filled with pain and beauty. It's a journey, a learning experience. You've always been a girl who has had to learn by doing, not by watching and listening – don't change that. Don't change now – you're too young.'

'I'm almost thirty, Grandpa,' I point out. My birthday is in two weeks.

'No, you're *only* thirty. Well, almost. Take it from your seventy-five-year-old grandpa, you've got a lot of living to do.'

As I hug my grandpa, the band begins to play Frank Sinatra: 'That's Why the Lady is a Tramp.' I smile. Of all the songs . . .

'Grandpa, would you like to dance with me?' I ask.

'I'd love to, Little Darlin',' he says. 'And I love to see that smile back.'

As my grandpa and I make our way out to the dance floor, he turns to me with a devilish look in his eye. 'You wanna *really* smile?' he asks.

'Absolutely!' I say.

'Okay,' he says quietly, 'watch this.'

As my grandpa twirls me around, I see Patsy walking in our direction but don't think anything of it until my grandpa dips me, and at the same time sticks out his foot and—

Oh my God!

Patsy goes flying through the air. As she does, I close my eyes to stop from laughing. When I hear her go down with a thud, I open my eyes, turn to my grandpa and whisper. 'I can't believe you did that!' Like a little boy, he giggles.

'I can,' he says quietly. 'That woman's had it coming for a long time!' Quickly changing his tune, he turns around and raises his voice. 'Patsy! I'm so sorry!' After making a big fuss, a big scene, he leans down to help her up. 'Are you okay?'

'Yeah,' Patsy says, brushing crumbs off her dress. 'I'm fine. I didn't mean to get in your way. Thanks for helping me up.'

'It was my pleasure, Patsy.'

'Mine, too!' I add.

As the band at the Starlight Roof begins playing 'Fly Me to the Moon', I twirl around the dance floor like a ballerina, while my grandpa – who looks like Warren Beatty, dances like Fred Astaire and sings in my ear like Frank Sinatra – makes me feel like the luckiest girl in the world.

Toward the end of the evening I decide to head back to my room so I begin looking around for Daisy, to say good night. After searching for a while, I still can't find her. I ask around, and a few people tell me they saw her go into the bathroom, so I head that way.

'Daisy?' I call out when I open the door. I hear sounds of someone getting sick. 'Are you in here?'

'Yeah,' says a weak voice, 'I'm down at the end.'

As I head to the last, large handicap bathroom, I hear more sounds of someone getting sick come from inside.

It's Daisy. 'Are you okay?' I ask, knocking on the door. 'Let me in.'

After I hear the click of the door unlocking, I pull it open and walk inside. Leaning against the wall is my sister, still beautifully dressed in her wedding dress but with watery eyes. 'What's wrong?' I ask.

'Nothing, I'm fine. It's just nerves.'

'Daisy, your wedding's over. How can it be nerves?'

She looks down, guilty.

Wait . . . 'Daisy, are you—?'

'Pregnant, yes.'

'Daisy!' Gasping, I swat her arm. Suddenly realizing I've just hit an expectant mother, I then begin to pet her. 'Oh, sorry!' I exclaim. 'So sorry!'

She laughs. 'It's okay – stop.'

'You're pregnant?' I cover my face in shock. 'I can't believe you didn't tell me!'

'I know. I just wanted to make sure it was definite before I told anyone, and it is.'

'Does Mom know?'

She shakes her head. 'No.'

Suddenly I remember. 'Wait – you told me that you and Edward were waiting.'

'Yeah,' Daisy says, cracking up. 'And I can't believe you bought it!'

'You mean you weren't?' I ask slowly.

'Obviously not!'

'I can't believe you.' Looking my sister square in the eye, I begin to shake my head. 'Okay, this might sound like a silly question, but it's very important that you answer truthfully, so listen carefully.' As Daisy stands up straighter, I continue. 'Do you remember when you told me how many men you slept with?'

'Yeah, seven,' Daisy says. 'Why?'

'Seven?' I screech. 'You didn't tell me seven!'

'I didn't?' Daisy asks, looking guilty. 'Are you sure?'

'Ah . . . yeah,' I nod. 'I'm positive. You told me four.'

'Four?' Daisy erupts in guilty laughter again. 'Well, again . . . I can't believe you bought it!'

'Daisy!' As my sister continues to laugh, I ask her for the truth, point-blank. 'I need to know. How many men have you slept with?'

She doesn't answer.

'Is it higher than seven?' I ask.

She nods.

'Higher than 10.5?'

She nods again.

'Daisy,' I say slowly, in the lowest voice I've ever used in my life, 'I can't believe you lied to me.'

'Oh come on . . . no one tells the truth about that.'

As I look at my sister, I erupt in laughter as well, and then wrap my arms around her. 'I can't believe you're pregnant!' I exclaim. 'I'm so excited! I know sometimes it might seem like I don't like little kids, but I do, I swear. Clean ones, that is.'

'Will you walk me to my room?' Daisy asks. 'I have to lie down. Edward already knows. He's going to stay with the guests a little while longer.'

'Yes,' I say, nodding. As I help my sister out of the bathroom and to the elevator, I decide to take advantage of her while she's weak and continue to dig. 'So, is it higher than fifteen?' I ask.

She smiles.

'Sixteen?'

She smiles again.

'Come on, just tell me,' I plead. 'I won't tell a soul.'

As the elevator doors close, Daisy leans over. When she whispers her number into my ear, all I have to say is . . .

Oh my God! Oh my God, oh my God, oh my God!

My sister is such a liar.

So Not Like a Virgin

After walking Daisy to her room, instead of going back to mine, I decide to take a walk. The air smells fresh, clean – it's been washed for days. As I stroll through the streets of New York and take in the smells, the noise, and the hustle and bustle of the city, I realize that I don't have undiagnosed ADD, I'm just more comfortable in chaos. Wearing my scarlet dress and my high heels, I walk down the street a proud woman. A woman flawed, but still, a woman who takes chances, a woman who has loved and been loved. To go out on a limb (or twenty – or forty or sixty, for that matter) is what life is about. It's about trying until you get it right. I'm okay with where I'm at right now. I still don't have a job, a loft or a husband and kids – but I have me. And I have Eva, too. My grandpa is right. I can *maybe* myself to death or make peace with the past, with any mistakes I might have made, and remember the good times and move forward. That's what I've decided to do. Because of this, I head somewhere important.

Once I arrive, after nervously waiting, I hear a voice.

'In the name of the Father, Son and Holy Spirit,' Daniel says.

'Amen,' I reply. I feel bad about waking him. I rang the buzzer of the church office about ten minutes ago and told a security guard that I had an emergency and needed to see him.

'Delilah,' Daniel says in a low tone when he recognizes my voice, 'this better be an emergency . . .'

'It was. It is. Well, kind of . . .'

'Kind of? Are you saying you lied to get me out of bed?'

'Well, maybe a little, but it was just a white lie and everyone knows those don't count.'

'White lies count,' Daniel says quickly.

'Well, then, I'm sorry. Please forgive me.'

'You're forgiven,' he says, sighing loudly. 'Now that I'm up, what do you need?'

'Well, remember when I said I was sorry for sleeping with *some* of the twenty men, that some of them were mistakes, but not all of them? Well, I've changed my mind.'

'Wonderful,' Daniel says in a cheerful tone. 'I'm glad to hear that you've finally come around.'

'Well, that's the thing . . . I didn't exactly come around to your side.'

'What do you mean?' The tone of his voice is serious.

'Well . . . I'm not sorry for any of them.'

'None of them?' he asks, sounding bewildered.

'No, none of them. My choices might not be right for everybody, and the Church might disagree with them, but they were right for me. They made me who I am. To be sorry is to regret them, and to regret them means they were wrong and evil, and they weren't.'

Daniel sighs loudly. 'I'm not sure I want to hear any more.'

'Well you have to. I might've stopped coming to church when I was eighteen, but before that I spent every Sunday of my life here and have listened to' – *fifty-two weeks times eighteen years, carry the one* – 'nine hundred thirty-six homilies, so please listen to one of mine.' I'm getting better at math.

Daniel laughs. 'You like to make up your own rules, don't you?'

'You have to in life, at least sometimes, because if you try to live by what other people deem right and wrong or above and below average – you'll drive yourself crazy.'

'Okay, fine,' he says, giving in. 'You have my ear, go ahead.'

'A very wise man once told me that when you think about the past, why not remember the reasons you did things as opposed to dwelling on why you shouldn't have. I mean, as long as you've learned whatever lesson there is to learn and have come out a bigger person, then it's silly to have regrets, which is why I'm not sorry.'

'You're not sorry for any of them?' he asks slowly.

'No, none of them.'

'Not even the last one? What was his name . . . Roger? I mean, you were really upset about him.'

'I'm not even sorry for Roger. He was a great dancer, and he made me feel wanted on a day when nothing but rejection was thrown in my face.'

'Okay,' Daniel says slowly, kind of getting where I'm going. 'Give me another example. One of the twenty.'

'Okay,' I say, thinking of a good one. 'I once dated a

guy named Wade who made me realize it's okay not to be a grown-up all the time, and I really liked that about him.'

Daniel laughs a little and then asks shyly, 'How about me?'

I smile. 'You know, you taught me one of the most important lessons there is. On a night when I was heartbroken, you made me realize there were more fish in the sea. That's something everyone needs to learn early in life.'

'I'm blushing,' Daniel says, after a bit of silence.

'You should be.'

After thinking about my new point of view, Daniel sighs. 'Well, well, well. I know you're not looking for forgiveness, but you have my blessing, Delilah. I'm happy you've come to peace with what you've done.'

'Thanks,' I say, smiling. 'Me too.'

'Will I see you at mass tomorrow?' Daniel asks.

'Probably not,' I say, 'but maybe we could go for coffee sometime.'

'Are you asking me on a date?' Daniel jokes.

'Well, you've seen *Thorn Birds*, right?'

Daniel doesn't say anything.

'I'm kidding!'

'Oh thank goodness!' he sighs.

Chapter Eighteen

Beep

Delilah, this is Jesus.
Listen, God and I got your file from Daniel.
After reviewing it and listening to your
argument, we've decided to forgive you even
though you didn't really ask for it.
Doorbell
Oops, someone's here, gotta go. Take care
and . . . Dad bless.

Beep

Del, it's Grandpa. I've given it some thought
and have decided to take my own advice and
go back to Vegas. I'm a young stud, and I need
to stay where the picking's good. Anyway, I
know I'm gonna see you this morning at
brunch, but I just wanted to let you know first.

Beep

Delilah, this is Jesus again.
Listen, after reading a little further, we're
gonna have to take back our offer. We're
sorry, but we had no idea you slept with
Roger. A braided belt? What were you
thinking? Sorry for the confusion.

The next morning I lie in bed alone at the Waldorf feeling
relieved, refreshed, but, yes, still sad about what happened
with Colin. However, there's nothing more that I can do
except say I'm sorry, which I've already done. From here,
it's up to him; the ball is in his court. As much as I want
to, as much as it kills me not to, I'm not going to chase
after him. I've learned my lesson with that. Daisy's right.
If something is meant to happen, then it will.

Daisy's post-wedding brunch begins in an hour, so after
getting out of bed, I take a shower and get partly dressed,
putting on my underwear, a T-shirt and a pair of heels. (As
nice as the Waldorf is, I will never forget what that TV
special said about dirty hotel rooms, so I won't walk on
the carpet with bare feet.)

Pausing for a moment, I turn on the TV. After flipping
around for a bit, I stop when I get to the Soap Opera
Network. After finding the information button on the
remote, I push it because I think . . .

Yes. Yes, I'm right.

A rerun of *All My Children* is on. I suspected it was
because while I was browsing around the Internet trying
to find out when Holden Jessup would make an appearance, I learned that the big storyline on the show right
now is a bunch of people being held hostage on a boat
out at sea. I was unable to find out anything about
Holden, by the way. After throwing down the remote, I
leave the TV on and continue to get ready.

As I'm putting on my mascara, I hear a commercial pro-
moting next week's episodes of *All My Children*. 'Next

week . . .' a man's voice says, 'a new man enters Pine Valley.'

A new man? I stop what I'm doing.

Could Colin make an appearance as soon as next week? No, it's too soon. There's no way. Looking back in the mirror, I resume putting on my mascara until I suddenly hear a woman's voice on the TV say, 'Holden . . . is that you?'

Holden? HOLDEN? That's Colin! Well, I mean, that's his character! Throwing down my mascara wand, I run over to the TV as quickly as I can.

Sitting down on the edge of the bed, I nervously bite my lip and watch as the camera slowly pans across a misty bridge. It's a rainy day in Pine Valley. Sappy music is playing. Suddenly the camera stops moving when it gets to a pair of grubby shoes. It then slowly moves up a pair of green cargo pants, a black tank top, and then . . .

This is it. This is the moment I've been dreading. I'm going to see Colin on TV and realize I made the biggest mistake in letting him go. I have a feeling I'm going to burst into tears.

As the camera continues moving up, I see his collar bone, and then his neck, and then—

Whoa, wait.

That's not Colin.

'Yes, yes it's me,' a strange man says, answering the woman. 'It's Holden.'

WTF?

I'm so confused. I mean, I know this is the right character and I'm positive this is the right show and Michelle said she saw him leave – wait, he did leave. I know he did. I mean, he hasn't been home. His apartment is quiet.

Suddenly my cell phone rings. After running over to where it is, I look at the ID and see that it's Michelle. I know she doesn't really talk to him, but maybe she can help me figure this out. 'Hey,' I say, answering quickly. 'Do you know if Colin—'

'Look out your window,' she says, interrupting me.

'My window?' I'm thrown for a loop. 'Wait, why?'

'Just trust me,' Michelle says quickly. 'Go to your window, open it up and look down. And don't hang up on me yet!'

I glance over at the clock; I don't have time for games. 'Michelle, I'm gonna be late for brunch. Seriously, just tell me what's going—'

'DELILAH, DO WHAT I SAY RIGHT NOW,' she demands. She's practically yelling at me.

'Fine, Jeeeze . . . No reason to get bitchy.' I slowly make my way to the window. 'Okay, I'm here. Now what do you want me to do?'

'Open it!' she yells again.

I undo the lock and pry the window open. As I do, I hear music. It's not just any music though . . . *it's Lionel Richie*. For a moment, my heart stops.

'Michelle, what's going on?' I ask.

'Do you see anything?'

'No . . .' I say slowly. 'I hear something though.'

'Music?'

'Yeah,' I say nervously. Something's not right here.

'Michelle, where are you?' I ask. I can hear her talking to someone in the background.

'Tell me when you see something,' she says, once again ignoring my question.

'See something where?' I'm so confused.

'In the street!' Michelle yells. She sounds irritated. 'In the freaking street, Delilah! Look down!'

'I am,' I yell back at her, 'but there's nothing there!'

And then suddenly, there's something.

Coming from the left, I see a white van of some kind slowly pulling forward. As it does, I begin to see letters that are written on the side of it. They appear to me backwards, one by one. D . . . P . . . Y . . . N.

Wait, NYPD. It's a New York Police Department paddy wagon.

Suddenly I see someone standing on the top of it and—
Holy shit.

It's Colin. Dressed in a T-shirt and yet another pair of sexy-ass Levi's, he's standing tall with his arms held high in the air holding what appears to be a boom box.

No, wait . . . it's a karaoke machine.

I drop the phone.

As the van pulls forward just a little bit more, I see that all of the Jimmys are standing next to him. When Colin sees me, the worried look on his face fades away and he smiles. And then I blush. Turning away from me for a moment, he says something to Jimmy O'Shaughnessy and the van stops. When it does, Jimmy picks up a police megaphone and talks into it.

'Ladies and gents of Park Avenue,' he bellows. He sounds like he works at a carnival. 'I'd like to thank you all in advance for allowing this good-lookin' fella to bother you yet again. What some of you might not know is that this is actually his second Park Avenue appearance. The first took place at a much less convenient hour, when he woke up half the block celebrating the Mother Earth, and—'

Jimmy Callahan rips the megaphone out of his hand. 'Gimme that, you asshole!' As a small crowd gathers around the paddy wagon, he speaks into it. 'Everyone, please don't let this man's past influence your feelings on what he's about to do today. He's got a slight wild streak in him, yes, but he's a fine gentleman. One of the best, actually. With that said, I'd like to introduce to you the one, the only, Colin Brody.' The crowd claps.

Colin hands Jimmy Murphy the karaoke machine but hangs on to the microphone. Jimmy Callahan holds the megaphone up to the speakers, and Jimmy Murphy pushes play. As 'Three Times a Lady' pours out of the speakers, Colin begins singing.

'Thanks for the tiiiime that you've giiiiiiiven me, the memories are all in my miiiiiind . . .'

Oh my . . . he's such a bad singer. He's the most gorgeous, perfect man, but he's an awful singer. However, I still can't stop smiling. I can't believe this is happening!

'You're once,' Colin sings, getting to the chorus. 'Twice . . . TWENTY TIMES a laaaaaady!'

Twenty times . . . I burst into laughter.

'And I luhhhhve you! I luhhhhve you.'

Oh my God. Oh my God, oh my God, oh my God!

As the music continues, Colin passes the microphone to Jimmy O'Shaughnessy and takes a large contraption of some sort from his father. As he puts a strap around his neck and attaches it, I realize what it is and bring my hand to my mouth to stifle a giggle.

It's a button accordion.

As Colin begins playing his squeaky accordion along to the music, all of the Jimmys sing Lionel's lead vocal and dance in unison.

'When we are together . . .'

Squeak! Squeak! Squeak!

'The moments I cherish . . .'

Squeak! Squeak!

'With every beat of my heeeaaaart!'

As Colin continues to squeak – I mean *play* – and the Jimmys continue to sing, everything becomes so clear to me. What was I thinking with Nate? Why was I willing to settle with someone when this is so right? I don't care that I'm taking a chance. I don't care that I may get my heart broken. If I don't at least give this a chance, I'll never be able to live with myself. I love this. I love this because it's funny. I love this because it's silly. I love this because I love Colin. I do. I love him, I love him, I love him!

And just like that . . . my heart goes boom.

When it does, I don't even close the window. I just run.

After I press the down elevator button a hundred million times, a car finally stops on my floor. As soon as the doors open, even though it's jam-packed, I quickly jump inside and begin pressing the close-door button repeatedly as well. Everyone is staring at me, but I don't care. The doors close and the car begins to move.

Hurry, hurry, hurry!

Even though it's a short trip, it seems to take for ever to get to the lobby. Once the doors finally open, I'm the first one out. Running as fast as I can to the Park Avenue entrance, I don't notice the allegory murals or the silk curtains – I don't notice anything – I just run. In a flash, I'm there; I'm down the stairs, out the door and in the street. I look to where the paddy wagon is parked, and my stomach drops when I see Colin.

Holy smokes.

'Hey, Darlin',' he says.

'Hey . . .' is all I can manage to say back because just like that, my heart goes boom again.

Looking around, I see Michelle, my mom, Victor, Daisy, Edward, my grandpa, Gloria, Ruth, and, yes, even Ally Hathaway standing in the crowd. Just as I smile, the music suddenly stops playing. When Colin and I both turn to see why, we see his dad standing next to the karaoke machine with a guilty look on his face. He looks at Colin.

'Sorry,' he whispers, 'but it was ruining the moment, son.'

Laughing, Colin turns back to me. As he jumps off the paddy wagon, I run and jump into his arms. He catches me and doesn't even drop me (which, with my luck, would happen). He picks me up and twirls me around, and our lips instantly lock. Again. And oh my . . . his lips are still so soft.

And then . . . *boom.* It happens again.

While I'm kissing Colin, I hear people cheer and begin to feel like I'm in *An Officer and Gentleman*, like Colin is Richard Gere and I'm—

No, no – wait. I take that back. This moment is nothing like that.

It's SO. MUCH. BETTER.

'Where've you been?' I ask Colin, when we finally stop kissing.

'LA.'

I'm confused. 'But you didn't take the soap opera role, I just saw—'

'No, I didn't take it,' he says, 'I didn't settle. I went for something else.' I'm confused until I see a smile creep across his face.

'Irish gangsta thug movie?' I ask. I'm practically screaming.

Colin nods big. 'Irish gangsta thug movie!'

And then we kiss again.

When Colin finally puts me down, the two of us turn and walk towards the entrance to the Waldorf. (No, not to do that, but I do need to get my things and get my dog.) 'Do I have to beat up someone upstairs?' he asks, as we step in the elevator. 'Because I'm prepared, you know, I got the Jimmys as my back-up.'

'No, no,' I tell him. 'I didn't settle either.'

As the doors close, he turns to me. 'By the way, nice legs.'

'Huh?' I'm confused.

'I said "nice legs",' he repeats. He then glances down and smirks.

When I look down, I realize that I forgot to put on my pants. All I'm wearing is a T-shirt, underwear and a pair of heels.

Oops. Now I really look like a tramp.

But I don't care, I just laugh. Life is funny; it really is.

Epilogue

The First, the Last, the Everything

Okay, fine. Colin might not be my first, but he's definitely my everything. I think. I hope . . . because he's right, you never really know.

Oh, scratch that – I know, I *so* know.

Two weeks later I wake up at Colin's to both the phones ringing yet again. (Yes, I made him wait two weeks – what do you think I am, a tramp?) Everyone's been calling us lately, if not to ask me about my new job as a designer at Vintage Vogue, then it's to ask me what I think of Elisabeth being found innocent, or to ask Colin about his new role, or to ask the two of us how we feel about making the front page of the *New York Post* the Monday after Daisy's wedding.

Yes, I was wearing my underwear in the picture, but the photo was taken from the side so it's not as bad as it could've been had it been taken from the back. I have my arms and legs wrapped around Colin while he's holding me, and we're kissing. Next to us is an article about finding love in the most unlikely places, like the article I read so many months ago about finding love on the F train. It's funny how things come around.

Even though it's Colin's phone that's ringing, I answer. I don't have to worry about things like this with him.

'Uh . . . hi . . . ' says an unfamiliar male voice when I do. 'I'm looking for Colin? Or actually, a girl named Delilah.'

'Uh . . . this is Delilah,' I say.

'Hi, this is Jim Nukerson. This is weird, but I got a message to call you. It was a while ago. I'm sorry to return the call so late, but I've been traveling for work.'

'Jim Nukerson?' I sit up.

'Yeah,' he says.

'*The* Jim Nukerson? As in Nukes?'

'Yep.'

Oh my God. Nukes. Too many Coco Locos.

'Do you remember me?' I ask. 'Cabo San Lucas? Spring break 1997?'

'Uh . . . yeah . . . yeah! Yeah, I do! Delilah from the—'

'Trampoline,' we both say in unison, and then laugh.

'Yes! It's me.'

'What's up? What do you need?'

'Well, the funny thing is, I don't need anything any more.'

And then in one big giddy breath I tell Nukes the whole story.

When I finish talking and exhale, Nukes doesn't say anything.

'Hello?' I ask.

'Uh . . . I'm still here,' he mumbles. 'I'm just a little taken aback and confused.'

'Confused? Confused why?'

'Confused because . . . well, Delilah, I know we were both drinking heavily the night we were together, but you must've been a little more out of it than I was, because the thing is . . . *we never had sex.*'

Never had sex? Come again?

'We came close,' Nukes proceeds to explain. 'But don't you remember? The trampoline was too bouncy. To be honest, we never even got naked.'

Never got naked? 'We didn't?' I ask.

'No.'

Suddenly, the night comes back to me and, by God, Nukes is right – we didn't get naked. He was just wearing really tight Speedos, that's all.

'So you and I never had sex?' I ask.

'Nope.'

Oh my God . . . this means that Colin is . . . Oh my God . . . it does . . .

I can't believe it. After everything I just went through.

'Nukes, I have to go,' I say. 'Thanks for calling back though. And good luck to you.'

When I hang up the phone, a smile creeps across my face. I can't believe it. I can't believe that after all that, now that I finally realize that it doesn't matter any more . . .

I turn to Colin, still sleeping next to me. Leaning over, I kiss his eyelashes, and then his nose, and then his lips. He opens his eyes and looks at me. As he reaches over and pulls me in closer, I snuggle into him and smile, my #20 . . . not that it matters any more. I hope he'll stay for ever, but even if he doesn't, even if he leaves tomorrow, I know I did the right thing. This moment, right now, right here, is better than living up to someone else's average.

I still find the thought of the sixty-year-old woman who's had sex with seventy-eight men a bit unsettling, but if I end up like her one day, I hope I will have stopped keeping track by then.

And now I have an announcement to make.

Drumroll please! (Drumroll begins.)

My name is Delilah Darling. I'm thirty years old, I'm single, and . . . I'm easy!

(Deafening applause.)

Thank you, thank you very much.

THE END

Acknowledgements

To my family – Mon, Dad, Mick, Todd and of course, my big sister, Lisa – thank you for always standing by my side. To my three best friends – Tracy, Naomi, Mark – thanks for being so supportive. (Mark, I mean that literally to you and David.) More thanks goes to Cristin Moran, Corey D. Wells, Dan Wells, Rod Pineda, Amy Shapiro, Sam Jacobs, Scott Woldman, Julie Wulf, and of course, Chrissy Blumenthal, for being a fabulous mentor.

I'd also like to thank the glorious Alison Callahan, Jeanette Perez, and everyone at HarperCollins, as well as the magnificent Linda Evans, Kate Marshall, and everyone at Transworld. To everyone at RLR, especially my agent Jennifer Unter, thanks for your input, insight, and friendship. More thanks goes to Jordan Bayer and everyone at Original Artists for always having faith in me.

A funny endnote . . . while writing this book my sister, editor and agent all had beautiful babies. Sex, sex, sex – it can be blood-tingling and hair-raising, or lackluster and lifeless. But when done with the right person at the right time, it can give you the greatest gift in the world!